CORPUS

BOOK TWO OF THE CULPA MAGUM SERIES

A.R. TURNER

Published by:
Cloaked Press, LLC
P. O. Box 341
Suring, WI 54174
HTTPS://www.cloakedpress.com

Cover design by Fantasy & Coffee Design
https://fantasyandcoffee.com/SPDesign/

To Anna,

If loving you was a crime, not even Felix could convince a judge of my

innocence.

And I wouldn't want him to.

-A

Contents

Part One: Ergo Sum

0 - A Deal

"Now, are you going to explain how you're dead and yet still here, or am I going to have to find another lawyer? It seems only fair if I'm going to tell you my life story that you should tell me yours."

Felix took a long look at the dagger on the table.

"Well, when you put it like that," Felix said, and told his client how he had died.

1 - John

Inanimate objects are, by and large, terrible conversationalists. I discount Racelsus in this, firstly because she is hardly what I'd call properly inanimate, and secondly because she'd beat me up. You remember Racelsus, yes? The witch's skull in the birdcage? Bit of an attitude?

Anyway, if you've ever tried talking to a door, or a well, or a thimble, you'll find the conversation more-or-less one-sided. This had been a completely acceptable state of affairs for most people (and the objects, as far as we can tell) for as long as we have thought about it, but there are always some who insist on taking matters a bit too far.

These days, it is well understood that most 'things' are *capable* of possessing that spark that can lend to it some form of life, allowing something (or a collection of somethings) to think, speak, and, appropriate appendages being present, move. Exactly what constitutes the 'whole' of the object largely depends on the person performing the animation. For example, if I were to perform the rather creepy act of bringing a little child's doll to life, what exactly am I animating? The fluff? The fabric? The little beady eyes? If I remove an arm, will it still flop around? If I breathed life into a bottle of wine, is it the wine, the bottle, or the combination of the two that I have, for want of a better word, birthed?

Perhaps I'm getting a little philosophical. What I really wanted to talk about was stabbing people.

The case wasn't one of mine, but rather the case of "Vinch vs Whom?", as it is recorded. The case surrounded the will of a wealthy old man named Vinch who had tons of cash and a tendency towards paranoia. One day, someone found him, quite dead, with a dagger in his back. That's not an attempt at maudlin poetry, I mean a literal dagger jutting from the man's ribs. Cue the despairing but also very pragmatic series of relations, friends, co-workers and other grievers all after a slice of the pie. The question was: who killed him? Whoever was found guilty would, of course, be imprisoned, and therefore not reap any of the spoils.

Unsurprisingly, nobody came forward as witnesses. The lawyer (and personal friend) of Mr Vinch, one Ms Cletzi, was a resourceful and indefatigable lawyer, unafraid of scraping the very bottom of the longest barrel if it would help her secure victory for her client. She moved in curious circles, and was on somewhat friendly terms with those on the cutting edge of 'new' magic (as it was then called).

What's 'new' magic I hear you ask? Depending on who you ask, it's either 'just what magic needs to stay relevant', or it's the 'death of the industry.' Old magic, or what is known by the practitioners as the more appealing sounding 'Classic Magic', consists of your well-known and reliable middle-of-the-road spells. You know, your Fireballs and Teleporting and whatnot. 'New' magic instead seeks to carve out entire new genres of spell-slinging, by experimenting with hitherto untested hypotheses and methods. For the fiscally-minded lawyer, there is quite a living to be made in the dogged pursuit of breaches of intellectual copyright for new spells, since wizards and their ilk are fiercely precious and protective over their achievements... but more on that subject a little later.

Back to the courtroom, then. Several days after the murder, and after several quiet meetings in dark rooms with unnamed collaborators, Ms Cletzi requested a public hearing during which a new witness was due to come forth and speak the truth to the Vinch affair.

All gathered in the courtroom and the hearing began, and all were surprised to see Ms Cletzi standing at the front, clasping a plain dagger. She thrust it into a cork stump that had been placed on a table, and turned to face the judge.

"This is the dagger that Mr Vinch was killed with. I have substantive paperwork to this effect collated in this file to my right, approved and verified by the lawmakers present shortly after the killing."

The judge, one judge Orch, nodded and gestured for her to continue. She bowed, and pointed to the knife in the corkboard.

"Your Honour, may I present my witness: John Dagger."

At which point, a tinny voice like a ladle hitting a spring floated through the room. "Your Honour, if it may please you."

Of course, mutters were whispered, whispers were muttered, no doubt moustaches were puffed out in consternation, but the judge raised a hand and waited for silence. He raised an eyebrow at the family lawyer, who explained that very recent magicks developed by the staff at Restastine University could bring mundane objects to life.

(Oh, a side note. Don't refer to a Vowel as mundane; they get a little tetchy. Vowel? Oh yes, let me explain.)

Unique Independent Entity Animate Objects, otherwise known as UIEAOs, are more commonly referred to as Vowels, for obvious reasons. It makes you wonder if the chap or chappette who invented the spell (and therefore the term) didn't start backwards with the naming just to have something to brag about, etymologically speaking. Perhaps, when quaffing a beaker of sherry, if the subject of the Vowel arose, they would push their fogged glasses further up their nose and lean forward with a knowing wink, then say: 'Hilarious name, wouldn't you agree? You know *I* came up with that?' Bleugh. I wouldn't put it past them. Where was I? Oh yes.

Vowels don't have the same set of senses humans or animals do. It tends to vary from thing to thing. Most Vowels can 'feel' and 'see' to an extent and 'hear' fairly well, but after that it gets a bit... well, to put it simply, weird. Let us return to the courtroom, and you will see what I mean.

A momentary pause from the judge. After some time, he nodded once more at Ms Cletzi, who asked John Dagger to start. What followed was a detailed explanation of the dagger's recollection of the night in question. How it had spent much of its time these past few years hanging decoratively on a wall within a dark cellar, only to find itself quite suddenly whisked away and, not five minutes later, plunged into the unfortunate victim.

Finally moved into speech, the judge leaned forward to stare at the witness. The witness did not stare back, because it didn't have any eyes. I know, it didn't have a mouth either, and yet it spoke. Look, I warned you that it would get weird, didn't I?

"Did you get a good look at the perpetrator?" asked the judge.

"No, Your Honour," said John Dagger.

"Did you hear them speak?"

"No, Your Honour."

"And how," said the judge to Ms Cletzi, with a sigh as if this was what he was expecting, "does this help our case if the, ehm, person on the stand cannot identify the attacker?"

"Vowel, Your Honour" said John Dagger, a touch indignant.

"...Quite," said the judge with an arched eyebrow. "The question still remains. How may we proceed if you cannot identify the perpetrator?"

"Oh, Your Honour, but I can," said the dagger. "I can *feel* the person that is holding my handle. Their *intent*. The way their palm *fits*. I would know that grip in an instant, without a doubt."

A surreptitious thumbs-up from Cletzi at the practised use of the magic d-word that lies at the heart of almost any legal case.

"Without doubt..." muttered the judge.

"Likewise, I can remember the warmth of every person I've been stabbed into."

"What?" spluttered the judge, standing. "Is this a sick joke?!"

"Please, Your Honour," Ms Cletzi said, a nervous smile on her face, twitching only very slightly. "John is not used to the rules of propriety and, ehm, decency." (It had taken her two hours to teach it the phrase 'Your Honour', and why it should definitely say it in a courtroom.)

"What *it* means is that daggers, spears, forks and other such objects have a sense they have come to call 'hold', and another called-" and she glanced at the dagger briefly - "called 'stab'. John has tried to explain these to me, but it is difficult for a human to grasp, in the same way that to explain 'smell' or 'taste' to an animated object is almost impossible. Yet, a human can recognise a distinctive taste, for example lemon, without a moment's doubt."

The judge squinted his eyes. "A moment's... Difficult to grasp, eh? I would like to hear... *its* explanation nonetheless." Judge Agorio Orch steepled his fingers. "John Dagger, what is 'stab'?"

John Dagger tried its best, but a human simply cannot understand how it *feels* to be wielded. Instead, tests were performed, in which members of the gallery (and of curious judiciary) were invited to take a number, then hold the dagger handle through a hole in a box.

This was to ensure no cheating was taking place, despite repeated assurances that John had no eyes and could not see. Nevertheless, did it possess some vision? Perhaps. Like I keep saying, Vowels are weird.

The test was to see how well John Dagger could recognise the hands that touched it. The volunteers from the public that were watching were lined up and given a number, then told to put their hand through the hole and grasp John's handle in whichever way they saw fit. Afterwards, John would be tested.

Each person walked up to the box and stated their number, then reached their hand through. Some of them wore gloves, or used their non-dominant hand, or held the dagger in unusual ways to try and trick John. One just prodded the knife with a gloved little finger. After each person had touched the handle, they made way for the next in line.

While this was going on, the judge made arrangements for a court Aleaomancer - that's 'chance-obsessed wizard type' to you and me - to be present. The wizard arrived within a few moments, wearing a tall brimmed hat, and oversaw proceedings. How did they arrive so quickly? If you ask one, they'll waggle their eyebrows knowingly and talk about how likely it is that they'll be needed on a given day, and the odds of them being in the right place at the right time so as to be ready when called upon, and other such insufferable chin-stroking intimations. Anyway.

After the twelfth volunteer had done what was asked of them, the volunteers were huddled in a nervous group. The Aleaomancer hushed them with a raised finger, then removed his hat and dumped a handful of wooden balls into it. Each ball had a number painted on the side in bold, golden letters. After jiggling his hat around, he reached in and lifted one out with a flourish. A quick glance at the ball, then he pointed at the person with the allocated number.

The chosen volunteer blinked a few times, then crept over to John Dagger's box. She reached her hand in, and no sooner had she touched the handle than John announced: "Number eight."

The wizard returned the ball to his hat, and started jiggling them again. "Odds of correct guess: one in twelve," he intoned. "Eight point three percent." He drew another ball out and pointed to another person.

"Number one," said John.

The Aleaomancer's mouth twitched. "One in one-hundred-and-forty-four," he said. "Zero point zero zero seven percent."

A third time. "Number eight again."

"Number eleven."

"Number five."

Sparks were flickering above the wizard's head while he watched and calculated.

"Number five again."

"Number twelve."

Every time, John was correct.

By the twelfth repetition, the chance wizard was sweating.

"Zero... point..." he was saying with great effort. "Zero zero zero... zero zero... zero zero zero zero zero zero zero..." he paused for breath. "...one percent." He reached into an inner pocket of his robe and pulled out a flask, taking a swig. "One in..." a flash of electricity arced from his head and formed a brief, crackling halo of blue light before vanishing. "Nine... trillion." He gasped and took another pull on his flask. After a few breaths, he turned to the judge.

"That is far beyond what could be reasonably considered to be chance, Your Honour," he said.

The judge grunted. "Thank you. You may go." The wizard nodded in reply, and walked to the chairs for the audience, before collapsing into one of them, a gormless, euphoric smile on his face.

A similar exercise was undertaken with randomised hunks of meat, fruit, fungus and mulch. John was stabbed into each one in turn, and then again in a random order. Each time, John correctly identified the material, even if the fungus made him, in his words, 'feel a bit peculiar'.

Once the mulch had been cleaned away (and the windows opened to let out the smell), the judge then turned to John. "How is it you can tell, witness?" He then started poking his finger into his palm with great intensity. "Explain 'stab' to me."

"There are many factors," John tried to say. "The resistance, the sliding, the heat, the grain… the pure *'stab'* of it," it said, almost with a sigh. The judge started poking his palm harder, a frown on his face.

"Meat is the best feeling," John finished, causing the judge to recoil. "*Much* better if it's warm. Uh, Your Honour."

After glaring at the chance wizard, who was still slumped on his chair, the judge carefully tucked his finger back into his robes. He grunted again, before he finally accepted that John Dagger could, with remarkable accuracy, identify 1) who had wielded it and 2) who, or what, it had been stabbed into.

"All that remains," he said, "is to find the likely perpetrators and test them against our new expert witness."

Rather anticlimactically, it turned out to be Mr Vinch's son, Finlay, who had purloined a dagger from the estate's armoury, done the deed quite without thinking of the possibility of getting caught, and assumed he'd inherit the lot. It was fairly obvious once he disappeared after the second day of testing, only to be found fleeing the city, newly inherited wealth in tow in the form of property deeds, expensive jewellery, and other small but ludicrously expensive artwork. He was the third to be tested, and the moment he grasped the handle, an unconvincing smug expression plastered on his face, John had yelled out that this was the killer. The smug look hadn't even vanished by the time he'd been seized by bailiffs.

The question, then, came after. What to do with John? It was suddenly brought to life (quite without its consent), and now its one use had been exhausted. Was John to just be left in a drawer? Returned to the armoury and forgotten? Hung on the wall? Smelted down? Or perhaps its consciousness was to be removed? Undone? Returned to a state of non-awareness? Was that not murder? The Vinch estate, to whom it technically belonged, wanted nothing more to do with it. That included Ms Cletzi.

I know. Lawyers.

Where do you go if you have no money, no hope, the world against you, and no clear legal path through?

Where do you think?

~

A gentle knock at the door of Lunchers & Co disturbed the relative peace of the morning. Mr Luncher, always dressed in his finest trim-cut black-and-white suit, answered the door, a mug of tea in his hand, a monocle on one eye. A young woman with a mildly concerned face, as if she was having a practical joke played on her and suspected this was the punchline, stood there. In her hands was a block of wood. In the block of wood was a dagger.

Mr Luncher had been around long enough to know that just because someone was brandishing a dagger, it didn't mean they necessarily wanted to stab you with it. Especially if the dagger was already stabbed into something else.

"Good day," he said, his mug wavering only slightly. "Can I help you?" The young woman shuffled on her feet.

"He, I mean it, said you'd give me three silvers if I carried it, I mean him, here," she said, in a restrained voice.

"Who did?" Mr Luncher said.

"I did," said a tinny voice. "I'm in need of some legal assistance." Mr Luncher looked down at the dagger, hesitated for a brief moment, then back to the girl. He cocked his head to the side and pursed his mouth in thought. After a brief consideration, he reached forward and flicked the blade.

"Oi!" came the voice. "What was that for?"

Mr Luncher reached some conclusion. He reached into his pocket, fished out a few coins and exchanged them for the block of wood, a frown on his wrinkled face. The young girl counted the coins, returned the extra that she had been given, then walked off without looking back. Mr Luncher returned inside, then placed the block of wood on the table.

A man walked in, holding a piece of paper in one hand and an orange in the other. He weaved between stacks of books and teetering piles of papers until he came to an untidy desk in the corner. He tutted, moving a still gently-smoking pipe from his mess of a desk onto another equally cluttered desk.

"Honestly, these things will kill you, you know," he muttered to himself. Before sitting down, he glanced up, noticing for the first time that he wasn't alone. He froze there, mid-sit, taking in the scene of his employer sitting by himself staring intently at a dagger sunk into a block of wood. "Er, is that a new decoration?" he said, deciding to stand up again. He waved a hand as he tried to find the right word. "Very... masculine?"

"It's our newest client," said Mr Luncher, turning to face him. After a second a shocked expression leapt onto his face and he turned back to the dagger. "I'm sorry, I didn't even ask for your name."

"Call me John. John Dagger," said the metallic voice.

Mr Luncher smiled at the man across from him.

"This is John. John, this is Felix."

"Mister... Dagger?" Felix said tentatively.

"Just John is fine," came the reply.

"How do you do?" said Felix, letting his manners fill in the void while his brain started whirring.

"How do I do what?"

Felix blinked and frowned, before reaching for a pencil. "Why don't you tell me everything."

"Why don't *you?*" John replied.

Felix's brows raised. "Pardon me?"

"I mean, you're clearly dead, right? What's that all about?"

Felix blinked to Mr Luncher, who looked back. "And why would you think that?"

"It's obvious to anything with a brain. Well, metaphorically speaking, a brain. Your imprint is all wrong."

"Imprint?"

"Yes, imprint," said the voice impatiently. "Now, are you going to explain how you're dead and yet still here, or am I going to have to find another lawyer? It seems only fair if I'm going to tell you my life story that you should tell me yours." The dagger shifted uncomfortably, conversationally speaking. In reality, it didn't move at all. "I say 'life'... you know what I mean. No offence, I hope."

Mr Luncher coughed in a way that could have been a disguised laugh. Felix shook his head. With a sigh he smoothed his hair back with a hand that turned from solid flesh to one pale and ghostly. Without having to exert an effort to remain 'physical', Felix felt he could relax. He gave the dagger a long look, then shrugged.

"Well, when you put it like that," he said, and told the dagger how he died, and how he didn't.

2 - Between - *before*

There wasn't any air in the afterlife. No gentle whooshing in your ears as you walked. No flutter of hair or sleeve. This wasn't the first thing Felix had noticed, but it was one of the things that he often thought about.

He walked, if walking was the word for it, over some nameless field he didn't recognise. The grass rippled and swayed as he passed, as if trying to avoid him, and moved back once he had done so. When he turned to look behind him, he saw that even as close as three paces away, the grass looked as if it had not moved at all. How long had he been dead now? Four days? Seven years? Who knows.

How am I even forming these thoughts? Are they really thoughts? I wish I'd paid more attention in philosophy classes. Do I even have a brain?

If he concentrated, he was able to stick his hand right through his own head. It passed through his nose and into where he presumed his brain should be, if he had one. It didn't feel like anything at all.

Withdrawing the hand, Felix looked at the field. It wasn't clear if this was a real field. It felt more like someone's interpretation of what a field should be, if that person had never seen a real field and only heard about it third hand. Almost completely featureless, it was the sort of a place that a mind might conjure if it needed to retreat somewhere calm and empty. The sky was entirely covered with grey clouds, and all around him was gentle, shin-high grass. From horizon to horizon there was simply nothing.

This is where he had woken up after that terrible incident. The demon Jurrekker, furious that he had lost his legal case to bring an end to Humanity, a case that Felix was defending, had flung a burning beam of black fire that pierced his heart, killing him. An old, rustic charm of protection had saved him before he had 'completely' died. Not a charm to protect him, which was the curious part. As far as he could understand, it was a charm that allowed him to protect others.

This field had been his home for an unfathomable amount of time. Not long, necessarily. It was literally impossible for him to gauge how long he had been here.

~

Upon waking that first time, he had risen, looked around, then, unsure of what to do, instinctively picked a direction and started walking. As he walked, he thought. At that time, he knew nothing of who he was or what he was doing there. It was difficult to piece together the fragments of memories that bounced around in his awareness. They would emerge like timid creatures from the fog, skittery and nervous, ready and charged to disappear into the undergrowth if approached in the wrong way. Patient contemplation was the only way for them to return to him. Despite his own name remaining out of reach, the names of his friends came to him, one by one. After that, he found he could even picture some of them, smiling and laughing. He gradually remembered his favourite foods, or songs he liked. Some memories, like his least favourite foods, or of the moments before his death, took much more coaxing. Seemingly vital facts evaded him entirely, like his profession, or his family, and still his own name. He definitely was dead though, that seemed fairly obvious. *So why am I able to think?*

Back then, a gentle pulling of his attention had stopped his walking. It was the smallest of tugs, but in a world of grey and silence, it felt like an urgent yank. *What was that?*

He blinked, and was aware of the silhouette of a figure before him, that of a woman slumped over a table. Her hands cradled her head, which was pressed into the table, and her back shook with sobs. Some unexplained feeling, some *instinct*, told him that this woman needed help. Specifically, help only he could give. *Legal help.*

Legal?

That's right, I was a lawyer.

A great wash of memories flooded through him, buffeting him like flotsam from the wreck of his existence, and he staggered to his knees. The whole latest chapter of his life seared into him, from the meeting of

Furbo, Helda and Racelsus to the great court case for Humanity, up until the confusion of looking down and seeing a burning hole where his heart used to be.

The shock faded, the tremors echoing into silence, but the memories remained. Standing up, he faced the silhouette. *Whatever is happening, whatever has happened, that can wait. Someone unable to defend themselves, someone undeserving of the dire straits they are in, needs serious legal help.*

And they're going to get it.

With a smile.

He stepped once through thin air, and found himself sitting at a cold, beaten table. He reached forward to take one of the pieces of paper, but his hands passed through it. By focussing his willpower, not dissimilar to tensing one's muscles, he found he could exert some physical influence on the paper, holding it as if he were made of flesh and blood. He lifted the letter and scanned it. It looked to be a fairly standard situation. Some money-grabbing and heartless landlord was squeezing everything from a tenant with nothing left to give. The letter itself, and more specifically the demand written upon it, was full of contradictions. It would be ripped apart in court like fresh lettuce in a sandwich shop. He could barely suppress a chuckle.

It's good to be back. This is where I belong. Eyeing the huddled form of the woman next to him, he decided to make it clear that he was there.

"Oh dear, oh dear. Someone is going to have quite the comeuppance," he said aloud.

The woman opposite looked up. Her red eyes were sunken with misery. The sight of her face, so full of anguish, both disturbed and steeled him. "Who are you?" she asked in a quiet voice.

I remember who I am.

He looked at her dead in the eye. "Why, Mrs Henria, I'm your lawyer. Now, let's get started."

She baulked at him, eyes bulging, mouth opening and shutting.

I remember.

"My name is Felix," he said.

~

The client was going to need a place to go to ask questions or check for progress, or to seek reassurance from seeing an old, fusty tower of books and documents. Knowing this, Felix had concluded the initial meeting with the recommendation that she take the opportunity to visit Lunchers & Co at her earliest convenience.

After that, Felix had gone straight to Lunchers. He wasn't quite sure how they would react, but it seemed the sensible thing to do. Standing outside the window, paying particular attention to the peeling yellow paint on the sign, he felt a terrible wash of nervousness. So nervous in fact that he hadn't paid any attention as to how he had actually arrived. One moment he was *there*, and the next he was *here*. Now, that raised another question. Should he just strut in, declare himself available again, then walk out? Send a letter? Or perhaps leave coded messages, or-

"Well don't just stand there, you great lemon, come on in out of the cold."

A stout woman with a tight bun of grey hair and a monocle was standing in the doorway, beckoning him in. Felix was taken aback.

"But, Mrs Zwelee, I'm-"

"Dead, yes, a ghost or something, yes, we all know. Come in, would you? I'm letting all the warmth out. Come in and we'll set it all straight. There are some people in here who are dying to meet- Ah, I mean, they're very keen to see you again." She did her best to hide her embarrassed flushing.

Felix, quite unsure of what else to do, did as he was bid.

~

Helda had folded him into a bone-crushing hug, or had tried to, the moment he walked in. Her arms had *swiffed* right through him, and she had looked awfully embarrassed as she'd tried to apologise. Furbo patted her arm and tried a different tack. He held out a hand to Felix, offering a shake of recognition. Felix started at it, then at his own hand, and reached over to take the old, wrinkled hand of Furbo the Wanderer. To the surprise of Furbo, he was able to grasp the proffered hand and shake it vigorously. Both their faces crinkled into smiles, Furbo nodded a head towards Helda. She held out her arms wide, giving Felix time to concentrate. When he nodded, she stepped forward, squashing him in a wide, loving hug that was as solid as if he were still alive.

They were both exactly as he remembered them. Helda, huge, scar-ridden, bright hair cut short. She had the physique of one who carries sacks of bricks for a living, but her face was quick to laugh and well practised at it. Furbo, still old, dark and curious. He had no hair on his head, and his eyes were wide and quick. His thin frame was at odds with Helda's bulky one, but the two of them had travelled together for many years before Felix had met them.

His heart burst at being able to see them again.

Pulling back, Helda wiping an eye, Felix's eyes were drawn to a desk by the door, on which rested a human skull in a cage. He eyed it up and down. The skull was white and mealy, and rested quite comfortably within the confines of a birdcage that looked like it had been recently polished.

He took a few steps over to the cage and raised an eyebrow at it. "How long have you known?" he said, folding his arms.

"Oh, I had my suspicions from the off. You're not so easy to get rid of, I think," came a low, lilting voice.

Felix narrowed his eyes. "And when were you certain?"

The skull quivered and clacked her teeth, which she did often, and for many different reasons. "Well, it was probably when a young woman came knocking on the door last night, and said that a ghostly lawyer had recommended she come here of all places."

Felix frowned, his arms unlacing. "Last night? I thought it had just happened a moment ago."

"Later, Felix. We'll go over everything later."

There was a brief silence, after which they both started speaking at the same time.

"It's wonderful to see-"

"I'm glad you're back-"

They both stopped, waiting for the next one to speak. Then they both started laughing. "Oh, I've missed you, you creepy old haunted skull."

"And I'm glad you're not completely dead, you infuriatingly chipper excuse for a lawyer," said the skull of the witch Racelsus.

A.R. Turner

A clatter from the doorway and an impeccably dressed man with a shock of white-and-black hair swaggered in, a smeary bottle of something dangerous-looking in one hand and a dusty bottle of something potent-looking in the other. Behind him trailed Yetty, Felix's mentee, carrying a tray of chipped and cracked glasses of various sizes, colours and shapes. The general state of Lunchers hadn't rubbed off on her; she was dressed as smartly as ever, dark hair tied in a ponytail against pale skin. She gave him a nod, which he returned, and she smiled.

"Now, onto the important stuff," the well-dressed man said, slamming the octopus-shaped bottles onto a nearby table, causing the papers stacked on it to shift alarmingly. "Can you drink the good plonk or will it just decorate the floorboards?"

Felix pursed his lips. "Well, Mr Luncher. I suspect there's a good way to find out."

~

"What I don't get," said Felix with a gurgle, "is why *this*," and he gestured at his faintly translucent body with a vague hand, "whatever *this* is, whether it's my own soul or psyche or some-higher-being's divine will and/or idea of a bad joke… whatever it is, why would they bother to give me hangovers?"

A chorus of grumbles and moans replied. It was the morning after his return, and Lunchers had celebrated it in proper Lunchers fashion. Within a smoky room with curtains drawn to keep the cruel morning sun away from where it wasn't wanted, Felix pondered his predicament while spread out on the floor. Around him, presumably, for he couldn't make out any definite shapes among the various jackets, pillows, blankets, knocked-over piles of paper and discarded bottles and pint glasses, were the rest of the usual suspects. It was only their tortured responses that revealed who they were.

A tinkle as a mound of bottles shifted, revealing a thick arm holding a thick head. "Foofff…" sighed Helda biliously, rubbing a palm over her almost-shaved scalp.

"I know," said Felix. "Okay, they also let me drink and get drunk, if I tried, but why do the next part? The rubbish part? Just do one part or none at all, I say."

"Grnnh," came a baritone groan that belonged to Furbo.

Felix rolled to his side to acknowledge him. "Exactly! It might well be part of some greater plan."

"Sshhhh," whispered Yetty, covering her ears with her hands from somewhere by the window. The issue with that is this left her eyes uncovered, so she moved them back.

"You're right, perhaps I should experiment," mused Felix.

"Perhaps you should shut up," came a mellifluous voice, undoubtedly that of Racelsus, her skull resting at an angle in her cage, which itself was precariously propped up on a treacherous-looking pile of stained steins. Another chorus of groans from the room, this time more of a groan of agreement than of dissent. Felix sat up, forcing back a wave of nausea that he was almost tempted to allow, wondering what exactly he would puke up from his ghostly form.

"Ectoplasm?" he mused.

"Ecto-shut up," came a gravelly murmur from what could have been Dago, one half of the pair of loyal clerks that kept Lunchers operating through peerless organisational acumen and unmatched attention to detail.

Well, matched only by his partner in crime, Merindhe, wherever she is.

"Unmatched doesn't mean good," he whispered to himself.

"Urh?" came the voice of Merindhe herself, from around the same area of Dago. *Ah, there she is.* A wooden clattering sound as she rolled to prop herself up on one arm, her dark hair standing out in a collection of interesting angles. "Whatchosay?" she wheezed, before slumping back to the floor.

The door swept open, and a figure strode into the room. With three brusque steps she had crossed the floor and ripped the curtains apart, bathing the room in a burst of bright light and fresh air. Even Felix joined in with the latest, loudest, most unhappy choir of irritable whines and sobs in response to this most unwelcome change to the state of affairs. Mrs Luncher, famous prosecutor turned legal-firm-partner, stood by the window, pipe clamped in teeth, steaming cup of tea in grip, surveying her crack team of expert lawyers as they whimpered and squirmed in various states of indignity. Her hair was in its permanent bun, tucked tightly behind her head.

"Oh dear," she said.

"I think I'm going to be sick," mumbled Yetty.

"I wish I was dead - no offence, Felix," said Helda.

"Gungh," said Furbo. "Oh Skrida, merciful Goddess of Death, save me from this torment," he said, before burping wetly and moaning.

Mrs Luncher, who had by no means stood idly by while the celebratory carousing was taking place, rolled her eyes and sighed. She walked to the doorway, muttering words like "constitution" and "light-weights". Once she'd crossed the room, she turned back, gave another sigh, then said:

"Right: Cooked breakfast at Gutcher's. I'm paying. Who's in?"

"Ooh, go on then."

"Yes!"

"You read my mind, ma'am."

She shook her head as she left the room to the sound of a handful of hungover reprobates struggling to their feet with various levels of success. A clink, a crash, then a series of swear-words that were four-hundred years out of date, and even she could not suppress a smirk.

~

By the time the staff of Lunchers & Co were leaving Gutcher's Ale & Breakfaster, they were feeling much rejuvenated by the charming combination of a hearty, well rounded meal swimming in grease and the 'hair of the dog that bit you', as Gutcher's famous 'Beer Gravy' was just as potent as the stuff that came in pint glasses. Whichever way worked for them, the assortment of lawyers, their associates and companions were back in at Lunchers and preparing for the day ahead by mid-morning.

In the back room, normally reserved for client interviews or used as the 'war room' in times of need, Felix sat opposite Furbo, Racelsus and Mrs Luncher. Mr Luncher was ensuring the normal day-to-day tasks were being run, which mostly involved reinforcing the support for the ever-growing structurally fascinating piles of paper or poking the clerks with a stick. Helda was asleep somewhere.

Felix fiddled with his cuff. When his concentration lapsed, his fingers passed right through it.

"I suppose I'd better explain everything from my end," he said at last, almost timid in his reluctance to share this inexplicable part of his life - or, more accurately, afterlife. "I remember sitting on the roof of Placenamia courtroom…"

3 - The First Return - *slightly less before*

"…and then I saw this woman just sort of appear out of nowhere, so I went over to her. It turned out she had some legal trouble she was in, so I, well, materialised in her dining room." Felix gestured with his hands in a 'I-just-sort-of-materialised' kind of way, and stared once again at his cuffs. "And, well, the rest you can probably work out." He glanced up after a moment of silence.

Mrs Luncher and Racelsus looked at each other. Well, Felix assumed Racelsus returned the look. It wasn't possible to be one hundred percent certain where the witch was looking, what with missing both of her eyes, but contextually it was usually simple enough to make an educated guess.

"I'm not sure if I have more answers to life's questions or more questions to your answers," said Furbo, rubbing a hand on his bald head. He broke into an avuncular smile that Felix realised he'd missed terribly. "But, what matters to me, my lad, is that you're safe and well. Uh, I think, that is. Are you well, I mean?"

"I think so," said Felix, patting the older man's hand. "Thank you for asking."

"Oh, you're most welcome, my lad." Furbo looked at the glowing white hand of Felix, placed carefully on his own. His face suddenly creased in a frown, as if he was trying to remember something elusive. When nothing was forthcoming, Felix asked a question he'd been dreading.

"How long has it been?" he said quietly.

"About five months," Furbo said, and Felix's eyebrows raised "That long?"

"Aye, lad, as long as that. You've been missed." Furbo continued. "I had a theory, but…" He paused, then frowned. "Erm, oh, what was it… It's tickling the back of my mind and I can't quite grasp it."

"Want me to have a prod around?" asked Racelsus, in the same manner as a plumber might offer to check out a leaky tap.

"Oh no, that's quite alright, I'll get it in a minute." And with that, he stood up and began pacing, lapsed into an intense silence.

"Well," said Mrs Luncher, tapping some tobacco into her pipe and lighting it. She drew deep and exhaled heavily. "I daresay we've all seen enough in our considerable lifetimes to know that what you've explained is entirely feasible, Felix. And, if my learned friend is still, hm, wrestling with his theory, I have one of my own I'd like to propose." She paused, almost as if waiting for his reply.

"I almost feel like I'm being cross examined by the famous Jucinda Luncher," chuckled Felix nervously, who had, in his entire professional life, been terrified by that very prospect. During his initial interview to join Lunchers & Co, she had grilled him as harshly as any prosecutor... and that had been enough. He almost felt sorry for any poor bugger that had to stand cowering in the dock with Ms Jucinda Diero, more recently Mrs Jucinda Luncher, ripping them to pieces. Mercifully for them, her prosecuting days were over. At least in the traditional sense.

She levelled that piercing, terrifying gaze at him, then looked up at the ceiling.

"BBvJB, BerBru v. JefBel, 1325," she said.

Felix blinked. Instincts drilled into him over years of case law flared into life, and his mind was filled with the details of the case, like levers of a locking turn-puzzle falling into place.

"That's... my old case. Bertruk the Bruiser, the barbarian who was tricked by the town of... uh..."

"Gurlton, outside of Plug Ford," said Mrs Luncher. He was surprised that she had such an intimate knowledge of his case, considering he'd flown solo on that one.

"Yes, that's right," said Felix. "How could I forget that case? Bertruk saved my life."

She nodded. "Then, 1336, HerFed v. JetCom. "

His mind raced. "That's another one of mine, isn't it? The ghost who was killed twice."

"Sounds like a bad play," Racelsus pipped in. Mrs Luncher narrowed her eyes at the witch, who seemed to Felix to sheepishly avert her gaze.

Mrs Luncher took her pipe out of her mouth and started gesturing with it, waving it like a swordswoman in a duel.

"In the latter of those cases, indeed one that you acted in, Felix, the defendant was, as you say, killed. He clung to this life, however, feeling that without some closure he could not progress onto the next life."

"Yes," Felix said, relishing the chance to appear knowledgeable in front of one of the greatest lawyers in the land. "He wanted to make sure everyone knew that his colleagues were trying to cover up their prank gone wrong."

She nodded, giving him the sort of a smile that a teacher gives an eager pupil. "That's right. Once he received his justice, he 'moved on', as it were."

Felix frowned. "But I don't think I have any… unfinished business, to borrow a phrase." Mrs Luncher waved her pipe from side to side.

"The first case, Bertruk's… tell me, how did that day in court end?"

"We won. He got off."

"He didn't 'get off', you admirably presented his defence and he was not found to have committed any breach of contract. Besides, what I meant was this: once the judge delivered their verdict, what happened between you two?"

Felix cast his mind back. It was difficult, remembering the details… It was so long ago, and…

~

Suddenly, he was there again, looking up at that great shaggy mass of scar tissue and missing teeth. The barbarian, thrilled to have been saved by the comparatively puny Felix (though almost anyone would be comparatively puny compared to the monster that was Bertruk), was chatting to him post-judgement.

"What matters is standing up for the right reasons, and doing the right thing. That's all I did," I said, turning back to my bag. I stopped, then regarded Bertruk.

He looked down at me, a thoughtful look on his battered face. He put down his axe then, and reached into a leather pouch strung to a belt. From it, he withdrew a tiny bottle of brown powder.

"What's this?" I said.

"Shh."

He unscrewed the tiny topper and carefully laid it down, before pouring the smallest sample of the stuff onto his grizzled palm. He considered it briefly, then poured out around a tenth the contents.

"I have a feeling you will need this," he rumbled.

"Need what?" I didn't know what he was doing, and I don't like not knowing things.

"Take a deep breath," he commanded.

Felix remembered that gritty, metallic powder coating his lungs. He remembered coughing while that great warrior clamped a hand over his mouth, forcing him to choke on it.

Bertruk had said an old friend had given it to him.

"It let us help one another."

Then, much later, in the courtroom in front of Habeus, Jurrekker and the rest... Bertruk had appeared out of nowhere, leaping into the path of the demonic Elder Prastor, saving Felix from being torn limb from limb. Felix had desperately asked Bertruk where he had come from, but that old hero had smiled enigmatically.

"I don't think I will be here long. I can already feel myself being pulled away."

I didn't want him to go. "Where? Back to the cave?"

"No, somewhere else. Somewhere, hmm, beyond. I left my body behind," said Bertruk.

Then he walked off and faded, vanishing completely.

~

"The powder!" Felix said. Mrs Luncher tapped her pipe on the table.

"Indeed." She sheathed the pipe back in between her teeth and inhaled, before blowing a perfect smoke ring. "I had a chat to Racelsus about that a while back."

The skull clacked in reply. "I've heard of that sort of charm before. It's very old-fashioned, quite hard to get right, but popular in certain circles."

"What circles? Which charm?" said Felix.

"A Charm of Sacrificial Protection," she said. "Not tremendously popular, as it involves you, well, sacrificing yourself for another in mortal danger. To some, it has a certain... heroic appeal."

Felix paused, missing the veiled compliment, too lost in thought. He'd had his own suspicions about what had happened, but at the time there had been so much going on.

"I want to ask you what happened to the bottle that Bertruk gave you," Mrs Luncher said.

"Well," said Felix, a little self-consciously. "I carried it around with me as a good-luck charm. A bit of nonsense, really..."

"And did you ever use it?" She was staring right at him, a single curl of smoke rising from her pipe.

"No." Felix thought back to that day, that fateful day. "Who would I... Actually, wait." He was lying on the rooftop of Placenamia Courtroom. His heart had been seared by the terrible magic of the demon Jurrekker. It was only the intervention of the God of Justice Habeus and the Celestial being Cherinda that were keeping him alive, and their own spells were wearing off.

Oh, Cherinda. I haven't thought about her for... for...

"Felix?" asked Racelsus, a note of concern in her voice.

He shook his head. "Sorry." He remembered lying on the roof, the sun setting, looking over the city that had once been his home for many difficult years. He had unstoppered the bottle, pouring the powdery contents to the wind... *why had he done that?*

"Yes..." he said. "Just before I... well, before I, you know, I opened that bottle and tipped it to the wind. It was carried away on a gust, and then that's the last thing I remember."

Mrs Luncher had a smile like a cat that had caught a particularly irritating mouse. "I knew it," she said. To Racelsus, she mumbled: "You owe me five silvers."

"Pft," Racelsus replied, an impressive sound for a skull with no lips to make.

Mrs Luncher turned back to Felix. "We think you might have, well, broken the charm. Not in a the-spell-is-broken, you-are-no-longer-cursed sort of way, but more like in a you-dropped-the-teapot-and-it-is-broken way."

"Still very much there, essentially, just in lots of pieces and scattered all over the floor," offered a grumpy Racelsus. "Five silvers, indeed…"

"The spell wasn't meant to be offered out to multiple people, you see," said Mrs Luncher, well into her flow. "So, when you spread it to the winds, you unknowingly - or perhaps, knowingly," she added with a meaningful look, "sacrificed yourself for the protection of thousands."

"But," Racelsus continued, her tone thawing with each word. "The spell, as I said, is quite old-fashioned. Only if you can actually *save* someone does it do anything. And, no offence, but a gallant warrior in shining armour you are not."

"None taken," said Felix, a little hurt despite it being obviously true. The old image of himself standing on a mountain of corpses wearing a chainmail thong burst unbidden into his mind. He waved it away like a bad smell.

"…So," the witch went on. "How can *you* help people? Why, by saving their *legal* life, of course. So the charm connected you with those in dire straits, back against the wall, no hope of rescue from those who would abuse the law… making you-"

"-The ghostly guardian of the legally destitute." said Mrs Luncher with a flourish. *Had she been saving that line?*

Felix stared at them both. It made sense in an unbelievably insane kind of way. He exhaled a breathless sigh. "Furbo, what do you make of all this? Have you remembered your 'theory'?"

Furbo twitched back into focus and blinked at him. "Oh, sorry, I was miles away. What was that, my boy?"

Mrs Luncher steepled her fingers. "What is obvious, I suggest, is that there are questions you still have to answer. Soul searching, if you will excuse the expression." She stood up, hands on the desk, looking down at Felix. "I imagine that will take some time. Until you are ready to move on, or whatever the next stage of your personal journey is, I would like to inform you that you still have a place at Lunchers & Co if you want it. We - I - would very much like to have you working with us again, for as long as you like and in whatever capacity you feel comfortable."

Felix had no idea what his future entailed, but he knew where he wanted to be for the present. He stood up himself and willed some corporeality into his hands, so that he could shake the hand of Mrs Luncher.

"I'd like nothing more, ma'am," he said, trying and failing to disguise an emotional wobble in his voice.

She nodded as if that was what she had expected, then grimaced slightly. "I'm more than happy to continue paying you for your services, but I'm not sure precisely... what the state of your estate is."

"As in, do I still have a bank account?"

"Well, yes. Legally, it's a little... unclear."

Felix laughed. "I'm sure we'll figure it out. Maybe we'll even set some precedent of our own? 'Felix's Law': The Right of the Dead to Own Property?"

Mrs Luncher sat down and gave him the smallest smile. "It's good to have you back, Felix." He lowered himself again, allowing a small feeling of pride and gratitude. The feeling warmed him and he basked in it, until Mrs Luncher cleared her throat.

"Felix? Don't you have a case you need to prepare involving one Mrs Henria?"

He hopped up to his feet again. "Oh yes, of course, right away!" And he headed through the door and back to his old desk, which was exactly how he had left it. Helda stood a few paces from it, dozily frowning at a huge ceremonial pipe that was fixed to the wall, while Yetty was reading through a document of some kind.

"Hi Held-" began Felix. Yetty dropped her document and jutted her chin in his direction. Helda yelped and jumped as if she'd, well... seen a ghost. She whipped around.

"Gods, you're quiet, Felix! Made me jump out of my skin!"

"Shall I moan and groan when I walk around to help your delicate sensibilities?"

"Maybe you should get some sort of ghostly bell?" said Yetty.

"Ooooh, oooooh, doooon't miiiind mmeeee..." moaned Felix.

"What about dragging some chains?" offered Helda.

"They're very last season, spiritually speaking."

29

They paused for a moment, in comfortable silence.

"It's good to have you back," she said, and Yetty nodded.

Felix thought the same thing.

~

By nightfall, Felix was reading through a few last notes for the case of Mrs Henria. A simple enough affair, just some grubbing landlord trying to take advantage. It'd come apart like a stale biscuit in a bucket of lobsters in court.

Mr Luncher was usually the last to leave, the one responsible for locking up, and he watched Felix for a few minutes before coughing to draw his attention. Felix looked up and waved.

"I'll be fine. You go ahead and lock up. I can always, you know..." and he waved a hand in the air and made a ghostly sound.

Mr Luncher gave a good-natured chuckle. "Now, my lad. I know you're a little, well, pale-" Felix gave a snort "- but I've been keeping an eye on you since last night. Just because you're dead, that doesn't mean you can't overdo it. I'd suggest you finish for the day. Have a rest."

Felix made to protest, but saw the logic. Truth was, even though he didn't feel the same earthly urges, such as drinking or eating (unless he wanted to, of course), he still found himself growing tired. But where would he go? Who'd want a dead man in their-

"You can stay with Jucinda and I," said Mr Luncher, as if reading his thoughts. "If you want to, of course."

Felix dropped his gaze. "You've already done enough for me. I couldn't ask you to do that as well."

"Felix-"

"No, please, Mr Luncher. I'll be fine. Honestly. Just a few more minutes to finish what I'm doing, then I'll go have a lie down. If I need some peace and quiet I can just float a few feet underground. One of the perks of, you know," he said, with a 'being a ghost' sort of a face.

Mr Luncher paused, giving him a long, searching look.

"The offer's always open," he said, before nodding once and turning to leave. "See you tomorrow, my lad."

"See you then," said Felix. The door shut and he could hear the lock turning. Just like that, he was alone again.

Closing his eyes, he opened them to find himself back on that plain, the endless sea of grass, the overcast grey sky. It was only here that he could completely feel at rest. An odd pulling sensation nagged at him whenever he walked the physical world, urging him back to this plane like the thought of a warm hearth and cup of tea on a winter's evening. It felt like an itch between the shoulderblades; easy to ignore for a while, but the longer he ignored it, the more it drew him. He'd noticed it getting stronger whenever he willed himself to physical corporeality. The more 'real' he forced himself to be, the more tired he became.

Laying down on the grass, Felix closed his exhausted eyes with a sigh. Sleep never came, but as time passed, the tiredness bled slowly away. Time was impossible to judge, but lying there thinking of nothing helped. When he felt more like himself again, Felix returned to Lunchers.

He was surprised to find the summer sun had not yet risen.

~

"There isn't normally anyone in when I arrive," said Mrs Luncher. If she was surprised, she didn't show it. She removed her coat and hung it up, then gave him a quick appraising glance. "Everything okay?"

Felix smiled at her and shrugged.

I returned to an infinite field of nothing because it's the only place I feel safe. Perhaps that's a little heavy first thing in the morning.

"I couldn't sleep. I don't mean I wasn't tired, I mean I literally couldn't," said Felix. "Just sort of floated off."

"It's far too early for jokes," she replied, straightening her blouse. "I'm going to need *at least* one cup of tea before I have to endure any awful chipperness."

"Hey, you're not allowed to speak ill of me."

She groaned as she climbed the stairs to her office, but froze when her eyes fell on his desk, which in life had been a haphazard jumble of papers, folders, scrawled notes and tea stains. Now, Felix's desk was utterly pristine. She narrowed her eyes.

"Are you well, Felix?"

He followed her gaze to his immaculate desktop and shrugged.

"Is it really so remarkable that I have such a tidy workspace that you think I'm ill?"

Her look said it all. He sighed and nodded. "I'm fine, Mrs Luncher, thank you. Still just getting *used* to it all. I want to keep busy, hence the organisation… It's a stupid thing, I know, but I worry that if I don't keep constantly occupied, then… well, I'll just sort of stop."

"Stop?"

"Yes. When I stop, my mind wanders. To be honest, in the dark, with no distractions, my mind is wandering to some pretty nasty places. I can still feel…"

Felix held a hand to his chest, resting on his lapel where his heart would be, were he still alive. He paused. Mrs Luncher didn't interrupt him.

"That feeling of death. It's so… final. I could feel it dragging me down, unstoppably powerful. Like great big gorilla hands wrapped around my legs, pulling me towards some terrible unknown. Some huge, dark vortex, like the sea in the dead of a starless, moonless night. That enveloping…"

He stopped and looked at her expression of genuine concern. He smiled and waved the thoughts away like a fly at a picnic.

"Oh, look at me harping on about dead-people problems. It's far too early for that sort of nonsense."

Mrs Luncher hesitated. "Felix, you sound-"

"Depressed?" he laughed. "Well, I think death will do that to a man. Oh, I'll get over it. Don't worry about me," he said, his smile inching slightly wider, almost falling from 'comforting' into 'insane'.

Mrs Luncher wasn't buying it. She started climbing down the stairs again. "I'm serious. You still have a brain, even if it's made of light or ectoplasm or whatever. And that means you are just as vulnerable to its many foibles and tendencies. What's more-"

At that point the front door opened and Furbo sidled in with Helda in his wake, and Racelsus swinging from Helda's pack at the rear.

"We will continue this another time," said Mrs Luncher, heading upstairs. Helda flung her pack off to thump on the floor, then collapsed into a chair with a yawn, immediately springing up at the squawk from Racelsus.

Ignoring the ruckus, Furbo settled down next to Felix. "Not... interrupting anything, I hope?" he said in a low voice, having observed Mrs Luncher depart more rapidly than normal. Racelsus stared at him from her cage, which had been placed on its customary spot on the highest filing cabinet in the corner of the room. Felix shrugged.

"Nothing serious, that's for sure. Tea, anyone?"

Furbo watched Felix head off to busy himself with the kettle. Meeting Racelsus's eyes, he frowned, and could have sworn she frowned back.

4 - Assessment - *The Present*

"Then," said Felix to John, "the case with Mrs Henria concluded around a week ago, or so," said Felix. "I was actually having a look through our paperwork for potential clients, looking for the next one that stood a chance. Not that that really influences our decision. In fact, we often throw ourselves at the cases that are not very likely... to..." Felix let the sentence dribble off.

John Dagger said nothing. Felix coughed politely.

"Succeed," he said. John Dagger continued to say nothing. "Any, erm, questions?"

"Is there really a country called Placenamia?" said John. "That's a ridiculous name."

"Not a country," Felix said. "It's a city. Well, it's also a royal district. I'll have tea, thank you." He rose in his seat and called out through the doorway to Mr Luncher, who had gone to make a round, and promptly forgot what Felix wanted. Lowering himself again, he continued. "The City of Placenamia is within the Royal District of Placenamia. One is the county, not country, and one is the city, and they both reside in the South Country, which isn't really a country, more of an area, and *that* is a part of the wider continent, which is called Fowermolde, sometimes just called Molde. Make sense?"

Once Felix had spoken it all out loud, he wasn't sure if he was sure. He rubbed his chin. "Or maybe it is a country?"

"But why that stupid name? Placenamia?" said John.

"Funny story," said Felix. "When the city was founded, the Queen, who had declared it to be her royal seat, had planned a great big ceremony to give the city its official status. It had been a town - the town of South Chickenpeck - but that wasn't considered a grand enough name for a city blessed by a royal. What to rename it to? They couldn't settle on a name, but there was still an awful lot of planning to be done, so they used Placenamia as a placeholder. Then, when the day of blessing came, someone picked up the wrong Royal Charter. They'd brought a draft copy, back from when the name was still the placeholder. The Queen didn't notice, signed the charter, and the City of Placenamia was accidentally created. Then the Queen died a few days later, and it was sort of forgotten about."

John had no face, but if he did, he'd have it screwed up in irritated confusion. "So… why is the Royal District called that as well?"

"That's simpler. It was named after the city."

"And what was it supposed to be called instead of the ridiculous name it has now?"

"You know," said Felix, rubbing his jaw. "No one actually knows. It's just one of those mysteries that forms part of our collective cultural tapestry. Now, what's really interesting about the naming of Placenamia is this…"

At that moment, Yetty walked in, much to John's relief. She had not technically reached full independent Legalite stage, but after Felix's disappearance, the firm had consisted of Furbo and Helda (non-legal personnel), Dago and Merindhe (clerks and admin staff), and Mr and Mrs Luncher (lawyers, but over-worked and past retirement age.) So, she had been the sole acting lawyer for the firm in the meantime, despite her junior status, and had subsequently morphed from a Journeyman-Legalite to a de facto lawyer without anyone complaining. She looked down at her dead former mentor giving himself a history lesson.

"Finally cracked, have we?" she said, unsurprised.

"No, this is our client," said Felix, gesturing. She followed his hand. "The table?"

"No, not the… Yetty, meet John. The Dagger. John Dagger."

John, true to form, said nothing. Yetty waited.

"John… Aren't you going to introduce yourself?" Felix said, leaning close to the silent knife. The knife, once more, said nothing.

After a moment, Yetty looked at the knife, then at Felix, lastly at the knife again, then nodded as if something had made itself clear. "Okay," she said, turning to leave. "I'm just going to go and talk to Doctor Blicksey at the clinic. No-one move."

"Look," said Felix, his face inches from the dagger and in a murderous stage whisper, "if you don't want to end up scratching grout from a pub toilet, I recommend you speak up, Mr Dagger."

"Sorry," said John, with what sounded like a smile. Yetty's eyebrows raised quite without her input. In a tinny voice, John continued. "Were you speaking to me? I was miles away. What were you saying?"

"Is it legal to murder a sentient knife?" Felix mused, rubbing his chin again.

"Good question," said Mr Luncher, walking in behind Yetty with two cups of coffee and an orange. "And one you are going to have to find out," he said, handing the fruit to Felix. "Incidentally, you must try that new coffee place everyone is going on about. They've got these crescent-moon shaped cakes, and the lass who makes the drinks will surprise you, I bet."

"Thanks," said Felix, "for the tea," he muttered, but he was just happy Mr Luncher remembered the drinks at all. "What's it called?" he said as he started examining the orange for the best place to start peeling.

"I think it was 'Myths & Mochas', whatever a mocha is."

"A weapon that can talk..." whispered Yetty, ignoring the two of them.

"I can do more than that, missy," boasted John. "Loads more. In fact, why don't I show you all? It could be a bit of a laugh. Have you got something weighty that you don't mind getting cut up? Like any fruit or something?"

They all looked at Felix's orange, which Felix was just about to peel. "Well," he said sadly, turning the fruit in his hand. "I suppose I could donate it... Will I get it back?"

"Oh yes," said John.

"...Alright then."

"Good!" said John. "Let's all go outside. Oh, I'll also need an unwitting volunteer. Here's why..."

~

A few moments later, they were gathered outside: Mr Luncher, Felix, Yetty and John. At that moment, Furbo and Helda emerged from the building. Helda spoke.

"We heard what sounded like Felix trying on his 'threatening' voice a minute ago. What's going on? Oh, cool knife." She went to pick it up.

"Wait!" said Mr Luncher. He looked at the dagger. "Actually, do me a favour Helda. Can you pick up this knife and go and stand about twenty paces that way?"

She looked at him with great suspicion, hand still hovering near the handle. Mr Luncher's pranks were like snakes in the grass. Deadly, cunning, and they always got you when you weren't expecting it.

"...And why would I do that?" she said.

"Uh, science," came the reply.

"Well, if it's for *science*," said Helda, gesturing towards Furbo. "Why not let the scientist help?"

Furbo blinked as if waking up. "Eh?"

"Hold this and stand over there," said Helda.

"Oh, okay, dear." He grasped the handle of the knife. As he did so, his eyebrows raised. "Oh, that's unusual," he said "Hmm." Furbo slid the knife from the block of wood and walked about twenty paces away. He stood facing the small group, dagger held loosely in his off-hand, a thoughtful look on his face.

"Now, Furbo, old chap," said Mr Luncher. "Would you do me a favour and close your eyes?"

The old man looked at him. "Hmm... This isn't one of your pranks, is it?"

Mr Luncher looked shocked and appalled. "Certainly not! It's for science." Under his breath he added, *"I'd never be so obvious about it."*

Furbo narrowed his eyes before closing them completely. "Very well. And now what?"

Mr Luncher met Felix's gaze, then threw the orange at Furbo. It wasn't a gentle throw as if tossing a ball to a child. This was a full throw as if trying to smash a coconut against a wall. The fruit blurred through the air, looking to collide directly with Furbo's wrinkled nose. The scholar, completely unaware, stood as still as a statue, moments from injury.

Helda, her instincts honed after years on the road, noticed a second too late what was going on. "Watch out!" she screamed, raising her hand.

In a streak of silver, Furbo's arm whipped up and sliced the orange deftly into two pieces. The old man yelped as his body was forced into sudden motion, pulled by the hand jerking against his will. He opened his eyes wide, stared at his arm, then dropped the dagger point-first onto the grass, burying the blade a few inches into the mud. There was a small clink as it landed in the mud. Furbo rubbed his arm, then wiped orange spray from his face. "Well," he said, spitting pulp. "I'm hoping that meant the experiment worked?"

"I'd say so!" said Mr Luncher, laughing. "Nicely done, old sport."

"Eugh, what is this?" said John. "Would someone mind picking me up again? It's cold and stabs weird."

That was unsettling, thought Felix, watching the scene unfold. *And the orange...* He went over to pick up the pieces, hoping some of it was salvageable. Upon stooping to inspect the remains, it wasn't sliced in two, as he had originally thought. *It's sliced into eight.*

Just what are we dealing with?

Helda, her fear forgotten and replaced with awe, clapped Furbo on the arm. "That was impressive, Furbo! There's fire in the old oven yet, eh?" Furbo rubbed his arm where Helda had slapped it.

"Oh, I wish I could say that was me. I had about as much to do with that display as you did." He stopped rubbing. "Felt jolly strange though, when I first picked it up. Almost like it was willing me to... well, I don't know exactly."

Mr Luncher had finished picking up John Dagger and wiped the blade off on a handkerchief. "Oh, you have a chip in you," he said, looking at the blade. "Did you land on a rock or something?"

"I think so, just now," said John. "It's nothing."

Mr Luncher looked up at Felix, who had one hand holding a mush of orange fragments and the other resting on a hip. The concentrated look on his face caused Mr Luncher to grin. He walked over to him.

"So, Felix," he said, sliding the dagger back into its wooden block then holding it forward as if presenting it. "Tell me what you're thinking about our new client."

Felix gathered his thoughts while everyone watched him. After a moment, he tipped his hand to let the orange fall to the ground. Then he walked over to John, still held in Mr Luncher's hand, and examined the chip in his blade. He willed his hand to be solid and flicked it.

Ow, he thought.

"Hey," said John. "Careful! That's tender."

Felix nodded and turned to face everyone.

"Here's what I think," he said.

They waited for him to speak. He stroked his chin.

"It's a dagger."

"You don't say?" said Yetty. Felix ignored her. He interlaced his fingers.

"It can talk."

"Wow, slow down for us smooth-brains over here," said Helda. Yetty gave her a wink, and Helda returned it with an eyeroll, to which both of the women suppressed silent giggles. Felix ignored them both, instead looking at the dagger.

"It has memories. It has a sense of humour and a sense of justice." He looked at the orange slices. "It likes to show off." John tried to protest but Felix carried on. He gestured at the floor. "It has things it likes to, well, stab, and things it very much doesn't. It can experience what could be described as pain. In short, it *feels.*"

"Meaning?" said Mr Luncher. Felix shrugged his shoulders.

"It's…" Felix hesitated, then corrected himself. "He's alive."

Mr Luncher nodded. "I agree."

"Me too," said John. "Though call me a show-off again and, ghost or no, I'll shave your eyebrows off."

They all laughed. Felix nodded his head as if reaching a decision. He glanced sadly down at his orange.

"I suppose I'll skip breakfast then and get right to it."

The excitement over, everyone began making their way back inside, talking about the morning's events. Felix did not speak, instead considering the next move.

I can feel that life in there. I know it. But how to prove it? A knife with a soul… An object that can feel…

I think I need to have a chat with Racelsus.

~

Felix found Racelsus resting on the window on the upper floor of Lunchers. She enjoyed sitting there, in her birdcage, watching the world go by. Not for the first time, she reminded Felix of a cat. He watched her for a few moments, taking joy in her peaceful silence, her gentle observation of life.

"Serves you right, you stupid bloody squirrel," she muttered.

"I've not interrupted anything important, have I?" he said, making Racelsus gasp.

"You know, I liked it better when I could hear you walking around," she grumbled, rotating her cage using some small effort of magic. She stopped when she could see him.

"We've been discussing that, actually," said Felix. "Helda has suggested a bell."

"I've heard worse ideas. As a collar or like a jester's hat?"

"Why not try both?" He grinned, then the smile faded. "Actually, Rass, I wanted to ask you something."

"About John?"

Felix gave her a suspicious look. "Are you reading my mind?"

"I don't have to, Felix. I know you," she purred. "You're trying to figure out what it's like inside his head, what with him being an object brought to life. So you thought you'd chat to me, because you think I'm the same. But you've forgotten that I'm not an object brought to life, I'm a living person, just without a body."

"No, that's... I mean... well, when you put it that way... Pretty much. Uh, yes."

She sighed. "No, it's okay. Despite differing origins, I'm the closest to John in many ways, so it makes sense to try." She took a moment as if mentally preparing herself. "What would you like to know?"

Felix lowered himself to the floor and leaned against the wall. "How does it feel to have a mind but such a limited physical presence? No legs,

41

no hands… To just be a *thing* in the world. What does that make you feel like?"

She hesitated. "To never strum a harp again, or climb a mountain? To never carve a wooden sculpture, or caress the face of a loved one?" Felix didn't reply. She sighed. A heavy, world-weary sigh.

"I didn't do any of those things anyway. To be honest, every time I feel frustration at that, at the missed potential, I just remember that without Furbo and Helda, and of course you, I'd either be still stuck in that bloody cave… or worse. So I cherish every day that comes, even if I'm just a skull in a birdcage."

Something about the way she spoke seemed off. Felix had to rub his eyes when he thought he could make out an expression on that white, featureless skull. Almost like he could see the brows furrowing, or the lips compressing. When he tried to focus on them, they vanished.

"What?" she said, a testy edge to her voice. "What are you staring at?"

"It's okay, Racelsus," said Felix softly. "You're still allowed to feel sad about all of those things." She didn't reply. "Just because you could have had it worse, doesn't mean that you aren't allowed to wish for better. It's okay. I know what it's like."

The witch paused before replying. "Well. Nevertheless. I'd suggest you remember that John has no point of reference. He has never had hands or legs, or what have you, so he can't miss them. Instead, he has his own vision of how he wants his life to go, and *that* is what I'd keep in mind. What you think of as a full and fulfilled life is completely different to what John thinks."

"That's… a really good point. Thanks Racelsus. I need to go and have a word with him." He stood and made to head back downstairs. "I'll speak to you soon. Remember what I said."

She smiled, or at least it seemed that way. "Don't worry about me, Felix. I'm fine." As he descended the staircase, she rotated her cage once again to look out the window, and experienced, for the first time, what it felt like to cry without eyes.

Journal Entry A - Copyrite

Reference case [GTvHh] (GerTun v. EldFur & FelSha & Fir et al), year 1295, Judge Greenway presiding.

It's a common enough storyline. The nefarious and mystical grimoire that contains spells so powerful that if the evil sorcerer were to read them, the safety of the very world would be at stake! Or maybe the story of the wizard obsessed with knowledge, putting himself in mortal peril just for a peek at Ye Greate and Teriyble Spellbouke Of Scethrog The Darke, or something. Let's face it; spellbooks are cool.

We all know they exist, of course, and not just in stories. But not many people think about *why* these spellbooks are written. What if I told you it's for the same reason that most things are written?

Artistic expression and the collective struggle for human advancement.

I'm kidding, obviously. The answer is cash.

People become wizards or mages or spell-breakers etcetera for a number of reasons. Some genuinely do want to make the world a better place, and so spend their days undergoing academic research, working and developing magicks of all varieties to answer life's problems, big or small. Most want to use their combination of brains and bureaucratic prowess to bleed each other dry.

Consider this: the classic light-globe spell. It's a dark room, you want to conjure a globe of light in order that you can see. Simple right? Well, the quickest, most reliable and most energy-efficient version of this spell is Lady Effa's Simple Light-Globe. I understand that it requires only a few specific gestures and no reagents at all. The problem is, if you want to learn how to do the spell, you have to either A) figure it out yourself, B) have an experienced wizard teach it to you, or C) read it in a book.

Good luck with 'A'. If you can do that, more power to you (literally.) 'B' only works if you have befriended (or blackmailed) someone, or coughed up enough cash to enroll at one of the universities, which rules most people out. So that leaves us with 'C'.

The going rate for a half-decent spellbook of, say, thirty spells (though these days, spellbooks seem less about the 'spells' and more about the 'art'...) is around sixty golds, give or take. Yep, two golds a spell. Pricey stuff! What's worse, if you want to learn the latest development from an experienced spell-weaver like Lady Effa, you can't just buy that one spell, oh no. It'll be included in 'Lady Effa's Mysterium-Arcane, Volume XII', along with twenty rites you already know. Does that reduce the price? Of course not.

Oh, and I use the word 'rite' here deliberately. As far as I can tell, a 'rite' is the same as a 'spell', but about fifteen times more expensive. I will hereafter use the word 'spell', because I'm not a snob.

If you want to remain on the cutting edge of magic, well, you'll have to fork out for these 'new' spells. I say 'new', because it's not unknown for books to just rehash existing magic with a slightly different aspect. Perhaps a spell of 'air displacement' instead of 'gentle wind', or a new 'spell of darkness' that promises to be 10% darker than the last one. Universities in particular have little choice but to cough up for the latest in magickery. A cynic might wonder if the book was padded out with bulk to increase the eye-watering sales price.

There's also the hype that surrounds a completely new spell. Imagine practising magic for twenty years, only for someone to announce a brand new, never before seen spell. It'd be like an artist being given a brand new colour.

(Incidentally, some wizards have claimed that they *have* invented a new colour, but no one has ever really believed them. Helda bought a jacket that is supposedly this new colour. It just looks like a greenish-yellow-purpley thing to me. The cat loves it, though.)

And how does one see or learn this new spell, this new facet to existence, this latest branch of the universe? Exactly. Cough up, matey.

So, it's no wonder that the thought of a hidden and unknown spellbook buried in the depths of an ancient tomb is enough to besparkle the eyes of many explorers or academics. It could be full of all manner of undiscovered spells… promising huge returns. Or, untold dangers. Perhaps both.

But what if you don't have the money to buy access to premium magic, or the wherewithal to go tomb-diving? There is… an option. You *could* try your luck with Gergle O'Tunken's Budget Magic For The Everyman, a hefty volume of one hundred spells for the bargain price of three golds. How could you say no?

Aha, you mutter knowingly, but surely the other wizards who make their living from the expensive spellbooks would object? And you'd be right. They did. And they took him to court.

"Page fifteen," whined Elder Furrow. "Icicle-Spray. It is exactly the same entry as in my own book, page seventeen: Furrow's Frozen Spears."

"And this," moaned the Witch Felicity Shadowmind. "So-called 'darkness spell' - it is a blatant copy of my own spell: Shadowmind's Cloak of Purest Night."

O'Tunken's lawyer stood up and shook his head. "I think you will find that there is a final step in each of my client's spells that you are missing." He flipped open the grimoire and stopped at page fifteen. "Step three, form the above shape with your fingers and thrust them forward in time with the words from step one. Step four, wiggle your fingers and say: habooba."

"That last step is totally pointless!" screamed The Great Warlock Firemouth. "It has just been inserted into each spell at random to make it *technically* different from the spells in our books!"

"So you admit that it is a different spell?" asked his lawyer calmly. Firemouth's face reddened even more.

O'Tunken lost the case and had to destroy all remaining copies of his work, as well as pay the assembled cadre for the alleged missed earnings. Apparently, he did so, almost instantly, with nothing but a shrug.

Mr Luncher told me he had a pint with the grand old mage, once. He'd recognised him from the back page of a copy of the above grimoire that he'd bought when he was a lad. When he asked O'Tunken about how hurt he must have felt, as well as the financial implications, the old man swigged his pint and shook his head.

"I made my money as a youth," he sighed. "But as I got older, I learned that true wealth comes from knowledge and kindness. The best way to spend it is to spread it." He had laughed, a broad, welcoming laugh. "Do you really think I destroyed *all* the leftover copies of my book? Of course, I destroyed all the ones *I* possessed. I had to. But I know for a fact that people still buy and sell illicit copies of it. How? Trust me. I can't tell you any more than that. And I tell you what…" He leaned in close. "That whole legal rigamarole? How many people do you think knew about my book *before*, and how many *after?*"

~journal entry ends

5 - Prep I

The summer warmth was filling the interview room with a close heat, not helped by the closed window and closed door. Neither of the two occupants, one dead, one made of metal, particularly minded. One of them, the dead one, spoke.

"So, John. What do you actually want?"

If John had had eyes, he would have blinked. "What do I want?"

Felix twiddled the pencil in his hand and tapped it on the blank page in front of him. "Mm. I want it in your words. Tell me, John Dagger: What do you want from life?"

He scoffed. "Well I... I want to do what I want to do, that's what!"

"Can you elaborate?" said Felix, writing a few words down.

"Yes! Of course!" There was a short silence. Felix did not rush him. "I want to be free to make my own choices and experience my own..." John made an embarrassed sound, like he was about to humiliate himself. "...destiny. Sounds a bit airy-fairy, perhaps, but..." his tinny voice dwindled.

"No, I get it," said Felix, putting his pencil down. "I really do."

There was a pause, after which Felix started writing again.

"So," said Felix, between scribbles. "You're here now. Here in Lunchers." He waved the pencil around to indicate this. "Why not call it quits? You're very welcome to hang around here and do whatever it is you want to do, provided it doesn't interfere with the running of the business, that is. We can forget all about everything that's happened to you and forge you a new life, right here."

John didn't reply.

"John?" said Felix, putting down his pencil again and looking at the dagger in earnest. "I mean it. It's yours if you want it. What do you say?"

"So I can just... be here? I won't get locked in a drawer, or smelted down or anything?"

"No."

John Dagger sighed, which was an odd sound for a knife to make. After a brief silence, he spoke. "Here's my take on it. I was brought into awareness without my say so to start with, right? And by a bit of luck and chance, I was given a day in the spotlight, with everyone paying lots of attention and fawning over me and whatnot. Then, quick as that, they forgot me, and would have left me stuck in a dark drawer forever, or worse. That's no kind of life."

A small cloud passed overhead, dimming the light in the room. "A bit more luck and I've found myself here, among you mad lawyers and wordsmiths. But I know I'm not the only one out there to have been brought into life and given no autonomy over it. Could I rest happy, knowing that through my inaction thousands more like me are suffering in silence? Doomed to lives of boredom? Seen as nothing more than tools, then discarded? Granted life, then denied freedom?"

The light glinted from his blade as the cloud passed on. "No, I don't think so. I want people to realise that if you breathe life into something, even a hitherto so-called inanimate object, you have some responsibility over it. Will it result in fewer living objects? Probably. But will it result in better lives for Objectkind? I think so."

He took a deep breath, more for effect than for any practical purpose. "So, Mr Sacramentum, in slightly fewer words, you can stick that suggestion where it won't catch sunlight."

Felix grinned and pointed with this pencil. "I was hoping you'd say that. Maybe without the suggested… Never mind. John Dagger, consider yourself represented."

He extended his hand and immediately felt like an idiot. Something guided his hand, though, gently nudging it to John's handle. He grasped it with as much warmth as a ghostly hand can muster, and a feeling of mutual respect flooded up his arm. He released the handle.

"Okay," Felix said. "What do you know about the law?"

"Bugger all," said John. "Only that you can't stab people, and yet people still forge swords."

Felix nodded as if this was what he expected. He leaned back in his chair and rested his hands together behind his head. "Okay. So. Back in the ancient days, there was a god called Habeus and a farmer called Corney…"

~

"…and so, generally speaking, we as a society all agree to follow these rules, or else face the consequences."

"And if you don't, some bearded madman from the sky kills you?"

"No, er, not quite. If you break these laws, then you are punished - again, according to the law. So the bigger the crime, the larger and more serious the punishment."

John mulled this over. "Makes sense. And you lot. Lawyers, Where do you come in?"

"Well, it is only fair that someone that needs to take an issue to court, to be heard by one of those judges I mentioned, then their argument should get as good a chance as it can get to be heard and judged. So, lawyers like me represent a person - with their argument - and do all the talking for them."

"A person?" said John.

Oops.

"Uh, yes, legally speaking. A person, human or otherwise, alive or otherwise, a dagger or otherwise." He offered a smile. John did not react.

"Why don't people just do it themselves?"

"They can, of course. But it's complicated and difficult, some say on purpose. And, more often than not, if it goes wrong and you lose in court, your life is going to change, and not usually for the better. So you want someone who knows how the courtroom works to help you and give you the greatest chance. Particularly if the other side are going to be doing the same.

"Let me explain it this way. Imagine if you were tasked to write a song, and then that song will get performed to a room full of song-writing experts. To truly show how great a song it is, you'd want someone who can sing really well to perform it, right? You might be a great singer yourself, sure, but the chances are there are plenty of singers out there who are much more experienced and know exactly how to take that song and make it, well, *sing*. Plus, they might offer their own observations on your undoubtedly fantastic song, little tweaks to make it shine that much brighter. Make sense?"

"Yes, I think so…"

The door opened and Yetty walked in and widened her eyes. "Whoa, it's warm in here." She walked over to the window and slid it open. Felix continued.

"So, now imagine if this singing contest was to the death, and…" he trailed off as he met Yetty's eyes. "What?" he said.

"A singing contest to the death?" she said, lowering herself to a chair.

"Yes! And, uh," Felix said, his confidence faltering. "Then, you could… Oh, I've lost my train of thought."

"But…" said John. "What if neither side had lawyers at all, and instead both sides just had to figure it out among themselves?"

"That wouldn't work, of course," said Yetty.

"Why?" asked John.

"Why? Because, well, it just wouldn't," she replied, looking to Felix for help. "It isn't the way things are done, and that cat is out of the bag. Now that people *can* employ lawyers, they sure as sure aren't going to *not* do so. Right, Felix?" she said, taking a sip of her water.

"Eh?" said John. "I'm sure that didn't make sense."

"John," said Felix, "I get where you're coming from, but for good or for ill, things are the way they are. When you're High Lord Emperor, we can take another look at the legal system, but until then: we're your best option. And we're not charging you, either."

"Lawyers charge people? Not much, I assume?"

Yetty coughed into her drink. "Uh, it varies," said Felix.

"And, that's another strange thing," said John. "Money, whose stupid idea was that?"

Felix stood and stretched his back out. Why, despite being a ghost, did he still have lower back pain? *If I ever meet the great creator, that's going on the list.*

"Wait until you hear about religion," said Felix. "Now that gets complicated."

Furbo's head poked around the door, with a mild pained expression. "We're talking about religion? And you didn't ask me?"

How did he hear me?

"No, Furbo, not right now."

"Oh," said Furbo. He looked genuinely disappointed. Felix sighed.

"I'm sure John would love an overview sometime later though?"

"I don't-" said John.

"Aha! Splendid!" said Furbo, tapping his nose. "I'll prepare the documents." With that, he vanished again.

"Uh, sorry," said Felix. "In advance." He stretched again. "I think that's all for today, if you are both willing. I need... rest." In truth, that yearning, that pulling sensation was getting stronger. He needed to return to the grey plain again.

"Not a problem," said John. "I'll just, well, sort of wait here I suppose."

"Do you want to rest on the windowsill alongside Racelsus?" asked Yetty. "Nice views from up there."

"I don't have any eyes," said John, and Yetty slapped her forehead. "But, why not. Yes please." Yetty lifted John in his stand and made to carry him upstairs, but paused at the door to look at Felix.

"Are you alright?" she said.

"Yes, I'm fine. Just tired." In reality, he felt worn through, like he hadn't slept in days. This feeling would come on him suddenly, and wear him down in minutes. "I'll speak to you tomorrow."

She lingered for a brief moment, then disappeared. Felix heard John's metallic voice as they walked away. "I think he's putting on a brave face, you know."

Felix sighed, then, an instant later, lay on the long, grey grass and looked up at the smooth, grey sky. He closed his eyes, unaware that he was being watched.

6 - Prep II

"Everyone," said Mrs Luncher one morning over coffee. "A letter has just arrived addressed to the representatives of John Dagger." The staff were getting ready for the day by sharing hot drinks and breakfast, as was tradition on starting a new case. John was on the table, in his customary holder.

"That was fast," said Felix, feeling much refreshed after a night of rest. "We've only really started taking instruction from him, well, this week."

"What's going on?" said John. "I haven't instructed anyone on anything, apart from Helda, and that wasn't really an instruction, just me telling her that her singing was bad."

"And I instructed you to bog off," said Helda, "if my learned friend do so recall."

Mrs Luncher handed the letter to Felix, who peered at it before turning it over. It was made of expensive paper with a glitter-shiny wax seal of blackish red. In the centre of the wax seal was an illustrated 'J'.

"See, this is what I keep thinking we need," said Yetty over a crumpet. "Look how good that looks! Intimidating, right? Serious, yes?"

"*Expensive*, agreed," said Mrs Luncher. Yetty rolled her eyes.

Felix ignored them and opened the letter. He was so distracted he'd even forgotten to make the joke about using John as a letter opener, and went straight for popping the wax seal off.

What did Jurviles have to say this early on?

He began to read aloud.

"To Luncher's & Co, the firm representing John Dagger.
It has come to the attention of the estate of Lady Vinch that the object calling itself John Dagger has taken steps to obtain recognition of its legal position as an autonomous and independent legal entity.
Being as the object in question belongs to the Vinch estate, and therefore any matters pertaining to it are the business of the estate and no other, please be advised

that Jurviles, acting on behalf of the Vinch estate, will take any and all action necessary to return the object to Lady Vinch so that it may be properly disposed of.

It is requested, therefore, that upon receipt of this letter, the staff of Luncher's & Co should make all reasonable efforts to return the object to the Vinch estate at their earliest convenience. Doing so shall be an end to the matter as far as the Vinch estate is concerned.

Failure to do so shall be met with direct legal action taken against the object in question and those attempting to abet it.

Warmest regards,

-Mettea Jurvile

Legal Counsel to the Vinch Estate"

"What the hell is this?" said John, a ring of panic in his tinny voice. "I'm not going back there!"

"Now don't worry John," said Yetty. "It sounds like a lot, but this is what we're used to."

"It sounds like they're trying to wrong-foot us," said Felix, who had started pacing. "They're trying to intercept us, before…" His voice trailed off.

"What are you thinking?" said Yetty. Felix's eyes suddenly opened wide and he leapt to his feet.

"Of course!" he shouted, making everyone jump. He started gesturing with his hands. "All we care about is getting John the legal status we all think he deserves, yes? No criminal case required. No real significant fear of going in front of a judge, because it's not like we'd walk out of there in any worse a situation than the one we walked in with. What we are after is more of a bureaucratic clarification, right?"

"Uh, right," said Helda, when no one replied immediately.

Felix clapped his hands. "That's why I'm here! I was starting to wonder! It didn't make sense. If you were in no real danger, why was I brought here to help?"

Furbo cleared his throat. "Racelsus and I were going to mention it when the time was right. It does seem that-"

"-whatever force brings me back to assist with these cases only does so when the person is in real, mortal danger," said Felix, quickly and excitedly. "Capital punishment on the line, destitution or poverty so extreme that death is a likely result, that sort of thing. So why would I have been brought back for your case, John, which is far from dangerous?"

"Uh," said John.

"Exactly! But whatever force it is, well, it *knows*. Gods, it knows. Of course!"

"What does it know, for goodness sake?" said John. Felix's eyes and hands were flicking around, moving at the speed of his thoughts.

"Look. Originally, this was a simple case of bureaucracy, like a will, or a name change, right? No offence, but not really the sort of thing I would expect to be 'brought back' for. But! What are the implications? Let's say you're given legal status as a living person. What then? The Vinch estate is suddenly responsible for you! They're the ones who brought you to life, as it were, or at least arranged for it to happen, and so will have to then look after you. They'll also have to answer some awkward questions about what happened to you after the murder case you were brought to life in. Not only that, but it starts to get inconvenient when dealing with inheritances and entitlements and other hereditary questions... Plus, we all know how amenable old, rich estates are to having to fork out hard-hoarded cash to help the needy and vulnerable."

Felix stopped pacing. "So, to stop that from happening, they think it's in their best interests to nip it in the bud, so to speak, and stop the question from ever being asked. They want to stop you from ever getting your day in court so you never get the opportunity to be considered a legal person, thereby skipping all this unfortunate business, from their perspective. Oh, those sneaky..." He shook his head.

"But what has that to do with you and your ghostly, er, ness?" said John.

"I'm only called back here when someone is in very real need or danger. When their life is at stake. This is proof to me that they are not just wanting to sweep you under the rug, John, but they want to... well..."

"Kill me?" said John in a small voice.

Felix nodded, starting to calm down. "Which is why I'm here," he said, softly.

"Uh, oh, hm, well, uh," said John. Felix walked over to the table and lowered himself into a chair, so he was next to John.

"That isn't going to happen, John," He said. "You're still our client, and we're still going to fight for you. Nothing has changed from our perspective. Not a thing. Well, that's not true," he said, straightening. "One thing has."

"What's that?" said John.

Felix grimaced. "Now I know they are clearly trying to hide something."

~

"There's no apostrophe in Lunchers," said Mr Luncher later that morning, scowling at the letter. He waved it at his wife. "Either they're idiots or this is a tiny yet calculated insult."

"Let it go, dear," said Mrs Luncher.

"The point of there not being an apostrophe before the 's' is that the firm isn't just one Luncher, it's the two of us."

"Just ignore them. If they feel they have to be so petty, don't let them see that it irritates you so much, or they win."

Mr Luncher scoffed, frowned and then sighed. "You're right, as ever." She walked over and gave him a peck on the cheek, along with a winning smile. "Attaboy," she said, patting his other cheek. He smirked back.

"You really are insufferable, you know that?" he said.

"I know," she replied, and began heading upstairs. "That's why my name isn't on the sign."

"Even though you're the one who actually qualified as a lawyer."

"Mmhm."

"And has all the brains."

"Of course."

"And looks."

"And modesty, don't forget that."

"What do you even need me for?"

"And the clocks are still chiming out of time with each other."

Mr Luncher snapped a salute. "Search continues for the thingy to change them, General!"

"Well, the sign still needs a lick of paint, you know."

"Aye, ma'am!" barked Mr Luncher. "Would ma'am like to sharpen her talons on my face while she's here? Perhaps she'd like one of my eyeballs for her latest poultice? I could spoon it out and straight into her cauldron, if she likes?"

"Just the sign will do, dear," she said, from near the top of the stairs. After a moment, her voice floated down. "Actually, I am creating a new husband from parts I've harvested, so anything you can spare would be fantastic. Your brain, perhaps?"

"Surely you have enough for the both of us?"

They both started to giggle, then got on with the rest of the day.

~

"So, are we the prosecution or the defence?" John's voice was as chirpy and twangy as ever, now he had had some time to process his situation.

"Well, since the Vinch estate are bringing a case against you, we are now the defence," said Felix, feeling much refreshed after a period of rest. It was the afternoon of the following day, and a bright, sunny day it had turned out to be. Felix and John were at one of the desks, with Furbo, Helda and Yetty nearby, mugs in hand. "You are the victim, you see, and we are representing your rights. In this case, your right to life."

He'd finished preparing the paperwork early that morning, and had filed it with the courts before lunch. His official reply to Jurviles had been short and satisfying to write.

"Dear Mettea Jurvile.

John Dagger respectfully declines your client's offer and invites you to reconsider your position.

If that is disagreeable, then we shall await a summons to court at your convenience.

Regards,

F. Sacramentum,

-Lunchers & Co

After dropping it off and spending a few minutes walking around the courtroom foyer, he was waved down by a clerk and was given a prospective date there and then, which seemed a bad omen. Clearly Jurviles had been expecting this answer. The date given was in three weeks' time. This speedy assignment was due to an unplanned gap in scheduling, and to his surprise it was being heard in Great Ogtown, West Country. The courtroom at Great Ogtown, was... well, it's bound to have come on by leaps and bounds since his last visit. It was probably going to be fine.

Felix suppressed a shudder, then shook himself.

"To give you an idea of where my head is, let me summarise my feelings on your case as a whole." Felix stood up and began pacing slowly, hands clasped behind his back.

"Once you were brought to life - against your will, certainly without your consent, of course - those who performed the spell and created your cogniscience then neglected to treat you in the way you deserved to be treated, as a newly conscious being - that is, portioning you with the means to fulfil your spiritual needs. Make sense so far?"

"Yes, though I don't know what you mean by portioning."

"Providing."

"Or cogniscience."

"Self-awareness."

"Well, why didn't you just say 'providing' or 'self-awareness'?"

Helda snorted. "Exactly!" she said, giving Furbo a meaningful look. "There's plenty'a words already without people making to use more than what they needed to. Makes'em awkward to follow, speaking-wise fashion." Furbo visibly recoiled from this butchered sentence, gripping his mug tightly with both hands. Felix rolled his eyes and continued.

"So, John, we argue that these people did not treat you in the way that a living, sentient being should be treated, especially one that they were directly responsible for giving life to. This morning, I suggested in a conversation with the lawyer representing the Vinch estate that we were seeking to obtain 'living person' status for you."

"Wait, how did they find you already?"

"When I dropped off our official response to their letter, I hung around for a few minutes, just to see if anything happened. And, what do you know, someone found me not five minutes later. Rich, influential families get priority treatment from the big, expensive firms, like Jurviles, and so word must have travelled around while I was there, and they must have had some pre-arranged script to follow. One of their lawyers came up to me and that's when we started speaking. He knew it all already, of course. They'd worked it out for themselves what we were going to do." Felix stopped. "I'm not completely sure how they found out about our intentions this quickly, though. That's a little concerning." He turned to Helda, Furbo and Yetty, who were all examining their boots, or fingernails, or the table with unnatural interest. "No one has been talking about John outside of Lunchers, have they?" said Felix, slowly.

They all looked immediately sheepish. "Have they?" he repeated.

"Well," said Helda. "John had really wanted to see the inside of the Duck In Flagon…"

"So we took him there when you had disappeared…" said Yetty.

"And he said that people seem to spend a lot of their time drinking," said Helda.

"And that it would be a worthwhile thought experiment to see if we could get him drunk," said Yetty.

"And it all got a little fuzzy after that," finished Furbo with a weak smile.

Felix stared at all of them. In their defence, they didn't hide their embarrassment. After a moment, Felix headed over to the doorway.

"Mrs Luncher," he called.

"Yes?" came the reply from somewhere out of sight.

"Do you still have those huge, thick books on Client Confidentiality and Authoritative Privilege? The ones penned by Cubb and Fekkit?"

"Yes, I believe so," came the reply. "Very big, dry books, those ones."

The three of them groaned.

"And Business Secrets, with Reference to Legal Strategy by Killok et al?"

More groans.

"Yes, I do. A *particularly* chunky tome, that one."

59

Helda lowered her head on the table and Yetty put her palms over her eyes.

"What about Morality of The Law by Professor Oakke Wrenna?"

"Oh yes, all four volumes."

Even Furbo, normally thrilled by the idea of large dusty books, was looking a little apprehensive.

"Can I borrow them for, oh, say, a month?"

"Of course," came Mrs Luncher's voice. "I can spare you a few notebooks as well?"

"What's going on?" said John. Felix gave him a borderline psychotic smile.

"Just arranging a little in-house training for three of the staff, John. Nothing to worry about."

"I, uh, can't read," murmured Helda. Felix's smile broadened. "Uh, that is… I mean, I can't… well… I suppose I can, a bit…"

Felix's smile lingered a moment, then faltered, and morphed into a frown. He then shook his head and shrugged.

"They were bound to find out anyway sooner or later, I suppose." He chewed his lip, then slapped his hands together. "Okay. Well. Right. Onwards and upwards. No use crying over spilled confidential information."

Helda perked up. "No studying?"

"*Absolutely* studying, Helda," said Felix.

"Wait," said John, ignoring Helda's expletive-laden outburst. "Hang on. So someone overhears a chat in the pub, then word moves around the country and into the ears of the Vinch estate already? And they've instructed a team of lawyers who are already preparing a case, and we're getting heard in three weeks? It all happens that quickly?"

Felix nodded, and started pacing again. "Yes, sometimes. Law often either happens agonisingly slowly or eye-wateringly fast. So, when the advice from the family had been relayed, this lawyer explained to me the official Vinch family response, which has presumably already been checked and re-written several times to be as precise and likely-to-get-the-result-they-want as possible."

He tutted. "Lawyers, right? They then decided to head it off at the pass, as it were, and have brought this case in which they will no doubt try to establish that you, and by extension other animate objects, should not be considered alive. Your defence - our defence - is that you are alive." Felix stopped pacing and sipped his tea. "All we have to do is prove it."

"How on earth are you going to do that?" said John.

"That's why you hire a lawyer," said Yetty, without missing a beat, and John laughed.

"Fair enough!" he conceded. "So what happens now?"

A knock at the door and Felix headed over. "Now," he said, reaching for a book that Dago had just held out to him from the doorway, "is the fun part. We read, we do our research, and we find a few reliable people out there who can provide testimony that will help our case."

"What, so random people will form part of my case? Do they get paid?"

"If they are an expert witness, that is, someone presenting a key skill or understanding of a complex area, they do get paid. If they're not an expert, i.e. a normal witness, they do not."

"They don't get paid? Then why should they care what happens to me?" said John.

"Because," said Felix. "One of the good and bad parts of our legal system is that everyone is responsible for doing their part. Most of the time, it's just obeying the law. Other times, it's using your unique collection of knowledge and experience to provide expert testimony on a specific area of interest for a particular case. Or maybe you are just some random person who happened to see something important that relates to the case. Then, if we want to hear what you have to say, you are *compelled* to attend court and explain what you saw. If you don't, then…"

"You get in *lots* of trouble," Yetty finished.

"So… you have to waste your time being questioned for no tangible benefit?" said John.

"Not at all," Felix continued. "You are part of the great machine of the law. Sure, you might be forced to spend a few days being grilled by a lawyer in front of a judge, for the benefit or detriment of someone you've never met, and doubtless you'd rather be in the pub or out in the woods or whatever. But it's part of what we are expected to do, because there may come a day when *you* are the one in the defendant's chair, fighting for your life and freedom. And if that day *does* come, you'll be glad that these mechanisms are in place."

He took a deep breath. Yetty stood up and spoke. "Well said. Now, after a lecture like that, I need a drink. Anyone want one?"

John considered his words. "So," he said. "Do you have a list of these witnesses?"

"We have a few ideas," said Felix, eyeing his empty mug, then handing it to Yetty with a nod. "Tea, please, if you're offering."

"Like who?" Yetty asked, reaching for the coffee.

And Felix told her.

7 - The Courtroom

On the evening before the case was due to be heard, the whole crew of Lunchers were in the garden behind the office, enjoying a summer evening of clear skies and a pleasant breeze. Dago was tending a grill above a narrow firepit, and Merindhe was experimentally roasting various unidentified sizzling morsels on sticks. The mood was good in the firm. Having Felix back had restored something to the general motivation of everyone, though he didn't realise that himself.

In truth, Lunchers had become a quiet, increasingly sad place after his departure. Each case fought in that three month period had been given the appropriate care and attention, but no one would admit it had become more difficult with each passing week.

"What would Felix have done?" was never spoken but often thought. Yetty especially found herself returning to that sentence. It helped, sometimes, but hurt more often. Helda and Furbo had quietly discussed their own plans, and when and where they were to head off to next, but something about the diminished and struggling Lunchers & Co made it hard to take those first outward steps. A week became two, became a month, became two, and still they remained, united in their shared grief and individual sadnesses. Even Mr and Mrs Luncher, often stressed but never angry, had felt a strain on their optimism, and had caught themselves sniping at one another (though never at the staff).

Since Felix's miraculous return, the firm had felt rejuvenated, and now, with a fresh and worthwhile case on the horizon, spirits were high. The prep had been done, the documents sorted and labelled, and it had been decided that there was nothing more to do, so they might as well enjoy the evening.

"Move your bloody stick," said Dago, waving a large, flat scraper at Merindhe. "You're in the way."

"Oh, there's plenty of room," she lied in return. "Besides, aren't you curious what barbequed snail tastes like?"

"Incredibly, no." He prodded and poked the food as it sputtered and hissed on the grill. "How do you even skewer a snail?"

Behind them, Mr and Mrs Luncher were examining one of the garden's small trees, inspecting it for problems or pests. A cherry tree, Felix guessed, though a botanist he was not. It hadn't bloomed yet.

On the other side, a red-faced Yetty was trying to compare biceps with Helda and losing miserably, but being cheered on by Racelsus. Furbo was snoozing in a hard, wooden chair, a half-smile on his face.

Felix relaxed on a similar chair, one of those carried from inside the office to serve as impromptu gardenware. Somehow, through some divine intervention, none of the towering stacks of paperwork or precariously balanced paraphernalia had been knocked over in the process of liberating the office of half a dozen of the wonky, awkward chairs. Getting them back in, though...

"Bet you five silvers that Helda knocks three things over in the course of the evening," he said to John, who was resting in his stand on a chair next to Felix.

John was quiet. Felix sat forward, lowering his drink. "John, are you okay?"

"No," he said. "I'm nervous and worried."

"That's natural," said Felix. "I feel nervous and worried before every case, no matter what it's about. Even the little ones."

"Is that supposed to make me feel better?"

"John, we've prepared as much as we can. I - we - have done as much as we can do, and tomorrow I'm going to stand up there and be the best bloody lawyer I can be."

"And if we lose and they decide to melt me down?"

"Then I swap you for a mundane dagger and smuggle you out of there," said Felix, without missing a beat.

John paused. "You'd do that?"

"Sure. I decided I'd do that the moment I agreed to take your case, if it came to it."

"But that would be breaking the law, wouldn't it?"

Felix reached for his drink and sipped it. "Maybe a bit, but in the grand scheme of things... I had a bit of an idea - you see, if they declare you *not* a person, then you will have no rights. So in effect, you would just be a *thing*. If they decide to be petty and try to destroy you, then I'm going to steal you. If we get a copy made, then maybe they just think you're giving them the silent treatment. How would they know? Worst comes to the worst, it all comes out, I get convicted of theft. And, uh, maybe something about perverting justice. But I'll worry about that if it happens." He sipped his drink again.

"You - a lawyer - would break the law?"

"I might be a lawyer, but I'm still a human. If I have to break a law to save a friend, then I'll do it, no hesitation."

"…Friend?"

"Of course, John," said Felix, smiling. "To save a friend."

"Huh," said John. "Is it too late to change my lawyer? Mine's crooked."

A comfortable silence passed between them.

"I have a question for you," said Felix, leaning back in his chair. "Something I've been wondering for a while."

"Oh?" said the dagger.

"Why 'John'? What made you choose that name?"

"What do you mean?"

"Well, I suppose it didn't strike me as a very… 'daggery' name."

"What should I be called? Slicey Jim? Stabby Pete?"

"Just Slicey or Stabby, maybe? Shanker? Ol' Sharp'n'Pokey?"

John gave a single small laugh, then paused. "I don't know," he said, his voice serious. "I heard someone calling someone else John, and I liked it. Then I learned people often have two names. One they're given, or they choose, and one that links them to the past. I didn't want to hide what I was or where I came from, you know?"

Felix swirled his drink in its cup, watching the liquid spin, but said nothing.

"Felix?" said John, a note of concern in his voice.

"Sorry," said Felix. "Got lost in my thoughts. What were we talking about? Something about me being corrupt? How about I slide you a gold piece and we forget all about it?"

They laughed together, and the sound carried into the evening, mingling with some gentle snoring and good-natured ribbing.

8 - The Morning

The case was to be heard, not in the City of Placenamia, but in the court of Great Ogtown, the capital of the West Country. Lunchers itself was located only half a day's walk from the city. Great Ogtown (often shortened by the locals to Togtun) was a far cry from the sophisticated metropolis that was Placenamia. Where the capital of the South Country had 'districts', Togtun had 'parts'. Placenamia had roads, Togtun had lanes. Placenamia had a grand, stone courtroom standing proudly as a testament to justice. Togtun had...

"Is this it?" said Helda. "This is the greatest courtroom in the West Country?"

Felix looked up at it. It hadn't changed since his death. It hadn't changed since his birth. "Yep. That's it."

It might have been imposing, once, but in the meantime it had given up any grandiose notions and settled into respectable decrepitude. Moss ran across every dark-stone wall, and at least a quarter of the tiled roof had ramshackle repairs on it. It looked like a stiff wind would knock it down. It almost had once, or so Mr Luncher says. *The whole town had to rally around it and brace it against the Big Bloody Storm, as they called it,"* he had said.

"It could be worse," Felix said. "At least it has all four walls." *As far as I can tell.*

"Don't let the outside fool you," said Yetty. "Despite appearances, this is still a sacred hall of law and justice, and the decisions made there follow the law with as much reverence as the courtrooms of Placenamia. The judge, too, will be a learned man or woman with as much authority as any judge found in the whole continent."

At that moment, a shout followed by the rapid patter of feet caused them all to turn, and they watched a woman covered in mud chase a small pig straight into the open courtroom doors. A rattle, crash and squeal, and she walked out, carrying the wriggling swine in her arms.

She coughed, snorted and spat on the ground as she emerged. "Burt!" she yelled. "I got the bugger! Oi, Burt!" She walked past the group and vanished into the milling crowd.

"Well, I think it's lovely," said Racelsus. "A real sense of rustic charm. Reminds me of home."

"The cave?" said Helda.

"I think," said Furbo, "that Racelsus was most likely referring to the place she lived in *before* the cave." Helda rubbed her chin.

"That makes more sense, actually."

The residents of Great Ogtown wouldn't look twice at a duo like Furbo and Helda, even if they were, as now, leaning to the occult side of regular, what with carrying a skull in a cage. They'd barely notice someone in a cloak openly carrying a dagger in a wooden stand around, either, as Yetty was currently doing. It was Felix, standing around looking awkward in his smart clothes and neat hair that really drew the suspicious stares.

"Anyway," said Felix. "If it's all the same to you lot, I wouldn't mind heading in. I've only ever been inside this courtroom as a spectator, so I just want to get my bearings. Find the chambers, the canteen and all that." The group murmured their agreement, with perhaps a concerned mumble about the sort of canteen they might find in a place like this, but in they went, leaving the locals to squint and mutter as they left.

"What's that one tryin' to prove anyway," one grumbled as they wiped a dirty pot with a dirtier rag, "with his fancy shirt and clean shoes?"

"Probably a king or sommat," said the other, throwing a whole unpeeled onion into the now 'clean' pot. "Trouble's what I reckon, either way, like."

~

The interior was much like the exterior, only without as much fresh air or sunlight (not that Togtun was a place blessed with much sunlight). Felix led the way, taking care not to slip on the mud, and approached what he hoped was a clerk or receptionist. Whoever it was, they were picking their fingernails with a splinter of wood, wearing an expression of complete and total boredom.

"Hello there," Felix said, a warm smile on his face. "My name is Felix Sacramentum, and I'm representing a client in this courtroom later today."

"Good for you," she replied, without looking up. A moment in which no one spoke passed. Felix widened his smile a touch.

"Should I... just go on through, then?"

"Why?"

Breathe. Well, not 'breathe'. You're dead after all.

The smile didn't drop. "Are you the courtroom clerk?"

She ripped her eyes from her task with the enthusiasm of a sleeping turtle and looked at him. "Clerk?"

"What's the hold up?" said Helda, shifting her enormous backpack. "This thing's heavy."

"Look," said Felix. "Which way to the defendant's chambers?"

"No chambers here," she said, returning to her fingernails.

Felix was almost on the verge of saying something impolite when a voice he recognised floated over to him. "It's this way, Mr Sacramentum." He turned to see Prosecutor Ettyson standing at the end of a corridor, watching him. It might have been an omen, having his opponent providing him with such basic assistance this early on. But, it was either that, or Felix be tried for murder after stabbing an unhelpful receptionist with her own nail-picking splinter. *I wonder if Yetty would represent me.*

Felix felt a little nervous flutter. It had been a long time since he had fought against Prosecutor Ettyson. In fact, he'd done so twice. First when Felix was defending Bupp the Despoiler, an unfortunate farmhand who had accidentally risen through the echelons of malevolence, in which Felix had lost, and second when it had been Racelsus's head on the block, and even then he had only won on a technicality.

I wonder if I can ever beat her properly, without any 'divine intervention?'

He tried not to think that thought too loudly, not when Racelsus was nearby.

"Oh! Uh, thank you," he said, trudging after her, his entourage in tow. In a few steps he had caught up to her. He always felt massively inferior as a lawyer when he was in her presence. Something about her demeanour simply exuded confidence and ability. Glancing at him as they walked, she spoke in a gentle voice.

"I haven't seen you in a while," she said to him.

"Uh, no. I've been, well, away," he replied.

"I gathered as much." They walked a few more paces and turned down a corridor. "I'm glad to see you're okay," she said, quickly and quietly, which caused Felix to look at her. She was avoiding his gaze, looking at a door that they were approaching. She came to a stop and pointed. "That one," she said, then turned and began walking away before Felix had a chance to reply. He frowned at her as she left. "Thanks!" he called after her as she disappeared around a corner, then pushed the door open.

~

Within the defendant's chambers - and Felix was relieved that there *were* in fact, chambers - Felix stood and watched his team file in. Yetty, putting on a brave face despite the stench, carrying John Dagger, standing upright in his makeshift stand. Furbo, seemingly in a world of his own, as per usual. Helda, shouldering her huge backpack, holding the cage that housed Racelsus in one arm, the witch herself bobbing slightly back and forth.

And me. A ghost who can't find his way around a courtroom.

Once they were all settled in, he cleared his throat and stood with his hands behind his back. Time to put their minds at ease. Time to let them set down their emotional burdens and allow him, Felix, to steer this ship through the rocky days to come.

I had better not go too far though. Best play it safe.

"We've done all the prep," he said. "So we should be fine. Any questions?" After a brief silence, Yetty raised her hand. "Was that your pep talk?" she said. He clicked a finger and pointed at her.

"Good question. Yes. Any further questions?"

There were none. Around half an hour later, a bell sounded somewhere in the town, and the woman who was so interested in her fingernails before entered their chambers without knocking. "Yer up," she said, then left without saying another word.

9 - The Start

If Felix had been hoping the actual courtroom itself would have been improved since his last visit. Thatgossamer thin cinder of hope soon sputtered out.

"What a dump," exclaimed Helda, who had once described the communal toilets at Gutcher's Ale & Breakfaster on a heavy Sunday morning, after an even heavier Saturday night, as 'all right, actually.'

The floor, in an effort to combat the encroaching muddy water, had been covered in an optimistically thin layer of straw and a creatively haphazard series of planks, which squashed and squelched as weight was laid on them. Every wooden wall had rising damp, and three of the windows had boards across them. Felix was not an expert in ceilings or roofs, but he was fairly confident that birds were supposed to make their nests on the outsides of them, and generally speaking the number of holes you want in them was 'zero'.

Whereas Placenamia had a large, raised dais for the judge to preside over, Togtun had a simple square table and an unadorned chair. On the table was a small piece of paper impaled with a stick that was wedged between two cracks. On it, in simple lettering, it said one word: 'judge'. Next to the table was the witness stand, though 'stand' might be a little grandiose. It was a stool.

There were still two desks and seating, one for each of the defence and the prosecution and their team, and a row of wooden benches for the public to watch. These seats were about a quarter full, mostly people in the same grubby clothing with the same grim expressions on the same mottled faces.

One woman, however, stood out. She was wearing a deep blue cowl, drawn up to hide her face. If she was trying to blend in, she wasn't. The woman met Felix's eye and looked away nervously.

"Well, it certainly has something in the atmosphere," said Furbo, his eyebrows raised.

"Yes, and if you strike a match, whatever it was would probably explode," muttered Yetty, covering her nose, then giving up the effort.

"I don't know what you two are moaning about," said Racelsus. "It's perfectly charming. Back in my day, Togtun, especially the courtroom, was a squalid dump. Look at it now!"

Felix glanced over and saw Ettyson, ready as ever on the prosecution side. She was dressed as usual, a predominantly black outfit, impeccably tailored. The only change was her usual shoes had been exchanged for some sailors' galoshes. What was unusual, though, was that she was not alone. A young woman sat next to her, as still and silent as Ettyson herself, dressed in similar getup and with even less emotion visible on her face. This new mini-Ettyson was staring forward, utterly ignoring everything that was happening. Ettyson seemed to sense Felix watching them, and so turned her head to meet his eyes.

"Defence Counsel," Ettyson said, inclining her head. "You found it okay then?"

"Yes, thanks, Prosecutor." *Why did he feel nervous all of a sudden?* Looking for something to change the subject, he remembered the person next to her.

"Who's this then?" he asked, gesturing at the new lawyer. Ettyson rolled her eyes. "Ms Twelly. One of the new Journeyman-Legalites from Jurviles. Brought her along for a bit of *real world experience*."

Something in the way she spoke suggested that this was perhaps a little more 'real' than Ms Twelly was used to, who let out a huff of breath and continued staring forward. Felix changed the subject again.

"Quite the ambiance here, isn't there?" he said, looking around.

"I couldn't agree more. You know, I've been looking for somewhere to set up a firm of my own," Ettyson replied, raising an eyebrow at the room in general. "How serendipitous, my visit today."

"And if it all goes south, you could chase pigs around," Felix replied, struck with the sudden image of Ettyson, in full court getup, springing through the mud to catch a squealing piglet. *Stop, infernal grunter!*

"Hmm. Perhaps. I've had worse jobs. Certainly more slippery opponents," she said, turning away to confer to Ms Twelly.

Was that a... compliment? Who are you, and what have you done with Rosetta Ettyson?

Felix turned to his client. "Are you ready, John?"

"If I say no, does it make a difference?" he replied in a small voice. Gone was the normal bluster that John usually maintained, and in its place a newfound timidity. This was probably a good thing for the case as a whole, but it still worried Felix a little.

"Uh, no. Not really," he replied.

"Then no, I'm not ready."

Felix gave him what he hoped was a reassuring pat. "It's going to be okay. Keep your chin up, or whatever else you'd keep up instead." John *hmm*'d.

"It can't go any worse than when Felix represented me," said Racelsus cheerfully. "Now *that* was rickety. He almost got us *all* killed, himself included, and I was the only one on trial."

"Must have been a mean prosecutor," said John.

"It was. In fact, it was her over there," said Racelsus, and then more softly, "I still have a score to settle with her..."

"What happened?" said John.

"It'll be quicker if I just..."

After a few seconds of silence, John whistled, somehow.

"Wow."

"I know, right?"

Helda chipped in. It was, after all, one of her favourite topics of conversation. "She's a smarmy, no good, uptight-"

"Everyone, please," said Felix. "The most important person is the judge. So long as they are, as they should be, a rational and balanced follower of the dogma of Habeus, we will be fine."

He didn't add that he had not yet met a judge who he would consider rational and balanced. Except perhaps old Habeus himself, and even that was pushing it.

Felix had attempted to reach out to the God of Justice on a few occasions, but with no success. He wasn't really sure *how* to do it. A few prayers here and there? Burning of sacred unguents? He'd even written a brief letter and just thrown it to the wind. It had seemed like a plausible idea at the time. Despite all of these, not a word. Nothing from Cherinda, either. He hoped the Celestial was okay. But then, if she was, then why wasn't she reaching out to him?

"Look lively," said Yetty, straightening down her clothing to appear more presentable. *As if that's going to matter here...*

The same door that Felix and everyone else in the room had entered swung open once more, and a fat, red-faced man started making his way down the centre. He had a few documents tucked under an arm and cup of something steaming in a pewter tin. He was dressed in stained, farmer's clothing, with a badge of some kind strapped to the front.

This must be the courtroom clerk. Though his uniform is a little sloppy...

Felix stood up as the man passed. "Good day to you. I wonder, would you be able to tell me when the judge is due to arrive?" The man's eyes boggled as he took Felix in. He looked him up and down, then said in a booming voice. "About now, I'd say." Seeing Felix's confused expression, he winked, then carried on walking past him, straight to the table with 'judge' written on it. Plonking himself down on the chair, he laid his papers and cup down, wiped his hands on his lapels and retrieved a tiny pair of spectacles from a pocket.

Ettyson was almost too professional to smirk.

Almost.

Idiot. Moron. Fool. Oaf. Idiot!

After a few moments of reading, the judge looked up at the two teams of lawyers who were standing to attention, and at the crowd behind them who were not.

"You can sit," he said, waving a hand. "We don't keep with all those southern customs here." They did so, and he stood up. "That isn't to say we don't keep with any, though. I'm Judge Burritt, and I expect to be treated with the same level of respect you would treat your prim and proper judges way over yonder. Yes?"

They murmured their assent, and Judge Burritt nodded. "Good. Now," he said, consulting his papers. "We're here to hear the case of one John Dagger. The prosecution suggests that just because a thing can speak, does not mean it is to be considered legally alive. The defence refutes that."

He lowered the paperwork and eyed both Felix and Ettyson in turn. "Is John Dagger here?"

"Yes, Your Honour," said Felix, gesturing to John.

"And it speaks?"

"Yes, Your Honour. Say hello, John."

"Hello, Your Honour," said John, in a small voice.

The judge looked at him for a moment, then clapped his hands. "Great stuff. Okay. So, let's get this show on the road. Time is…" he started making a few scribbles on a piece of paper. "Okay. So-"

A voice from the small crowd of observers piped up. "Wait a minute Morrit, int this the case for t'pub waterin' down their beer'n'that on account of 'em being proper stingy, like?"

The judge frowned at the interruption. "No, Bett, that's three days from now, by my reckoning."

"Oh, right. Sorry, Morrit, 'scuse me, sir," the lady who had spoken was making her way down her aisle to leave. Two others joined her, muttering. Once they had left, the judge sighed. "Well, Prosecutor Ettyson," he said. "I'd say it's time for an opening statement. This case has begun." With that, he struck the table with a small gavel he had produced from somewhere. Felix looked at John, and felt his nervous energy. *Oh John, we haven't even started yet…*

10 - Opening Statements

Prosecutor Rosetta Ettyson stood with practised confidence and looked slowly around the court. If the fact that she was standing in what could optimistically be described as a real fixer-upper for the DIY-minded judge bothered her in the slightest, she didn't show it. She didn't show much, as was typical for her.

Which is why it's so odd that she was being quite friendly earlier. Must investigate that later.

Each and every case brought before a judge in the whole of Fowermolde started in the same way. The prosecution, that is, the lawyer representing those with the axe to grind, would deliver their opening statement. It was in this that they would lay out their argument, start to finish, and set the tone for the rest of their case. It was the defence's job to listen closely and pick holes in everything. The problem was Prosecutor Ettyson. She didn't just look neat and tidy; her arguments were typically smooth as marble and just as solid.

Which reminds me, I need to take notes.

With nothing but a thought, a small pad of papers and pencil materialised in Felix's hands. The first time it had happened had spooked him. He didn't know where they came from, or where they went when he was done, and had decided that some questions were best left unanswered. For now, at least.

Ettyson took a breath. "Six months ago, a gruesome and nefarious plot was brought to a conclusive end. The patriarch of the Vinch estate, one Festin Vinch, was brutally murdered in an attempt to seize control of the family's estate. The weapon? The defendant, a.k.a., this dagger."

She gestured at John, and the eyes of the judge followed her lead, settling his gaze on John. "How do we know this?" she continued. "In that case, a new and relatively unknown incantation was used to 'enchant' the dagger. This spell would grant the dagger the means to produce audible speech, and to retrieve and recount its so-called 'memories'. This allowed it to be used as the star witness in the case, thus securing a conviction. It did this by recognising the feeling of being plunged into the back of the victim."

Felix stood. "I must object, Your Honour."

"This early on, young man?" said the judge, looking up from his paper to glance at the dusty brass clock on the wall.

"Uh, yes, sir," said Felix, stumbling a little.

"Objecting on what grounds?"

"To correct something my colleague said. It was not the 'feeling' of being stabbed that sparked the recognition that thus led to the conviction of the case; rather, it was the memory of the hand that held the handle."

Judge Burritt made a few scribbles. Without looking up, he spoke. "Prosecutor? Is this correct?"

Ettyson took this in her stride. "I shall adjust my phrasing. It was the memory of the grip that thrust its sharp, metal blade into the back of Mr Vinch that sparked the alleged memory."

Is that much better? Felix sat down. Ettyson continued.

"The case was concluded, and justice was done. This dagger had fulfilled its purpose, and now, like all tools, was ready to be stored away. However, in this particular instance, the dagger carried with it the ghoulish memory of the killing of her husband, and so Lady Vinch took means to dispose of it, as was her right."

She started to pace. "The dagger belonged to her, for her to do with as she saw fit. I believe it is not farfetched to say that it is understandable that a woman in her position would seek to remove, even destroy, a relic of such terrible memories. Thankfully, she had done the necessary: removed the dagger from her life, granting herself time and space to grieve in her few remaining lonely years."

Ettyson paused. "Imagine the poor old woman's distress in hearing that the very dagger that killed her husband had not only resurfaced, but was using its experimental enchantment to somehow take a position of 'victim?' Demanding certain rights be granted to it, including the right to be compensated by the Vinch estate for abuse suffered? For a dagger?"

"I must object," said Felix, rising. "No such request for compensation has been made."

"Is this true?" said the judge, drawing his brows in and aiming them at Ettyson, who inclined her head.

"No formal request, I admit, but informally through the use of suggestive language…"

"Please adjust your statement, prosecutor," said Judge Burritt.

"I accept that there has not yet been a *formal* request, Your Honour."

The judge nodded. Ettyson didn't look the slightest bit put out. She merely continued as if no interruption had taken place.

"And to top it all off, the threat of dragging this poor widow back to court again, for what, exactly? To welcome this traumatic memory-made-real into her life and home?"

Felix made to rise again, but the judge got there first. He leaned forward and clasped his fingers together.

"Prosecutor, it is my understanding that the whole reason this case is being heard in a court is on the insistence of the Vinch estate. Has the defendant made any such demands on the estate, or on Mrs Vinch herself?"

"The estate is taking such measures as necessary to protect itself, Your Honour," she replied.

Judge Burritt thought about this and leaned back on his chair, gesturing to her to continue.

Ettyson slowly shook her head. "It is with regret that Lady Vinch has had to corral what dignity and independence she has into bringing this case forth herself. If it were up to her, this would never have seen the inside of a courtroom. And yet, here we find ourselves. It is the prosecution's intention that we shall demonstrate that this dagger, this defendant, as I must call it, is nothing more than an empty shell; a toy, a child's trick, a splint of metal controlled by invisible strings of mischief. It is not alive, and never shall be. We must not open the floodgates and treat it as such, for when will it end? Will your toast that you have for breakfast be granted the rights of property ownership? Will the privacy of clouds be protected, so that we may not gaze upon them?"

She stopped. "No, it is a slippery slope that threatens us. We must nip this in the bud, and at the same time, grant an old woman some peace. We intend to prove the above, so that this dagger may be taken into the street and melted down, and thus turned into something useful. A new bucket handle for the well, perhaps. With your permission, Your Honour, I would like to call upon a series of witnesses that will put an end to this farcical idea of the autonomy of inanimate objects."

"Objection," said Felix, the heat rising to his ears.

"Again? On what grounds, Mr Sacramentum?" said the judge, pencil at the ready.

"Animate," said Felix, before sitting down again and staring forwards. The judge tilted his head to one side, considering Felix. After a moment he seemed to make his mind up and turned to Ettyson without writing anything down. "Permission granted, prosecutor, though I would first like to ask if the defence would like to make their opening statement?"

Felix forced himself to calm down. Ettyson was going for the throat. Melting him down? In the street? Bucket handle? No, that wouldn't do. He stood up and doused the flame that was roaring within him, letting the cool mask of professional advocacy filter his inner thoughts and rising fury.

I'm sure I never used to get this emotional… Not this early on at any rate. What's going on?

Felix looked at the judge, who was waiting for his reply. "I would, Your Honour, if I may."

The judge nodded back. "Go ahead, lad. This ought to be good," he added under his breath.

Felix stood and immediately felt woozy. It felt like a lack of blood to the head, but Felix supposed he would have felt that earlier, lacking any blood at all. Something was wrong. He was tired, he realised, and not the tired that could be treated in the physical world. A small wave of nausea rose through him as he found his feet sinking slightly into the stone floor. He blinked away the blurriness and focussed on John, willing his body to remain corporeal and his thoughts to sharpen.

This was for him. For John. If he really must be all melodramatic and ghostly, he could do that on his own time. Felix stood and touched his fingertips together, then realised his mouth was dry.

Every time…

"Life," he announced, "comes in many forms. There are plants and insects so small and inconsequential that it is hard to imagine they are alive at all. Doubtless there are some among the higher powers beyond our understanding that think the same of us."

I should know, I've met a few.

"My client, John, is alive. He is alive by any measure that matters - this I shall demonstrate beyond doubt. The question will thus become: how do we treat him? Society can be measured by how it treats those at the bottom of the ladder. John is hanging by a thread, dangling below that bottom rung. It is within our power, the power of the court, to make the decision on whether we grant him the rights that we ourselves hold so dear, or whether we dismiss them out of convenience. To reach down and help him up, or to cut that thread and let him fall."

He opened his hands and widened his arms. "This will, of course, raise questions. We shall have to make changes to accommodate him and lay the framework for more of his kind to be treated in the way he has been treated. This sounds like a lot of work, granted, but it is my dearest hope that we shall do what is right, not just what is convenient."

He finished and collapsed into his chair. He could feel sweat prickling his non-existent back. "Thank you," John whispered. "That was - say, are you alright, Felix?"

"I'm fine," he said, through gritted teeth. His eyes looked a little more sunken, his skin that little more taut. "And you're welcome. But we're just getting started. It's about to get a lot less polite."

Judge Burritt flipped over a second piece of paper and read the back. "Prosecutor, when you are ready," he said, barely looking up. Ettyson stood up.

11 - Philosopher I

"For the first witness for the prosecution," said Ettyson, "we call Lady Esmeralda Tincture."

Furbo sat up in his seat and raised his eyebrows. "Did she say Esmeralda Tincture?" He smoothed his crumpled shirt and rubbed his bald pate. Helda rolled her eyes and tutted. "Oh gods," Furbo muttered.

"Who?" said Yetty, but Helda pinched her nose.

"A philosopher that Furbo happens to have a childish crush on," Helda said, and sighed. She affected a deep, whining voice. "Oh Helda, her views on the cosmos are just so dreamy. Oh Helda, her diatribe is so enswillingly troppopulous. Oh Helda-"

"Hush!" said Furbo, waving a hand at her. "She's coming, oh my, there she is…" He sat up straighter even than before, and Felix heard his back audibly crack as he did so. To his credit, Furbo barely flinched.

The door to the witness chamber had indeed opened, and a rakish woman of an age similar to Furbo began sauntering down the central walkway, utterly at home with the ramshackle surroundings. She was dressed in clothes that may have once been fashionably shabby and were now just shabby, and her hair, a mad mess of grey frizz, was tied back with a red ribbon. Furbo watched every step she made.

Felix caught Ettyson watching Furbo stare after her witness, and caught a small grin on her face as she looked down at her papers. She glanced up and met Felix's gaze, at which her expression instantly shifted to professional indifference.

Did her cheeks just flush? Was that… emotion from Prosecutor Ettyson?

"I owe you a silver," he muttered to Yetty, who had also noticed the rare emotive outburst from the otherwise impassive prosecutor. She tapped her temple to suggest she'd made a note in her 'who owes me what' mental notebook, in which Felix had never asked for a detailed account of the size of his debt. All he knew is that he was definitely in debt.

With a flicker of optimism, Felix considered that maybe this Lady Tincture wasn't going to be one of those word-twisting philosophers that take five hundred words to say nothing at all. Maybe she'll be a straight-shooter; a no-nonsense, taciturn breed of philosopher who answers life's largest questions in as few words as possible. Felix glanced at Furbo, who was still lost in unconcealed admiration, then felt his optimism sputter out. He supposed the kind of person the old scholar would admire would probably belong quite happily in the loquaciously verbose club.

You never know though. I'm probably just being pessimistic. Oh Habeus, please make her speak like a human being.

Once Esmeralda was settled, Ettyson nodded to her. "Witness," she said. "Please state your name and occupation."

"Why?" came the lugubrious response. Esmeralda spoke slowly, drawing out each word. "Why, Prosecutor Ettyson? What is an occupation, anyway? Am I an occupation, or am I a state of being, merely *occupying* an event? Is that what you mean?"

Oh well.

"Miss," boomed the judge, causing the witness to visibly flinch at the word. The volume made Felix jump. The judge leaned on the table to give her a pointed look, then pointed a thick finger at her. "If you don't take this seriously and answer properly, I'll bloody lock yer up." Felix's eyebrows rose involuntarily, and he tried to regain control of his face with mixed success.

I think I'm going to like this judge after all.

Lady Tincture sighed and tilted her head back. She raised her hands. "That's fair enough, I suppose." Sitting bolt upright, she shot daggers at the judge. "But don't call me 'miss' again."

The judge coughed. He met her gaze and shrivelled a little. "Ahem," he said, in a much less commanding voice. "Please continue, mi-, that is, witness."

The witness settled down and once again affected her air of gloomy nonchalance with a louche slouch. "My name is Esmeralda Tincture, and I'm a philosopher."

Philosopher...

Felix looked at the witness again. There was something… unconcerned about her. Her actions suggested she could take it or leave it, whatever it was. Yet… something about the way she lounged, something about the way she dressed. Was it genuine carefree-and-damn-you-all? Or was it meticulously planned to appear that way? A genuine disregard of all societal norms, or a contrived idiom to simply seem thus?

This is going to be interesting.

Ettyson nodded at the judge, who steepled his fingers. "You may begin, prosecutor," he said.

After a brief mutter with her young associate, Ettyson walked to stand in front of Esmeralda. "Witness," she said.

"Yes?" came the reply.

"What is life?" asked Ettyson, in the same way as a night-watchman might ask *'What's that smell?'*

Without missing a breath, the reply came. "It is unsummarisable."

Is that a word?

Ettyson bristled. For someone like her, the only giveaway was a closing of the eyes, but it was clear to those who knew her that she was fighting back some serious irritation.

"Please try," she said. "As briefly as you can."

The witness scoffed. "*What is life?* You expect me, an ageing and experienced philosopher, to sum it up in a sentence?"

"Yes."

The witness sighed. She narrowed her eyes and pursed her lips, staring hard at Ettyson, who, in her defence, stared back without flinching. Tilting her head from side to side, Esmeralda took a deep breath, and let it out slowly. She did everything slowly.

"It's love."

"Love?" said Ettyson.

"Love," said Lady Tincture. "Passion. Lust. Fear and pain, joy and sorrow, defiance, justice, unfairness… All wrapped up in one dull mortal eggshell for a brief, beautiful flickering burst of light in an endless black expanse of nothing."

Furbo sighed with pleasure. "Oh, my," he said. Helda nudged him with an elbow, causing him to splutter, and Racelsus gave a quiet *hmmm*.

"Bit bleak, isn't it?" she whispered.

"And," said Ettyson. "What are emotions? If I may, specifically: *what is love?*"

Felix was expecting some endless, wordy metaphysical essay on spiritual connections, of the yearning of the soul, of a golden chain from heart to heart, purpose to purpose, mortal to god. The answer given was much shorter.

"Chemicals," said Esmeralda, shrugging.

Furbo's brow furrowed. "Chemicals?" he muttered.

Chemicals?

"Can you please elaborate, witness?" said Ettyson.

The philosopher nodded. "I'd be delighted to. You see, love, like all emotions, is a label that society has created. Love specifically... It's the name for a certain type of feeling that our bodies experience when we find that certain special other person that we think gives us, and perhaps our genetic material, the best chance to survive. That feeling, that instant, earth-defying *need* for another person is not some deep, primal connection of souls; it's merely our bodies trying to find someone to provide us with shelter or a vessel for our children. And, guess what fuels that need? That unquenchable desire?"

She waited for a response.

If Ettyson answers that I'm going to object.

Ettyson did not answer, to Felix's disappointment. The witness, seeing that no one would, shrugged again, palms up.

"Chemicals. It's all just chemicals. A bit of our body squeezing out some of that love juice into another bit, driving our minds wild. On such meagre liquids are empires brought to ruin, etcetera."

Furbo looked heartbroken. Helda scowled at the philosopher, her hand on Furbo's arm. She looked ready to either spit words or throw fists, and it was clear who the target would be in either case.

"What I have here," said Ettyson, retrieving from her desk and holding up a piece of paper covered in messy notes, "are the results of some medical trials conducted at Restastine University. During the trials, various chemical compounds were introduced to a number of subjects, with the intention of monitoring their emotive responses. The summary of the third trial, conducted by Dr Gerlo Threshwin, is thus…" She held the paper in front of her and squinted at it, evidently trying to decipher the terrible handwriting. "…and I quote: 'The introduction of these certain chemical substances dramatically altered the subject's feelings of what we have typically labelled 'love', in some cases removing such feelings in long-married couples and in others inducing it in pairs of stranglers.'" She frowned at the paper and squinted. "Excuse me, 'strangers.' End quote."

Ettyson returned the paper to her desk and turned to the witness. "Is this study known to you?"

"It is," came the reply. "I know Dr Threshwin very well. In fact, it was from a discussion we had in private one evening that sparked the idea for the experiment. After a few glasses of something strong and expensive, we were discussing the effects alcohol had on the human mind. There is, or was, a well-equipped alchemy lab at the university. One thing led to another, and the study was commissioned. Once the results came out, I felt my own mind had been altered. Suddenly I saw the world for what it really was. Love? It's a scam perpetrated by our organs, and monetised by every flower seller in Fowermolde and I daresay beyond."

Felix had had enough. He stood up. "Objection."

"Yes?" said Judge Burritt, eyebrow raised in expectancy.

"This is not a biology lesson," said Felix, arms held out wide. "How is this relevant to the case?" The Judge looked at Ettyson.

"Why," said Prosecutor Ettyson, turning to face Felix. "Would this be irrelevant to the case?" The Judge looked back.

"It is not for me to explain why something is irrelevant, prosecutor," said Felix. "Rather, it is you who should be proving that it *is* relevant. Perhaps you missed that day at law school?"

"Perhaps, or perhaps you are merely clutching at straws? Can you give an example as to why you think this testimony is not pertinent?"

"Despite my having just told you that it is not up to me to do so," said Felix, keeping his voice calm and level, "Since you have asked so politely, I *can,* in fact." He held up a finger. "For one my client hasn't got any organs." As soon as he'd said it, he knew it was a mistake. He opened his mouth to say something else, but nothing came out.

Ettyson smiled. A cold smile. "Exactly. Do you wish to keep going?"

Felix did not.

The Judge cleared his throat meatily. "I don't know how you two practise your craft in the big city, but if you have finished squabbling, it is usual for the judge to respond in some manner between your statements, to assess the merits and whatnot. It is, after all, my opinion as to whether what you are saying is at all relevant, is it not?"

Felix looked sheepish. Ettyson did not.

"Regardless," said the judge, leaning back on his simple wooden chair, causing it to creak in protest. He was moving his mouth around as if chewing a particularly defiant piece of gristle. "I believe the point the prosecution is trying to make is that, according to this expert witness, life is defined by emotions, such as love, and to feel 'love', or the chemical cocktail that one thinks of as love, one must have organs which the chemicals can, hm, affect. Consequently, if the client has no organs, they therefore cannot be affected by these chemicals, and therefore cannot feel love, and therefore cannot be considered alive." He looked at the philosopher. "Is that about right, mi-, uh, witness?"

The philosopher smiled at him. "I couldn't have put it better myself." The judge smiled back, looking immensely proud of himself, and started making notes furiously.

"So," said Felix, trying to dig himself out. "How do you explain the feelings John does say that he feels?"

"'It', not 'he'," Ettyson said, waving a hand. "But shouldn't you wait until it's your turn to cross-examine to ask the questions, Defence Counsel? Or did you miss that day at law school?"

Felix sat down and felt his colour rising to his cheeks. An odd sensation for one with no blood. *That was a stupid mistake. Idiot!*

Focus!

Prosecutor Ettyson waited for the judge to finish writing his notes. When he was done, he looked up, grinned at his paper, then gave Ettyson a nod.

"So," she said, facing her witness. "In the case of the defendant here, John Dagger. It has no heart. No brain. No capacity to store or create chemicals. Therefore, according to your testimony, it has no ability to experience emotion. Correct?"

The philosopher nodded and gave a small, sad smile in Felix's direction. "Yes, prosecutor. And without emotion, what is life?"

12 - Philosopher II

"I have no more questions," said Ettyson. She returned to her desk without any further discussion and sat down quietly. Twelly asked no question or made no comment. The room seemed a little more melancholy, somehow, after that testimony. Even Twelly's expression had shifted from a blank mask of nothing to a slightly concerned mask of almost-nothing.

Bloody philosophers. I'd ask them what the point of them is, but they'd probably enjoy the question.

Felix leaned over to Furbo, who looked the saddest of all, and felt guilty. *They're not all bad, I suppose.* Felix whispered to him in a hurried tone. "Furbo. How many books has the witness written?"

"Hmm?" came the reply. He looked up at Felix with red-rimmed eyes, and Felix felt a sympathetic twinge. *There'll be time for emotional support later.*

"The witness. How many books about philosophy has she written?" Furbo sighed. "Oh. About fifteen, I think," he said. Felix patted him on the arm. "Thanks. Gotta go."

"Mr Sacramentum, lad," said the judge. "Are you ready to proceed with yer cross-examination?"

"I am, Your Honour."

The judge gestured with an open hand. "In yer own time, then, lad." Felix approached the witness, who appeared even more laid back than before, if such a thing were possible. He still hadn't settled on whether she meant it or not.

"Lady Tincture, you have written broadly and extensively-" *so I'm led to understand based on a fifteen second conversation conducted barely a minute ago...* "- about life, and its many facets and variations, correct?"

"I have, but what is life, really?" she sighed.

Felix fought back the urge to roll his eyes. "Lady Tincture, we have heard your answer to that in quite some detail just a moment ago. I would like to ask you some questions as to how your definition applies in several scenarios. For now, we are concerned with one life in particular."

"This… John character?"

"Indeed. Now, if I may-"

"Can I talk to him?" She was watching Felix from under low lids.

"Excuse me?"

She sat up and opened her eyes fully, suddenly interested. "John. Can I talk to him?"

What's her angle… did Ettyson put her up to something?

Felix gave the prosecutor a suspicious look, but she was sitting staring straight ahead. Then he turned back to the table where John was standing, and crossed his arms. "It is not usual for a witness to speak to a defendant like this, Lady Tincture."

He tried to catch the judge's eye for support, but he was staring at his steepled fingers as if lost in thought.

But… Maybe…

"If… my client has no objection, I can introduce you if you like? He's just over here." Felix jerked his head towards the defendant's desk, on which John stood in his makeshift stand. "That's John Dagger, our defendant."

"How do you do," said Lady Tincture.

"How do I do what? Oh, I mean, fine, thanks," said John, perhaps a little icily. "How do you do too?" The witness smiled, whispered *"how quaint,"* then turned to Felix. "I'm ready for your questions."

"Don't answer then," Felix heard John muttering. Felix paused for a heartbeat, not that he had a heartbeat, and then began his question.

"You have stated clearly that you believe life is defined by emotions that humans feel-"

"Not just humans. Animals, other species, all feel emotion," the witness interrupted.

"Please wait until I ask a question before answering," said Felix. Esmeralda's face darkened, the languid good humour melting away. "Is that understood?" She didn't reply, her face retreating further into a severe brood. "You can answer now, please. Do you understand?"

"Yes," she said.

"Thank you, witness. Now. Does a tree feel emotion?"

"Yes, I believe so."

"You believe so? Why?"

"Because they have chemical balances and imbalances, just as we do."

"I see. What emotions do they feel?"

"I don't know."

"You don't know? Can you elaborate more?"

"Yes."

"…Please do, then. Why do you not know what emotions a tree experiences?"

"Objection," said Ettyson. "The witness is not a botanist." The philosopher gave Felix a smug smile.

"That is true," said Felix. "But I am not asking about the tree part of being a tree. I am asking about the part that the tree shares with all other living things, or so your witness insists. Or was she mistaken?"

The smug look vanished, and Ettyson raised an eyebrow. The judge coughed. "I will hear the question. Witness, please answer."

"For clarity," said Felix. "I asked why the witness does not know what emotions a tree experiences."

Lady Tincture shrugged. "Because the chemicals they contain are not like that of a human, or a dog, for example. They have their own emotions that we cannot understand, so I have no idea what a tree might feel, only that it does feel, because it has chemicals and imbalances, as I've already said."

"So, let me see that I have this straight," said Felix. "The tree, or plant, has its own range of emotions that are beyond human comprehension, triggered by chemical imbalances?"

"Yes."

"How can we possibly know that?"

"It's logical. The tree yearns for more water, more nutrients, to satisfy a chemical imbalance. That is the same as what any human does. They are driven by their emotions, which are just our chemical-creators tricking us into correcting imbalances."

"What gives us the right, then, to chop down a tree to use it for lumber? Or firewood?" Felix leaned back on the defence's desk, remembering to make sure he didn't float through it. The witness gave a bitter chuckle.

"What indeed? What gives us the right to treat the poor and destitute in the way that we do, working them to the bone, day after day? Are we not stealing their lives, branch by branch, to fuel the fires of the rich?"

"So you are saying: we do not have that right?"

"I am. And yet," the philosopher said, looking over to the judge. "My pencil is made of wood. Humans are very good at living with what they cannot morally justify."

A flashback of a sheep on the stand, giving testimony. The hairless demonic prosecutor, Jeast, asking questions of him. Felix noticed the judge frowning at the pencil in his hands. *Time to change tack...*

"I'd like to ask you about something else." He paced the concourse, if a muddy, sodden straw-strewn random assortment of planks could be considered a concourse. "If I ask John how he is feeling - in fact, John, how are you feeling?" he said, turning to the dagger.

"Irritated, to be honest, he replied. "Angry, and perhaps a little sad. Stabby."

The judge was brought from his focus on the pencil and leaned forward, raising an eyebrow. "Feeling 'stabby?'" he said.

"Uh, thank you, John," said Felix quickly, hoping the judge wouldn't reprimand him. He carried on pacing, his steps making faint squelching noises. "John tells me he feels angry and sad. Why does he say that, witness, if he is unable to feel these emotions?"

"Because, as I understand it, he was enchanted to pretend to feel them."

"What do you mean by that?"

"I mean these so-called 'emotions' were put there by a wizard or some such when John was created."

"You are saying these emotions are not real? They are fabricated, magically?"

"I am."

Felix returned to the defence's desk and leaned back on it again.

"Assuming that is true... In your professional opinion, how does a fabricated emotion differ from any other emotion?"

The philosopher hesitated. "Well, one is created organically, naturally, without interference, and one is manually created. A painting of a rose is not the same as a rose."

Felix chewed his lip and fought down a rising nervousness that started to float up through his stomach. *This isn't going as well as I had hoped. What to say… I feel like I keep putting my foot in it.* Perhaps he should just stop there? Before he makes it any worse?

Yes, probably the best option.

Felix sighed and prepared to thank the witness for her time when he felt a touch on his arm. He turned to see Furbo rising to his feet. The old man's face was unreadable. "In that case," Furbo said, in a quiet voice that nonetheless carried. "If I look at the painting and think the rose is beautiful, am I being tricked into false emotion?"

"Objection," said Ettyson, rising. "This man is not a legal representative in this case."

"Mr Sacramentum?" asked the judge. Felix looked at Furbo, who didn't waiver as he met his gaze. Felix felt the nervousness in his stomach shrivel as he looked at the old man, so full of purpose. He turned to the judge and spoke in an assured voice.

"This man is as much a part of the legal team of Lunchers & Co as I am, Your Honour," said Felix. "And provided our client does not object, I do not see why he cannot perform cross-examination on his behalf."

"Neither do I," said the judge. "'Tis the client's choice, after all. And, hm, John? Do you object to this fella representing you?"

"I don't," said John. "I think," he added quietly.

The judge sat back. "Then proceed, please."

Furbo turned to his idol. "The question, I believe, was this: if I look at - in your words - a so-called 'false' representation of something, for example a painting of a rose, and feel an emotional response, especially of a kind that I would feel if I were to consider a 'real' rose, am I not, in fact, feeling a real emotion?"

Felix's eyebrows raised in surprise. He glanced at Ettyson, who, for a woman normally as readable as a brick, had her eyebrows raised as well.

There is a you-shaped hole that the legal system has sorely missed, Furbo.

A squint, then Esmeralda furrowed her brow in thought. She shifted her weight from side to side. "Well," she replied eventually. "I would say that you are feeling a real emotion. You are reminded of the rose, and feel beauty." Furbo nodded, as if this was what he were expecting.

"The beauty I feel might well be the same as if I were looking at a real rose, would you agree?"

"...Yes, I would say so."

Felix sat down. Furbo pressed his fingertips together. "More so, perhaps, depending on the skill of the artist."

A shrug. "Maybe?"

"And artists do not just paint roses. They paint lust, fear, pain, joy, sorrow... Or even love. Yes?"

"Yes, I suppose they do."

"You suppose they do?" Furbo scoffed "Kokolio's 'Heart Torn Asunder' is considered one of the greatest paintings, or indeed works of art, ever created, and its subject is love, is it not? There is Queen Lylia's 'Tempered Rage', a masterwork of the boiling anger of the spirit, or Mistress Cattail's 'Eyes Closed at Midnight Tower', a terrifying painting indeed, all of which instil such tremendous emotions in their observers, as has been agreed by all who value such things. Do you agree?"

The philosopher waved a hand. "Yes, fine, you are right. Tremendous paintings all. Your point, however?"

"These... artificial emotions, transformed from mind to paint... They are powerful, able to instil tremendous emotive responses, yet they are not real emotions?"

"They are very real."

"The emotions created by the artist as a result of their work being experienced - those are real, you say?"

"Yes, I do, for the fifth time."

"And so, an enchanter, an artist in his own way, has filled John with the capacity to speak, doubtless after his own fashion, for he must have had inspiration from somewhere. And, I would warrant, the same enchanter gifted John the ability to feel emotion."

"Well, I would-" started Lady Tincture with an impatient expression.

"Witness, I have not asked a question yet," said Furbo. The philosopher did not reply, save a sharp intake of breath. After a pause, he continued. "The emotions granted to John do not perhaps correlate to your own, one-dimensional definition. But! They *are* emotions. They *are*. I have seen this fellow angry and disappointed. I've seen him laugh and crack jokes. Good jokes, bad jokes. These emotions, whether chemically sourced or not, are real. John inspires emotion in me. He can be an incorrigible arse, granted, but he is full, *stuffed full* of feeling. And these two," he said, gesturing first at Felix and secondly at Racelsus. "Two of my dearest friends. One is a *skull in a cage*, sustained by her own magic. Not a chemical in sight. She is a charming, manipulative, boorish, surprisingly lewd at times, guilt-ridden, childish, vulnerable woman who has one of the purest spirits I've ever seen, and I've seen a lot, believe me. And the other, this very lawyer, is a ghost! He *died,* you see, and yet here he is, returning from the great beyond to spend his time *helping the needy.* Why? What's in it for him? Nothing. But it is the *right thing to do.* It makes him feel happy. And so he does it. Do you see any chemicals? Because I don't, and I can literally see right through him on a bright day."

He straightened up, piercing her with a glare Felix had never seen before. "I put it to you, Lady Tincture, that by your own definition, these people, these wonderful people, are alive. As for John... His emotions are not chemically created, but they are as true and beautiful as a painting of a rose. If you remembered what drew you to this profession, and had any respect for those truly in difficult circumstances, instead of those who pay for your fine wine and expensive tailoring, you would agree."

Furbo sat back down without ceremony and stared at his hands in his lap. Helda gripped his shoulder and whispered something to him, but Furbo shook his head.

The witness was not moving. Her head was resting on her hands which were clasped together under her chin, and was tilted to the side. Her eyes were half-closed and unfocused, and her mouth was closed. She was absolutely silent. Something about this change in demeanour made Felix finally see her as she probably yearned to be seen; a thinker, pondering life's great questions. It wasn't her clothes or verbal affectations. It was the genuine act of searching for a purpose. A goal. A question, even.

Gods, philosophy is contagious.

The judge broke the silence. "Perhaps my ears need cleaning, but unless I missed it, I did not detect a question in that examination. Do you *have* any further questions, Mr, hmm… Mr Sacramentum?" he asked. Felix looked at Furbo, then back to the witness. Neither had moved.

"Just one, Your Honour. Witness," said Felix, rising to his feet. "Is John Dagger alive?"

The witness hesitated, then shrugged, her expression unchanging. *Good enough for me.*

"We have no further questions," said Felix, lowering himself back down. The judge made a note, then cleared his throat.

"Then you may leave, witness. Thank you for your time."

Lady Esmeralda Tincture stood up, nodded her head towards the judge, then walked away without saying a word. Felix watched her leave, then turned to look at Ettyson, who met his eyes. She nodded her head at Furbo and mouthed *not bad*, causing Felix to smirk involuntarily. He was about to reply when the judge interrupted with a second noisier throat clearing, then glanced down at another piece of paper. "I believe the next witness is another for the prosecution. In yer own time, Ms Ettyson."

Momentary camaraderie dispelled, Ettyson's face fell back into its characteristic non-description. "The prosecution calls Yan Vo Mouletter to the stand."

Journal Entry B - Mind Reader

Reference case [VJvGC] (VeeJel v. GoC), year 1304, Judge Neffin presiding.

Imagine you are sitting around a table with two people. You speak language A, and only language A. The person sitting to your left, henceforth called Lefty, speaks language B and only language B. The person to your right - Righty - speaks both language A and B. Clever old Righty.

You want to buy something from Lefty. Righty is here as your translator. You meet her outside the bar, and agree on a fee. Back at the table, you tell the translator what you want, and she dutifully relays this to Lefty. Lefty nods, reaches down into a satchel by his feet and pulls it out, placing it on the table. After a few more words, Righty tells you Lefty's price. It's expensive. Far more than you were expecting to pay.

You question the price, and Righty translates. Lefty's eyes narrow and he starts grumbling. Why is he grumbling? Righty tells you that Lefty's not happy with your haggling. Righty then tells you that Lefty made some snide comments about your family, your mother in particular, suggesting that she entertains sailors by moonlight. Just before you throw a punch, a total stranger walks by and informs you she can also speak languages A and B, and that your translator is lying to both of you, clearly trying to capitalise on a bit of false animosity. She offers to step in and help, for the same price as whatever cut you're paying to Righty. Righty protests, of course, proclaiming this newcomer to be a charlatan and insisting that their own translation is true, honest and correct.

What do you do? Who do you believe? Stranger, or Righty?

As far as a philosophical puzzle goes, assuming that both of these translators are strangers to you, and that you have no means of communication with Lefty, they are equally unknowable. Because you lack the knowledge of language B, you simply cannot know which translator is telling the truth.

But Felix, I hear you say. Why don't I find a third translator?

You do, and this one immediately agrees with Righty.

But how do you know that *they* are honest?

A little while ago, it was common practice in law courts to employ (prepare yourself) a Cerebrilectorem - that's "Mind-Reader" to you and me. It makes perfect sense. Why bother going through all the rigamarole of getting your robes on and shouting at witnesses for a few hours when a learned academic could walk in and literally recount for you an exact play-by-play account of what happened? Of course the accused would protest at this, but they do that anyway.

These Mind-Readers, the most reputable of which were trained in the various universities scattered over Fowermolde, charged exorbitant fees. Wouldn't you, in the same shoes? Yet they knew it was still cheaper to hire one than risk a lengthy trial with all that bothersome expensive stuff like lawyers and due process. Crime rates dropped, incarcerations skyrocketed, the legal profession dwindled - a positive result for almost everyone. Everyone except lawyers.

Whether motivated by a sense of moral justice or a serious case of running-out-of-cash-itis, it was one such mere lawyer, Cattara Makeamend, that started theorising about the potential for a mischievous mind-reader to manipulate testimonies in court. What if they've been lying to everyone, falsifying results? She arranged for a second mind reader named Hyacinth Lopside, (who happened to be another rare individual concerned with potential chicanery instead of grabbing all the cash they can get their hands on,) to accompany her to a case being heard, between a rich landowner and poor farmer. The farmer had accused the landowner of the theft of a flock of his sheep, which the landowner denied. The mind-reader employed by the land-owner proudly declared that he had read the mind of the plaintiff and that this unscrupulous vagabond of a farmer was merely attempting to abuse the system for his own profit. Seconds before the judge's gavel slammed dramatically down, sealing this liar's fate, Makeamend's own telepath heroically stood up from the audience and accused this other mind-reader of lying, and that the plaintiff was saying - that is, thinking - no such thing.

The judge's response was to retrieve the services of a *third* Cerebrilectorem, and demand that they read the mind of the plaintiff without speaking with anyone else. This third expert did so, and explained without preamble that the farmer was lying to take advantage of his employer.

The judge threw the man in prison, forfeiting his worldly possessions to his landowner, and arrested Lopside for perversion of justice. However, the judiciary conceded that, based on the *clearly* corrupt and immoral Lopside, it was possible for a mind-reader to fabricate testimony. (Of course, as it later turned out, the third mind-reader had, upon being summoned, read the mind of the other two, then realised that it would be vastly more profitable to go along with the first version of events, and so had done so. But how could anyone prove that?)

The judiciary's solution to this conundrum?

From then on, two independent Cerebrilectoria were required for any case that wanted to use one, much to the delight of the mind-reading industry, who suddenly found their demand doubling. Invariably, every randomly selected backup mind-reader called upon a case would agree with the first one, and, for a time, faith was restored.

Because, the Cerebrilectoria argued, what were the chances that *two* of them were corrupt?

Very low, as it turned out. They were *all* on the take.

When you have a network of erudite practitioners of this secretive and complex art, before long everyone knows everyone; fresh-faced graduates, ancient and respected artisans, everyone in between… and every newcomer to this wealthy profession is sat down and given *the talk*. Anyone who shows the slightest moral qualm is given another talk, and, if they are still unconvinced… Well, I'm not sure what exactly happens, but I'm certain it's not pleasant. All I know is that they are quietly removed from the register.

Why not just lie, I hear you ask? You do remember which guild we are dealing with, don't you?

Eventually, one enterprising and tenacious Cerebrilectorem with a sense of moral justice as red-hot as Solhiti's eyebrows managed to lay it out for everyone to see. They unleashed a flaming exposé that left out no morbid detail or sordid scheme. When they did, it caused an uproar, not just in legal circles but in society more broadly. Mind-readers were vilified by the masses, their various headquarters burned to cinder, and anyone calling themselves a Cerebrilectorem was beaten, exiled, arrested, or worse.

Needless to say, mind-reading in courts nowadays is generally considered somewhat of a 'no-no'.

...So how did all this come to light? The whistleblower was a wizardess named Petunia. Petunia Lopside, niece of the unfortunate Hyacinth.

She was something of a prodigy, and, not only was she a talented Cerebrilectorem, while she was a student she invented two new spell techniques that are still used to this day (though only by those with express permission by the state): Petunia's Emotive Transplantation, which can read the memories and emotions of one person and share them with another, and Petunia's True Hiding, a spell that does nothing except hide the wizard's magical prowess from those with the power to sense such things.

It was a combination of these two that helped her infiltrate the community of mind-readers and emerge unscathed, then spread this story far and wide, driving the practice of mind-reading deep underground, where it stays to this day. Justice returned in its well-worn form; two lawyers slagging each other's clients off in front of an angry and/or bored judge.

A paranoid reader might theorise that Petunia could have falsified memories or feelings using her own creation, and therefore doom the mind-readers guild to oblivion for her own unknowable means. Is it possible? Sure. Can we prove it? No, because we cannot question the architect of all of this. Why? Petunia was assassinated by the dissolved Guild of Cerebrilectoria at the first opportunity, obviously.

~journal entry ends

13 - Blacksmith I

Abroad, powerful man appeared through the door at the end of the room and began a slightly lop-sided walk down the thoroughfare towards the witness stand. His arms were as thick as Helda's thighs, and he had the kind of face that would give a hungry bear second thoughts. Once he settled into the witness stand - or small wooden stool, which all but disappeared beneath the man's girth - Ettyson walked over to him.

"Witness," she said. "What is your name and occupation?"

In a voice like rolling gravel, the man coughed and answered. "Yan Vo Mouletter, and I'm a smith. A blacksmith." He coughed again and his large mustachios quivered nervously, then began speaking before Ettyson could continue. "I works with iron and steel, y'see. Mostly, that is. Or copper." Ettyson tried to speak, but he interrupted her again. "Or any metals I suppose, unless I-"

Ettyson held a finger up, and the smith stopped speaking. "Sorry," he mumbled, looking down, fiddling with his buttons.

"Just answer what I ask you to, witness, clearly and without wandering," said the prosecutor. The smith nodded and settled into silence. Without turning, Ettyson gestured at John. "Do you recognise this dagger?"

The blacksmith fiddled with his pocket and retrieved a huge pair of scratched and beaten spectacles. Holding them to his face, he peered at John under black bushy eyebrows. After a few seconds, he lowered the glasses and faced Ettyson. "Yes, I do, miss. I made it."

Felix heard John gasp in shock. "Father..?" he whispered.

Ettyson asked the witness how he had made this dagger, and how he could recognise it as his own work. Yan Vo Mouletter explained the process for forging, the melting of the iron, the smelting over coal to form steel, the pouring into the mould, the sharpening of the blade. When moving on to the handle, he explained that the pommel is where he recognised his own work.

"Everyone does theirs a bit different, you see," he said. "Might look similar to someone who don't look at metal every day, but someone like me can see a sword'n say, 'oh that's Tib's work', or what-have-you. As fer me, I has a particular way of shapin' the fuller and t'pommel. It's the outside shape, you see, that sort of five-sided shape with the little filigree around t'edge. I can't see it from here, but I'd bet sure as sunset you'd see my symbol on the base of t'pommel: it's a 'Y', a small 'V' and an 'M' all linked up inside a circle."

Any hope of proving that this smith was mistaken melted; Felix knew every inch of John, and even now could see the small signet mark on the pommel. *Strange that such a brutish looking man could make such a small, detailed mark.*

"Do you have any particular feelings towards this dagger?" asked Ettyson. Yan considered this, then shrugged his huge shoulders.

"Hmm, proud o' a job well done, I 'spose."

"In the same way a baker would be pleased with a loaf she has baked. Any other emotional connections?"

"No, not really," said Yan.

"I'm going to ask you a few questions about daggers in general, witness. I want you to answer with a simple yes or no. Understood?"

The blacksmith nodded.

"Can a dagger eat?"

"Pardon?"

"Yes or no, witness. Can a dagger eat?"

"No, of course- uh, no."

"Does it produce waste?"

"Doe- I mean, no."

"Can a dagger reproduce?"

The blacksmith's eyes boggled slightly, as if he wasn't sure if the lawyer had gone mad, or he had. "No!"

"Can it grow?"

"No!"

"Can it repair itself?"

"Look, what-"

"Yes or no, please."

The smith took a deep breath and let it out. "No."

"Thank you," said Ettyson, and looked down at a piece of paper on her desk as if she hadn't just asked a bizarre series of questions of a bewildered blacksmith.

Ettyson looked up and turned to face John. She gestured at him with a hand, before addressing the blacksmith. "Would you consider the dagger you forged, that one over there, to be alive?"

The blacksmith grunted and waved a dismissive hand. "Alive? What sort of a... No, why would I? 'Tis just metal and wood and such."

"With no capacity for emotive cogitation?" said Ettyson.

"Eh?"

"I mean, not able to think? To feel?"

The witness shook his head. "Didn't I already say that? No."

"But I can! I do!" shouted John from Felix's side. "I do think and feel! I do!"

"Eh?" the blacksmith grumbled, looking out towards Felix. "Who asked you, lawyer?" Felix met the man's gaze and held it with some difficulty.

"I didn't say a thing. He did," he said, and looked down at John. Yan followed his gaze and looked at the dagger. He scoffed. "I don't believe it, 'tis just some trick of the voice," he said.

"It isn't!" said John, his tinny voice taking an edge of desperation. "It's me!"

"Your Honour," said Ettyson. "My examination of the witness is being interrupted."

"Hmm, yes," the judge said, and waved at Felix. "Discontinue these interruptions so the prosecutor can complete her questions, or else I shall have t'take action. You'll have time for questions and comments later, as you well know."

Felix bowed his head. "Of course, my apologies." To John, he said, quietly: "This is a lot to take in, I know, but don't worry. We will have time for our own questions soon. You just have to sit tight for a bit, okay? I know this is hard."

John did not reply.

"I notice, witness, that you did not mention at any point that you employed the use of wizards or other magically-inclined persons in the creation of this weapon," said Ettyson. "Is that right?" Yan made a sound as if he was about to spit, then glanced at the judge and changed his mind with a nervous swallow.

"No, never. I hate magic, and magic users, and magic makers, and magical objects, magic spells, magic creatures, all of it. I hate magic. Causes nowt but trouble and misery, magic."

"Nowt but trouble?" It sounded strange, hearing Ettyson with her voice so used to long, elaborate sentences in a court of law saying words normally heard in a farmer's pub. Felix had a sudden image of Ettyson, covered in hay and muck, trying to order a pint of scrumpy down at Wart Bottom. He was snapped from his daydream by her voice. "Can you explain what you mean by that?" The blacksmith gave a mirthless chuckle.

"I gets magical items brought to me, sometimes, y'see. It's always the same. Some magical self-stirring cookpot has gone berserk and started chasing granny across the kitchen. Or maybe that magical door hinge that opens by itself when you approach has decided it doesn't want to open for you anymore, so you need muggins here to remove it from the wall. Of course, once these things are pumped full of magery, that's it, isn't it? No chance of getting it back to being useful. It's always going to be a bit unusual. No good for anyone. Best off just melting it all down and dumping it down a dry well, in my opinion."

If John had eyes, he'd be gazing downward. Ettyson, unperturbed, continued her questioning.

"So, if I were to tell you that someone had enchanted the dagger you'd made, the one over there in fact, so that it could seem like it's speaking and moving a little, what would you think?"

Yan glared at the dagger. "I'd think: what a shame, that's a waste of a perfectly good dagger."

"Thank you. I have no further questions." Ettyson nodded at the judge, then at Felix, and returned to her desk.

14 - Blacksmith II

"Yan Vo Mouletter," said Felix, approaching the witness stand.

The smith stared at him. "Aye?"

"I'd like to pick up on a few words you used a moment ago, if I may." When the witness did not reply, Felix began. "You said: 'some magical self-stirring cookpot has gone berserk and started chasing granny across the kitchen'. Yes?"

"Aye."

"You also said: that magical door hinge has decided it doesn't want to open for you anymore.' Am I right?"

"Sound it," he grunted. "What's yer point?"

"A rock wouldn't go berserk, or decide something. A clump of mud couldn't go berserk or make any sort of choice."

The smith didn't answer. Felix didn't need him to. He started counting off on his fingers.

"'Gone berserk.' 'Decided.' 'Doesn't want.' These are words that describe decisions or behaviours, aren't they?"

Still no reply. "Witness?" Felix probed. Yan shrugged. Felix ploughed on.

"What I'm trying to get across is that you didn't say: 'The self-stirring pot broke', or 'the door hinge malfunctioned.' You were using words that we would typically use to describe something alive."

"I was?" came a voice beneath furrowed bushy eyebrows.

"I would argue that way, yes."

"Well, good for you, lad. That stuff in't alive. It just in't."

It's unusual for someone to be so profusely anti-magic, especially a smith...

There are dozens of spells specifically designed to help with smiths and smithing, arguably revolutionising the vocation; spells of durability, heat-resistance, sharpness, etc. Most smiths swore by them, much to the chagrin of those old-in-the-tooth smiths who suggest that all these modern, young smiths don't know which end of a hammer to hold, and how the whole industry's gone to the dogs.

I wonder if…

"…Witness," said Felix. "Have you ever had a run-in with a magical object? Perhaps something that went wrong, and has perhaps caused you some sort of trauma?" He glanced at the prosecutors bench, where Ettyson was simply staring blankly forward, pencil in hand, yet not writing.

The smith scowled. "No."

I know I must be roughly along the right lines, otherwise Ettyson would have jumped down my throat for being irrelevant…

Or is that wishful thinking? Am I clutching at straws? Reading the prosecutor is like reading a brick.

"I remind you, sir," said Felix, affecting a borderline imperious tone. "That if you are lying right now, you could get into some very serious trouble." The smith's scowl deepened. "We're talking fines, irredeemable reputational damage… even prison time."

The judge cleared his throat pointedly. "Leaning more towards the former than the latter…"

"Ahem, yes, Your Honour."

Felix lowered his voice.

"I ask you one last time: have you ever had any sort of run in or altercation or similar from an incident involving a magical item of some kind?"

The smith didn't respond. Felix held his gaze until Yan Vo Mouletter's eye twitched.

"What happened?" Felix asked softly.

Yan leaned to the side, then reached for something. After a sound of a buckle or two unlatching, he sat up straight again, and slammed a boot on the edge of the judge's table next to him. A piece of metal with some sort of bracket on the top protruded a good few inches from the top of the boot, where the leg would go.

Where the leg would go…

The smith held the boot with one hand and yanked the metal rod with the other, revealing a crude, foot-shaped block of dull metal on the end. He pointed it at Felix, eyes blazing.

"Here, are ya happy?" he said, waving the metal leg. "I had an 'incident', as you right chipperly put it, with an anvil. That bloody wizard, that fraudster, had offered to cast a spell on it, my anvil, in exchange for a set of new shoes for his horse. I was poor, but also young, intrigued and stupid, so I ignored the thought of honest coin and said, sure, what have you got? He said, how heavy is yer anvil? About a pigsweight, says I, which is true. Maybe a pigsweight-and-a-half. Heavy thing, right? Well, says he, I can make it light as a feather, but still strong as iron, so you can move it if ever you needs to. Great, says I, not that I'd ever seen a future where I'd have to move it much. But, being stupid as I was, I thought it a nifty trick. So I farriers his horse good and proper, and once I'm done he gets out his book, reads it, then waves his hands with his wiggly fingers and click, poof, kazam! The spell is woven. He lifts my anvil with one finger, balancing it like it was no more than a wicker plate. Then he lowers it and asks that I strike it with my hammer, so I does, and it stays stock still, ringing true as it ever has. Well, I was delighted, imbecile that I was. Great, I says, and I meant it. I shake him by the hand, and off he goes.

"Later that day, the wife comes home from seeing her sister with the sprogs, and I show her my new anvil. Look here, says I, and lift the anvil with one finger. Well, I try with one finger, but it's a bit too heavy for that. This wizard must have had strong fingers, I thought. It takes both my hands but I lift it anyway, right above my head. My wife is mighty impressed. I'm smiling, but thinking, here, this anvil's getting heavier, or maybe I'm not as fit as I thought. I need to put this damn thing down before it crushes me. The little ones are running around by my feet, laughing and pointing. Look how strong pap is, they say. I nod and smile, but really I'm gritting my teeth. We've only a small house. Not much floor space, yes? Nowhere to drop the damn thing. Okay young pups, I said, barely able to speak for the pain in my arms. Move now, pap needs to put his anvil down. They don't hear me, they're squealing and laughing. Move, I says louder. Move! They finally hear, and scatter, and by this time I can barely stand with the effort of holding his huge, heavy bloody anvil in my arms.

"I go to drop it, but something in my back twinges, and it falls wrong. It lands on my leg with the full weight of a blacksmith's anvil, all cold steel and hard edges, and pins me to the ground. I'm shouting and screaming like a mad billy goat, and my family are shouting and screaming too. They fetch four strong lads from the village and together they lift the anvil from me. The pain... You can't imagine it. The moment they shift it, it's obvious that my leg ain't good for anything anymore. I spent the next few bitter months designing this metal leg, and a poor substitute it is, despite years of trying to improve it. A few people have tried to offer ideas, some even saying that there's these amazing new magic legs that feel just like the real thing, but I'd soon as trust a hammer made of glass."

He finished by sighing. "So, Mr Lawyer, yes, forgive me if I find it hard to trust these magical types and their schemes. Last time I did, it cost me a leg."

Felix let the smith calm down, while mulling over the story. He glanced at Ettyson, who turned to regard him. She had the good grace not to look smug. Felix shook his head. "Mr Vo Mouletter. Let me first say that I am saddened to hear of your story. It must have been a dreadful experience."

The smith shrugged. Felix continued.

"If I swing a fresh, new sword at a wooden training dummy and the sword snaps in half, am I to blame?"

"Not unless you were stronger than Halmar the Strong, which, and don't mean any offence, I very much doubt..."

"None taken, witness. So, is the sword to blame?" The smith blustered his moustaches.

"Eh? No, not at all. A sword is only as good as the man who makes it," he said. Felix nodded his head towards John.

"You must be a decent man, then, based on this dagger." The smith did not reply.

"'Only as good as the man who makes it,' you said... Could you not say the same as your anvil's spell? It sounds like the man who enchanted this anvil for you was, to put it simply, not very good at casting spells."

"Objection," said Ettyson. "Mr Sacramentum is not a qualified wizard of any sort, and so how can he make this suggestion?"

The judge looked at him. "Good point. Are you a secret sorcerer, lad?"

"No, Your Honour, but I would draw your attention to a part of the testimony given, for it reveals the answer." He turned back to Yan.

"The enchanter. He wiggled his fingers, yes? Like this?"

Felix wiggled his fingers up and down while keeping his palm steady. The smith frowned at him. "Yes, exactly like that."

"Did he then say the word: 'habooba'?"

"Now you mention it, I think he did... mighty odd, it sounded."

Felix turned to the judge.

"That almost certainly means our magician was reading from 'Gergle O'Tunken's Budget Magic For The Everyman', a spellbook notorious for being, shall we say, readily available for just about anyone who wants to try and cast a few spells. I know this because that particular instruction, 'wiggle your fingers and say habooba', is part of every spell in the book."

"Possession of that book is illegal, is it not?" asked the judge, with a severe look at Felix, who blinked and flashed a nervous smile.

"Ah, yes, that's true. I, hm, read about it in the case notes."

"Indeed," said the judge, and with a short pang of horror Felix saw him make a note.

Note to self: hide book.

Yan shook his head, mustachios flailing. "What does this mean?" he said to Felix, doubt in his voice. "What are you saying?"

"I'm saying the so-called wizard who cast this spell is no different to a slapdash or amateur smith forging a poor sword: the spell is not to blame, and nor is magic. Rather, it is the ineptitude of the man who *cast* the spell that is to blame. He was, I suggest, a charlatan, or at least an unskilled amateur, who used his charm and small skill to trick you into a free horse-shoeing."

The smith considered this, stroking his magnificent facial hair. "Well... I mean, that makes sense, I suppose."

"I would suggest, Mr Vo Mouletter, that perhaps your thoughts are clouded by this understandable trauma suffered at the hands of not *bad magic*, but a *bad magician*. Perhaps this has tainted your opinion of magic as a whole, and is shutting you off to a world that is eager to help you."

The smith was clearly in some deep thought. His furrowed brow twitched with the effort.

The judge coughed. "Mr Sacramentum, fascinating that this all is, how does it relate to the current argument of whether the dagger, here named John, is truly alive?"

"I hear you, Your Honour." Felix turned to the smith. "Mr Vo Mouletter, I'd like you to try and put aside your previous thoughts on magic for a moment and introduce you to someone who is aching to meet you. Meet John."

He gestured to John. The smith put his glasses back on. "John?" he said, tentatively.

"Uhm, yes... p-uh, Mr Vo Mouletter," said John. "You... made me, uh, sir."

"You're alive?"

"Yes, sir, I believe so, sir."

"I... but..." said the smith, rubbing his chin. "You can't... That is... Well, it's nice to meet you, lad."

"It's nice to meet you-"

"Objection," said Ettyson, rising. "This is not the time and place for this charade. For this to be cross-examination, there surely must be questions from a legal representative that are, at least tangentially, related to the case in hand."

"That's okay," said Felix. "I'm done, Your Honour."

He sat down, and the judge informed the witness he was free to go. He replaced his leg, then started walking towards the doorway at the back of the courtroom again. He paused when he approached the defendant's desk.

"I'd... like to get to know you, lad," he said to John.

"Thank you, sir, I would like that too," said John. Yan nodded with a grunt, then made his way, not to the door, but to the back of the courtroom, where he took a seat in the corner.

Felix turned to John, who seemed quiet and reserved. "Are you okay?" Felix asked.

"A little all over the place, to be honest," John said. "I hope there aren't any more surprises like that." Felix gave him a pat on the hilt. "I'm sure there won't be," he said, but as he said it, a thought dawned on him. He looked at Ettyson.

She wouldn't. Would she?

She probably would.

She definitely would.

Oh.

"John," he said. "I think-"

Ettyson stood. "For our next witness: we call the Metallicumancer Sal Yul Sel to the stand."

She did.

15 - Wizard I

Sal Yul Sel was an old man, completely bald, dressed in a shimmering grey robe of some fabric woven with metal. He had a belt of iron links, and, from the way he sounded when he walked, either his pockets were stuffed full of coins or he was wearing a set of chainmail unmentionables. Ettyson had just asked him a question, and he was looking at her with impatience over his thick spectacles.

"Yes. I was the one who cast the spell to animate the dagger." His voice was deep and clear, as if used to talking at length and with authority, but it was obvious he wasn't making any effort to hide his irritation.

"Why?" said Ettyson.

"So it could give testimony during the murder case, of course. I should have thought that was obvious."

Ettyson didn't react to the wizard's sharp tone. She was a professional, after all. "This would be the Vinch case?"

The witness sighed. "Yes."

"How did you, as you put it, animate the dagger, witness?"

Sal Yul Sel gave a single mirthless laugh and followed up with a humourless smile. It was the smile of an expert whose favourite part of being an expert is the feeling of superiority among those they believe know less than they do. "It's an uncommon spell developed by a specialist department at the university, of which I am the faculty leader. The spell itself is rather complex. Forgive me, but I don't know what level of detail you require?"

Ettyson, didn't blink. "Just an overview, please, witness, suitable for a layman."

The wizard raised his eyebrows and shook his head. "I shall try, but I don't know what use it will be. When one dedicates a life to the study of the mystical and the higher arts, one forgets sometimes the average understanding of the typical layman." He looked at Ettyson, who still wasn't biting. "Please stop me if I say anything too, hm, *esoteric*. I'm used to dealing with other scholars or advanced students in the arcane, you see. With people who have a grasp of not just the basics, you see, not with…"

His voice started to falter a little when it was clear that the prosecutor was not going to be impressed or cowed by anything the wizard said.

"Witness," said Ettyson. "Just explain, please. I will ask for clarification or further explanation… if any is needed."

Sal Yul Sel's eye twitched, but then he seemed to concede something within himself and shrugged. He settled into the stool, hands folded across his stomach, assuming what appeared to be his natural lecturing tone of voice. Ettyson started slowly pacing back and forth, head bowed, listening intently.

"Essentially, the way an animal or human moves around or talks, for example, comes down to what we call 'signals'. These are jolts of energy from the brain to the part of the body that needs to move. Then, signals are sent back, and the brain reacts. For example, you move your leg to take a step forward, then you step on a stone or similar, so you lift your foot. This is a signal moving from the brain to the foot and back again. Does that make sense so far?" He spoke to the seasoned prosecutor like she was a child.

"Yes," is all she said, without breaking stride.

"Hm, good." He leaned back in his stool. "So, these signals… They are intangible in that we cannot touch or hold them, or see them even, but they do exist. I am certain that I need not explain to those assembled here that just because we cannot see something that does not mean that it does not exist?" The wizard gave an exaggerated look around the room, waiting to see if anyone required clarification. His haughty gaze finally settled on Ettyson, and he waited, with apparent - but clearly mocking - earnestness.

"That will not be necessary," she said. "Please continue."

The wizard gave a self-satisfied smirk, then folded his arms.

"The spell itself is named - and forgive me, for we haven't settled on the final name yet, and as the spell is not fully published, there is still time - the spell is named 'Yul Sel's Animanatomy.' The fundamental nature of the spell is to instil these signals into an inanimate object so as to allow the object some form of higher cognitive process."

"And these signals… they can create the illusion of speech? Or thought?"

"Oh, absolutely. When it is performed with enough *skill*, it is possible for even the most *mundane* of objects to appear intelligent and vivacious." His eyes moved slowly over to John, then back to the prosecutor, his mouth fixed in a small, smug smirk. Ettyson stopped walking, laced her fingers behind her back and faced him.

"And can we confirm for the court that it was you, yourself who performed the incantation on this dagger?"

"Yes, it was. The university was approached as part of the case, and as the head of the department, I volunteered to perform the rite. It went swimmingly, if I may say so myself."

Ettyson looked to the ceiling as if in thought.

"I'd like to ask you about something you said a moment ago. 'It is possible for even the most mundane of objects to appear intelligent,' you said. 'Appear?' Why did you use this word, witness?"

The wizard shrugged. "Because it is not real. It is just an illusion."

"Illusion? It is trickery, then?"

The wizard snorted. "Indeed, it is, in a manner of speaking. It's the magic which is granting these responses, and if the magic were to run dry, or be dispelled, the illusion would dissipate, and any animation of thought or movement would end in a heartbeat."

Ettyson walked back over to her desk and leaned on it, arms folded. "But, in the Vinch case mentioned earlier, this dagger was a key witness. Are you saying that its testimony was suspect? Unreliable, as it was based on fraud?"

The witness barked a single, harsh laugh and dismissed the notion with a wave.

"Oh, absolutely not. The memories that the object possesses are very real, just as a footprint in a muddy pathway is real. All the spell does is let us see that footprint in a different way."

Ettyson narrowed her eyes. "Lastly, witness. That dagger there." She indicated John with the smallest of inclines of her head. "It can speak, and will claim it has emotional capacity. Is it alive?"

A.R. Turner

The wizard shook his head. "It is not, no more than a puppet is alive, or a candle."

"Thank you, witness," said Ettyson. "I have no further questions."

118

16 - Wizard II

Felix stared at the wizard for a few moments before standing to begin his questioning. Why was he putting in so much effort to appear erudite? Did it matter to him that much that everyone knew he was well-educated? Is he trying to impress someone in particular?

Or, he thought as he remembered a tiny nervous twitch of the wizard's eyes when Ettyson told him she would ask for clarification if required, *was he feeling inferior and trying to prove that he was the intellectual equal of these lawyers?*

A grand wizard with an inferiority complex?

"Witness," said Felix. "Mr Sal Yul Sel."

"Hm? Yes?" came the reply. "More questions, is it? I'm a busy man, so *do* please hurry up."

"I'll try to be as quick as I can, witness. But first, I would like to clarify something, if you wouldn't mind."

The wizard scoffed, removing his glasses and examining them. "Is that not what you are here for, Mr..?"

"Sacramentum. And yes, I suppose so."

He started to pace. *If I ever get tired of being a lawyer, I'll go into business selling padded socks for legal representatives. Extra tough for all that courtroom-level pacing. Even the most perambulatorily-minded lawyer can march back and forth in comfort, or your money back.*

"You are primarily a man of learning, yes?" said Felix.

"My boy, you don't get to head up a faculty at Restastine University if you are not!"

"A yes or a no will suffice, witness."

The wizard's eye twitched again. "Yes," he said, exaggerating it with overt theatrical emphasis.

"In many ways," said Felix, "the actual results of the case are irrelevant to you. Your involvement in this case is just that of an expert witness. Not the victim, or the perpetrator. Not an injured party, or an accused accomplice. You are merely here to offer your expert opinion and help us collectively arrive at the truth and therefore administer justice. Yes?"

"Yes."

"Well, now that we mention it, not an 'expert' witness as such. You are here mostly because you were the one to cast the actual spell on John, not for your expertise, as such. So you are not here as an 'expert' witness, merely a witness."

The wizard narrowed his eyes in an attempt to control the fluttering eyelid. "Yes," he said. "But I am an expert in this matter regardless. The spell is named after me, is it not?"

"It is," said Felix. "But, as I said, the actual outcome of the case doesn't really affect you, except perhaps regarding professional interest. Whichever way our honoured judge rules, it won't affect your life in the slightest. Am I right?"

The wizard sniffed. "You are. I am merely here to do my duty as a citizen of the kingdom. I was called, and I am here to serve."

"Good." Felix said, then stopped and considered the wizard, tilting his head to the side. "So, why then are you telling lies under oath?"

His moustache actually blustered outwards in apoplexy. "How dare you?" the wizard spluttered, eyes bulging. "Accusing me of... I am telling the truth, you... you rabble-rouser!"

A few of the locals who were spectating seemed to wake up and start excitedly mumbling to each other. Felix overheard one of them say "'Bout time it start t'pick up. Say, what's a rabbit-riser?"

"Objection, Your Honour," said Ettyson, resting her hands on the desk in front of her, then immediately lifting them and wiping them on her coat with a grimace. "We are indeed seeking the truth, not throwing unsubstantiated insults at witnesses."

"Mr Sacramentum?" said the judge, leaning over. Felix held a hand up, palm forward in apology. "Maybe I should explain?" he said.

"I think that would be wise." The judge settled back, watching Felix like a bull that was trying to decide whether to charge or not.

Note to self: less theatrics with the judge...

Felix pulled out a piece of paper and considered it, then tapped a line of scribbled notes with his finger. "Wizards, by and large, are a proud lot. Desperate to slap their name on anything. 'Yul Sel's Animanatomy,' you said the spell was called. You also reminded me the spell was named after you mere moments ago. Correct?"

The wizard scowled. "Yes." A small nervous shuffle. "I also said the name was not finalised…"

"Yes, I noticed that. A curious caveat to add. Why haven't you settled on the name? You were very proud of it a moment ago."

Ettyson rose. "Objection, why do we care about the name of the spell? This is irrelevant."

Felix spun on her before the judge could speak. "If it turns out your 'expert' witness is the sort of man to lie under oath, surely it is relevant as to whether we take his 'expert' testimony to heart when deciding the life-long consequences of my client?"

Ettyson's face darkened to a frown that vanished as quickly as it appeared. Felix turned to the judge. "May I, Your Honour?"

"By all means," came the reply. Felix addressed the witness.

"Why is the name of the spell still in flux?"

"We just… haven't decided on whether we want to call it that yet." Sal Yul Sel fidgeted like a child caught eating sweets before dinner.

Oh really?

"I see." He let the silence stretch. "You are a learned wizard. A faculty leader, you said. Have you heard of a wizard called Thweylin?"

He shifted uncomfortably and mumbled something noncommittal. "Please speak up," said Felix.

"I have… heard of her."

"Good. So have I. In fact, I've done quite a bit of research on her. Did you know, in fact, that three years ago she published an essay on what she called 'Discussion on Implications of Animation and Re-animation?' It was to act as her dissertation, of sorts, during her final year at Restastine University. A final academic document, a culmination of years of research, and her gateway from student to wizard - providing her academic superiors accepted it as a well-rounded and researched document that furthers the industry."

Walking back to his desk, he reached into a satchel and produced a small hard-back book of around fifty pages. Sal Yul Sel's eyes bulged. "Where did you-" he began, before stopping himself and shutting his mouth with a snap. Felix raised an eyebrow at him, watching him squirm, before looking down at the book in his hands.

"It's a fascinating read. She, in collaboration with a necromancer named…" Felix paused. It had been a long time since he had thought of that particularly tragic case. Composing himself, he continued as if nothing had happened. "Forgive me. Along with a necromancer named Hyreit, she considers the ramifications of breathing life into that which does not have any, whether the body of a now-dead animal or person, or the bringing to life of an inanimate object. She then goes on to detail how she has successfully created a spell that will, in her words, 'breathe life into the lifeless', but declares that it should not be used unless in the most dire of circumstances, for the potential suffering that would be created on the part of the animated object."

The wizard scoffed. "Your point being?"

"You see, an odd thing happened. From what I can deduce, the essay was submitted, then, according to my own research, Thweylin was dismissed from the university mere months before her graduation, for reasons I cannot seem to find details for. What I was able to find, however, was that this happened three weeks before you yourself were elevated to department head, following - according to the University's campus newsletter - a 'significant breakthrough in a new area of spellmanship'. What was that breakthrough, witness?"

"I… it is too complex to explain."

"Was it animanatomy?"

"This is baseless conjecture."

"Is it?"

Felix turned to the audience of a half-dozen locals and gestured to a young woman wrapped in a blue cowl. She stood. Felix turned to the judge. "This woman's name is Thweylin. I can call her as a witness to testify to everything I have just said, if you like. Or, our witness currently on the stand can save us a large amount of time and simply admit to stealing the research and passing it off as his own. Which is of course why the name of the spell is a lie. It isn't "Sal Yul Sel's" anything. The guilt that he feels from stealing the spell means the witness can't settle on a name, especially one that hides such blatant thievery-"

"I didn't steal it, you buffoon!" shouted Sal Yul Sel, red in the face. "It was paid for! Every silver! That lying…" a coughing fit overtook him, choking his angry words to nothing. He took a sip of water from a bottle and glared at the woman.

Paid for?

Felix gestured to the woman in the blue cowl to sit down, and she did so. Her name was indeed Thweylin, but she wasn't the one who had written the essay. Felix's relief in his bluff not being called was overshadowed by this development he wasn't expecting.

"What do you mean, witness?" he asked. Sal Yul Sel closed his eyes, took a deep breath, then flicked them open again.

"You were right, lawyer, up until a point. This young lady did come up with some *quite* interesting research on inanimate objects. Of course I remember it. I'm the faculty leader, as you say. When it came time for her to submit her dissertation, a dissertation I was *rather interested* in reading, she called me for a meeting, which I, of course, accepted. There she told me of the trouble she was in, financially, you understand."

The wizard sneered.

"It turns out she had borrowed money from the wrong people to try and impress a man, or somesuch other nonsense. She asked if it was possible to sell a spell. I said that it is unusual, but it has been done before. Then, she offered to sell the spell to me, and I accepted."

He waved a finger at Felix, as if admonishing a misbehaving pupil. "I paid a fair price for the rights to it. Why she then disappeared from the university, I don't know. She could have worked on something else, perhaps, and submitted it. But one day she simply was not there. I have not made public knowledge of any of this for several reasons. One, I don't want to put her in any further danger. Two, I don't want to draw any of that danger upon myself. Three, such discussions are private affairs between wizards, or wizards-to-be."

He smoothed his bald head with an old, shrivelled hand and gave Felix a grim smile. "Does that satisfy you, Mr Sacramentum? Am I still a liar?"

Felix turned to his team who were not meeting his eye.

Well… Time to move on, I think.

~

The yearning for the grey fields came upon him like a slap, and exhaustion washed over him. Felix stumbled, and whipped an arm out to catch himself before he fell. Instantly Racelsus's voice was in his mind.

What's wrong?

Nothing, Rass. Just tripped.

Ghosts don't trip.

Standing up straight, Felix shook his head from side to side like an animal, trying to focus his mind. He clasped his hands behind his back and started to pace as if nothing had happened. "I'd like to ask you about another topic, Mr Yul Sel," he said.

"I don't doubt it," the wizard spat back. If he had noticed anything wrong with Felix, he wasn't mentioning it. "Hopefully something with a little less artistic licence."

Hmm… Artistic…

"You were the individual who actually performed the enchanting on John during the Vinch case, yes, witness?"

"Yes, I was. I've already said this."

"Indeed. In many ways, Mr Sal Yul Sel, you could claim to be one of the parents of John."

"Ridiculous," the wizard said. "Parent, indeed! It's just an object, for goodness sake. You might as well say I was the parent of my morning expulsions." Felix ignored this particular image and continued as if he hadn't been interrupted.

"It was the combination of your expertise with magic and the smithing of Yan Vo Mouletter that led to the creation of this individual, with his thoughts, dreams, opinions, likes, dislikes… He even has your accent."

"Ridiculous." Sal Yul Sel waved a hand dismissively. "All illusory. It is all illusion. It-is-not-real!"

"How do you know?" said Felix, his mouth twitching into a tiny smile.

"Excuse me?" said the wizard.

"How do you know they are illusions, and not real emotions?"

"Because *I* created them."

Felix crossed his arms over his chest. "Earlier, I felt shame at misunderstanding the situation with the spell. Could you not say that you also made that emotion for me? I wouldn't have felt that way if not for you."

"That was you creating that feeling, not me. Your brain, your body. *Your* mistake."

Felix quashed his frustration. Since the revelation with the ownership of the spell, his momentum had started wobbling dangerously.

I'm not getting anywhere with this pig-headed, overblown-

A small metallic ting sounded from behind him. Felix realised it was John. "Can I say something to him?" he asked, very quietly, so only Felix could hear. Felix chewed his lip.

"It's not usually a good idea, John."

"Please."

Something about the way he said it made Felix look at John intently. Maybe it was that he'd never heard that plaintive tone in his voice before. Felix turned back to the wizard.

"...I have only one last question. My client, John, would like to say something to you, witness."

The wizard shrugged. "If it will cause this senseless excuse for a cross-examination to end, then fine. Bring out the puppet, pay no attention to the strings."

Felix nodded to Helda, and she lifted the wooden block that John was resting in so he was at eye level with the wizard. The room was silent, straining to hear what he had to say. The expression on Sal Yul Sel's face was that of a bored parent watching their child perform the same magic trick they've seen a dozen times already. As the silence stretched, he rolled his eyes and opened his mouth to speak. John spoke before him.

"I've missed you," said John.

Sal Yul Sel's haughty expression fell from his face, but his eyes stayed on John. He leaned forward a touch. "You have?"

"Yes. An awful lot."

The wizard blinked, then rubbed his eye. "Yes, well."

"You... don't think I'm real?" John's voice sounded small.

"Well, it's... you see, it's very complicated, my boy," said the wizard, in a soothing tone completely opposite to the one he used with Felix.

"Objection," said Ettyson, rising. "This is not cross-examination. This is idle chatter."

"I'm inclined to agree," said the judge, making some notes. He jabbed his pencil at Felix. "If you have no more questions, I think it is in the interests of the court that you cease this. You can always continue this afterwards, whatever it is."

"Understood, Your Honour," said Felix, nodding at Helda again, who took John back to the table. "I have no further questions, witness. Your Honour." Felix walked back to the desk and sat down. Racelsus and John were whispering together.

"I think we shall have a short break," said the judge, peering at the dusty clock. "One hour, I reckon." With that, he produced a small bag from somewhere and unpacked a few small paper parcels. He unwrapped them. They contained pastries. The judge read through his notes and started munching on his lunch, completely ignoring everyone else as he did so.

The wizard Sal Yul Sel left the witness stool and walked past the desks, stopping briefly to turn and look at John. After a moment, without saying anything, he strode to the back of the room and found a space on the bench beside the blacksmith, Yan Vo Mouletter. They sat in silence next to one another, avoiding each other's eyes. Yan picked at his apron, while Sal Yul Sel examined his fingernails. Eventually, Yan coughed and leaned over.

"Look, I think we'd better-"

"I would like every other weekend," Sal said. "And one full month in the summer."

The smith stared at the wizard, then held out his hand.

"Deal," he said.

The two men shook hands.

"There's a pub around the corner, want t'get a quick one in before the recess is over?" asked Yan.

"I should like that very much," said Sal Yul Sel, and they both got up and left together; the wizard and the smith.

~

Felix paced in the defence counsel's chambers, brow furrowed. He stopped abruptly and turned to his team: Yetty, Helda, Furbo and Racelsus. They all waited for him to speak.

"I think it's going... okay," he said. Their expressions varied from enthusiastic agreement to pained dissent. "You don't agree?" he said to Yetty. She raised a hand, held it flat and tilted it side to side.

"The blacksmith went well. The wizard went poorly. The philosopher... Although Furbo did a pretty fantastic job, I have no idea which way that's gone."

"I agree," said Felix, tapping his chin. After a pause, he checked the wind-up clock in the chamber. It was even dustier than the one in the courtroom. Fifteen minutes to go.

"What we need," said Yetty. "Is a killer witness. Someone to knock the pants off of the judge. Someone with a silver tongue and a passionate spirit, who can ignite the sympathy in every single person in that room."

"Someone to get the juices flowing," said Furbo.

"Someone with dark, rippling... arguments," said Racelsus, smirking. *Did she smirk? Did I imagine that?*

"I hear you," said Felix. He ran through the list of defence witnesses in his head. None of them seemed to fit the bill. *Except...* He snapped his fingers. "I have just the guy! Let's get this bonfire burning."

With only a few minutes to spare, he stepped from the room to find the witness and instil into him the importance of letting his unbridled charisma shine through.

17 - Bureaucrat

"Naturally, if, ehrm, John, were to be declared *legally* alive, that is to say, a non-object, therefore it follows it, ehrm, he, would become an automatic citizen of the kingdom, then of course he, ehrm, it, would be subject to all applicable laws and obligations that any other, ehrm, person would be subject to."

The man speaking took a long breath as if to continue, but Felix cut him off. He almost missed his opportunity. Wulte Gribb was a senior taxation administrator, and had about as much unbridled charisma as a curtain.

"And so," Felix said, making up for Gribb's ceaseless monotone by reflexively overdoing his own vocal undulations. "In your professional opinion as a taxation administrator, there should be no blocker to John becoming a live and legal citizen, provided he can and will follow all taxation requirements and other bureaucratic necessities?"

After a moment of prolonged, utterly silent contemplation, Gribb nodded. "Yes, I should say so, that is to say, provided the courtroom today finds no legal, erhm, impediment, then there is…"

Felix turned his eyes surreptitiously to his crack team, watching him with mixed expressions from his desk. Racelsus met his eye and spoke into his mind.

This is your secret weapon?

"Well, no," whispered Felix as Gribb droned on. "I'd have thought that was fairly obvious."

What is… this, then? Even the judge looks bored.

It was true. The judge's eyes were glazed over. If he had had a particularly large lunch, the somnolent effect of Gribb's circumlocution could be in real danger of sending the judge to sleep.

"The actual witness I'd sent for is delayed…" Felix whispered. "It was much easier when we could just magic them up out of nowhere."

Oh, I don't know about that. Magic is never free, you know.

"…pursuant to zoning regulations," Gribb finished.

"Thank you, Mr Gribb," said Felix. "I have no further questions."

After a pause, Felix repeated more loudly: "I have no further questions, Your Honour."

The judge blinked and coughed. "Very good, very good. Ms Ettyson, would you care to cross-examine the witness?"

She stood and gave Wulte Gribb a lightning-fast appraisal. "No, thank you, Your Honour."

Felix sighed inwardly. If even Ettyson didn't want to speak to this witness then he knew that the testimony would be almost useless.

"Very well. Mr Gribb, you may leave," said the judge. The bureaucrat did so, nodding once to Felix and Ettyson, then to the judge, before shuffling towards the back of the room. Felix overheard Helda saying, perhaps a little too loudly to be unintentional, "never let Felix plan any surprise parties for me, unless it's a surprise sleepover."

"Does the defence wish to present another witness at this time?" said the judge, yawning. Felix shifted a little.

"Yes, Your Honour, but, well, she's not here yet."

"Not here?"

Felix gave a pained expression. "Uh, no, Your Honour. I think she is, well, delayed."

The judge leaned over and tapped his pencil on the table. "That won't do, Mr Sacramentum. We cannot wait around for every tardy malcontent to arrive when they fancy it."

"No, Your Honour."

A pause.

"So..?" said the judge.

"Your Honour?"

"Do you perhaps have *another* witness you might want to call up?"

Felix blinked. "Uhm…"

"Perhaps," said Ettyson, rising. "I could call another? It might give the defence a little more time to… get their thoughts in order."

The judge considered this.

"That is a little irregular," he said. "But, provided the defence is willing?"

"Uh, yes, of course, Your Honour. Very kind," said Felix, who wasn't very willing, and didn't think it was particularly kind.

Ettyson pressed her hands together. "Excellent. The prosecution would like to call John Dagger to testify."

Journal Entry C - Commonwealth

Reference case [GMvHRH] (GreMal v. HRH), year 1299, Judge Neffin presiding.

What does it mean to be a person? What sort of a ridiculous question is that?

You might remember from earlier case notes of mine that I've had a few run-ins with non-humans. There was the nosgoot, Gluk. A couple of dragons. Great Croaker, the wizard-frog of the swamplands, of course. There was also the goblin, Burrimo, whom I met twice; once where I helped him, and once where I failed him. Why was I even representing him at all? He wasn't human, and humans are the dominant species on this planet (as far as we know - and gods excepted, naturally.)

It's a story with a good part and a sad part.

It was much before my time when the first goblin case could be said to have been heard. But I must jump a little further back before I can start.

Goblins are small creatures compared to humans. In other respects they resemble us near enough. The same number of arms and eyes. The same needs and wants. Their own cultures and histories, mythologies and artistries. The same ability to hold a spear or reload a catapult. You can probably see where I'm going with this.

When the goblin cultures were encountered, it was the first time the human empires had met a significant non-human civilisation. It could have gone one of several ways, but blessedly the hand of unity was extended to them by the monarch of the time. Come and share our medicine, said he. Learn the ways of modern science. Teach us your ways with jewellery. Enter mutual protection pacts. Oh, and occasionally join in a couple of border wars as expendable auxiliaries, nothing serious.

The threat was never made explicitly, the history books say, but what do they know.

So, after a few generations of goblins being sent off to hellish battlefields, a few of the more enterprising and curious ones decided to settle in human towns. Again, it went about as well as you expect, but goblins are hardy folk, and they stood their ground. Those that settled experienced a new way of life. They built houses and shops, became nurses and administrators. A new leaf had been turned for goblinkind, and for the rest of the empire, the humans, it was proof that we were not all that was out there.

Why am I telling you all of this? Well, the law had, in its characteristic lethargy, not caught up with the military charter. Oh, they were of course welcome to join the army and get slaughtered, but could they legally own a square foot of dirt? Check back in around fifty years. What about those shops and houses they had built? Well, they could only be owned by a legal person, and guess who wasn't considered a legal person? When this was discovered, there were threats of violence, speciest scuffles, seizings by jealous locals, the works. It was not a good time to be a goblin.

What they needed was legal protection. The state didn't want to have to do any of the hard work. They were happy with things as they were. Goblins signed up for the armed forces in exchange for food and lodgings, and a blind eye could be turned to the issues in the towns and cities.

If they weren't even represented as something more worthy of rights than a cabbage, you can bet your last copper that no sane judge in the land would allow a goblin to represent themselves in court.

Thankfully, Judge Ulnola was not sane.

Mallimo was an extraordinary second-generation goblin who taught herself to read, then taught herself to read law. In between fending off local idiots and helping in her parents' bakery, she was able to, through her own ingenuity, trick the courts into allowing her to stand in court and represent herself in a fight against the state. The charge? Fraud. Misrepresentation. She argued that the empire of humanity had approached goblinkind under false pretences, and had not delivered on any of their promises of shared knowledge and protection. She listed each and every promise made by the late King Eof the Friendly, and then explained how each of them were still unfulfilled.

How could humanity expect continued friendship and cooperation from goblinkind, she said, if goblins were not even considered persons in the legal sense? This was a one-sided exploitation-based relationship, and it was going to end one way or another.

By contemporary accounts, she was incredible. Not only were her arguments sound and well-researched and her delivery mesmerising, but she personally was a paragon of the ingenuity and tenacity of goblinkind. Humanity weren't the smartest kids in the playground anymore. If they didn't take a long look at themselves, they could end up biting off more than they could chew.

Ulnola, as I said, was borderline insane. It was the days before you could strike off a judge for being of unsound mind. However, he also had a heart. I like to think it was the latter that caused him to immediately conclude that goblins were henceforth persons, and accorded the same legal rights as humans. I can't say for certain though.

Since then, provided an appropriate representative of both the empire and a new civilisation are in agreement, anyone can join, and enjoy the rights accorded to any member of our civilisation in more-or-less any way they want to be, so long as it doesn't infringe on the rights of anyone else in the empire.

Sorry, that was dangerously close to a history lecture. Let's keep things spicy and interesting with a joke. Why don't philosophers make good lawyers? Because they like to ignore evidence.

Furbo didn't like that one, but Yetty thought it was great. Racelsus responded with her own lawyer joke, but it was terribly rude and I won't sully these pages with it.

~journal entry ends

18 - The Knife Speaks I

Ettyson pressed her hands together. "Excellent. The prosecution would like to call John Dagger to testify."

Felix choked, which was hard to do, as a ghost.

"Does the defendant object?" said the judge.

Why did I walk right into her trap?

Oh Ettyson, you sneaky…

"No, Your Honour," said John. The judge nodded.

"Very well then. Please proceed."

John was carried carefully by Helda and deposited, in his customary hunk of wood, on the witness stool. She stood there awkwardly before catching herself and trotting back to the desk. She avoided Felix's eyes. Yetty didn't.

"I hope you know what you're doing," she whispered.

"Of course," said Felix. *Of course I don't.*

Ettyson swept to her feet and walked over to John. "Witness," she said, peering down at him.

"Yes?" said John in his tinny voice.

"Please do not reply unless I ask you a direct question," came the icy and well-rehearsed response.

"Uh, okay," John replied. "Wait, does that include - actually, never mind."

The prosecutor assessed him in the same way a snake assesses a mouse. "Witness, how old are you?"

"Well, that depends on when you think I was born."

"Made, not born. You were not born."

John made no reply for a moment. "I feel the need to say that that isn't a question, so I'm not responding."

Not bad, John.

A lesser lawyer might have bristled, but Ettyson simply ignored him and continued. "When were you forged, then? When was the metal that forms your blade poured and hammered? How long ago?"

"Couldn't you ask Yan Mouletter? He's just over there you know," said John. Felix looked across at the two men who were sitting on the back row, looking a little merrier than they had earlier in the day. Yan waved a cheery hand, but Ettyson ignored him.

"I want to ask *you*, witness. Can you please answer the question?"

John tutted. "Suit yourself. Just trying to help. Fifteen years, give or take a little, I think," he said. A little twinge of worry nagged at Felix's mind.

"You think?" said Ettyson, no doubt sensing the same thing, but with wholly different intentions.

"Yes. My memories are a little fuzzy from that far back."

"Fuzzy how?" said Ettyson, starting to pace slowly back and forth. John considered for a moment.

"I was not really alive at that point, you know. Life was simple. I merely existed with no perception or thought. So, in order to remember that long ago, I have to really concentrate, and, despite that, it's a bit... fuzzy."

"Fuzzy?"

"Look," said John. "I don't have eyes, or fingers, or skin, so when I describe something as 'fuzzy', please know that I'm doing my best based on what I have been told the feeling that I am feeling is best described as." After a raised eyebrow from Ettyson, he added sheepishly: "I hope that sentence made sense. I'm sort of new to this sort of conversation."

Ettyson stood in silence for a few moments, then started slowly pacing again, this time with her hands clasped behind her back.

"I understand, witness, you have some skill at arms, by which I mean an unskilled wielder of, well, *you*, can, through some manipulation provided by yourself, find themselves performing daggercraft at the same level as a seasoned practitioner. Is this true?"

"As I said, I'm still sort of new to lawyers and their unique form of conversation, so give me a moment... If I've understood your rather lengthy and comma-laden question as well as I think I have, then yes."

Perhaps he's being too difficult...

Felix frowned at Ettyson. She was a difficult person to read. She had a history of blindsiding him. That nagging sensation returned.

Why do I have a bad feeling about this… What is she up to?

"How does that work?" said Ettyson. "Do you mind-control them? Possession?" John laughed; a small, tinkly laugh.

"No, not really. Nothing like that. Well, it's hard to explain. I just sort of… help them move me to the right place."

"So you can cause them to slice you through the air, or deflect a blow, that sort of thing?"

"Yes, that sort of thing," said John, his voice brightening. "I'm quite good at it, you know."

Perhaps I'm worrying over nothing. Felix relaxed. Ettyson nodded her thanks to her newly cooperative witness, then stopped walking and faced him directly.

"Witness, how many people have you killed?"

Oh.

"Excuse me?" John said. Ettyson took a step towards him.

"How many people - human people - have you killed, John Dagger?"

"None!" he said. He twitched slightly, sending a short, sharp *ting* to ring through the air, as if he had just been flicked or tapped with a metal coin.

Felix stood up. "This is wholly inappropriate. I suspect the prosecution is attempting to confuse the defendant through rampant spreading of bu- uh, nonsense."

Before the judge could respond, she whirled on him. "I think I'm confused, Your honour. Either 'John' is an object incapable of thought or action, and therefore also incapable of holding blame in the event of someone using 'it' to kill someone, or 'he' is a living person capable of *not only* conscious thought but actual movement as well - movement via manipulation of direction and speed. If the latter is true, which you argue, and 'he' has been involved in the death of a human person, 'he' could have chosen to alter the thrusts or slices by whomsoever was wielding 'him' - that is, chosen *not* to kill."

She paused for effect. "But," she said, more quietly. "If 'he' did *not* do that, that is to say, had the understanding *and* the opportunity to prevent a death, a death that would be caused *by his own body*, then that is something I think worth discussing."

A.R. Turner

Felix stood, struggling to hold her gaze. That fiery, superior, victorious gaze.

Damn.

"I don't think I followed that one," said John, in a quiet voice almost imperceptible.

"…An interesting philosophical question," said Felix to the judge, noticing a small itch of sweat prickle his lower back. *Who knew that ghosts could sweat?* "But, I fear, irrelevant, as John has not been involved in such an event, not since the spell of animation was cast and he was brought to life."

"Mr Sacramentum," said the judge in a grave tone. "I do hope you are not answering on behalf of a witness currently under cross-examination. I believe he - it - has not yet actually provided an answer for the question posed."

"But, Your Honour, if it is not relevant, then he does not need to answer."

"How will we know if it is relevant until the witness answers?" said the judge.

Felix felt a little heat rising in his cheeks, and had to fight back his initial remark.

"Well," he said, "you ask the lawyer who posed the question." The judge narrowed his eyes.

"I don't need to. *You* did. And I have heard her reasoning, and would like to hear your client's answer." The judge gave a small sneer, a lip curl that twisted his face into a cruel mask that had heresofar been absent. "Is that enough for you, *My Lord?*"

Felix squared his shoulders and crossed his arms. "Look, whatever bee in your bonnet you've got towards metropolitan lawyers has nothing to do with me. So stop being difficult and grow up, you overblown self-important wart-hog."

…is what Felix wanted to say. But he also wanted to have at least a chance of winning the case, so he bowed his head and swallowed his pride.

"I apologise, Your Honour." The judge's expression softened, all traces of the sneer vanished. Felix turned towards John who, if he had had eyes, would have been avoiding Felix's.

140

"Well, now that that is over... witness?" said the judge, turning to face John. "Have you been involved in any killings since you were enchanted? By which we mean, have you been used as the weapon by which a killing has occurred?"

All eyes turned to the dagger, which suddenly looked very small, and very sharp.

"I have the right to remain silent?" said John.

The judge shook his head. "No, you don't."

"Think about it," said Felix under his breath. "That wouldn't make any sense. It's okay, just answer honestly."

John hesitated.

"Then I... yes, I have," he whispered.

Sharp intakes of breath from those within earshot. Ettyson and the judge did not react.

"And," said Ettyson, in her stride. "Were you in any danger of death yourself, and thus forced to kill to protect yourself?"

"No, but it-"

"And did you exercise your own physical abilities to prevent the death of the victim?"

"No, but-"

The prosecutor returned to her desk and stood with a hand resting on the tabletop.

"And was the killing justified in any legal sense, for example to protect another, or in wartime?"

"I don't know..."

"You don't know? You killed someone, and you don't know why?"

"No! I had just been brought to life, and-"

Ettyson slapped her hand on the table beside her. "Witness," she said. John silenced himself. "If you are, as you claim, a living, thinking, feeling 'person', then you are also subject to those laws by which all creatures of higher sentience are obliged to follow. You must not steal, for example. Of course, the most obvious and important of these: you must not kill, unless for a small set of very specific circumstances. I suggest that you do not know the circumstances of this murder. You simply went along with it, which, I regret to inform you, is no defence in the legal sense." She crossed her arms. "If you want to be considered *alive,* and part of our society, you must respect these rules, these edicts entrenched in law, or suffer the consequences."

"I-"

Ettyson held a finger up, silencing him. "I did not ask a question, witness."

John was silent. Ettyson returned to her seat.

"I have no further questions."

19 - The Knife Speaks II

In the heavy silence, Felix got to his feet and walked slowly over to his client. The dagger was completely still and silent. He didn't have a face, but if he did, Felix could imagine an expression of inward dejection.

"John," said Felix quietly. "I am going to ask you about the circumstances of that killing."

The dagger said nothing. *Can I blame him?*

"Just tell me everything you remember, as clearly and simply as you can. Okay? Can you do that?"

"…I don't want to…" said John, quietly.

Felix gave a smile that did not tally with how he felt, but sometimes all you need is a brave face. "Trust me," he said. "I'll get you out of this."

"You will?"

"I will." *Sometimes a gentle lie, too.*

The dagger did not reply for a moment, then appeared to take a shuddering breath, despite not needing to breathe.

"Okay," he said. "Ask me what you have to."

Felix stood back and crossed his arms, trying to figure out the right place to start. *Start with the simple questions.*

"Where were you on the day of the killing in question?"

After a pause, John began.

"It was just before the case…"

"Which case, John?"

"The Vinch case, the one I was brought to life for."

Felix nodded. "Thank you. Continue, please."

"The case had not yet begun, and I was waiting in a back room somewhere. I think I was being stored where the other pieces of evidence were kept. My thoughts were firing off in all directions. I mean, I'd never *had* thoughts before. It was a very confusing few days."

"Days? You were kept in there for days?"

"Yes, I think so. It was hard to tell. Everything was so confusing. But I saw the light change a few times, which I later learned was the passage of the days." Felix unfolded his arms and started pacing.

"Do you remember being brought to life?"

"Yes, sort of. At first, I had no memories. No way of thinking. Then, after a bright flash, suddenly… *there*. Or, here. I could think. So much to take in… Not only that, I could remember so much of my life before."

"Before you were able to think?"

"Yes, and I know that sounds crazy, but it's true. Years of endless nothing, and the occasional, well, excitement."

John was warming up. It seemed he was enjoying this detailed discussion of his life. *Another piece of proof, John: your favourite subject is yourself. If that doesn't scream 'I'm a person', what does?*

"Had anyone spoken to you at this time?"

"No, not at that point. I kept looking around for the blacksmith, but I couldn't find him. There was nobody there."

A pause, in which Felix had to force himself not to look at the blacksmith, watching from the stands.

"I had memories, too, of another man. A wizard, I now know they are called. He used to speak to me before, just before I awoke. He'd chat about this and that… mindless things, perhaps, but I enjoyed it immensely. I found that when I spoke, it was his voice I spoke with."

Felix nodded, again fighting the urge to gawp at the wizard in the gallery, if you can consider three rows of benches full of half-drunk bumpkins as a gallery.

"What happened then?" he said.

"All of a sudden there was noise. A door opened, a set of feet walked in, and I was being carried. It was an odd sensation, I can tell you that. Then, someone put me down, and a voice started speaking to me, telling me what was going to happen and what I needed to do."

"What did they ask you to do?"

Ettyson stood. "Objection."

"On what grounds?" said the judge, making a note.

"Leading the witness," said Ettyson. "I will elaborate: how could the witness possibly understand what they were saying, and whether he was being told to do something? You were only days old by your own reckoning, which is far too little time to understand the nuances of a language as complex as ours."

Felix crossed his arms once more and stood between Ettyson and his client. "Would you like me to call upon the wizard again? Because I'm sure that in as much as we need to know, the answer to your question is simply: magic."

Ettyson narrowed her eyes. Felix turned to Sal Yul Sel, whose eyes, from where Felix was standing, appeared a tad damper than they were before.

"Excuse me, wizard? Is the answer to my colleague's question: magic?"

Everyone in the room turned to look at the wizard, who stood up, rubbed his eye and cleared his throat. "Well, pretty much."

"Thank you." He returned his focus to Ettyson, eyebrows raised. "Well?" he said.

She then lowered herself to her seat.

"Thank you. So, John. What were these voices saying?"

"I don't know how I understood them, but I did." John said.

"That's okay, John, you don't have to answer that part. Just tell me and the court what they were saying you had to do."

"Oh, sorry. They told me I was going to be asked a number of questions, and that I needed to answer them."

"That sounds familiar, eh?" said Felix, with a smile. No one laughed, except Helda, who quickly quietened. "Sorry, John, Please carry on."

"I didn't know what that really meant, but it sounded pretty serious, so I agreed. I was still amazed at how I could even understand what was being said or asked. A few moments ago I hadn't spoken to another living thing."

"Continue, please."

"I answered all their questions, and did what they asked. After the case, Finlay's mother, the widow, came and found me in the evidence room. She was with someone else. I recognised his voice from before. The one who gave me the instructions. She picked me up. I remember the feeling of her grip from before. It was so cold…"

"Then what happened, John?"

"She walked with this someone to a back room somewhere, then outside. I heard running water. They talked. Their voices started to get angrier. I remember him saying 'you owe me more than that', and she said, 'I'll give you what you've earned, nephew'."

"Nephew?" Felix wracked his brains for details of the case. *Such a convoluted family tree… what was his name…*

Yetty nudged his elbow. "Grent," she whispered.

"Was his name Grent?" Felix said.

"Objection," said Ettyson, standing again. This time, the judge didn't need to hear her reasoning.

"Now that is leading the witness," said Judge Burritt. "What are you playing at, man?"

Felix wanted to slap his palm over his eyes and disappear into the floor, but settled for what he hoped was a conciliatory nod of the head. "I apologise, Your Honour. I would be able to provide case notes that prove the name of the nephew, however, and as this was not a fact that was in question, I hope the court might forgive my oversight in wishing to arrive at the next stage of questioning more speedily."

It's worth a shot!

The judge made a short note on his paper, which he underlined several times. He looked up. "Do *not* do it again."

"Yes, Your Honour. Apologies once again."

The judge waved a hand at him, which Felix took as a sign to continue.

"John," he said. "This nephew. What was his name?" The dagger sighed.

"You were right. It was Grent," John said, and Felix gave Yetty a small and quick thumbs up and a pained grimace.

"What happened then?" he said.

John paused. "Then they, that being the widow and the nephew, Grent, well they stopped walking, and she used me to stab the man in the back, then pushed him into the river."

A few gasps from behind Felix somewhere, and Felix had found his eyebrows had raised quite without his input, and had to force them down again.

"The mother? The widow Vinch? She stabbed her nephew, Grent Vinch, in the back?"

"Yes, that's right," said John.

Felix blinked, and shot a glance involuntarily at Ettyson, who returned it without expression, but a narrowing of the eyes.

"Why did she stab him?" asked Felix.

"I don't know," said John.

"Did you know she was going to stab him?"

"Yes. Sort of. I could tell she was planning to, and when she was about to."

Something in Felix's mind was screaming, clanging warning bells and waving like mad, but he couldn't stop.

"Did you try to stop her, or fight against the stab?"

"No," John replied quietly.

"Why not?"

"It sounds terrible…"

"John, please tell us," said Felix, wanting to shut down this line of questioning yet unable to force himself to do so. He needed to hear what John was thinking but dreaded the answer.

"…I didn't really know why I should try to stop her," said John. "And… I didn't know what it would feel like. I hadn't been stabbed into anything living since I came to life. I was… curious."

Another smattering of gasps and mutters from the members of the audience that were paying attention. The judge's face was unreadable, creased into a frown beneath low brows. Felix's thoughts were running in ten directions at once.

Focus!

"John, that…"

A small light flickered in the corner of Felix's mind and he paused.

"Wait," he said, holding up a hand, mind racing. "Going back a moment. The conversation before the court case, when the man was talking to you. What specifically did he say to you? Do you remember?"

John thought for a moment. "I do. He said: The lawyer was going to ask me a series of questions, and I had to answer them."

"Did he tell you... *how* to answer them?"

Felix gripped his fingers without meaning to. A nervous habit.

If I'm right, then this might be your only chance. Come on, John.

John did not answer immediately. The entire court was waiting, breaths drawn in - except Felix, who had no breath. Felix's head started to swim a little, the wooziness returning. Just as he was about to prompt John again, the dagger started to speak.

"Yes, he did. He told me what to say and how to say it. He told me that I had to declare Finlay Vinch the murderer, or I'd be thrown into the sea, and I'd rust into nothing."

More murmurs and mutters from the small group of onlookers behind the benches. Felix ignored them.

"John, hang on a second. This voice. Grent Vinch. He told you to point the finger at Finlay Vinch?"

"Yes."

"Was Finlay the killer? Was he guilty?"

"No, he wasn't. His mother was."

"His mother," hissed Yetty to Felix, who couldn't stop now. He took a step towards John.

"*She* was the killer of her husband? His own wife?"

"Yes."

"John," said Felix, as calmly as he could, taking another step forward. "Are you admitting to us now that during that case, the Vinch case, when you were acting as a witness... that you *lied* in the courtroom?"

"Uh," said John. "I-I said what they asked me to say. I didn't want to be thrown in the sea!"

"How do you know who the original killer was?"

"I'd r-recognise her grip anywhere. That cold clutch... She wasn't t-tested in the courtroom. I think she was due to be after Finlay."

The judge squinted his eyes at John.

Which is why it was so important that they pointed the finger at Finlay...

Ettyson stood up. "Objection. How could he possibly know that the widow was after Finlay in the testing order? Such information would have invalidated the test."

"Witness?" said the judge.

"They told me the order in advance," said John, in a small tinny voice. "I don't know how they knew, but they knew."

Felix felt for his friend. "Nearly there, John," he said, in what he hoped was a reassuring way. "Returning to the second, uh, killing. That of Grent. What happened afterwards? After the stabbing itself, by the river?"

"He fell into the river, then she threw me in the river, too. I floated around for a bit, then landed on a bank somewhere." John had started to speak more quickly, a tiny note of panic entering his voice. "Someone found me, dried me up, tried to figure out how much I could sell for. Of course, once I started speaking, they thought that was a neat trick, so they kept me tied up hanging on a wall in a pub for a while, I think around a year. I had a lot of time to think, and truth be told, I was bored, you know? I wanted to see the world, but no one would consider carrying me around. They preferred me acting as a toy on the wall."

He took a deep breath, or gave as close an approximation as someone without breath can do, and continued in a slower voice. "You hear a lot in a country pub. One day, I overheard someone mentioning how a frog up in the north country had been given some rights by some ridiculous lawyer somewhere, and thought, perhaps I could get the same. If a frog can get representation, so could I. I asked them who the lawyer was, and what a lawyer was."

John sighed. "Eventually, I convinced one of the younger children with a promise of a few coppers to bring me to Lunchers & Co, which they did... and here I am. Uh, that was quite a long answer. Sorry."

Felix stopped chewing his lip. "John... Why didn't you tell us this before?"

The dagger would have looked sheepish if it could. "I... learned later, on the wall, people don't like the idea of being stabbed, and don't much like talking about it. So I... kept it to myself."

The judge leaned over, causing a stab of panic to jolt through Felix. "Mr Dagger…" he said. "Do you understand now why it was wrong, though? Wrong to kill?" A pause followed in which Felix could feel his heart thumping in his ears, or would have, had he had a real heart. Or real ears. Eventually John spoke.

"Yes, Your Honour. Having had time to consider, and having been gifted this new life of mine, I have come to realise that having it taken from you is… well, awful. I would hate to have my life taken from me, and I would hate for any of my friends to have their lives taken from them."

"Do you regret your part in this killing?" the judge asked. This time, John answered immediately.

"I do. I regret it terribly. I wish things could have been different."

"Carry on, Mr Sacramentum," said the judge, sitting back.

"I have no more questions," said Felix, willing his voice to stay calm, and failing.

20 - Closing Statements

Helda brought John back to the defendant's desk without speaking. The judge watched them go, then turned his attention to Felix.

"Any sign of your witness, Mr Sacramentum?" he asked, knowing full well that no one had entered or left the room.

"No, Your Honour."

Was that it, then?

Judge Burritt shook his head sadly. "I don't know how you do it in the capital, my lad, but here in the West Country we take these things seriously. If your witness has decided not to attend, I'm not going to wait any longer. There are cases lined up to be heard tomorrow, you see. Besides, you've had plenty of notice. So, unless they walk in that door in the next ten seconds, we will have to move on."

Felix's eye twitched. "Yes, Your Honour."

Felix. The voice entered his mind without ever passing through the air. He turned to look at Racelsus.

What?

She isn't coming.

A few weeks earlier, Felix had written to the College of Spelc on Mrs Luncher's suggestion. Once he had done so, he hadn't thought much more about it. Mrs Luncher had been rather quiet and mysterious about it, but that was nothing new. The reply that arrived not two days later had been as surprising as it had been promising.

Dear Mr Sacramentum,

Thank you for your letter. The curator read it and sent it my way.

I'd be delighted to attend as an expert witness in your case, pro bono of course. That is how you lawyers say it, yes?

The case sounds fascinating, as does John, who I am looking forward to meeting. I'll see you in the courtroom.

Yours,

Melana Furne'

Melana Furne was a mind reader. A literal mind reader. One of the only few that had publicly declared the fact. She'd had success in a few cases in years gone by, and Felix had no idea that she would be the one to reply to his enquiry at the college. When he'd told Mrs Luncher, she just smiled.

"Owes me a favour," she said, and left it at that.

The plan had been to use her famed skills to read John's mind. Her prowess was that she was able, as had been proved, to read the mind of one person or creature, then pass the thoughts and feelings onto another. It would have been a perfect way to impress upon the judge the depth of John's psyche.

Felix? Racelsus's voice brought him back to reality, and he sighed.

No, I think you're right. She's not coming.

But why? He'd included the date and time, the directions, checked and double-checked.

The judge leaned forward. "Time's up, I'm afraid." He settled back into the chair, which creaked in protest "Am I right in thinking there are no more witnesses from either party?"

Felix chewed his lip.

"I am not in the habit of repeating myself," said the judge with a dangerous edge to his voice.

"Yes, Your Honour, you are correct," said Felix. "No more witnesses." Ettyson nodded and bowed.

"In that case, would you both please offer your final closing statements, after which I shall retire to my chambers to consider the case. Ms Ettyson, if you would."

Ettyson stood up and took a few moments to gather herself, then brushed an imaginary speck of dust from her sleeve and began.

~

"Life is biological in nature. That much is obvious. Whether human or animal, plant or fungus, there are a list of commonalities. The consumption of energy from fuel, be that food, water or light. The expulsion of waste. The means of growth and reproduction. The ability to repair damage sustained, whether physical or emotional. The natural decline with age. Any of which would, if missing, mean an end to life as we know it for one reason or another.

"The defendant in this case can do none of these things. It cannot eat, reproduce, consume, grow or repair. It has no chemicals, and therefore cannot feel emotion. It cannot love, and without love, what is life? It is not even undead, for in order to be considered as such, one must have had a life to begin with.

"It was forged by an everyday blacksmith to be an everyday dagger, and then a spell was cast upon it by a wizard, who, by his own admission, has declared that the dagger is not alive. His magic simply creates the illusion that it is by emulating speech and surface-level mannerisms.

"This murder weapon is simply a reminder of a terrible crime that has hung over my client like a raincloud. As if this wasn't enough, we now have to listen to this farcical bumf of a narrative, suggesting my client was in some way involved in the initial murder!" She tossed her hand dismissively. "This whole sorry saga should be concluded with the destruction of the dagger, and the entire rotten business can be forgotten about."

She moved back to her seat and lowered herself into it. The judge nodded as he made a few scribbles, then looked up to Felix.

"In your own time."

Felix stood.

~

"Life is not as simple as the prosecutor would have you believe," said Felix. "Take it from me." He had hoped that at this comment the judge might crack a smile or even stifle a chuckle, but this judge was made of sterner stuff. Felix continued.

"Emotions are not chemicals. Love does not define a life. These are sweeping, unprovable opinions made by a philosopher that left this room unsure of her own convictions.

"John started life as a mundane dagger, unable to express himself or understand his feelings. You know what? So did I. Who I am now is not who I was.

"The spell created by Thweylin and performed by Sal Yul Sel was created with one purpose: to create life. So significant was this, that the spell's creator declared that it should only be used in the direst of circumstances. Why? Because it *creates life*, and that is not something to be entered into lightly.

"What better evidence of this can there be than the compelling demonstration of Professor Melana Fur-" Felix coughed. "Ahem, ignore that. Excuse me." The judge raised an eyebrow, but Felix ignored him.

"We have heard opinion after opinion from a string of witnesses. They each held a belief about whether a dagger could be alive. But each of them shared a few words with John, and, just by looking at their faces, it is plain to see that their opinions were not the same once they had done so.

"Why? Because John is alive. He is a bright blazing soul occupying a small, metal frame. He is not a trick. Not an illusion. He is an opinionated, emotional, interesting, magnetic, genuine *person*. If the court does not agree, then it will be robbing not just John of his life, but the world of a wonderful soul. Thank you."

Felix sat down again at his desk, looking down so as not to meet eyes with anyone. The judge made a single note, then stood.

"Thank you both. You shall be called for." He tapped the table with his gavel and stood up, then left the room with no further ceremony. Felix lowered his head into his hands.

"Is that good?" asked John.

21 - Verdict

Felix waited. His team would strike up conversations with him, but he found it hard to reciprocate, and so they would talk among themselves in hushed tones.

It'll be fine. The arguments were sound. The witnesses were good. Mostly. Well, they were fine. It'll be fine. What's taking him so long? If only Furne had turned up.

It wasn't only Furne that had been a no show. There had been a man he knew from a previous case that Felix had represented. A magician. Not the kind that can perform *actual* magic; rather, a slight-of-hand specialist. Felix hadn't been lying when he said that he'd smuggle John to freedom if he had to.

A new voice brought him from his introspection. "Guessing a judge's mind is like guessing what happens after you die; impossible to know for sure, but you'll worry about it forever regardless."

Felix looked up to see Prosecutor Ettyson standing a few paces from him. She was holding her hands tougher in front of her, as if awaiting inspection at a military parade. *How does she stand so still and move so quietly? Was she trained as an assassin? It would explain a few things.*

"Was that a joke?" he said.

She shrugged. "No, not really. Just a saying. You looked like you might benefit from it."

Felix frowned. "You're not normally this friendly. Who are you and where is the real Prosecutor Ettyson?" She smiled - actually smiled - at him. It was a surprising warm smile.

"It's good to see you back," she said. "Look lively."

Before Felix could reply, she swivelled and returned to her desk. It was then that Felix realised the judge was making his way back towards his own desk, walking solemnly down the centre of the seats.

Oh gods.

What was it with these life-or-death cases that always involved his friends? Why not a harmless prank-gone-wrong or fraud cause? Or a simple divorce?

Oh Habeus, please send me a simple, straightforward divorce case…

They weren't pleasant as such, but at least people rarely got executed.

Judge Burritt cleared his throat, silencing any remaining babble from the meagre audience. "It seems to me," he said. "That there has been much to consider. This individual… John…" The judge looked at him, apparently still deep in thought. "I have heard much from him and those who know him. I have heard regret, and I have heard deceit. I have heard logic, and irrationality. In short, I have heard that which any living, sentient creature experiences."

The judge glanced down at his notes. "In addition to that, I find that the arguments from the prosecution are not correct. I do not believe, on the weight of expert opinion, that John Dagger is merely an 'impression' of life. He is the real thing. Hearing him speak, and hearing his reasoning and internal struggles with his own emotional landscape convinces me. His capacity to suffer, likewise. Who am I to say that John Dagger does not possess life, when I can conjure no reason sturdy enough to argue that point? I cannot declare a green sprout is dead, or that a rock is alive, for these are simply untrue facts. And I cannot say that John Dagger does not live, for I would be incorrect."

With a severe expression that any statue would be proud of, he lifted his gavel. "To conclude: I declare that John Dagger is to be considered a living being for all intents and purposes, and has been since the day that his sentience was bestowed upon him."

Felix felt relief wash through him. Turning, he caught Helda's eye, and she returned a toothy smile. Yetty was frowning forward, eyes fixed on the judge. Why wasn't she smiling?

Wait. What was that last part… Since the day..?

A cold sensation started to fill him from the pit of his middle. The judge had not sat down, nor had he lowered his gavel.

He's not finished.

The judge took a breath. "This means, however, that I must regrettably bring attention to the murder of Grent Vinch, and the perjury committed in that case. I do not find any legal reason as to why John Dagger would be exempt from a charge of murder and perjury, being, in his own words, of sound mind and complete faculty at the time of the killing. The perjury can, to some extent, be mitigated, if it was indeed coerced. The rest, however…"

The judge scowled. "John had the means and foresight to prevent this senseless death, and chose to exercise neither. Then, equipped with unique knowledge of both this circumstance and of vital information in the killing of the elder Vinch, John did not do his duty and make this information publicly known. Would he have acted differently, in the way that a reasonable person would, both a death and a wrongful life imprisonment would have been prevented."

He paused, glaring at John. "The prosecution is seeking the destruction of the dagger to excise a reminder of a terrible, personal tragedy. This request would only be lawful if John Dagger was merely a piece of property. I cannot grant this; John Dagger is not property. However, taking into consideration the weight of new evidence brought forth regarding the second unlawful killing… I must sentence John Dagger according to his crime and his status."

What..?

"As an accessory to the murder of Grent Vinch, I hereby sentence John Dagger to death."

No!

"The method of the death must be adjusted, for hanging clearly will not be appropriate. I hereby suggest death by melting. Until that time, John Dagger: you are to be held under arrest."

The gavel finally fell, and that wooden thump sounded like the lid of a coffin closing.

~

"Your Honour!" said Felix, jumping to his feet.

The judge paused, mid standing. He eyed Felix.

"Mr Sacramentum, I have delivered my judgement."

"Yes, sir, I understand, Your Honour. But-"

"-But?" The judge stood, his brow lowering, casting his eyes into deep shadow. "That is a dangerous word in this context. The next thing you say had better be exceptional."

"Your Honour," said Felix. "Back when I was a Journeyman-Legalite, I was taught to respect the knowledge, will and authority of the judges, and I believe I have done so, and will continue to do so, until my dying, er, until my time has come."

"Indeed?"

"I think it would be remiss of me not to raise an objection when I feel that a legal opinion is-"

Don't use the word 'wrong.'

"...is..."

Think of another word!

"...wrong."

Argh!

The judge did not react immediately. "Wrong?" he said. "You think my judgement... wrong?"

Felix remembered a conversation with Mrs Luncher, in which she grilled him upon their first meeting. It was honesty that won the day, then. Honesty and conviction. He stood up straight and looked the judge straight in the eye.

"Yes, Your Honour. I think that it is wrong to convict a person without giving them a fair trial."

"But, sir," said the judge, an icy formality in his voice. "You seem to forget we have just had such a trial."

"A trial to determine whether John Dagger could be considered living, yes. Not one as to whether he is guilty of murder. For that, he should be able to mount a defence, should he not?" The look the judge was giving Felix deflated his sudden burst of ego. "Er, Your Honour?"

The judge looked at Felix for a few moments more, then at John. He stroked his moustache.

"Well, well, well," he said, and the smallest smile tugged at the corner of his mouth. His eyes widened, eyebrows raised, and the smile turned into a frown.

"What does-" said Helda in a stage whisper, before Yetty kicked her leg in an attempt to shut her up.

The judge's face reset to its normal placid state. "Mr Sacramentum has raised a good point," he said. "And I have learned a lesson today in propriety." He looked at the large clock set on the wall. "In that case... John Dagger, you have been accused of the most grievous crime of murder. The murder of Grent Vinch. How do you plead?"

"Er," said John.

"Guilty or Not Guilty, please."

"Not, I mean, Not Guilty, please? Thank you."

"It must go to trial, Your Honour," said Ettyson, standing up. "For the good of the realm, the death penalty should be considered."

"Not necessarily," said Felix, standing up as well. "I think-"

"Hold it, both of you," said the Judge, looking at the two of them, his meaty finger raised. They both silenced themselves immediately.

A long moment passed.

"I must think on this," he said, standing. "Should John Dagger be put on trial for murder? A serious question. I will go to my chamber and consider. I will hear your arguments upon my return. One hour."

With that he tapped his gavel on the plate and walked from the room. Felix watched him go, then looked at his team. "We'd better get started."

"What is going on?" said John.

~

In the defendant's chamber, Felix stood looking out of the window. It was just himself, Yetty and John. Furbo and Helda had remained in the courtroom with Racelsus, to, as the witch had put it, 'not get in the way'.

Yetty looked at Felix. He seemed... thin. Not in the sense that he hadn't eaten enough, but more in the way that the light shone through him a little, like through paper on a sunny day. She wasn't used to seeing him look stressed, but... he looked terrible. His hair, normally neatly swept back, had started to loosen and dangle in front of his eyes. Those eyes... dark. Darker than she had remembered, before...

She took a deep breath, and he turned to look at her. She willed herself to meet that gaze. "Interesting situation," said Yetty. "Any ideas yet?"

Felix grunted, and turned back to the window. "Not yet." Less than an hour to think of a reason why his client, John Dagger, despite having stabbed someone to death, should nevertheless not be tried for murder. If he were deemed justiciable, then he'd be as good as condemned.

"…I've had a thought," Yetty continued after a pause.

"Oh?" The last time she had had a thought, Felix had almost sacrificed himself to an eternity of torture. *Had that been real? It had certainly felt real. It was all so fuzzy, that terrible, fateful day. Fateful day? Really? Careful, I'm starting to sound like a melodramatic poet.*

"Doubtless that stuck-up Ettyson character is taking heaps of detailed notes now, concocting a thousand reasons why John should be melted into scrap. Probably in that tiny, perfect handwriting of hers."

"Mm."

"So, why don't you… you know, with your ghostly powers…"

"Mm?"

"Why don't you float over to her chambers and read her arguments? You could find out what she was going to say, and think of the perfect counter-arguments. It's foolproof!"

"Float… Over?"

She took a step towards him. "Exactly! Through the walls, or ceilings, or whichever. No one would know. How could they? Those rotten prosecutors cheat all the time, anyway, I'm sure of it."

She clenched her fist. "We both know John is innocent, that's obvious. It's that judge… If Ettyson mutters her poison into his ear in the wrong way, and we're not prepared… So we're doing the right thing. We're just making doubly sure that John is not executed in a terrible miscarriage of justice!"

Felix paused, apparently deep in thought. His brow was furrowed, and he tilted his head. Yetty waited for his reply. Eventually, he shook his head, his lank hair whipping side to side.

"No, that's not right at all."

She scowled, not disguising her distaste. "Listen to yourself! You could learn everything. All her plans, her questions, the evidence she's keeping to herself… Not just today either. In all your future cases with other prosecutors. You'd *never* lose." The look she was giving Felix was intense, bordering on feverish excitement.

Felix turned from the window and fixed her with his gaze. The light played around his edges, causing him to shimmer in the slightest way. "I don't think you're seeing it how I'm seeing it." He tapped a finger on the tip of his nose and nodded. "Yes, you have it wrong."

She looked as if she wanted to reply, but didn't know what to say. The sun was setting behind him, and in his semi-translucent state, it was filling Felix with a golden glow. He looked like some spirit from the stories. He looked a little like… *her*. Yetty's mouth opened and closed twice. Felix continued.

"It's not about winning or losing. It doesn't even really matter what you or I think about the client, or what we believe. If I sneak into the prosecution chambers and eavesdrop on everything they're saying, I will be able to pre-determine answers to all of their questions. This is true. They will have no surprises. They won't be able to blindside me. Perhaps you're right, and they wouldn't stand a chance. But is that fair?"

He looked at her again, his golden eyes piercing her. Her frown wilted. "The prosecution is expected to try their damnedest to get the defendant convicted, *within the rules of the court*. The defence will do the same, *within the rules of the court*. We can argue, cajole, accuse, grandstand, wheedle and infuriate… But it's all done with the pure intention of answering a question: Is this person guilty? We, as lawyers, represent both sides of that question, and we have been appointed to hash it out in a public court of law and find the answer to it. Once we've both had our say and argued as best we can, the judge considers our points, our suggestions, our qualifiers, and sifts it through the mantle of experience and authority. When their verdict is announced, the stuff that bubbles to the surface is what we call justice. It doesn't matter what the man in the pub says to you, or what the lady cutting your hair *reckons* is right. Until it's there in a courtroom, with two highly educated and motivated people *going at it like rutting stags*, justice has not been served. The question is unanswered. But, once that decision has been settled upon by one of the most learned scholars in the land, then, legally, *that is the thing that happened.*"

He leaned on the wall and gazed out the window. His eyes settled on the statue outside the front of the courtroom. "Those rules of the court I keep going on about haven't been decided by me. Not even by the judge hearing our arguments today. They're the result of our collective civilisation's experiences, opinions, gut-feelings, moral obligations and more. Every wrongdoing, every intentional misdeed, every act of negligence that someone has been wronged by has been fought over and thus categorised in courtrooms just like that one. Each one of *those* lawyers stayed within the law themselves, for if they didn't, how could we say justice had been done?"

A cloud moved over the sunset, and his colouration shifted from golden hues to murky grey. His face darkened. "If any of those lawyers had decided to take the law into their own hands, to ignore the rules, to spit in the face of all those who came before them… If they were ever found out, the punishments levelled on them were severe. Barbaric, almost. But what else could we do? The very people at the beating heart of our law-making were themselves law-breaking… if they were bending the rules to make the rules… well, they deserved everything they got."

Felix's voice softened as he sighed, and the cloud passed. "That isn't to say that things never changed, that new rules weren't written, or old ones abandoned. But it was always done with consensus. Someone would put their argument forward, saying: 'I don't think it's fair if we, as a collective jurisprudence, continue doing 'x', 'y' or 'z', and here's the reason', and a representation of the profession would debate it with her. Either they agreed or they didn't. And if they did, the law changed, and the law, and thus society, became fairer."

Unfolding his arms, Felix looked back at Yetty. "How can I, knowing all that, having been through everything I've been through, decide that Felix Knows Best? That it's okay if *I* break the rules, because my intentions are pure? According to me, of course. History will either forget us or deem us as manipulative scoundrels. And, the worst part is this: If I cheated, and I won, I would always have this thorn in my heart, this thorn of guilt. Someone, somewhere was wronged once, and sought out a lawyer's help, and then wronged twice, because I did not let them have a fair trial."

Neither of them spoke for a long minute after that. Yetty's temper had melted, and she fidgeted with her cuff. She rolled her eyes, took a deep breath, then let it out slowly. "Well, when you put it that way…"

He cracked a grin at her, and she couldn't help smiling back. His colour had returned to normal, his whole being seeming more solid again. Whereas before he had seemed unsettled and worried, now he struck her as confident and in control. Even his hair seemed to have returned to its normal state of tidiness. "I *do* put it that way," he said. He glanced at the clock on the wall and slapped his hands together. "Now, let's win, and let's win fair and square." He gestured to the exit, and she headed towards the door, her mind racing with inspiration.

"Oh, and Yetty?" came Felix's mellifluous voice. She turned, and beheld an expression on his face that froze her blood. The room darkened, and all she could see was that terrible ghostly face, those terrible hollow eyes, that chthonic light bleeding from him, bathing her in dreadful menace.

"I don't want to ever have to explain that again to you," he said.

Her throat felt dry and she nodded, desperate for this feeling to pass. "O-of course," she said.

The expression left his face and he smiled again, the room returning to normal. "Good. Shall we?" He walked past her and out of the room. She watched him leave, smoothed her hair with a shaky hand, then followed.

~

They returned to the courtroom and took their places. Within moments, the door to the judge's chamber opened, and the judge walked over to his seat, but did not sit down. He stared at them all with hard eyes set in a face full of purpose.

"I have considered the question of whether to try John Dagger for murder," he said, without preamble. "I find myself hovering, as it were, on the brink. I can think of reasons why, and an equal number of reasons why not." The eyes of every person in that room watched him, including the particularly dedicated village-folk who were still present.

"Therefore," said Judge Burritt, "I open this question to the floor. I would like to hear discussion from Mr Sacramentum and Ms Ettyson. I shall then make my decision."

"If I may," said Ettyson, rising. "I believe the most sensible course is to move to trial. We must treat the defend- that is, John Dagger, as a full, legal person, subject to all the laws of Fowermolde. Surely, it is as simple as that." The judge looked over to Felix, saying nothing.

"I would suggest," said Felix, standing to face Ettyson, "that it would be inappropriate to judge John on crimes he committed before he was a legal person. To him, at that time, the law did not apply."

"John could understand speech immediately," said Ettyson. "John could reason, discern, consider. It - he - was in a fit and ready state to follow the laws of the land in the best way he could based on his situation. That should have been simple. As an enchanted dagger, he is not likely to steal or embezzle, or trespass or commit fraud. The only realistic crime he could commit is murder or other harm, and that is all he needed to *not* do."

"How would he know what was right and wrong to do?" said Felix. "We cannot prove what he was taught when he was created."

"Actually, we can," said Ettyson, swivelling to search the seating area for Yan Vo Mouletter and Sal Yul Sel. "Wizard," she said, pointing. "What did you talk to John about when you first created him?"

"I," said the wizard, standing, looking flustered. "Well, this and that, you know."

"Did you teach him right and wrong?"

Sal Yul Sel hesitated.

"Answer immediately, please," said Ettyson.

"Uh, yes," said the wizard. "I explained how things - people - work."

Ettyson gestured to the wizard, eyebrows raised. "Mr Sacramentum?"

"It's not as…" said Felix, before stopping. Ettyson waited. Judge Burritt waited. Sal Yul Sel slowly lowered himself to his seat, slumping a little lower than he had before.

Felix held his hands together, his eyes closed.

Okay. It's okay. You're not justifying murder. It isn't murder. Not really. Not from… his perspective.

"There is a certain concept that I would like to explain," said Felix. "If my learned colleague will permit me."

Ettyson shrugged and sat down. "Of course," she said. "We are in no rush. Take your time." She produced a pencil and a small stack of notes written in a tiny script, then waited for him to start speaking.

Before, Felix might have found this intimidating, but he was used to Ettyson now. It wasn't the first time she had notepadded him.

"The concept, then" began Felix. "It is what some call 'ness'. For example, if I were to hold up an apple, what about it would indicate its apple-ness? What defines how much of an apple this apple is?"

To demonstrate, he gestured to Helda, who rummaged in her pack and produced a slightly squashed and bruised apple. Felix held it aloft.

"This fruit has a distinct look and flavour. It even feels like an apple. Has a certain weight. It contains seeds and a stalk. What is its purpose? To grow, to be eaten, to spread its seeds, and to grow again. This seed," he said, pulling the apple apart and fishing out a shiny seed. "This seed will act according to its nature. Its apple-seed-ness. If I plant it in fertile ground, it will sprout, and eventually become a tree. To do anything else would be against its very essence."

A pause.

"We do not blame the seed if the tree pokes a hole in a fence. It does not exist on the same moral spectrum as us. To expect it to deny its own nature and live according to human law is simply unrealistic."

"But," said Ettyson. "Your whole argument for your earlier case, need I remind you, is that John should be treated as a living person. How could he be a living person and not be subject to our laws?"

Felix walked over to his desk and produced a blank blackboard and a piece of chalk. Holding it up, he began to speak.

"I think there are a few distinctions that I must demonstrate," said Felix. He drew four neat squares arranged in a two-by-two grid. Above the top-left square he wrote 'Alive'. Next to it, above the top right, he wrote 'Not alive.' To the left of the top-left square he wrote 'Human', and beneath it, to the left of the bottom-left square, he wrote 'Non-human'. Above the whole grid he wrote, in large letters: SENTIENT BEINGS.

Sentient Beings

	Alive	*Not alive*
Human		
Non-human		

"This grid can help illustrate what I am trying to say," he said, pointing. He took the chalk and wrote 'Furbo' in the square where 'alive' and 'human' intersected.

"I believe we can all agree that Furbo over there is an alive human," he said.

"Thank you, I think," said Furbo, itching his head.

"Neither of these characteristics are in question. By virtue of being an alive human being, Furbo, along with everyone else in this grid, is expected to behave according to the laws of the land."

Felix moved his chalk to the square intersecting 'human' and 'non-alive'. In this, he wrote: 'Felix.'

"I am not alive," he said matter-of-factly, ignoring the twinge he felt at speaking it out loud. "But I am human. And," he tapped the top of the grid. "I am sentient. Therefore, I am expected to follow the laws laid down by humans."

He wrote the word 'brick' in the box that intersected 'non-alive' and 'non-human'. "I don't think anyone would argue that a non-alive non-human would not be subject to human laws. I perhaps have cheated here, writing brick. It's because I can't think of anything that is sentient, non-human and not-alive."

"A zombie?" offered Ettyson.

"Technically human," said Felix.

"A zombified cow?"

Felix thought about this, rubbed out 'brick', and wrote 'undead cow'.

"Would an undead cow be expected to follow societal laws?"

Ettyson considered in turn. "No," she admitted. Felix nodded, then moved on.

He lowered the chalk and stared at the one remaining empty box. He tapped it. "This is where John sits. The grey area. Should we expect him to ignore his nature and follow our laws? Despite not being a human, and not sharing many of the characteristics that form the human essence? The human-ness?"

He paused. "Though he is not alone in this area."

Felix wrote the word 'wolf' in this square. "A wolf is a sentient non-human. It kills as that is its nature. We cannot try it for murder."

He wrote 'Jurrekker', and suppressed a shudder. "This is the name of a demon I know. A demon is an alive, sentient non-human. It lives according to its own rules. It cannot be tried for murder. It can, however, be tried by higher courts for other crimes, but that is a discussion for another day."

He thought about Cherinda. What was she up to? Why hadn't she contacted him since he… returned? And Habeus?

Had he imagined everything?

The nagging pain in his chest flared briefly, and he felt his corporeal form wilting, yearning to be released so he might return to the Other place to rest.

Ignoring that, instead focussing on the blackboard, Felix wrote the word 'John'. "So what happens to John? He is a sentient, alive, non-human, being tried for crimes that humans have defined. An action by a human, against a human, that contravenes human rules. How can John be tried for that?"

"But," said Ettyson. "If we can ignore that crime… That means John can go about killing as many people as he likes, with impunity?"

"John," said Felix, turning to the dagger. "How many people would you like to kill?"

"None," said John.

"But you did," said Ettyson.

"Did you, John? Kill someone? Or, were you *used* to kill someone? And, then, acting according to your nature, did you fulfil your purpose as a weapon? Did you act on instinct?"

"But," said Ettyson. "By his own admission he did not prevent the death!"

"I would suggest, by what we know of the nature of the accused, this murder would have happened by hook or by crook, whether with John or without him. It just so happened that in this instance, John happened to be nearby, and the lady took advantage of his juvenile emotional state."

Felix took a deep breath and let it out slowly, not that anything actually came out.

"Swap John for a child. A young child, born to a single parent, raised outside of civilisation. Imagine this child had been taught to hunt and kill to survive, and never been taught otherwise. Is it fair to expect him to follow all of our laws and rules immediately?"

Ettyson, unusually, had no response.

"Ms Ettyson?" prompted the judge. Ettyson shook her head and lowered her pencil.

"I have no more arguments," she said suddenly. She looked, for the first time in Felix's memory…

Tired.

Judge Burritt rose.

~

The judge sighed. "I must admit, this day has turned out to be an unusual one." He tapped his fingernails on the tabletop in front of him. No one spoke for several moments. The judge then turned to look behind him, at the stained-glass portrait of Habeus, God of Judgement.

"Mr Sacramentum. Your arguments are sound, and I agree with them. I do not think John Dagger should be tried for murder."

Thank goodness.

That ever-eager sense of relief flared up again, until the judge continued speaking.

"However, I must also take a stand here. If… animated objects are to be considered alive, then I must take action for the sake of the future, and be mindful of setting precedents. Ultimately, a man is dead, and John is, in some small way, partly responsible. So, my quandary is this. Where does John and his kind sit on the legal spectrum? How should he, and therefore others of his kind, be treated?"

"Your Honour, at this stage, John is not human, and therefore not subject to human laws," said Felix.

"Goblins are non-human," said Ettyson. "Yet you yourself represented one at court. Burrimo. He was tried according to human laws."

"Yes," said Felix. "Goblins agreed to become subject to human laws when they joined the commonwealth, as said in case GreMal versus HRH. Since then, they have been treated in the same way as humans, legally speaking, that is."

"But," said the judge. "Something must be done. The courts of the land have the power to govern both humans and non-humans, as Mr Sacramentum has said. It has happened before. In each case, such agreements were reached after discussions with an appropriate representative of the species, race or being."

"Yet, in this case, no such representative exists," said Ettyson.

"Not yet," said Felix. "John?"

"Felix?"

Felix waved at Wulte Gribb, the bureaucratic witness from earlier, who was sitting at the back of the courtroom, watching the case with intense scrutiny. "Mr Gribb," he called. The clerk blinked and coughed.

"Uh, yes?"

"What is the lowest form of rank that can be accepted as a diplomatic representative when dealing with foreign nations?"

"Uh, well, one moment... that would be 'Crown Prince's Third Royal Consort,' I believe."

"Uh, what about a non-royal rank?"

"Anyone considered to be in the employ of the government can represent it as a diplomat, in theory."

"John," said Felix. "As of this moment, you are the sole existing member of the Animate Objects race, hereby declared as living by this very courtroom. You must therefore require some form of government."

"Uh, I do..?" said John.

"So, in this new Animate Objects government, which you have just formed, what is your rank and seniority?"

"Uhm," said John. "Chief Dagger, and, uh, Lord Seniority."

"Congratulations on your promotion, My Lord," said Felix, bowing low. "Now, I am but a mere member of a foreign nation, but might I recommend reaching out to the government of Placenamia and asking for entry to the commonwealth of nations?"

"Uh, well, yes, okay. How do I do that?"

"You just ask Wulte over there," said Felix, gesturing at the confused bureaucrat, who looked like he quite wished he'd made his excuses earlier.

"Oh, right," said John. Then, more loudly: "Uh, Wulte, as the Chief Dagger of the, uh, Animate Objects, uh, kingdom, can we please enter your commonwealth?"

Wulte had gone pale. "I can't... that is, I don't have the..."

Felix chipped in. "Forgive me. You said 'any member of the government.' That includes you, yes?"

"But what if, I mean, they find out, and I'll-"

"Wulte!" said Felix, his voice intense. "This is your chance to go down in history! Don't worry about what the higher-ups will say. Seize this moment! All your years as a public servant have led to this moment. A delegation of the highest ranking members of a foreign state is asking you, Wulte Gribb, if you would do them the honour of welcoming their fledgling nation into the commonwealth. What is your answer?"

Wulte's face looked more horrified than before.

Come on...

Wulte looked at Felix. Felix looked at Wulte. Something changed in his face. His eyes hardened. His demeanour strengthened.

"John Dagger, Chief Dagger of the Animate Objects nation," said Wulte, all tremor in his voice vanished. "As a member of His Royal Majesty's government, I welcome you and your kind, well, people into the Fowermolde Commonwealth of Nations." He puffed up his chest and strode over to John Dagger, hand outstretched. When he realised there was no hand to shake, he instead patted John on the hilt.

"So it's done?" said Felix. "That's enough?"

"Well," said Wulte, his old self creeping back. "It's highly unusual, but, I suppose, on balance... yes, it's enough."

Felix grinned at John. "Welcome, John, to the commonwealth, and all the laws and protections contained therein." He turned to the judge, who suppressed a smirk. Abruptly, it vanished and the normal sombre look returned.

"John Dagger," said the judge in a booming voice. "As befitting your status as a member of the commonwealth, I must charge you according to our laws. But based on your particular and unique cultural background, I shall adjust the ruling. You are hereby found *not* guilty of murder, but I must find you guilty as - quite literally - an accessory to murder. Therefore your punishment is adjusted as befits your cultural and biological status. I sentence you to five years community service, stationed in the charitable food stations in the poorest quarter of the city. You may not intentionally harm any member of the commonwealth during that time, nor, if you can do so in any way, allow any to come to harm. In addition, you must perform all acts requested by your appropriate legal sponsor, to be determined at a later date. Oh, and I shall require you to perform one official function for me, which shall be explained later."

With a final glance around the room, and a tiny smile pulling at the corner of his mouth, he struck his gavel on the plate.

"Dismissed."

Felix closed his eyes and let out the non-breath he was holding.

"However," said the judge, rising to his feet. He pointed at Felix. "See me in my counsel room, Mr Sacramentum, and bring John, if you would be so kind."

He strode smartly back down the central passageway. Felix grabbed John's stand and followed, almost but not quite slipping on a muddy puddle in his haste to keep up. He would have muttered a light curse, but was too nervous to remember.

~

What did I do?

Felix and John followed the judge down a series of dark corridors, passing nobody. At a door that looked indistinct from the others, Judge Burritt pushed it open and held it for Felix, who dutifully entered. The room itself was not so much a Judge's Chamber as a glorified junk shop.

Felix scanned his eyes around, trying to understand what this room was for.

One man's garbage is another man's... slightly different garbage?

There was no other way to describe it. The room was stuffed full of junk. There were a few tables ladened with clutter (one of which did have at least some official looking paperwork on it), some broken chairs piled in a heap by an empty fireplace, and a single set of drawers labelled *Burritt's - keep out on pain of imprisonment* on it.

Case notes? Precedent? Written opinions on the cases of the day? Is he going to whip out a code of conduct that I've broken and disbar me?

Judge Burritt, face like thunder, gestured to the desk with the papers on it, and Felix took one of the two identical chairs and lowered himself into it. He made to deposit John on the desk, but there was no space. Felix gently shifted a few things around - a mug and a sextant, of all things - until there was enough room, then plonked John down.

The judge himself had opened the bottom drawer of his cabinet and was rooting around for something. Felix would never dream of poking about in a judge's private documents, of course, but was nevertheless seized by the smallest tickle of curiosity. It was far outweighed by the sense of dread, however.

What would that do to me? Would I still appear like this, to help people? If I'm disbarred... Should I?

"Aha," said Judge Burritt, seizing something from the depths of the drawer. Felix couldn't bear to look, but couldn't look away. The judge slid the drawer shut with a creak, then walked over to Felix and sat down. He shifted a few things around on the desk in a much more haphazard way than Felix did, sweeping a small collection of detritus into a heap on the floor. When he was finished, he thunked down a metal tin.

A tin? What's in it? Something to banish a ghost? Manacles? Some sort of-

Burritt yanked the tin off with a grunt, and the smell of ginger wafted into the room. He tilted the tin at Felix with a smile.

"Biscuit?"

~

"It's a habit of mine," said the judge, brushing crumbs from his shirt. "Always have to have a little something after a big case like today's. Helps settle the mind. Especially when we have some more thinking to do straight after."

"I understand," said Felix, polishing off his own ginger biscuit. "More thinking, Your Honour?"

"Oh, none of that in here, lad. Just call me Burritt."

Argh!

"Of course, uh, Burritt." It felt wrong on around fifteen levels to call a judge by his last name like this, with no honorific or title. Well, wrong to his face. "You said something about more thinking?"

Burritt had taken another biscuit. "Aye." Before taking a bite, he waved the biscuit at John. "We have a few things to talk about."

John, who had been uncharacteristically quiet up until now, squeaked. "Yes, sir," he said. "Just please don't melt me down."

"Nonsense, lad, you're a citizen of the kingdom now. I couldn't melt you down, even if I wanted to. Not legally, anyway. I should know, it was me what made that decision!" He chuckled. No one joined him. He considered his two companions and cleared his throat.

"Yes, well," he said, finally taking a bite. "The Vinch family."

Ah yes. Them.

"If what you say is true, lad - and I don't doubt it - then this group of miscreants are out there, unpunished." Burritt reached down the floor and picked up a notepad and a pencil. He flipped a couple of pages until he found a blank one, then he looked at John with a fire in his eyes.

"This is what I want you to do for me."

~

It only took two days to find and apprehend Lady Vinch once the order went out. She was in her summer retreat. When the peacekeepers found her, she was making preparations to leave the continent and travel to places unknown. She had tried to resist, ordering her various servants to defend her honour and liberty against these tyrants, but a few stern looks and loosened coshes quelled any rebellion before it started.

The widow was taken to the Great Ogtown courtroom to be tried in front of Judge Burritt, who listened to her rail against the government, the judiciary, the courtroom, Ogtown, Judge Burritt himself, before trying to throw each and every member of her remaining family under the wagon. The judge let her wear herself out, then informed her they would test her using what he called 'The John Method'. Lady Vinch paled at the smile he gave her. Her lawyer tried to object, but Judge Burritt shook his head.

"It was good enough for you then, Ms Cletzi, it's good enough for you now."

At this point, John was brought in by an attendant, and Burritt declared that there would be a lineup of everyone present in the courtroom. Each person would grip the handle of John Dagger through a gap in a curtain, and John would announce when he recognised the hand that held him as he killed Mr Vinch, all those years ago.

Lady Vinch was, of course, recognised instantly. That was enough for Judge Burritt, who charged her with two counts of murder, and a whole ream of Justice Obstruction for good measure. The fortunes of the Vinch estate were seized and distributed, and John Dagger was thanked for his service to the kingdom, and sent home.

22 - Punishments

"You don't think it looks a bit... flouncy?"

"No John, it looks very nice," said Yetty. Mr Luncher nodded his agreement.

"Nice?" said John. "I don't want a scabbard to look 'nice'."

"Why not?"

"I don't know, it just doesn't seem my style..."

"Look," said Yetty in a tone more typically used with fussy children. "We all went through a lot of trouble finding someone who would make one to your specifications. Most of the smiths and tanners laughed at us when we asked for a scabbard with a solid cork interior, so the least you can do is be grateful."

"I am! I am, Yetty, very! It's just... did he really have to carve that flowery bit on the side?"

A knock at the door. "That'll be the postman," said Mr Luncher, waving at the man he could see through the window. "Wonder what old Burt has for us this late in the evening..."

Stooping to pick up the stack of papers, one caught his eye. A very serious looking note on luxuriously thick, expensive paper.

"Any of you lot expecting a High Court Declarative Order?" he asked in the same tone as if he had said 'which of you was having the strawberry tart?' He turned to the table in the centre of the room, where Helda, Yetty and Felix were sat, with John resting point-down on a board, next to a flouncy-looking scabbard. Racelsus was resting in her cage, positioned on a shelf by the door.

A frown, then sudden recollection on Felix's face. "Yes," he said. "John is. About where he has to perform his 'charitable deeds.' I wondered when that was going to arrive." He took the letter, then rubbed it between thumb and forefinger. "Whoa, nice paper."

"Isn't it?" replied Mr Luncher. "Makes you wonder, perhaps we should-"

John made an odd noise, like someone without a throat trying to clear it. "Oh," said Felix, "sorry John." He unfolded the paper and began to read aloud.

"To His Excellency, Lord Chief Dagger, John Dagger."

"Excellency?" said Helda, stifling a giggle.

"Hush," said John.

"At once, *Your Majesty…*"

Felix ignored her and carried on.

"In furtherance to the ruling passed down in the case blah blah on the date yes yes yes, very impressive…

"…you are henceforth as of receipt of this letter commanded to spend every complete second day until five years hence performing duties with the charitable organisation known as Fellow's Free Meals, located at 15 Dock Road, Oaken District, Placenamia, Placenamia. Your sponsor will be keeping in weekly contact with the appropriate authorities, and is duty-bound to report any reluctance or refusal on your part. The court will not treat favourably any reticence by yourself, considering the lenience you have been shown with your sentence.

"Your sponsor's name is-"

"Oh, now that's interesting," said Felix, holding a hand to his chin. "I almost can't believe that. How very interesting."

"What's interesting?" said John, a nervous edge to his voice. "What is it? Oh, don't leave me in suspense. Who's my sponsor?"

Felix put the paper down and pointed at Mr Luncher. "It's him."

Mr Luncher had lit a pipe and was letting the smoke curl from it. He shrugged. "You volunteer at Fellow's Free Meals?" Helda said, incredulous. "That place that just *gives* people meals, no questions asked?"

"I don't volunteer there; I own it," said Mr Luncher, matter-of-factly. "Just a little side project." He puffed on his pipe.

"Well, it sounds as if you've gotten off easy, John," said Yetty. "Imagine getting a friend of yours as your legal sponsor. Talk about good luck."

"Oh, I wouldn't think of it like that," said Mr Luncher, his smile broadening a little and his eyes widening a little more. "I happen to hold the opinion of the courts in *very* high regard, Yetty, and *rest assured*, John, that I shall be making *great* use of your assistance."

"Uh, that's, well, thanks," said John. "I look forward to it."

"In the meantime," came the voice of Mrs Luncher as she entered the main room from her office upstairs. "You are welcome to stay here as long as you need to, unless you would prefer to make other arrangements?"

"Well, my, er, fathers have asked if I want to spend time with them."

"And do you?"

"Yes, I think so… but I don't know them very well. I hope that I might be able to, er, come back here if it all turns out to be, well…"

"Not a problem. You are hereby welcome here indefinitely." Mrs Luncher turned to the kitchen, then stopped and shot him a glare. "*Absolutely* no stabbing anyone, or I'll grind you into a toothpick. Understood?"

"Yes, ma'am!"

She nodded, then disappeared to make a cup of tea. If John had had breath, he would have let it out. Mr Luncher swept his coat on in one smooth gesture and sighed. "Well, the night is drawing in. We'd best be off."

"We?" said the dagger.

"Yes, John. I happen to be heading to dock street this evening, so your service starts tonight. What an asset you shall be. May I?" With that, he strapped on the new leather scabbard that John had been so concerned with, and deftly lifted John and sheathed him.

"Don't worry lad, I'll go easy on you for a few days. After that, you'll soon get used to the high pressure, rough-and-tumble world of catering. Oh, I hope you like the feel of turnips…"

"Oh gods," said John. "Have I not suffered enough…"

"Ah! That reminds me," said Furbo, hopping to his feet. "Why don't I walk with you? I can give you the lesson I promised you on the religions of the country."

John groaned. Furbo either didn't hear, or didn't care, and pulled on his coat.

"Now," he said, as Mr Luncher and he headed towards the door. "Where to start? In the beginning, the gods created everything. This is widely accepted in most major faiths… But, did you know there are some documents that suggest another god created the gods?"

"Oh, that's hogwash," said Mr Luncher, opening the door.

"Humour me, sir," said Furbo. "Consider the following… where did the gods come from?"

"But if you're right, where did *this* god come from?"

"Why, another, greater god, of course…"

"Argh!" said John.

Their voices faded away as they left the building and headed off.

The involuntary smile faded from Felix's face as he felt the pulling. The familiar tugging on his soul. He had stayed in this world for too long, and his spirit yearned for the endless grey plains of… well, wherever it was.

"Are you alright, Felix?" said Racelsus. "You don't look well."

"I'm okay," he said. "I just…"

"I know what you need," Helda said, slamming her palm on the table. She raised a clenched fist high in the air.

"To the pub!" she said.

Felix was feeling tired, and could sense the longing pull of the grey fields. Despite wanting to spend time with his friends, that exhaustion had its hooks in him, and he felt he couldn't shake them off. The urge to return to that place, to lie in the grass, tugged at him with every motion he made.

Still, he thought. *I'm sure I can ignore it for the length of a pint or two.*

"To the pub," he said, hiding his discomfort in a grin.

"To the pub!" agreed, well, everyone else. It was customary to visit one of the local establishments when a case concluded, to celebrate a victory, to commiserate a defeat. In those pyrrhic or bittersweet cases where the outcome was neither wholly positive nor wholly negative, the pub was as good a place as any to consider the possibilities of what could have been, what might have occurred, and just how many empty pint glasses you can stack on top of Racelsus's bird cage before she noticed.

"Just so long as we don't go back to that place we went to last time," said Helda. "Do you remember that barman?"

Yetty waggled her fingers. "The blue one with too many arms? He wasn't all bad. At least, I think it was a 'he'."

"It wasn't the arms that disturbed me the most."

"The singular eye?"

"For me," said Racelsus, "it was the underlying aura of psychic tentamenta that pulsed from him."

"Psychic tenta-who-now?" said Helda.

"I think it means sort of like tendrils or tentacles," said Felix. To demonstrate, he did a similar hand-gesture to Yetty's, mostly involving wiggling his fingers about, but with added sound-effects.

"It wasn't malicious," continued the witch, lost in her own thoughts. "Quite gentle, really. It's just what you expect from a bartender. Almost like a caress."

The others were looking at her. She blushed, as much as a skull could blush. "At least he, er, it, er, he, always knew how you liked your drinks," she finished. "So, pub, was it?"

Journal Entry D - Treasure

Reference case [NPvQH] (NumPol v. QuiHal), year 1335, Judge Purnisto presiding.

Imagine the following.

You are wandering through an abandoned-looking area of the woods. This part of the forest is full of all manner of unfriendly creatures and treacherous bandits. The weather turns, and it starts to rain. After turning up your collar you scan the surrounding area for any sort of shelter. You find a fallen tree that has landed unusually on another tree, providing a rudimentary shield from the elements. After scrambling beneath this sanctuary of dryness, you are shocked to find a sizable wooden chest half-buried in the dirt next to you.

The chest has a severe looking lock and is banded with iron rings for strength. It appears sturdy and robust, but weathered with age. Do you:

    a)   Ignore the chest, or

    b)   Open the chest and loot the contents.

People I've talked to about this seem to fall into two distinct camps, either of which you yourself might have already entered. I think I can summarise both with the following thought experiment.

On the one hand, somebody somewhere has taken the time to store their valuables in a chest, a locked chest, and hidden it to protect it from looters. On the other, what kind of person stores their valuables in a chest in the woods? Probably a criminal, so the contents are almost always guaranteed to be stolen anyway. But then again, they might just be the result of an overactive paranoia... but if the contents were important, why leave them in an abandoned chest in the woods for years?

Now, to make it more interesting, let's say you opt for option c), which is:

    c)   Poke around a bit and gather more intel.

You discover that the chest appears to be booby-trapped; set up to administer a lethal case of stab-someone-with-a-knife to anyone foolhardy enough to break the chest open. How does that change your opinion?

Well, clearly only a villain of dubious character would put an actual life-threatening booby-trap on a chest, shoved out in the woods where a child might find it. Or, someone utterly desperate to protect whatever is contained within it at all costs. It could be an entire family's livelihood, being stored out of sight to protect against robbers or thugs.

~

"Sir, I didn't find any treasure, or gold, or anything like that," said Numple, my client. She was a wiry lady of middling years, dressed simply. "Nothing but that booby-trap and the ringing bell contraption."

"Lies," said the lawyer of my opponent. "Why would my client go through the trouble to hide an empty chest in the forest? You have clearly stolen the vast wealth contained within and ferreted it away."

"I was nearly killed!"

"I'm sure the stolen gold was worth it."

The whole of the questioning went like this. Quite pointed, quite aggressive. I did my best to keep everyone calm, and instead posed the questions I started this story with. If it was that important, and legally obtained, why leave it in the woods? In my argument, that's what it all boiled down to. If I had some valuables that I wanted to protect, I'd leave them in a bank, or in my house, or somewhere safe, as any reasonable person would. Without direct proof, mustn't we consider the reasonable person, whoever he or she or they is or are? Sorry, that sentence got away from me for a moment.

Back to the case. The judge went off to mull over the arguments while we waited in awkward silence. Before long, he re-entered and gave us all a long, pondering stare.

"I have given this some consideration. I believe that it is likely that the chest did contain some considerable fortune at one point. However, I do not think sufficient proof has been given that the defendant in this case was the thief." The merchant's face turned red with suppressed anger. The judge had looked at him and paused, as if considering whether to say something or not. Eventually he came to a decision.

"In order to assist with any investigations, I think the authorities would benefit from a detailed inventory of the contents of the case."

The merchant narrowed his eyes at this. "Why?" he said, but the judge ignored him, instead holding a finger up to signify he was still talking.

"And," he said, "I should like to know your reasoning for hiding such wealth in that way. I should also like to see an affidavit from your local tax collector to ensure that you are paying your fair share. If the contents of the chest really are as valuable as you say, I should wager that our gracious state is owed no small part of it. Shall I send the taxman around, say, this afternoon?" The judge steepled his fingers. "In fact, I could send him home with you. There's plenty of space in your carriage, by the looks of it."

Under the weight of the judge's regard, the merchant's jowls quivered furiously. I could hear him grinding his teeth. "That would…" he began, before stopping. He shot daggers at my client, then coughed. "Perhaps it is easier for all involved if I just accept that the chest and its contents are lost due to the *most unfortunate of circumstances*," he growled.

"Perhaps," said the judge, peering at him. "Perhaps, indeed." He turned to my client. "What did you say you found in that chest?" She sprung to her feet, the relief causing her to speak too quickly. She fumbled the words out.

"Your Honour, thank you, I found naught but a spring-loaded booby trap and a loud ringing bell contraption, thank you again, sir."

He had raised an eyebrow at the merchant who was steadfastly not returning his gaze. "Curious. I believe we are done here."

And indeed we were. I'd asked the team about that last comment later that evening in the pub, and no one had understood it. No one except Helda, who cradled a pint in her hands.

"It's a dirty trick," she said. "Old bandit trick, that. The bell rings, then the idea is if you're nearby and in the know, you head in that direction and rob'n kill whoever you find. Some poor sod with a knife in his gut and a purse on his belt, maybe. More often just some poor sod with a knife in his gut and nothing but the shirt on his back."

I hadn't asked her how she knew that.

~journal entry ends

23 - Pubishments

The Duck in Flagon was as welcoming as ever, with sturdy, slightly sticky tables and large, smeary windows. The barman, Burt, nodded as the Lunchers procession entered, and started preparing a row of pewter pots. He grabbed one in a meaty fist and started filling it with something brown and frothy.

"Wotcha, Burt," said Helda, causing the publican to stop his pouring and squint at her. He grunted once, then carried on pouring.

"He's in a good mood today," she said, as she lowered herself onto a table. The bench beneath her creaked in protest, but then, everything in the Duck creaked or groaned or threatened to collapse into a heap of splinters. It was part of the charm.

"Now, tell me," she said, after a long sip of a broad cup. "Is it true that some lawyers once wrote a cease-and-desist letter to a river?"

"Oh not the bloody monks again," said Yetty. "Look, it was just a story!"

Felix grinned to himself and decided to poke the fire. "Not the way old Pike tells it," he said, prompting another outburst from Yetty. "Very serious business, I heard..."

~

An hour or so later, the door swung open, breathing a quick wash of fresh, cool air that was immediately swallowed by the resident smelly, smokey, warm fug. Furbo looked around and spotted them, walking between tables to join them. He sat down on the table beside Helda, who shook her empty pot at him. "You have some catching up to do, lightweight."

The old scholar scoffed, a small smile on his face. "Oh ho! Lightweight, is it? I've been quaffing rotten beer since you were just an impulse after dinner, young lady."

Helda froze, her brow lowering. The Lunchers staff felt the atmosphere shift as if the sun had just passed behind a cloud, and their conversation died away. Even Dago and Merindhe stopped their whispering. They turned to look at the massive bulk of Helda, hunched over her drink, murder in her eyes.

"What did you say?" Helda growled. Furbo's smile faltered.

"Uh, well," he said. "Now there, Helda, dear, I didn't mean…"

Helda slammed her fist on the table. The echoing crash silenced the entire pub instantly. A dozen sets of eyes were watching her, some nervous, some excited.

"What's goin' on here then?" said Burt, the barman. He cracked his knuckles. "No fightin' inside, Helda, you know better'n that."

Helda pointed a thick finger at Furbo. "I've been waiting for this day for a while now, old man," she snarled. Furbo looked horrified. Helda swung her hand back and pointed at Burt.

"Burt," she said. "You still got a barrel of Dead Man's Grout?"

"Aye. It's a bit mature, mind."

"Fetch it," she said, leaning back. "And two mugs."

~

Burt dropped the barrel onto the table with a thud, then placed two mugs down beside it. Felix could make out a few faded words on the side of the barrel.

'Dead Man's Grout'. And what's that beneath it…

He squinted.

"Keep away from hallowed ground?" he read aloud.

"This drink don't mix well with what ya might call *consecrated spaces*," said Burt. "Tends to get a bit upset." This shocked Felix. Not just with the idea that a drink could be considered unholy, but also that Burt knew what consecrated means.

Furbo, his confidence restored, slid a mug over to Burt. "I'm ready when you are, barkeep." Helda stretched her neck from side to side, then nodded.

Burt picked up Helda's cup, then turned the tap with a squeal. A wet slurp sounded from somewhere inside the barrel, then a thick, viscous fluid, more like a gravy, sludged its way into the pot. It took about twenty seconds to fill, not because of the size of the mug but due to the speed of the liquid. When it was done, Burt repeated this with Furbo's.

Lastly, he handed each of them a spoon.

"Go," he said. Both contestants lifted their cups and began.

~

Another hour later, Furbo was slumped face-down on the table, making no sound or movement.

"He's fine," said Racelsus, following Felix's eyes. "Relatively speaking. I'll keep an eye on him. Well, not an eye. You know whattam saying."

"You sure you want *another* beer?" came Yetty's voice. She was leaning on Helda's shoulder. The large woman snorted.

"I need sommat t'wash that slime down with," she said, prodding the empty barrel of Dead Man's Grout with a finger.

"I can't tell if I'm impressed or horrified," said Felix. "Well done either way, I suppose. Quite an achievement." Yetty returned a moment later with another drink, and Helda took it with the hit-and-miss precision of the totally inebriated.

"Achievement," Helda murmured, then she blinked, then raised a hand. "I've'd an idea," she said, thunking her wooden mug on the table. Foam splashed from it and dribbled down the side.

"Is it meat-flavoured beer?" said Felix, watching the foam on its doomed descent to join its fellow foamy comrades in a sticky puddle on the table. "Because you've had that one already."

Helda raised her eyebrows. "Thassa good idea," she said. "What sort of meat?"

Felix gave her a look. "You said you had an idea?" he prompted. Confusion, then understanding dawned on Helda's face.

"Oh yeah!" Her face took on a serious expression, only slightly marred by the fact her eyes were blinking independently. "You'r'a man of the world, right? Achievemently? I mean, lawfully speakin'."

187

"I suppose so."

"As in, you've seen all sorts of stuff happening in the courtrooms and stuff, right?"

"Mmm," said Felix, taking a sip of his own drink.

Helda snapped her beefy fingers, or tried to, but missed.

"You should write a book."

Felix choked on his beer. "Oh, very funny," he said, wiping the front of his shirt. "Anyone know how to get the stains out of phantom linen?"

"I mean it," said Helda. "You've seen loads, and you're real good at explaining stuff to me, so I think y'should write it all down so other people can read it to." She turned to Furbo's prostrate form. "You'd read it, wouldn't you?"

"Oh gods I miss him, Helda," said Furbo, groggily. "Will we ever find him? The poor boy, the poor boy."

"None of that now, old man," said Helda, stiffening. "None of that." She patted him on the back of his bald head, gently despite her obvious discomfort. "You need more drinks is what. Eh? Oh, he's asleep."

Felix shook his head.

Maybe I could get out my old journal, put a few bits together, take out the boring bits... Oh, but who would read it? Who would it be for?

He dismissed the idea with a wave of his hand. *Nah, waste of time.*

~

Another hour and many drinks later, Felix stood.

"Everyone, I'm off to bed."

There were a few moans and boos, but he waved them down.

"Are you okay, Felixsh?" said Racelsus, with a slight slurring. For the animated skull of an ancient witch, she could really put them away if she was in the mood.

"I'm okay, thanks. Just... tired. I'm going to go rest for a little bit. I'll see you all later." With that, his vision blurred, and before he knew it he was back in the grey plain. It was completely unchanged from the last time he had visited. He lay down on his back in the grass and watched the grey sky roll past, and fell into a dreamless sleep.

He awoke suddenly, disturbed, and sat up to find he was not alone. A figure was watching him. The figure of a woman. She wasn't close enough for him to recognise her. At first, he was too startled to speak, then he began waving frantically at her.

"Hey!" he said. "Hey! Who's there?"

The figure turned and disappeared. Running to where she was, Felix saw no evidence that there had been anyone there at all.

Who was that?

Whoever it was, it was someone he didn't recognise. At least... well, there was something familiar to her.

Racelsus?

24 - A Rest

The next morning, Felix returned to Lunchers. Upon arrival, he gathered everyone around the always-cramped meeting room, ignoring hungover protestations and complaints.

"Hello everyone," he said, then raised an eyebrow at Helda, who was pressing palms into her eyes. "Good night last night?"

"Gurrgguh," was the reply. Furbo was completely silent.

"I'm not going to ramble on," Felix continued. "With John's case concluded, it's time for me to go."

Everyone's voices started up at once.

"Go where?"

"Why?"

"I expected this would happen…"

"Gurugh?"

He silenced them with a raised hand. "I can't really explain it very well. There's this feeling, right here-" and he gestured to his chest "- that doesn't sit right. It feels as if I have this chain that's tightening, and it's pulling me back to the… other place. When I was working on John's case, it was fine, but now that it's done… I have to return."

"You can't just stay?" said Dago. Felix shook his head.

"I'm sorry, I can't."

"Will you come back?" Yetty asked. Felix shrugged.

"I don't know. I think I will. Whenever I go back there, I see and hear people, people in trouble. Legal problems. Just like Mrs Henria a little while ago, I am drawn to them, and while I'm working with them, this pain… fades. So, provided Lunchers keeps working with those in trouble, I daresay you'll see me again."

He smiled, but his worried eyes rested on Racelsus. The witch's skull was resting in her customary birdcage. She sensed his gaze, and rattled slightly.

What? What is it? she said, directly in his mind. *You look concerned.*

Rass, thought Felix. *You didn't… visit me, did you?*

191

Visit you? What do you mean?
You didn't visit me in the grey plains?
No, Felix.
Oh. Okay.
I tried, though. I really tried to reach you. A couple of times.
You did?
Of course.

Felix smiled.

You saw someone there? Someone besides you?
Yeah, I think so.
That's peculiar. Let me have a dig around.
Thanks Racelsus. Oh, I don't want to worry the others...

The witch clacked her teeth again.

What, in case someone kills you?

He shifted uncomfortably.

Oh, fine.
Thank you. Sorry to be a burden.

If the witch could have waved a hand, she would have done so.

"Right," said Felix, looking around. "I best be off." And so it was. After their conversation was concluded, Felix let himself be dragged back to the grey plain, where he lay down and rested for a time.

When Felix had gone, Yetty looked at Racelsus with narrowed eyes. "What were you two talking about?"

"Who? Me?" said the witch. Yetty wasn't convinced.

"I know when you and he are brain-talking. He gets this concentrating look on his face, like he's trying to thread a needle. Practically pokes his tongue out. Come on, spill."

Racelsus rolled her eye sockets. "Nothing you'd find interesting."

Yetty crossed her arms. Racelsus clacked, trying to think of something.

"Just, hm, philosophical discussions on... the nature of death and, hm, stuff," she mumbled. Furbo perked up at this.

"Oh?" he said, eyebrows raising. "Do tell."

Racelsus sighed.

~

Once Felix was feeling ready, he stood up, and started exploring. Just like before, the endless grey sky stretched forwards, and the gentle grass spread in every direction. Infinite nothing and forever to explore it in.

I should have brought a book.

There was no sense of time. No sun, no moon, no clouds. Felix wandered. He would see vague shapes, like shadows through a mirror, and approach them. Doing so would yield short snippets of conversation, almost always regarding legal troubles. Many would fade, but some would sharpen. Those that became full, clear images of people - viewed as if Felix were standing by them - were those that resonated with him. The truly destitute or victimised, with the littlest hope against terrible odds.

Over the next five months, Felix made himself visible to three of them, each time approaching them first alone and then recommending they head to Lunchers, whereupon he would meet them and take their cases. They were a small-time baker being strong-armed by a local gang; a patient whose doctor had, without informed consent, prescribed her experimental treatment for his own research; and a young lad falsely accused of theft from the armed forces. Each time, the cases were fought and won, with Felix taking the lead and the staff at Lunchers providing support. Each time he reappeared to the staff, they would welcome him back and rush to support the case with renewed vigour, and whenever he left, they would feel the loss of their friend once again, hoping he would return, but never being certain. The longer the period of time between cases, the heavier his absence was felt.

On quieter, lonelier days, some members of Lunchers would guiltily wish for a case that would bring Felix to them for good, or at least a long, uninterrupted period of time. As has been the lesson taught by old stories whispered by experienced mouths from cradle to grave, they should have been careful what they wished for.

Journal Entry E - Relative Value

Reference case [SBvHRH] (SunBuc v. HRH), year 1314, Judge Ewslef presiding.

I am not attracted to 'valuable' things that are only valuable for the sake of being valuable. Famous artefacts, expensive wines, fine shawls… I've never seen the point. Money is a consequence of civilisation, and commerce, bartering etcetera must be endured for modern survival. The idea of taking money, this cold, metal air that we must all breath to survive (in the purchase of food, for example) and wasting vast quantities of it on worthless tat baffles me. The relentless pursuit of prosperity drives people to despair, destruction and death.

Of course I'm tremendous fun at parties, why do you ask?

Yet, human beings are not alone in this obsession with wealth. Goblins in the South Country formulate great expeditions to mine deeper and deeper into the mountains in search of crystals or precious metals. Even a magpie will grab something shiny to show off in the hopes of attracting a mate.

Perhaps there is something that speaks to our very souls when it comes to material worth. For, ultimately, what makes something valuable? Is it the shininess of the gold, or the value we assign to it? Why did we kill each other for it, even if we were rich beyond the dreams of the common man?

There have been attempts to quantify what makes wealth so appealing. Could gold and gems *contain* something, some element, terribly addictive, which caused us to ascribe it value? Else, how could the goblins, and certain other creatures, seek it out with no other frame of reference? What else explained the furore with which the ultra-rich seek endless heaps of the stuff?

Attempts to quantify this element - unimaginatively named 'valulium' - were fruitless. No attempt to boil, crush, spin or mix any kind of high-value treasure resulted in any discoveries, and the scientists lost heart.

That, and it was of course very expensive when what you are experimenting on costs more than what you make in a year.

This argument resurfaced again when I read about a case some time ago. It involved an affluent estate and a dragon.

The goblins I mentioned earlier? The reason their expeditions to the mountains were so dangerous is that for whatever reason the search and discovery of such high-density riches attracts... well, dragons. Goblins claim they can *smell* gold and gems, which is why they're most suited to the task. They just *know* which way to dig. Dragons seem to share this instinct, but won't get out of bed for anything less than a veritable hoard. Upon finding or gathering said pile of treasure, they like nothing more than bathing in great heaps of the stuff. Similar to cats and certain types of mint. They'll roll and roll, then curl up to sleep on their hoarded piles of cash.

So what does this have to do with our estate, way in the North Country?

Our patron was a seller of fine art. Indeed, the most successful there was. Before Mr S. M. Buckles, artwork was only worth what the struggling painter could get you to throw at him in order to stop him following you down the street, waving his painting at you. You might toss a copper or a silver at a landscape you liked particularly, or, if you were particularly lavish, you might commission an artist to paint or sculpt you. The picture itself was practically worthless to all except the subject, of course.

Enter Mr Buckles.

Over the course of four years in the East Country, Buckles created a narrative. He created desire. He created *envy*.

He would invite his friends over to his house and walk them through the paintings that covered his entire home, wall to wall, ceiling almost to floor.

"Oh that? The painter died shortly afterwards, most tragic, yes, considering it is, as you can plainly see, a portrait of the Goddess of Death herself. Note the braid and the basket. That face... Quite a marvellous scene, such beauty. I can almost hear her voice when I examine it. I'm glad I bought it when I did."

"Ah, this one is by Debouchli, a blind sculptor from the North Country. It is what he imagines colours to look like. Astounding, yes?"

"Well, I might be willing to part with it, I suppose, but I am most terribly fond of it…"

"Yes, Countess, I think that would look marvellous above your dining table. It is one of a kind, did you know that?"

Before long, the great and the gullible begged him for the chance to view his wonderful gallery, and threw such huge sums of money at him for the chance to obtain one of these *masterpieces.*

To this day, we still don't know exactly what the exact moment of critical mass was, but at some point on an evening in Spring, just as Mr Buckles was getting ready for what he promised was 'the greatest unveiling yet', a great shadow swept over his luxurious estate. A swooping shape smashed through his roof with a roaring crash, dust swirling in the unseasonable wind. Patrons and punters alike scattered for cover, and, as the chaos subsided, a sense of dread sat on that place like a blanket of snow.

Pulling back the lavish double doors to his gallery with a trembling hand, S. M. Buckles was horrified to see a huge golden-scaled dragon scooping the priceless paintings into a pile. It gave him a look as if to dare him to make a move, then settled comfortably on the pile of debris, nostrils steaming, tail flicking.

Dragons are a tricky legal sticking point. They're not beholden to any laws, particularly, mostly because no one can enforce them. If a dragon decides that it doesn't agree with your ruling that it should *not* keep stealing sheep, then good luck to you, and goodbye Flossy. For this reason, it was assumed that the dragon simply *was* a factor, and the question became: how to deal with it.

Buckles argued that the East Country's king should rally some troops and fight it off, especially considering the sizable tax contribution he makes to the royal treasury. The king disagreed, saying, rather pithily, that the great art collector and trader had brought it upon himself by creating the greatest concentration of wealth in the whole damn country. What dragon could resist? The judge agreed, saying that, in essence, Mr Buckles was out of luck.

So what did he do? Without his paintings, he had no status or money. The dragon was in his house, and none of his friends wanted to associate with him while his social status was uncertain. He only had one escape plan, and, I admit, it was a brave thing to do.

Standing in court, S. M. Buckles admitted that all of the works he had sold were lies. He had painted them himself. They were uninteresting, pointless, contrived and passionless shams. The stash, his stash, was therefore completely worthless. His outraged social circle agreed, and started their own complex litigations against him, accusing him of fraud and all manner of other things. In an instant he went from darling to the stars to reviled scamster, from a wealthy celebrity to a penniless fraud.

Did it work? Well, his speech to the court was given at Midspring sunset in the capital. Witnesses back in the East Country say they remember on Midspring seeing a great winged shape soar into the sky from his estate just as the sun was setting, never to be seen again. I'll leave the inference to you.

~journal entry ends

Part Two: Speculo

1 - The Plains

Felix lay in the grass on the ground, watching the stalks swaying gently, despite the lack of wind. Tiredness eventually overtook him, dragging at his heavy eyes. Felix slept.

When he awoke, he did not sit up. Instead, he stared at the sky. The plain grey clouds stretched from horizon to horizon and did what they always did: nothing.

Is this it, then? Forever? Waking up, finding someone who needs help, helping them, exhausting myself, disappearing from their lives, returning here, falling asleep... repeat? Until when? Until the sun dwindles into nothing, and the earth freezes into a frozen ball of mud? Why am I still here? What am I doing?

I'd kill for a cider. I wonder if I could represent myself? Could I get away with a crime of passion... fruit?

Felix laughed at his own pathetic joke, then paused. This wasn't the first time that these particular thoughts had travelled this particular path across Felix's thoughtscape, especially the cider one. In fact, so well-travelled were these thoughts that they were acting as voluntary guides for other thoughts; showing them the sights and landmarks, telling the history and charging admission.

No use sitting around and moping. That won't get me anywhere. Certainly won't get me a cider.

With a groan he rolled over and stood, stretching his back out and smoothing down his jacket. Quite why he was wearing a jacket, and why it needed to be smoothed down, were some more of the questions he asked himself regularly with similar levels of success.

~

Felix walked through the grass, as he often did, focussing on nothing but the steps, letting his thoughts meander along with his feet. Within a space of time between a few moments and a few hours (it was not easy to be more precise than that), he started to see a dark shape sat on a stool. As he approached, it sharpened into focus. A man of middling years, staring at the floor. Felix stepped towards him, willing himself to appear beside him, and the scenery around him morphed from an endless plain of nothing to the inside of an unkempt living room. Unkempt was perhaps putting it kindly. The floor was littered with loose papers, broken furniture, smashed bottles and other signs of a person that didn't care anymore. Felix approached the figure and cleared his throat.

"Hello," said Felix. "Don't be frightened."

The figure glanced at him, but made no other sound or physical movement. *That's odd. There's usually a little more... well, something.*

"I'm here to help," he said.

The man scowled, twisting his face into a silent snarl of anger, then abruptly burst into tears. "How? How can you possibly help me?" he sobbed, gripping his head with both hands, then collapsing into wails and moans.

That's more like it.

Did I really just think that?

"I don't know exactly how yet," Felix said in a soft voice. "Why don't you tell me what's been going on and we'll go from there?"

The man groaned. "You won't believe me." He sniffed. "No one believes me."

"Oh, I've seen my fair share of unbelievable events. Try me."

The man sniffed again and wiped his nose. "The guards didn't believe me. My own wife... Why should I bother?"

Felix flipped an upturned stool over and lowered himself onto it. "What have you got to lose?" he ventured. The man considered this for a moment. His red eyes scanned from side to side. Eventually he shook his head.

"What sort of bloody…" He glanced up, meeting Felix's eyes for the first time. Felix forced himself to return that haggard, vein-broken gaze, and said nothing. Another moment passed. The man leaned over and plucked up a bottle from the floor, examined it, took a swig, coughed, then began to speak.

"It went like this:"

2 - The Boatbuilder

Erran lowered his hammer and wiped his brow, then wiped his hand on his vest. His arm burned and his fingers were numb. Looking at the sky, it must have been nearing midnight. On his right he heard a grunt followed by the sound of a hammer dropping to the floor.

"Guv," Pettee said to the foreman. "I'm dead on my feet."

Erran could see the foreman was carrying huge bags under his own eyes. He could almost sympathise with him, until he spoke. "You ain't on your feet," was his reply. "You're on your arse."

Pettee looked set to spit something venomous in reply, but Erran let his own hammer slide to the floor, making sure it made a decent *thunk* as it landed. Both Pettee and the foreman glanced over at him. The foreman swallowed nervously.

"Fine," he said, turning back to Pettee. "But sunrise tomorrow, first thing. We don't get this frigate finished soon, we're as good as done." Fifteen voices groaned.

"We know," said Pettee with irritation, rubbing her shoulder with a calloused hand. "You bloody said already."

The foreman pointed at her. "I'm sick of your jibs and jibes, Pettee. One more of them and you're off the job, no pay."

"Without me you'll never get the boat done, guv," she said. The foreman sighed. He pinched his nose. "Don't remind me," he said. He waved a hand around in front of his head, vaguely circling. "Alright, pack up everyone. See you all tomorrow."

As Erran stood and started dragging his exhausted feet to the door, the foreman touched him on the arm. "Erran," he said. "I need a quick word." A momentary panic fluttered through him. Was it the gesture with the hammer? He was too heavy-handed, Jylin always said so. Not subtle enough to be sneaky. Or was it sneaky enough to be subtle? Was he going to get sacked? He needed this job, what with the little one…

"Uh, sure thing, guv," he murmured. Pettee glanced back at them and frowned, but the foreman waved her off. Once everyone had left, Gort, for that was his name, struggled with how to start.

"How's the little one, Erran? Little Perra?" he said, not meeting Erran's eye.

"Fine," came the reply, perhaps too quickly, perhaps too loudly. Erran took a breath to slow his thoughts, then looked at Gort. He wasn't a bad foreman, all things considered. They'd known each other years, dozens of years, and Gort was the good sort. He just got himself tangled up, sometimes. Erran could see Gort was trying to figure out how to bring up something awkward, so he came to his aid.

"She's started schooling."

"Good news, yes, good news."

A silence. Erran could bear it no longer.

If you're going to sack me, just sack me! He plucked the courage to ask the question, no mucking around.

"What-"

"We're not going to finish the boat in time," said Gort. "We just ain't. You know it. I know it. In fact, the only person who doesn't know it is his high bloody majesty Prince Ulaco."

Erran didn't react. It was true, of course.

"I been asking around," Gort continued, more quietly. "I found a wizard, or witch, or lady wizard, or whatever you want to call her, who don't cost the earth who can help."

Something about this didn't seem right. Perhaps he was just tired, and the tiredness was making him suspicious. Erran replied in a voice just as hushed as Gort's.

"Help... how exactly? Magic up the boat?"

"I wish... Nothing so useful as that." Gort glanced from side to side, then leaned in a little closer. "She tells me she has a spell that can make a man work twice as hard without breaking a sweat. In fact, they can do twice the work and rest twice as much as well."

"Well, that sounds too good to be true, Gort."

A frown on his friend's face. "Well, it might be. But it might also not be." His face softened. "I got the money for it, but only for one casting. I was hoping you might volunteer…"

"Me? Why?"

Gort sprang to his feet and started pacing.

"Because you're the best worker I know, and you're the strongest man I know, and you're the oldest friend I know. That, and you know as well as I do that if we don't get this boat done - and we won't - then we're all in trouble. The Prince won't pay me for this one, which means I can't pay you, and we won't get any more work from him. He's also a vindictive weasel, so chances are his displeasure would dry up all the work in the area for us. Sometimes I reckon he's doing this on purpose for some reason, trying to make us fail where we can be seen to fail."

This was an unusual selection of words for Gort, who was typically a short-word sort of a man, and not prone to conspiracy. Erran reckoned he was quoting something that had been said to him. He realised Gort was waiting for him to say something.

"Uh, would it hurt?" he said. Gort, sensing his friend coming around, perked up.

"Not a bit," he said, coming closer.

"Any chance it'll go wrong?"

"None at all. She made that very clear." Gort's hand went to his pocket and closed around something.

Erran sighed. The chance of getting no pay was… unbearable. He'd heard from his cousin that work was drying up downriver, and *he* had heard it from his friend that a nephew of his brother-in-law had to sell his children for a loaf of bread. It sounded far-fetched in the warmth of the pub, pot in hand, when he'd laughed into his pint as he heard it. But on cold nights in harsh times… Perra *was* looking scrawnier, he reckoned.

She won't starve. Ever.

He sighed. "What do I have to do?"

Gort smiled widely and clapped Erran on the arm with his free hand. "Very little, my friend, very little. I need a little sample of your blood, then that's it."

Blood?

That didn't sit right with Erran, whose grandma's own mother had told him of stories of blood-drinkers that still sometimes came unbidden to his mind on long, dark nights like this one. There must be some other way.

"Guv... Ow!"

Gort whipped his other hand backwards, and Erran saw he had prodded him with some kind of sharp needle, causing a tiny bead of blood to appear. Before Erran could say anything else, Gort had held a tiny dry cloth over it, then secreted it back into a pocket. "Sorry, Erran, but that's it. We're done." Erran glanced down at the tiny drop of red blood welling on his arm.

"You said it wouldn't hurt."

Gort laughed. "That didn't hurt you, surely? Big tough man such as yourself?"

Erran gave Gort a withering look. "Uh huh. I see you didn't volunteer yourself?" The foreman snorted and gestured down at his ample frame.

"Look at me, Erran. I'm made for organising, not hard labour." He patted a hand on his pocket and gave Erran a wink. "All done," he announced.

"What now?" said Erran.

"Now? My friend, now you take tomorrow off."

"What? Seriously?"

Gort smiled. "Yes, Erran. Seriously. Come down after sunset and do your shift then."

Erran's eyebrows had risen without his knowledge, causing his old friend to laugh. Gort slapped his meaty thighs and stood. "You've just saved this company, Erran. Thank you."

Without thinking, Erran shook Gort's outstretched hand and left, quite unsure of what had just happened. He would have thought more about it as he tossed and turned that night, but he fell asleep as soon as he lay down.

3 - The Event

The next day, Vinna's Day, a day of honest work for the God of Honest Work, he slept in. At least, until his daughter woke him and his wife up at sunrise. Still, even this was better than the times he *had* been waking. His wife didn't believe him at first, raising an incredulous eyebrow as he swore to Halka that Gort had given him the day off.

"You've been telling me for weeks that there's too much to be done," she said over breakfast. "And now you've got a day off?" She shook her head. "That Gort isn't the giving kind. You two are up to something."

Despite these suspicions, the day was spent in comfortable domesticity; helping around the house, playing with his daughter Perra, surprising his beautiful Jylin with an impromptu stroll down by the river. Swept up in good humour, he even treated his family to a rare luxury, particularly given their financial situation - a small pouch of rock-toffee, purchased from the half-blind and affectionately grumpy old lady in the round hut.

Erran handed one to his daughter and one to his wife, choosing the smallest, saddest looking sweet for himself.

"Now eat it slow," said the shopkeeper as Erran paid. She waved at Perra, who hid behind Jylin's skirts. "Don't bite it too hard or you'll hurt y'self."

"Nonsense," Erran said in mock machismo, gurning and grunting with arms flexed. "A sweet can't hurt a big, strong man like me! I fear no sweetie!" In answer to Perra's childish giggles, he chomped on his own sweet, and flinched and yowled when he heard the *crack* in his mouth, followed by the stab of pain in his back tooth.

"Are you sure about that, oh great hero?" Jylin said, trying not to laugh and failing. Erran jabbed in his mouth with a thick finger.

"Neurgh," he said, feeling the tooth loosen. To his horror it came loose with a single poke, and he held it up in front of him, glistening and slimy, much to his wife's disgust.

"I told'ee," said the shopkeeper, waggling a finger. "Now, off with you, before you break your leg on my doorframe."

Even this pointless injury couldn't dampen Erran's mood on a morning like this morning. He loved his family, and carefree days spent with them were the days he lived for, broken tooth be damned.

After a dinner of soft bread and warm soup (which may or may not have had something to do with a certain tooth-related accident), as the sun started to dip, Erran prepared to kiss his family goodbye and make his way to the workshop, though not before telling Perra a story about ducks and geese dancing and singing. As he went to close the front door behind him, Jylin grabbed him by the elbow and threw her arms around him. After giving him a squeeze, she released him.

"I've had such a wonderful day, Erran," she said. "I felt like we were newlyweds again."

Erran smiled. "We did have a lot of fun back then, dint we?"

Jylin bit her bottom lip and leaned in close to him. "I'd say we still have fun now," she said. She leaned in even closer, and in a low voice, barely above a whisper, said "Might even have time for some fun later."

Erran's eyebrows shot up, and he blushed. "Well, how'm I supposed to go do a shift now?" he growled back.

She brushed a hand down his cheek. "Oh, you'll manage. I'll be waiting for you." With that, she kissed him one more time, then twirled, her skirts flaring outwards as she crossed the threshold to their home. She smirked as she closed the door. With an enormous, stupid smile on his face, Erran straightened his cap and headed off to work.

~

On the walk there, he passed the village pub, named Gaman's Pot, after the God of Revels. He could hear a few voices floating out, and for a moment Erran thought to pop his head in. Once he approached the door, he moved to push it open, but stopped. Thoughts of Gort reminded him of the dire position he was in, and he'd already acted frivolously by buying those toffees. Rubbing at his aching gum, he changed his mind, and continued to the workshop.

Once he arrived, he found to his surprise no sounds of working, save a single, methodical hammering. Instead of the sounds of a dozen or more, it sounded like just one. Gort spotted him approaching and came out to meet him. His foreman shook his hand warmly.

"Nice day, Erran?"

"Yes, Gort, very nice."

"Good, good…"

"Where-?" said Erran, looking around.

"Is everyone?" Gort laughed. "Come along, mate, there's something I want you to meet."

Something?

He led a bemused Erran into the main assembly workshop. Someone was waiting for them, sat down, with their back to the pair. Gort walked over to the figure and held a hand open as if showing off a new painting, a huge grin plastered on his face.

The figure, hearing the two approach, stopped hammering. It let the hammer in its grip slide to the ground, landing with a decent *thunk*, then wiped its forehead with a sleeve. The figure then stood up slowly and turned around. Erran's heart skipped a beat. Gort clapped his hands together excitedly.

"Erran, meet… Erran."

The man, who was a complete duplicate of Erran, smiled and held out a hand calloused with rough work. "Nice to meet you, mate," he said, in a voice Erran knew very well.

~

"Hang on a moment," said Felix, rubbing his temple. "You saw… yourself?"

"I did," said Erran, lowering his head into his hands. "It was the strangest thing I ever saw, but it was also the most familiar thing I ever saw, too."

"But… how?" His mind flew back to a case from his past. Gurrinko. A wizardess who had split herself into three. In Gurrinko's case it had ended up going wrong. It had started fine, but ended predictably badly. *What had she called it… Some sort of Rite?*

Felix snapped his fingers. "A Rite of Splitting! Was it a Rite of Splitting?"

Erran waved his empty bottle dismissively. "I don't think so. Listen, I'll get to that bit," he said, putting the bottle down and rummaging for another. When he'd found one, he took a swig and coughed.

"I still remember that stupid look on his face. So pleased with himself, he was."

~

"You're my best worker, Erran, and now, bless my stars, I got two of you." Gort's wide grin did nothing to disarm Erran's unease.

The double looked a little awkward. He held up his hands in a conciliatory fashion, palms open, facing forward. "I know this is pretty weird… Erran." It seemed to have difficulty saying the name out loud. "It's weird for me, too. We have the same cogs and whistles up here, you see," and it tapped its head, "so I really do know how you're feeling."

"How did this happen?" Erran murmured, lowering himself to a bench. Gort cleared his throat and fiddled with his shirtsleeves.

"Well, I was chatting, as you do, to a friend. This friend had another friend in earshot, you see, who heard my, erm, thoughts about our worker situation. They offered to put me in touch with someone who might be able to help, so I, well, I said yes."

He dropped onto the bench opposite Erran. "I was desperate! You've seen how I've been. You know what's at stake here. I had to try something, Erran, or we'd all have been buggered."

"I wish you'd told me," said Erran quietly. He met eyes with his double, who was watching him intently. More quietly he said: "It's hardly like we can just undo what you've done, now, is it?" The double stiffened in exactly the way Erran would have done, giving nothing away but a narrowing of the eyes.

"Sure we can," said Gort, shrugging. "Once everything's all sorted, we'll go back to the wizard and reverse the spell."

The double's squinted eyes suddenly boggled. "Excuse me?" he said, with a tone Erran recognised as restrained anger. "What do you mean: *reverse the spell?*"

Gort flustered as he stood. "Now, wait, hang on, what I mean is-"

"Why not just chop my head off with a saw, instead? It'd save you the hassle," the double spat through clenched teeth.

"Be reasonable, that's not what I meant-"

"You'd *kill* me?"

Erran stood up. He knew what would calm himself down. "Listen, Erran." Using his own name to refer to another felt all kinds of wrong, and he could see why his double had stumbled earlier. "He's not going to do that to you. He will - *we* will - I don't know, find somewhere you can go, or something."

The double held his gaze. "What if I don't want to go?"

A cold feeling writhed in his stomach. "What do you mean?" he said, knowing full well what he meant.

"You - we - have a wife and a child. I love them just as much as you do. Why shouldn't I get to spend time with them?"

Erran knew how much he loved his family. He knew what he would do to protect them. He knew what he would do if someone - anyone - tried to take them away.

His double moved quicker than he did. A shove, and Erran went sprawling. Gort started to yell, but Erran heard nothing. The double stepped smartly over to him and swung at the side of his head with his strong, workman's fists, and Erran blacked out.

~

When he came to, he found Gort, wiping his brow with a cloth. He groaned and tried to stand. "Erran, lad, don't-"

"Off me," said Erran, forcing himself to his feet and staggering with the effort. It was full dark outside. How long had he been out? "Be back... talk you soon," he said, his words coming thick and halting through the fog of his bruised brain. It was hard to walk quickly when the room swam and tilted, but he moved as quickly as he could to the door.

211

He had to stop once and let the world stop spinning. Leaning on a tree, he tried - and failed - to not throw up. *Keep going, you bloody oaf.* What would he do when he found his double? *Worry about that when you actually do.*

There was light in his house. He shook his head and marched straight to the front door and yanked the handle, but it didn't open. It was locked. Erran blinked a few times, then leaned on the door, thumping it with a fist.

"Open!" he yelled. "Open, you bloody… thieving-"

The door opened and Erran was shoved backwards, stumbling over his feet and onto his back. He lifted his head to see the open doorway to his beloved family home, and silhouetted against it was his double, looking at him with a face filled with… was that pity? In his hand was a club. His club.

"Turn around and go, shapeshifter," his double said. "Last warning."

"No. Not," said Erran. Gods, his head hurt. Names and faces swam and melted, forming and unforming. If he could just *explain.*

The double hesitated, then took a step back. Erran's wife and daughter, Jylin and Perra, stood there, looking terrified. Erran almost choked. "It's me," he said, his voice thick with pain and confusion. "My Jyla. Little Perryn. Perra."

"Stand back, monster," Jylin said, her voice harsh. "Turn around and never return."

"What you saying? It's me, Jyla! Jylin. *Jylin!*" He coughed then, a great racking cough, and blood dribbled from his head wound. He touched it for the first time and his fingers came away wet and red. Perra cried and hid behind Jylin's skirts. He took a gasping breath and stared at them, his bloody hand outstretched. "This… this *thing* fool you!"

Jylin sneered at him, an expression he had never been on the receiving end of before. "Erran told me you'd say that. We know all your tricks, shapeshifter. Now leave before we set the town on you." She looked over his shoulder. Dumfounded, Erran followed her gaze.

There were people. People he knew. People he'd known his whole life. They were arriving, standing, some holding pitchforks or spades, some holding nothing. They all stared at him with undisguised hatred.

"Foul imp", one of them said.

"Witchery," said another.

"Get gone," came a third.

"What you all saying?" Erran said. He dragged himself to his knees and beat a fist into his chest. "Erran! I'm Erran! I know all you all my whole life!" He spotted Gort at the edge of the crowd, and rose to his wobbly feet, then stepped towards him, stumbling as he did so. The crowd readied their weapons, but Erran ignored them. "Gort! Gort, tell them thing you told me!" Tears ran down his face, mingling with the blood. "About the... wizard, with the..." His mind was so foggy since that head blow. What was it Gort had said? It was important. *Oh, my head...*

Gort scowled at him. "Begone, impling. Get out."

Erran didn't understand. "What are you..."

"Get away, monster!"

The weight of what was happening hit him like a spear in the gut. The next few minutes were a blur of shouting, jostling, shoving and hooting. Before he knew what had happened, he was on the edge of town, sheltering his head from stones being thrown at him. He ran, confused, heartbroken, terrified.

He ran until he collapsed, then huddled under a tree at the side of the road.

~

"If I'd just gotten to my family first..." He scowled at his bottle and tipped it up, drinking the last of whatever was in it, and grimacing at the taste.

Felix pressed his lips together. "When was all this?"

A tinkle as the bottle was discarded to land among the rest. "A few days ago."

"And what have you been doing since?"

Erran gestured around him.

"Mmm." A silence stretched between them both.

"Good news," said Felix. "I think I can help."

The man gave a mirthless laugh and gave Felix a long appraising look. "Are you a wizard?"

"No."

"A curse-breaker?"

"No."

"An assassin?"

"How would that help? No, I'm not."

Erran shook his head. "Well, what are you then?"

Felix grinned and spread his arms out wide. "A lawyer."

Erran stared at him, eyes boggling. "How the bloody hell is that going to help me?"

Felix told him.

Journal Entry F - Curse

Reference case [LCvO]] (LupCob v. OldJil), year 1339, Judge Jeckob presiding.

'Curse you!' I might yell if you steal my purse and run laughing from me in a crowded street. *'Curse the very ground you walk on! Curse your cat and all her kittens!'*

I, however, am but a humble lawyer, and so my curses are simply words on the wind. There are, I am sure you will be astutely aware, people whose curses possess a certain tangibility. That is to say, their curses are more than just words. Cross one of these folks and you might find your milk turning sour, or your crop failing, or your baby being born a squalling demon-child with billowing black plumes of smoke for eyes, or your toothache not going away for ages.

Those smaller curses are a favourite of your stereotypical remote-village bog-witch/crone, or, perhaps more accurately, the favourite of those men and women who want to *blame* such unluckiness on someone, and so find the nearest old woman to pin such misfortunes on.

"She caused all my bottles to leak!"

"My window keeps falling out! Tain't natural!"

"No matter what I try, my breath smells rotten! 'Tis a curse, and no mistake!"

Etcetera.

It's a sad truth that often the best way to deal with these small-minded bigots is to, well, threaten them with curses. You say I'm causing your pumpkins to deflate? Well, you best keep your mouth shut or I'll turn your ears to cauliflowers, that sort of thing. If a bumpkin is scared enough that he blames you for his pumpkins, chances are the lumpkin'll believe you if you threaten him with more. It's the ones that *don't* seem to care about follow-up threats that you have to watch out for.

For example: Luppy Cobbler.

You can probably figure out most of it so far. Essentially, fifteen prize foals and fillies that belonged to Mr Cobbler all up and died within a week of each other, seemingly of no natural cause, nor could anyone see any strangle-marks, cuts or other evidence of slaughter. The dog that guarded the herd didn't bark, and neither did anyone see any footprints in the frost or dew in the fields around the paddock.

There's only one explanation. It must be witchcraft!

My client, Old Jilly, was a toothless, warty, bent-double lady of some advanced years who lived in peaceful solitude on the edge of the village of Brownleaf Way. She emerged once a month to sell plants and poultices at the market, but otherwise was mostly left alone (saving, of course, the occasional desperate villager with some problem or other. These acts of kindness and assistance are often forgotten by those obsessed with demonising witchery and encouraging witch-hunting.) By all accounts that I could gather she was seen as a perfectly harmless old lady, kept to herself, and that was that.

Luppy, however, was an angry man. An angry man that just lost twenty-five golds worth of prime young horse, and someone was going to pay for it.

The day before market, he whipped up the townsfolk into a froth of outrage, spouting how he was sick to death of this witch, this hag, this harridan living by her own rules at the edge of town, cursing and hexing anyone she felt like. He, for one, wasn't going to stand for it anymore!

"She ain't done nothin' to me," one responded.

"Ah, but didn't you say you reckoned this winter was colder'n last, Spurro? That's her doin', make no mistake!" Luppy spouted. "And you, Mrs Bubbins, your pies in the winter fair came second to last, but you won last year! Who mucked with the taste, hm? Who do ya think?"

Thereafter followed other such spurts of clumsy demagoguery. Sadly, it had the desired effect. Row upon row of angry citizens with a focus for their hatred. A focus that, mere moments ago, most hadn't had a bad word to say about.

"We need to sort this witch out!" bellowed Luppy, to a collective roar of support.

"But she'll curse you, sir!" came one worried reply.

"Quick as look at you," another continued.

"Sure as anything!" the last squeaked, a fearful look over his shoulder.

And this, reader, is where a man who *genuinely believed* that a witch was out to get him would pale, swallow nervously, and conclude that probably some things are best left alone. Would you like to hazard a guess as to what Mr Cobbler did?

A flaming torch in hand, he stormed off to her hut with a few select men brave enough, or perhaps well-paid enough, to follow. Miraculously, she wasn't murdered by the mob, and so through one means or another her situation was brought to our attention.

The crux of the case was proving that anything or anyone was cursed. How do you *prove* that? Even the Cursebreakers, those esteemed specialists of the noble armies of Fowermolde, will tell you that the name is mostly for show.

"It's bloody hard to detect a curse," one had said while tugging at his moustaches. The prosecutor was trying her damnedest, but he was implacable. "Ninety-nine percent of the time it's just bad luck, see?"

"And what about the other one percent?" growled the prosecutor, fingers tapping on her desk.

"Oh, then it's an inside job," my man had said. The prosecutor seethed, dismissing the irritatingly calm soldier with a wave.

The Cursebreakers break more faces than they do curses. Their main plan of attack is: break face, hope curse also breaks. If not, repeat the plan. That being said, they are often thrown into where the highest concentration of deadly magic is likely to be, often laced with anti-magic runes or blessings. As such, they have an admirable laissez-faire attitude to most things, as I suppose anything is a relaxing boat ride compared to charging towards a cadre of warlock-screamers, purple lightning crackling from top to toe, spitting blood and feathers at anyone not possessed by demonhood.

They aren't bloody cheap, either, so maybe their relaxed frame of mind comes from their huge, sagging money pouches.

Anyway, the case. Old Jilly was a nervous but resolute witness that swore blind that she didn't have nothing to do with no horses. Nothing the prosecutor could threaten would change her story, and with no evidence to present, perhaps it might have ended there. We'd never have found out the truth.

Luppy might have gotten away with it.

I'd asked around the village before the case - not that I doubt those sent officially to investigate such alleged crimes, of course. However, sometimes physically being there to see things with your own eyes can open up new possibilities, and if you're willing to get your hands dirty, it's amazing what you can uncover.

I went to see the paddock where the horses were kept, and where they were found dead. It was a wide, well-kept meadow of tightly cropped grass. Mostly grass. At a few spots were seedlings sprouting up. I'd brought Furbo with me, suspecting that there might have been some sort of poison, and knowing that the old alchemist often had something useful to add (as well as a lot of less useful things).

When I pointed to the small, purple sprout, he 'hmm'ed.

"Hmm," he said.

"What?" I said.

"That there is either Guire's Petal, which is completely harmless, or..."

"Or?"

"Hmm?"

"What?!"

"I think we'd better get out of this field, Felix."

He explained that, upon closer inspection, that particular shade of purple on a sprout this small was almost certainly King's Roon, a majestic purple flower whose seeds are said to make horses run faster.

"But it's a myth. In tiny doses, it does nothing. Anything more than that, it's deadly to practically, well, everything," he said, shaking his head. "Plus it spreads like no one's business. There's a reason it's illegal, my lad."

"Mr Cobbler," I said, back in the courtroom. "We found traces of King's Roon in your fields."

"How? I mean, uh, what's that?" said the plaintiff, with a nervous cough.

"We suspect it might have been fed to your horses, who dutifully passed it through their systems, before dying suddenly to a massive poisonous overdose of it."

"That can't be. It's that witch, I tell you," said Mr Luppy, dabbing at this brow. I put on my serious voice.

"Mr Luppy. That flower is deadly. Its seeds are deadly. Its leaves are deadly. Left alone, it could spread through the paddock that we found it in, possibly contaminating every patch of grass within a half-mile, from which it would spread, and before you know it His Majesty's Most Noble Pyromancers would be visiting your village and turning it into a hearth."

I leaned forward and studied him through my eyebrows. "Now, if you were to simply admit that there is a chance that King's Roon has ended up in your fields, for example through your ill-advised but perhaps understandable desire to increase the market value of your horses, we can request his Majesty deal with your field immediately, and you will most likely get a relatively minor reprimand for Misleading the Course of Justice. Or, we can wait for a few weeks, perhaps a month, when the problem is too large to ignore, and you can return to this very courtroom and plead your case against a much scarier lawyer than me as to why you have caused Mass Threat to Life."

The man in the witness stand ground his teeth, bulged his eyes, throbbed his veins... but relented. It worked. He caved. Luppy admitted that a friend had suggested the idea to him, and that he had sourced the illegal flora from a mutual contact. The deaths of the horses were the doing of his own greed and ignorance. The judge was not impressed, and fined him heavily, telling him he only avoided prison time because of his previously spotless record.

Afterwards, once the judge had left and everyone was filing out, Luppy approached me as I was gathering my things.

"I suppose I'd better get someone to look at that field then," he said, mopping his brow.

"No need," I said, shouldering my bag and heading for the door. "We had an alchemist deal with all the sprouts when we first saw them. The field will have to lay farrow for a season, but the seeds have been destroyed."

A.R. Turner

"But you said! You made me- You said we'd need a pyromancer!" Mr Luppy's face started to turn redder as his voice became more hysterical.

I didn't respond, and left him spitting and swearing at my retreating back. Perhaps even mumbling a curse or two.

Of course we destroyed the plants as soon as we saw them. Despite them being vital evidence, we couldn't risk them spreading. I'm just glad we were able to get him to confess.

Budding curse-breakers: chalk up another one-percenter.

~journal entry ends

4 - Prep

"Erran, meet the team. Team, meet our latest client."

A few nods and greetings from the crew at Lunchers. Erran gave a nervous wave back, which was returned with a firm handshake by Mr Luncher. "Pleasure, my lad. Pleasure. Do you smoke?" he asked with his bushy eyebrows raised.

"Uh, no, sir."

"Oh, that's a pity. If you fancy one, just give me a nod."

"Uh, okay, thanks."

Felix touched him lightly on the shoulder. "We've prepared a little room in the back. Why don't you come with me and we'll outline the ideas we have."

Erran followed Felix and was in turn trailed by a young woman that had introduced herself as Yetty. She hadn't explained why she was carrying a skull in a cage, and Erran didn't feel confident enough to ask.

They squeezed through stacks of paperwork mounted high on desks, every surface littered with mugs, notes, pipes and half-eaten things in various states of decay. As they did so, a clock *thunk*ed from somewhere in the canteen. At last they passed through a doorway into a medium-sized meeting room, with an empty blackboard, a few chairs and a table, upon which was a teapot and a few biscuits. Upon arriving, the clock in this room *ting*ed.

"Ignore the clocks, we've lost the thingy to change the time on them. Help yourself," said Felix, gesturing at biscuits. "I can't guarantee the outcome of the case, but I can guarantee the tastiness of the biscuits. They're Mrs Zwelee's secret recipe, the precise blend of spices utterly unknown to any creature, alive or dead, or so she says."

Yetty reached for a biscuit.

"You can't guarantee the outcome?" said Erran in a small voice. Yetty's hand froze and after a brief calculation she decided that perhaps the delicious treat could wait.

"No," she said. "We can have what we believe to be the greatest case ever put to paper, with iron-clad proof, a judge who happens to be your kindly grandfather, a donkey for an opposition lawyer, and yet some oblique judgement or reasoning pulled out of thin air can mean we lose."

"Oh." Erran looked defeated.

"But," said Felix, giving Yetty a look. "That is not to say it's not worth trying. And, for what it's worth, I think your case is one that we have a good shot at."

"Mm."

Felix walked over to the blackboard and picked up a piece of chalk. "So," he said brightly, and began to draw a stickman. "This is you." Erran blinked at it.

"Okay," he said. Felix drew another stickman.

"And this is your... Is there a word for it?"

"For what?" said Yetty, eyeing the biscuits again. Felix waved his chalk in a circle as he struggled to find the word.

"You know, a... copy-double-person."

"Copy-Person? That could work?" she said, reaching for the teapot.

"No, it sounds... weird. There must be a better word."

"Duplicato?" said Yetty, gathering the few teacups scattered on the table and pouring a cup for everyone.

"What? No. It has to be something that we can use in the court that isn't going to sound... weird."

Erran burst into sobs. "My family don't want to know me," he said. "I don't care what they're called."

"They're called a 'doublekin'," said Racelsus, which caused Erran to stare madly about him. "Down here," she said, clacking her teeth. "The pale one in the cage."

"Who?"

"I'm Racelsus. I'm smiling, but you can't tell. Anyway, call them doublekin. That's their proper name. If you're going to call them anything, might as well do it properly." Erran blinked twice, then accepted the steaming cup of tea pressed into his hands by Yetty.

Felix wrote 'doublekin' over one of the figures. "Okay, that will work." He wrote '=/=' between the two figures. "Now. We don't know

222

what spell or potion or ritual etcetera created this duplicato - I mean, doublekin. We think we know *why* and we know what happened after. Namely, this doublekin took advantage of an opportunity to rip your life from under you and cast you out." Felix's eyes darkened briefly, then he shook his head and continued. "The crux of the argument is going to be proving that you are the original, and, as such, are legally the rightful husband and father to your family. We intend to argue that no one, not even a copy of yourself, has the right to take those from you."

Erran sniffled and reached for a biscuit from the plate Yetty was holding. He examined it. "And how would we do that? We're exactly the same. We even have the same thoughts." He started trembling. "You don't think he can read my thoughts right now, do you?"

"I'll have a check," said Racelsus, and Felix was aware of a faint hum that he hadn't noticed previously. It was like some great brass instrument playing several miles away, and only by straining could you even detect it. But it was definitely there. He felt it.

"What's going on? I feel all weird," said Erran. Holding a hand to his head, he lowered his cup and moaned.

"Nearly done," Racelsus purred. The humming increased. "Just a little pressure now, nothing to worry about. Aaand... there we are."

The humming stopped, and Erran blinked twice at the skull again. "That was you?"

"Yes. I'd suggest having a sip of tea. It will make you feel better." Erran did so, reaching for the steaming mug before he'd even realised what he was doing. Once he'd had a long swallow, Racelsus explained.

"What I did was have a quick look in your mind. I only did it to make sure there was no one else piggybacking on your thoughts. If there was, I'd have been able to spot them and possibly give them quite a shock. I'm happy to report you are completely clean, at least as far as thought-spying goes."

"Racelsus," Felix said with a sigh. "I'm pretty sure I've had to say this to you before, but please ask next time."

"I did!" said the skull. In response to the look Felix gave her, she lowered her eyes, or would have if she had had any. "Or did I just think about it without actually doing it..? I'm sorry. I keep forgetting."

Erran coughed. "When you were… in there, were you able to find anything that can prove I'm not the doublekin?"

Racelsus clacked her teeth. "No, sorry. Without the doublekin here to compare, I can't make any sort of deduction. Even if I could, it's quite unlikely that the court would just take my word for it. I'm not a recognised *expert witness*." She said these last words with exaggerated pomposity. "Like they'd know real magic from their grandad's ars-"

"Thank you, Rass," said Felix, ignoring Yetty's splutter in her tea. He turned back to Erran. "No, that method is too risky. Rass brings up a good point. We have very limited access to the defendant before the trial, so we have no idea how he will be different to you. But, rest assured: there will be something."

He drew a horizontal line on the board. On the left, he wrote: *Sample is taken*. On the right, he wrote: *The doublekin meeting*. He pointed at the left of the line. "This is when your employer and lifelong friend, Gort, took a sample from you without your consent." He pointed at the other side. "This is when you met this doublekin, and all the other stuff that happened afterwards." Lastly, he pointed at the middle.

"I need to know precisely what happened here, in as much detail as you can remember. Without this, the case is doomed."

~

"There!" said Felix, pointing his pencil at Erran. "Say that again."

Erran repeated the last sentence he had said. Felix grinned.

"That's it." He looked at Yetty. "You caught it, right?"

Yetty's eyes were switching left and right, and they gradually widened as she clicked her fingers. She laughed. "Of course! It's so simple when you think about it."

Erran looked between the mentor and the mentee. He had no idea what they had figured out.

"I have no idea what you've figured out," he said.

"Allow me to explain," said Felix. "But before that… can I tempt you to another biscuit?"

Erran took one tentatively, wondering why both of these lawyers were staring at him so intensely as he took a bite.

~

A few hours later, and after a final shake of hands, Erran nodded once more to them and walked through the front door, Yetty shutting it behind him. She turned back to Felix, who gave her a small smile.

"You reckon we've got everything we need?" he said.

"I think so," she said. "Just have to track down a few witnesses to set the scene and figure out how to phrase it all." She leaned against a table. "You don't normally prosecute, do you?"

Felix shrugged. "No, not really. I have once or twice. I tend to find myself on the defending side, more often than not."

"You remember how to prosecute?" she asked.

"Sure I do. It's still mostly done by the docks, right?"

It took Yetty a second to realise the awful joke, and upon doing so, she groaned and rolled her eyes. "Ugh. I thought at least I wouldn't have to hear any of your terrible jokes any more after... after..."

She stopped and swallowed. "...you know," she said quietly.

"I know."

A short silence stretched between them, before they both started speaking at the same time.

"I'd better-"

"I should-"

"Yes, okay, see you tomorrow."

"Yes, see you."

Yetty nodded and walked away, careful not to let Felix see her face. He watched her go, then, once he was alone, retreated to the grey fields, and lay down. He thought of the figure he saw the last time he was here. Who was it? Why did she look familiar? If only he had gotten a good look at her face.

Who could come to this place? This place of death?

Was he no longer alone? Had he ever been?

When sleep finally did come, it was broken and agitated.

~

Tracking down the witnesses didn't take as long as they had thought, and a slot in the courtroom schedule opened up just before the end of the month.

Time passed.

The day before the case was due to be heard, Felix found Erran sitting in the garden. He was hunched over, his back to the entrance to the garden. Felix settled down next to him, and noticed that Erran was resting his face on his hands, in which something was clasped.

"Not long now," Felix said, with what he hoped was a reassuring smile. "Then this will all be done and dusted."

"But what happens if we lose?" sniffed Erran, red-eyed. He tucked whatever he was holding under his shirt collar, where it hung on a small chain. "What will become of me?"

"If we lose, we try again. Then we try again, then again, until we're out of options. And that won't be for a long, long time."

"I don't want a long, long time, if it's without my old life. My family…."

Felix gripped Erran's hand. "I know this feels horrible right now. Just know that we've done everything we can, prepped everything we can, and planned for as many eventualities as possible. And tomorrow, when you're sitting on the prosecution bench and I'm standing there on the concourse, you're going to see that I'm not always as charming and polite as I am right now. I can be a right arsehole."

Erran coughed. "I never doubted that for a minute."

"Oh, I see! Maybe I've changed my mind, I don't want to represent you after all. Good day!"

Felix stood at that with a theatrical huff, flicking his hair back with a maudlin hand. "Never has a lawyer been treated so poorly in all my years." He glanced down at Erran, who had a small, sad smile on his face. With an enormous eye-roll, he sighed. "You know what, I forgive you. I will represent you again, but for double the fee."

"I thought I didn't have to pay anything?"

"For that remark, I'm charging you triple."

Erran chuckled, and sniffed again. He fished into his shirt and pulled out a little metal trinket that hung from the chain around his neck. It was small and rough, but Felix could make out what was probably meant to be a head, two arms and a tool of some sort in the trinket's hand.

"I was wearing this on… the day. It's meant to be Vinna, the God of Honest Work. My little girl, Perra, made it for me. You know how it is, though. I find I pray to him for just about everything at the moment. I don't know if he listens, or cares. Do you pray at all, Felix?"

Felix let his eyebrows raise as he exhaled. "Me? Oh, no, I'm not into that sort of thing."

"You don't believe in a higher power?" said Erran, looking skywards.

"Oh, quite the contrary."

"Eh?"

"I've met some of them, actually."

"You've *met* them?"

"Yup. Well, one of them."

"Yup?! You've met one of the gods and all you have to say is 'yup'?"

"…Yup."

Erran shook his head.

"Erran," said Felix. "I am many things, but a liar is not one of them. Tell you what. I'll tell you about it after the case. Over a pint. Deal?" Felix held out his hand.

Erran blinked, then laughed for the first time since Felix had met him. "Deal," he said, grasping that surprisingly cold hand and giving it a single shake.

"Now get some rest," Felix said, looking up at the setting sun. Erran could have sworn he could see the light through Felix, as if he were made of stained glass. He shook his head and rubbed his eyes, and when he looked up again Felix looked normal. The lawyer looked at him and smiled. "Big day tomorrow."

5 - The Courtroom

The courtroom was in Alondsbury. It was not as fancy as the Placenamia court, but several ranks above the Great Ogtown courtroom, in the same way that Rytingur, Swordsman of the Gods was several ranks above Twirling Burty Bluntblade, the silent soldier-clown of Penchly Bog circus. Technically true, but perhaps missing important context.

The room itself was large enough to house a good dozen rows of benches, with ample space for lawyers to strut about while giving their speeches. At the front was a small concourse, flanked by benches - one for the defence, and one for the prosecution. At the centre was a wooden chair on a small raised platform for the witness to sit in as they were questioned, and behind that a raised wooden dais, upon which the judge would loom, watching proceedings and enforcing propriety.

Judge Deccana was unknown to Felix, but she immediately struck him as either tacitly calculating or utterly airheaded. The reason for this is she barely spoke or reacted to anything anyone said or did. That meant either she was taking everything in and weighing it all up, ready to deliver a perfect judgement in the way a lion pounces upon a stalked prey, or she was thinking about what to have for dinner and would make up a judgement based on whatever she felt like at the time. She was flanked by a large man in bailiff's robes, and a middle-aged woman armed with a stack of paper and a series of pencils.

His counterpart, Defence Counsel Losoja, was more talkative. Though that was not a particularly high benchmark to attain; Twirling Burty Bluntblade would be more talkative than Judge Deccana. One of the wordless monks of the Southern Isles would be more talkative than Judge Deccana. An elm tree would be more talkative than Judge Deccana. Losoja wasn't familiar to him, but in the few brief words she and Felix shared before the case started, she seemed well-presented; composed, watchful and prepared.

A.R. Turner

Why does every other lawyer seem to be in complete and total control? Am I the only one who bricks it at the start of every case? Like I'm making it up as I go along, regardless of how much prep I do?

"Pleasure to meet you, Defence Counsel," said Felix, holding out his hand. She shook it, and replied with a bright but professional tone.

"Likewise, Prosecutor. Good luck, and may we together deliver justice where justice is due, Mr Sacramentum."

Oh, she's new!

Felix smiled. Was he ever this optimistic? Was he still?

"Hear hear. And good luck to you too, Ms Losoja."

They took their respective seats on their benches. On the defence's side was Losoja and Erran, and no one else. For Felix, he had Erran beside him, along with Yetty, and Racelsus in her cage on the table. Behind them were Furbo and Helda.

It had been quite a shock when they'd entered. Despite knowing the nature of their case, of course, seeing Erran, hale and hearty, laughing with his lawyer while at the same time seeing Erran bedraggled and downtrodden, gaunt-eyed and hollow, standing next to him. His Erran had vacillated between glaring at his double, who was ignoring them in return, and positioning himself so Felix, Helda or whoever, was blocking him from sight. Right now, Felix's Erran was sat on the bench beside him, head in hands.

Somewhere behind them (on the defence's side of the room) was Erran's family. Earlier that day, Felix had warned Erran not to approach them.

"It won't go how you imagine," he had said. "All it will be is painful, both to you personally and the case. It's going to be hard, but keep away from them." Erran was doing so, to his credit. He was snatching the occasional glance between nervous twitches, but was otherwise not engaging. Felix pretended not to notice.

Judge Deccana tapped her gavel on her wooden plate. She gestured at the bailiff to her right, who rose to his feet and filled the room with his booming voice.

"The case to be heard is Erran versus Erran, the honourable Judge Deccana presiding. Prosecutor, please begin with your opening statement."

Felix stood up and straightened his lapels, ignoring the sudden dry feeling in his mouth.

Why didn't I prepare a glass of water?

"Good morning, Your Honour."

6 - Opening Statements

Felix stood straight, his hands resting on one another in front of him. In his head, he counted slowly to three, then began speaking.

"To unlawfully take the possessions of another is a crime. This we know. We refer to this act as 'stealing'. The stolen possessions are then either sold by the thief, or they are kept by the thief, to use as their own. To unlawfully take another's life, that is, to take their life away... this is also a crime. In this case, the life is eradicated, not retained. It is taken from the owner and destroyed."

Felix paused, as if in great thought, as if he hadn't rehearsed this speech a dozen times already.

"But to *steal* a life? To retain ownership of the very essence of someone else's experiences, while denying it to them? That is not so clear cut, for it is not often possible. How can one steal a life?"

Another pause, as if expecting an answer. Felix unclasped his hands and began slowly pacing. "It takes a very specific set of circumstances, along with a lapse in judgement and the refusal to see reason. All of these have indeed happened, as I shall explain and demonstrate using the evidence of witnesses and their testimony."

He came to a stop, and clasped his hands behind his back this time. "A crime committed for an understandable reason is still a crime, and there is still a victim. It is perhaps understandable that a doublekin would attempt to seize the life - and all its accessories, such as family, friends, occupation - of their progenitor. It is worth remembering that this is not stealing a life unfamiliar to you; rather, a life you believe is truly and completely yours. The chance to live a full and complete life, *your* true and complete life, at the cost of committing a grievous crime against another? Of robbing someone else of a life of their own? It is a consideration that many of us thankfully do not have to make. Alas, there is someone in this room that did have to make that choice. And, tragically, the choice they made was as selfish as it was cruel."

The eyes of the doublekin were focussed on Felix's. Felix did not flinch away as he met them. The hatred he could feel emanating from the defendant, that furious mouth, those burning eyes... would his client be wearing the same expression if their positions had been swapped? Would he feel the same way towards Felix?

He turned from the defendant's bench to the judge's dais and tried to make his voice sound reasonable and sympathetic, instead of obstinate and overbearing.

"As I stated earlier: a crime committed for an understandable reason is still a crime. To steal from the rich to give to the poor may be understandable. But it is still a crime, and there is still a victim. To kill a man whom you believe is secretly plotting to kill you is, perhaps to some extent, understandable... but is still a crime, with a broad ripple of victims." As he walked back to his own prosecutor's desk, Felix took on a more authoritative tone.

"It is my intention to prove to the court that my client, Erran, is the right and proper Erran. The first and true Erran. And, though to them their reasons might be understandable, the Erran sitting on the defence's bench acted unlawfully and disgracefully when stealing my client's life from under him. It is our intention that by the time we conclude the proceedings today, the right man, my client, will have his life justly returned to him."

Felix sat down and nodded his thanks as reached for a glass of water that Yetty had prepared for him, along with a small thumbs-up. Defence Counsel Losoja had taken to her feet in the meantime, and was waiting for her cue to begin.

The judge met her eye and nodded.

"Thank you, Your Honour. If I may, before I begin, might I make a suggestion? In order to head off any confusion before it becomes a problem, I would like to suggest a means of referring to the two separate Errans. Perhaps we could call my client Defence Erran, and my colleague's Prosecution Erran?"

A good idea. I should have suggested that...

Deccana leaned forward, looking first at Erran and secondly at Erran. She pointed at them in turn, and spoke for the first time.

"Derran. Perran," she said in a low, smoky voice.

A second of rumination from Losoja before she pursed her mouth. "Derran for Defence, and Perran for Prosecution?" An affirmative grunt from the judge. A smile from Losoja. "Thank you, Your Honour."

"Which one is ours again?" Felix heard Helda whisper.

"Ours is Perran," said Racelsus. "It's a good job he didn't have the same name as my uncle Enis."

"Why's that?"

"Uh, never mind, love."

"Hush, you two," said Furbo, though Felix could tell he was suppressing a childish giggle. He knew, because he was too. His focus snapped back to Losoja, who was gesturing with both hands as she spoke.

"...A tragic and uncomfortable incident, no matter which way you cut it. However, if the prosecution's case is to be successful, there must be absolutely no doubt *whatsoever* that Perran is the original. It is through the evidence we provide, and doubtless from the lack of certainty in the evidence of the prosecution, that we shall determine conclusively that Derran is the real Erran, and bring this difficult chapter in the lives of Erran and his family to a close."

She returned to her desk and to her seat. The judge looked at Felix and gestured with her hand in a 'get on with it' motion. In response, he rose to his feet and planted his hands on the desk.

Here we go.

7 - Perran I

"I would like to call my first witness," said Felix. "Perran. That is, my client; Prosecution Erran." He touched Erran lightly on the shoulder, and the man stood. He dragged himself over to the witness stand, back hunched over, hands clasped.

"Witness," said Felix. "Perran. Please state your name and occupation."

"I'm Erran," he said in a small, croaky voice. "Perran." He looked on the verge of tears. "I was a boatbuilder and a family man." He chanced a look at wife and daughter, who were staring at him with undisguised disgust. The witness flinched back, his lower lip trembling. "Now, I'm... well, I don't know what I am."

Felix nodded. "Are you a doublekin, Perran?"

The man's eyes snapped up to meet his, and Felix saw in them a smouldering ember that had hitherto been hidden, like a coal burning through a smothering cloth.

"No." His voice was solid and low, utterly devoid of any wobble or quiver. He held Felix's gaze for a few seconds, then his eye twitched, and he drooped his head down. "No, sir, I'm not."

"And this man," said Felix, gesturing to his exact clone, minus the weeks of obvious hardship and emotional toil. "Is he a doublekin?"

"I don't know for sure, sir, but yes, I believe so. I can tell you for certain that he isn't the real me. I am."

"Thank you." Felix smiled, trying to reassure his client before what was going to be a challenging few minutes. "I'm going to ask you some questions now about the evening before the day you met your doublekin."

Erran stared at Erran, who stared back. His eyes narrowed. "I'm ready," he said.

~

"You were working at the boatbuilders as per your normal routine?" said Felix.

"I was. It was the end of a double shift, as it had been every night for two weeks prior to that."

"What happened at the end of the shift?"

"Pettee got tired and asked Gort to end the shift, and he… agreed to. So we got ready to leave."

"And did you? Leave, that is?"

"Everyone else did, but Gort asked me to stay behind."

"What happened then?"

"He confided in me that the job was not just running behind a little, but it was looking like it wasn't going to be finished in time for the Prince's deadline. I knew this already."

"How?"

"You notice things. We started cutting corners. Gort would get angry messengers in official looking garb. Plus, just knowing what I know about boats, I could tell that it simply wasn't going to be ready in time."

"What else did Gort say to you?"

"He said that he had found someone who could cast a spell, something that would make his workers twice as efficient, or somesuch. He said that he only had enough money for one casting, at least to start with. One casting would only affect one person."

"And did he ask you to volunteer?"

"Yes. He wanted me to be the one they cast the spell on."

"Did he explain in any detail what the spell would physically do?" said Felix.

"No."

"Did he warn you of any potential problems or the likelihood of any complications?"

"He told me there was no way it could go wrong."

"And did you agree to his request?"

"…I did. I was damn unsure to start with. Something about it didn't smell right."

"Yet you agreed? Why?"

"I've known Gort for years. I've worked with him for over a decade. I knew the business was in bad shape, and he looked so desperate… That, and I needed the money. How could I say no? So I agreed."

"Then what happened?"

"He stabbed me in the arm with something to take a sample of my blood, and told me that was that, and that I wouldn't have to do the day shift the next day, only the evening one. Then I went home to my f-" He choked on the word. "I went home."

"At this point, what did you think the spell might do?"

"Objection," said Losoja. "Conjecture. The witness is not a student of the arts, and so any guess at this point would be simply that: a guess."

The judge blinked, then nodded her head. She pointed at Felix to continue. Losoja, unsure of what had happened, lowered herself back to her seat.

That's two of us… I think that was sustained?

"I'll rephrase. Erran, did you have any worries that evening?"

Erran frowned. "I did, aye. My gran used to warn me about blood magic. Warned me it was nasty stuff, best avoided."

Felix nodded. "Thank you, Erran. I'd like to move on to the next day, please." He watched as Erran visibly hunched over and held his head in his hands, pressing his palms into his eyes.

"Okay," he said.

~

Perran told them of the day he had spent with his family. His eyes lit up as he did so, and was more than happy to go into great detail about it. It was as if he had committed the whole day to memory, and delighted in reliving it. Perran told Felix and the courtroom of the late breakfast, the walk through the village and the visit to the sweetshop.

Felix nodded along, occasionally flicking his eyes to Jylin, Erran's wife. She sat impassively through the whole testimony, not reacting, barely blinking, looking as if she wanted nothing more than for the misery to end. Eventually, Perran sighed, then finished.

"Then, after I walked everyone back home, we had a dinner of stewed carrots and potatoes, with thyme and sage, then I put Perra to bed. I told her a little story about geese and ducks having a royal ball, then headed straight to the workshop." He smiled and rubbed his eye.

"When you got there," said Felix, "what did you see?"

Perran scowled, his face twisting. "I saw Gort. He led me through to the main workshop area, and I saw… I saw…"

Perran closed his eyes.

"I saw me."

Felix paused to let the works sink in.

"Then what happened?" he said.

"Gort introduced us and explained that this other… this other me had been created by magic, from my blood."

"And then?"

"Then we started talking. Gort clearly thought we'd get on well. That we'd work in tandem to help him build this bloody boat. I said I wish he'd told me what he was up to, because it complicates things. Gort told me that once the work was done he'd reverse the spell, and the double, that is, the other me, overheard, and got angry."

"About what?"

"Well, Gort was basically saying that he'd end his life once the work was done. Kill him, even."

Felix glanced over at Losoja. She hadn't reacted. *She was expecting that… Hmm.*

"And then what happened?" said Felix.

"Talk turned to our - my - family. Him… *the double*… he said he loved them too and was entitled to spend time with them. But before we could discuss it, he attacked me and ran off. He hit me right in the head." Perran rested a hand lightly on his temple.

"In the head you say? Did that affect you in any way?"

"Yes, it did. My memory became fuzzy, my vision became blurry, and I found it hard to think of words and speak them properly for a while."

"Then what happened?"

"Well, I knew that if he was like me, he'd go back to my fa- my family. So once I'd recovered, I followed him. My head was spinning though and I kept getting confused and falling over."

"Then?"

"When I made it home, my family didn't want to know me. They spoke to me like I was a monster. They cursed me. My double had gotten there first, and turned them against me. He threatened me with a club - my club - and called me a shape-shifting monster. The whole town had gathered to jeer and heckle, then they chased me off."

"And what did you do?"

"I begged Gort to set them straight, but he didn't. He joined in. Then, I ran, and hid, and spent the next week at the bottom of a bottle. Then you found me, somehow, and that was around two weeks ago."

"Thank you. That's all I have, Your Honour," said Felix, taking his seat. The judge nodded, then pointed at his counterpart. Losoja straightened her immaculate cuffs and stood.

8 - Perran II

"Perran," said Losoja. "I am going to ask you for some more detail on some of the things you have said." The witness said nothing, merely watching Losoja as she spoke. Felix watched him in turn, silently hoping that Erran remembered the conversation they'd had some days back.

"This is probably the most important part to remember, when you get up on that stand," he had said, laying down his pencil. "The defence will have one job, basically, and that's going to be to poke holes in whatever you say and call you a liar, uh, in front of everyone."

"Why?" Erran replied, looking horrified.

"They're going to try and discredit you. Our job, as the prosecution, is to present a case that cannot be denied based on the evidence we supply. The evidence will come in many forms, but mostly through witnesses explaining what happened. If the defence can discredit a witness, by catching them in a lie, intended or not, then it raises the question: how can we believe or rely on what they say? And if that happens, it weakens our case. Rinse and repeat until the whole case falls to pieces."

Erran had looked at his hands, then clenched them in defiance. "Well, I'm not *going* to lie, so that doesn't matter."

Felix shared a look with Yetty. Erran glanced up and saw it.

"What?" he said.

~

When Erran didn't reply, Losoja began.

"Please cast your mind back to the day in which you spent the morning with your family." Erran glared at her, to which she only smiled. "Allow me to get the order of a few events of the day in my head. You spent the day walking with them, then went to a sweetshop. Then you went home for dinner. This we have established." She twirled a hand in a circle, almost as if encouraging herself to get on with it. "Then you went straight to work. Yes?"

"Yes," said Erran.

"You didn't stop by anywhere else?"

"No, I went to work."

"You didn't, for example, stop by the local pub, known as Gaman's Cup?"

Erran chewed his lip. "No, I didn't…"

Losoja pressed her palms together, fingers pointing down. "This is important, witness. Please be sure you are telling the complete truth. Did you stop by the pub on the way to work?"

Erran's eyelid fluttered. "I… I went up to the doorway, but I didn't go in."

"You didn't go in?"

"No, I just went up to the door. I could hear people in there, you see, and I was going to pop my head around. But I thought better of it, and so went to work."

"So you did go to Gaman's Cup?"

"Yes, I went to the Cup, alright?"

"Why didn't you think to mention this before?"

Erran gave an irritated shrug. "I don't know, I forgot. I mean it just didn't seem relevant."

"Well which one is it? Either your memory of the day in question is not reliable, or you decided it wasn't relevant for the court to know your precise movements at a time where your precise movements are of grave concern to everyone assembled?"

"I… That is… The latter. I didn't think it was relevant. I didn't even go in."

"Someone might have spotted you through the window. Perhaps someone recognised your footsteps, or maybe they were taking the air when you approached. Any one of them might prove instrumental in this case. Yet you deem it not relevant? Are you concealing anything else, witness?"

Felix stood. "I must object, Your Honour. The defence counsel is both speculating based on a lack of evidence, plus badgering the witness."

The judge tapped her fingers on the table in front of her, then looked down at the bailiff, who addressed Losoja.

"Her Honour requests that you rephrase your question."

Losoja gave a curt nod, barely registering the objection. "Of course, Your Honour." She turned back to Erran. "To your knowledge, are there any other aspects of the evening you might have failed to mention?"

Erran scowled, and hunched forward on his chair. "No."

"You said yourself you took a mighty blow to the head. So much so that your speech and memory was affected. Are you sure that you are not confused?"

"Yes I'm sure!"

"And you haven't suffered any memory problems since the day in question? No confusion?"

"No!"

"Witness," said Losoja. "What's the name of the pub in your village?"

Erran blinked. "Uh, Gaman's Cup."

"Are you sure?"

The witness's eye twitched, but he didn't say anything.

"Witness," said Losoja. "The pub is called Gaman's Pot, not Gaman's Cup. Yet you tell me your memory is not affected?"

Dirty trick, thought Felix. Then he sighed. *Quite clever, though.*

Erran fidgeted. "Well, I just said what you said."

"A sign of short-term memory-loss is to take inspiration from what is immediately visible or audible, and to supplant missing memories for it. For example, if you hit your head and didn't remember how it happened, if you woke up and saw a heavy wooden beam on the floor, you might well convince yourself it was a falling beam that caused it. It presumably works the same for Duplicatos."

Felix leaned over to Racelsus and whispered.

"Now I hear it more… I reckon Duplicato sounds much better than doublekin."

He could feel the withering stare she gave him despite her having no eyes. "And I think," said the witch, "'Ow, please, Racelsus, you're hurting me' sounds better than whatever you have to say next."

"Shh!" said Yetty, giving them both a look. Abashed, Felix returned his focus to the cross-examination. Racelsus gave a *harrumph*.

"I don't have memory loss!" said Erran. Losoja continued, ignoring him.

"A more severe physical trauma might cause more memories to become confused, and so the mind can rush to fill in the gaps with quite remarkable agility. There's even a word for it. Confabulation."

Erran said nothing. Losoja tilted her head.

"Depending on the severity, it might even be possible that one's own identity could come into question. Whether one is a duplicato, or a human, for example. Just how hard did you hit your head, witness?"

"Objection," said Felix, rising. "My witness did not *hit his head*, he was struck by the defendant. And, while he is no doubt a strong man, is he strong enough to inflict such wildly damaging and long-lasting effects with a single punch? Only a medico could say, and even then, maladies of the mind are very complex to fully clarify."

"My learned colleague is correct," said Losoja, to the judge. "But I hazard that any medico we ask would say that, while unlikely, it is possible. As you say, the mind is complex, and damage to the mind doubly so. The court knows as well as I that we cannot rule out that it is possible."

They stood in silence for a moment, staring at one another. Felix narrowed his eyes. Losoja raised her eyebrows. As one, they both looked at the judge, who tapped her fingers once again on the desk in front of her. She shrugged.

"Possible," she said. Felix fought the urge to throw up his hands and scoff, and instead inclined his head, then sat down.

Losoja started to pace. As she paced, she spoke.

"If it is very difficult to tell apart a duplicato from their progenitor, and you are admitting, witness, that you took a significant blow to the head, and you have demonstrated that your own memory is, for want of a better word, sketchy… then how can you know that you are not the duplicate, and my client Derran, is not the original? How can any of us?"

Erran did not answer. He simply stared down at his hands. Losoja stopped walking, then returned to her desk.

"No more questions," she said.

9 - Derran I

Erran returned to the bench and flumped down between Felix and Helda, who gave him a pat on the arm. "Don't worry, I've seen worse," she said with forced cheerfulness. Erran did not reply.

Felix shook his head, fighting off the thin, dragging feeling that was prodding at his senses. The urge to return to the Grey.

Time for that later.

He stood.

For now, it's my turn.

"The prosecution would like to call Derran to testify."

~

In contrast to his double, Derran strode over to the witness stand as if he was getting ready for a fight. He puffed out his chest and squared his jaw as he sat down. Once he had done so, Felix considered him for a moment.

"Witness," he said. "Please state your name and occupation."

The witness tossed his head, like a bull preparing to charge. "My name is Erran, and I'm a former boatbuilder, recently turned labourer."

Unsurprisingly, his voice was exactly the same as Perran's, except where Perran's was soft and pained, Derran's was proud and brash. So too did they physically match one another, except for their bearing and clothing; Perran appeared unshaven and unkempt despite their attempts to smarten him up, and he wore some ill-fitting spare clothes they had lying around in Lunchers, which were made for a man thinner and shorter. Derran looked in the peak of health and presentation. Losoja, for Felix presumed it was her, had even put him in a suit. A suit that fit, he noted with slight annoyance.

"Witness, are you a doublekin?"

"Absolutely not."

That's a pity. If only he'd just said yes.

"You heard the events as described by Perran a few moments ago. I'm going to ask you about the same events, but first: Can you explain your first memories after the spell was cast and you were created?"

Derran narrowed his eyes at Felix. "I don't have any memories like that, because I wasn't made like that."

Worth a shot.

"Of course," said Felix with a smile. "You were once arrested by the local peacekeepers and given a caution. What was it for, and how old were you?"

"What, so if I don't answer this, that proves to you that I'm the double?" scoffed Derran. Felix shrugged, which causes Derran's eye to start twitching in the same way as Perran's.

"I notice you didn't ask *the fake* all these questions," he said.

"I notice you haven't given me an answer yet," said Felix. "Or do you not remember clearly?"

"I remember clearly!" said Derran. "I was fifteen, and it was for stealing a keg of beer from Gaman's brewery."

"And what was the punishment that-"

"Look, what's your game here?" said Derran. "You gonna ask me about me whole bleeding life, now? My favourite kind of cheese, what I had for breakfast, or what?"

"Witness," said Felix. "I am merely asking you some questions about your past. Not just to help paint a picture of the sort of man you are, but also to help understand the connection between my client and yourself. Surely you can see the logic in my doing this? As for why my client, Perran, wasn't asked these questions as well, you will have to take that up with your lawyer." Losoja shot a look at Felix, which Felix ignored. "But, for now I am satisfied."

He paused for a few moments. "I will assume that your testimony up until the point that Gort Redspun, the supervisor, took a sample of blood, will be identical to my own clients. Do you accept this assumption, witness?"

Derran gave Felix a suspicious look. "Yes," he said.

"Thank you. In that case, I would like you to tell me everything that happened from the moment you woke up the following day."

Losoja rose to her feet. "I don't understand. Surely it is the same testimony again, as my colleague has himself just attested to?"

Felix turned to her. "Are you raising an objection, Defence Counsel?"

She met his eyes for a short second, then dropped her gaze, and lowered herself into her chair, grinding her teeth. Felix put his hands behind his back and started to pace.

"As my colleague has noticed, yes, I sound like I'm contradicting myself. I am willing to forgo certain parts of your testimony, assuming that they are the same as my witness. But, there is a clear and definite divergence point between the two Errans. One went to bed as normal, then woke up next to his family." Felix glanced at Erran's wife, as did both Errans. He turned back to Derran. "The other did not. He was created by some sort of magic, woke up or was otherwise created, and spent the day working. So, witness, I ask you this: Can you please explain to me what happened from the moment you woke up?"

Derran shifted a little. He glanced at his lawyer, but Losoja was irritably writing something on a piece of paper. "I... woke up next to my wife, as normal."

"I see. And what did you have for breakfast?"

This time, Losoja did object. "Objection, Your Honour. What could this possibly have to do with the case?"

The judge looked at Felix, who inclined his head.

"Your Honour, there is a reason, but if I must explain it, then it changes from potentially vital evidence to irrelevance."

Judge Deccana raised an eyebrow. The bailiff spoke on her behalf.

"Prosecutor, it is not through such means that objections can be side-stepped. You must either explain the relevance to your point *now*, in front of everyone, or accept that it is irrelevant." The judge agreed by steepling her fingers and leaning in to hear Felix's words.

Felix sighed, and raised his hands. "Please allow me to explain. The hours spent with Erran's family leading up to the altercation were experienced only by the real, original Erran. The double did not spend the day with his family. On this we can all agree. Now, during the testimony of my client, he explained, in some detail, his movements that day, from his breakfast, to his quality time with his family, even down to their dinner and the bedtime story he told his daughter." He turned to face Jylin. "Throughout all of that, his wife, Jylin, did not react. I would have expected that if my client had spoken some mistruth, perhaps making things up as a sort-of disguise, then Jylin would have reacted in some way. Perhaps a shake of the head or a confused expression. But she did not, meaning, I suggest, that everything he was saying was true."

Jylin turned to look at him, a look of wide-eyed shock on her face.

"Therefore," said Felix. "I intend to question Derran about the same events, and look to see if the reaction on his wife's face is the same. For example, what if he is unable to recall any of the specific events of that day? Or perhaps doesn't know any of the detail? Of course, he has heard the story already once from my client, so even if he does have gaps, he might be able to remember them. But… all of them? This is what I intend to test."

The judge considered this, then shrugged. "Interesting," she said.

"It would have been," sighed Felix, "but I fear that explaining it might have also ruined it."

Losoja had leaned over and was talking to Jylin, who was biting her lip, her eyes still wide open. After a moment, Jylin's expression hardened into stone, and Losoja straightened. "Objection withdrawn," she said, sitting down. Felix pondered this.

That's interesting. I was expecting her to leave. I would have advised her to. Hmm.

"So, after all that, witness: What did you have for breakfast?"

Derran's mouth and eye twitched together. "I don't recall," he said.

Felix raised his eyebrows. "Don't recall?"

"A lot happened on that day, and a lot has happened since. I don't remember some of that stuff. Only the important stuff."

Jylin's mouth tightened.

"So the day of quality time with your family wasn't important?" said Felix.

"No, that's not what I meant! I mean, with the double, and everything."

"What bedtime story did you tell your daughter that evening, witness?"

He blinked several times in quick succession. "Uh, it was about ducks and, hm, geese."

"I see. And where did you all go during the day?" said Felix, immediately after the answer, not letting a moment of silence build.

Derran fidgeted. "The, ah, sweetshop, and the, the river. I don't remember it all, I've told you!"

"What did you have for dinner?"

"Potatoes! With sage. Potato soup."

Throughout these questions, Jylin's face attempted to remain as hard as stone. By the final one, it was starting to crack.

"What did you say to your wife before you left for work?" Felix asked. Derran chewed his lip, avoiding his wife's gaze.

"I said…" he coughed. "I said: 'don't wait up for me, I'll see you later', then I kissed her on the cheek and left."

"That's all? No-"

He was interrupted by a small scuffling sound from somewhere behind him. Turning, he saw Jylin had stood up, red faced, but Losoja was ready for her. The two women exchanged heated whispers, but Jylin shook her head and began stomping off, dragging her daughter behind her. Derran watched her go, a pained look on his face.

"I'm sorry!" he called after her. "I've had a lot going on! I haven't been able to remember everything like I wish I could have!"

He looked at his wife's back as she left the courtroom, then slowly slid his eyes to Felix's. Felix, for his part, was the very picture of sympathy.

"You can understand my concern, witness," he said. "It almost seems as if you have no clear memory of the day in question. Do you have an explanation for this?"

Derran narrowed his eyes. "I've had a lot on my mind," he said eventually.

"I see," said Felix. "I have no further questions," he said, returning to his chair.

10 - Derran II

"Witness," said Losoja, standing up. If she was feeling frustrated, she was hiding it well. Derran looked at her, his eyes pleading for help. "Thank you for your testimony. It is clear you have had a challenging few weeks, and I would argue that anyone going through such a period of heightened stress would find their memory a little shaky." He chewed his lip, then nodded. She turned to the judge.

"I would ask the court to consider something. Duplicatos, or Doublekins, or changelings, are creatures of shadow and mischief. They copy their victims, insinuating themselves into their image for their own purposes. Their very life depends on going undetected. For this reason, these creatures are adept at lying. They must be able to lie confidently, at length, and with such skill that no one would question their accuracy - not even their own loved ones, on some occasion."

"Objection," Felix said, and stood. The judge didn't react, which he took as permission to continue. "Excuse me, Your Honour, but is my learned colleague suggesting that the entire testimony of my client was a fabrication, and that it went undetected by Erran's wife? You must accept that it is a stretch."

"Does the prosecution know Jylin's demeanour?" said Losoja. "Perhaps she is a quiet person, unlikely to break into emotive outbursts, even when hearing uncomfortable testimony? Can they prove that Jylin was even listening? Perhaps she did not want to interrupt court proceedings with her misgivings? Or she was withdrawn into her own thoughts, simply wanting this event to end?"

"Then, Your Honour, why did she attend, if it was not somewhere she could cope to be? And she clearly is prone to outbursts, otherwise why would she have left just now?"

"She is here to support her husband. My client-"

"Stop," said the judge. She looked at the bailiff, who nodded.

"Unless you are calling the wife as a witness," said the bailiff, "such speculation will not continue. Does the prosecutor wish to call the wife as a witness?"

"Prosecutor?" said the judge. Felix pursed his lips.

Hmm.

He sat down, saying nothing. "I withdraw my objection, Your Honour." Losoja continued.

"To summarise; I posit that any creature that bases its existence on impersonating a sentient being - particularly a human - must be a very good liar. I also suggest that any human undergoing such a stressful time as my client has undergone is perfectly able to experience memory loss, or confusion. Therefore, we cannot with certainty say that the testimony given by Perran is true. Not without subjecting Jylin to testify, which she is not in a fit state to do. And should a wife testify against her husband? Can we be sure of unbiased answers? And she is upset, as can be seen by her departure. Can we rely on her for a cogent response?"

The judge considered this. After a few moments she gave a shrug. Erran gripped at Felix's sleeve, or tried to, his fingers passing through his ghostly clothing. "What are they saying?" he whispered.

"That the only way to prove what happened on the day before the altercation is to question your wife, but they're suggesting she's both biased and not emotionally stable enough to answer," he replied. "I don't think we're going to get her on the witness stand. That might be a good thing."

Losoja took the judge's shrug as an affirmative. She turned back to Derran, who looked as confused as Perran. "Witness. Are you the duplicato?"

He shook himself back to focus. "No!" he said.

"Thank you. That is all," said Losoja, settling herself back down. Derran, confused, slowly stood up, and went to join her. They shared some whispered conversations. The bailiff cleared his throat.

"Next witness," he said.

11 - The Supervisor I

"I would like to call my next witness," said Felix. "Gort Redspun, owner and supervisor of Redspun Shipwrights."

The doors towards the back of the courtroom opened and a portly red-faced man walked through, decidedly not glancing at either Erran as he did so. He made his way to the witness stand and settled in it, looking thoroughly miserable as he fiddled with his bedraggled shirtsleeves.

"Witness," said Felix, staring at Gort Redspun, who visibly shrivelled from the scrutiny. "State your name and occupation, please."

"Ugh..." The witness gave a thick, wet throat-clearing, and mopped his brow. "Gort Redspun, and I'm a supervisor, uh, Your Majesty."

Felix raised his eyebrows. "I appreciate the respectful address, but I am sadly not a member of the royal family, Mr Redspun, and unless you know any single and desperate princes or princesses, that's unlikely to change." He darted an eye at the judge to see how she reacted, but she was as inscrutable as ever. *Immune to jokes, as well.* "What do you supervise?"

"B-boat building, milord."

"I own no land, much to my disappointment, so I am not a lord, either. Where do you build boats?"

"Uh, down at West Feasty, Your Honour."

"You're getting closer, witness, but I am a mere lawyer, not a judge. If you find it easier, you can call me Mr Sacramentum, or simply 'mister', or even leave any sort of address off entirely. Okay?"

"Oh, uh, okay." The man seemed to relax a fraction.

"Wonderful," said Felix. "First off. A quick question." Felix stood in the middle of the floor, equally spread between the Defence and the Prosecution benches. He raised his hands outwards, palms forwards, then slowly closed each fist until one finger pointed at each of the two identical men sitting on opposite sides of the room.

"Which of these is the original Erran?"

255

Gort sniffed and looked between them.

One, well-dressed and smartly presented, sitting upright next to Defence Counsel Losoja with his hands folded in his lap, the picture of proud dignity and quiet determination. The other, ragged, filthy, nervous, desperate, hunched over, staring back at him with bloodshot eyes that twitched spasmodically. He gestured at the one on the Defence's side. "That one is the original." Felix did not react.

No real surprise there.

"You are sure?"

"Quite sure, sir, uh, Mr Shocromentam."

Wrong.

"Okay," said Felix, tapping his fingers together. "So, you are a supervisor for a boat-building company down at West Feasty. Tell me, how is business?"

Gort looked visibly relieved to have gotten over the question he was clearly most nervous about. To be able to complain about his work was a realm he was much more comfortable in. That, or perhaps he thought this simple identification of the correct Erran was all that was required of him, and now it was done, the rest would be easy.

Wrong.

"How *was* business, you mean," he said, with a sigh.

"Are you no longer in the trade, then?"

"No, not right now. Since all this happened, I've lost all my contracts, and I won't get reimbursed for the time spent, nor materials wasted neither."

Felix began to pace slowly back and forth across the concourse, clasping his hands behind his back as he did so. Gort followed him with his eyes, and fidgeted with the sleeves of his stained blue shirt again.

"Cast your mind back to the day in question," said Felix. "How was business at that point?"

"Well, very good, I suppose. We had no end of work. Too much, really."

"Too much? What do you mean by that?"

Gort wiped his balding head with a hand. "We had a huge order to make a new frigate for Prince Whats-his-name, and we weren't going to finish it in time."

Felix stopped. "You weren't going to complete the boat in time for the agreed contracted date?"

"No, sir, uh, milord. Mister."

The pacing returned. "What caused you to fall behind?"

After taking a deep breath, Gort sighed again. "Oh, you know how it is. Someone calls in sick, or makes a mistake, or fails to deliver a key component. Then that has a knock-on effect, you see. Without the component you can't fit this part or that part, and your team of specially hired carpenters can't do nothing, and before you know it you've lost a day's work. Consequential losses. That's what it's called." He reached for a glass of water and took a sip.

"Calling in sick, making a mistake, failing to deliver… Consequential losses. I notice none of the problems you've listed are your fault." Felix whirled around to face Gort, a face like thunder. "Do you often blame others for your own failings?"

Gort coughed and spluttered. "Excuse me?"

"It's a straightforward question, witness."

"I… that is, of course not! I mean, I don't just blame everyone else. I'm a man of honour."

"You are?"

"You accuse me of lying?"

"Not at all, witness. I am merely asking you questions. Such as: do you often deflect blame for your own professional failings?"

Losoja raised her hand. "I object, Your Honour. This is, uh, badgering. I think."

"Prosecutor…" rumbled the judge.

"My apologies," said Felix, nodding a head to Judge Deccana. He turned back to Gort, whose attitude had flipped from nervous to vengeful. *A short fuse? A good actor?*

"Allow me to turn, if I may, to the specific job in hand. The Prince's frigate. It was running behind. Why?"

"I already told you," he grunted. "Weren't you listening?"

"No, you have given me examples of reasons why a job might run late, not why this specific one was. I ask you again, why was this job running behind?"

"I don't remember." He leaned back, looking smug. "Sorry, your holiness."

"Witness," said Felix, in his most reasonable tone of voice. "I'm trying to understand something quite fundamental here, and your cooperation would be most helpful."

"Hm. What are you trying to understand, exactly?"

"What would drive a man to fall so disastrously behind his own work schedule that he felt compelled to start magically duplicating his workforce, regardless of the psychological and logistical, not to mention legal, repercussions." He took a step towards Gort. "I want to understand at what point you began to consider this frankly bizarre step, and why you didn't spot the signs of trouble in your business sooner. I want to understand why you didn't simply hire more people, or outsource the work, or accept that the job was going to fall behind schedule and own up to the Prince, perhaps to ask for an extension. Or, why you did not turn the job down, knowing that you were never going to be able to make it on time, unless you asked your overworked staff to go above and beyond to deliver this impossible project." He took another step. "I suppose, witness, to boil it down to a single question: What went wrong?"

The bluster had ebbed away from Gort. He was opening and closing his mouth. "I..."

"Yes, witness?"

"I just..."

"Please speak up."

"I just didn't think."

Felix raised his eyebrows. "You didn't think?"

Gort held his head in his hands, rested his elbows on the ledge of the stand. "The money was too good. And the team... they haven't ever failed me, so I thought they'd cope. Each time I worried we were falling behind, I put it out of my mind, and instead thought of all the future contracts we would get. If it all went to plan, I could finally... I'd... I'd..."

"Retire?"

He raised his head up, eyes shining. "Well, yes."

Felix crossed his arms. "A life of peace and relaxation, unburdened by the memories of the burnt-out husks of your so-called friends that worked themselves ragged for you?"

"Objection."

"I'll rephrase. Did the welfare of your employees ever concern you?"

Gort coughed. "Of course it did! I always had their best interests at heart!"

"You did, did you… Do you think your employees had a good quality of life for the couple of months leading up to this incident in question?"

"Yes! I've paid them well for their labour. Fair wage for fair work."

"Have you? Paid them, I mean?"

The supervisor hesitated, and did not meet Felix's eye.

"Well… They have been accruing payment obligations, which I shall render to them once I have more money to hand. Once our customers have paid me, that is."

"I see. So, you've paid them nothing?"

"Not nothing, don't be ridiculous. I've paid them their standard wage."

"Despite the almost doubled working hours?"

"We're all in this together, you know! I'm also doing those shifts. It's exhausting."

Felix raised his eyebrows. "You said earlier that you were no longer in the trade. That you had lost all your contacts."

The supervisor squirmed.

"Which is it, witness? It cannot be both, surely?"

Gort swallowed. "Well," he said. "You know how it is."

"No, I don't," said Felix. "Which was the truthful answer?"

"Look, I… I lost lots of the work, you see, so now I'm having to do more myself. Okay?"

Felix let the answer hang in the air for a few seconds longer, after which he walked back to his desk and rifled through a few papers. Finding the one he was looking for, he looked up at Gort..

"And how much are you paying yourself?"

A pause. A pause that grew.

Felix lowered the paper then leaned back on his desk. "Am I right in saying that what you pay yourself is more than what the rest of the staff are paid?"

"It is only right that the supervisor get paid more," came a small reply.

"Am I right in saying it's more than double?"

"A little."

"Am I right in saying you have paid yourself for every worked hour, including overtime, while your staff accrue what you called 'payment obligations'?"

Gort did not answer, but instead looked down at his hands. When no answer was forthcoming, Felix put his hands in his pockets and began to pace.

"Back to my question. Your staff are working double shifts for single pay, accruing 'payment obligations' for any extra work performed - i.e., not being paid for it. Meanwhile you pay yourself more than double the rate of any other worker, and for every hour of every shift worked. And you consider this 'fair work for fair pay', and claim you are concerned for their welfare?"

"...yes..."

"Indeed. I'd like to ask you about something else. Have there been any accidents in the shop? Anything that might have prevented someone from doing their job, for example?"

His face blanched. Felix raised his eyebrows. Gort's face twisted with discomfort.

"I know where you're going with this," he said, quietly.

"Please speak up."

"I said I know where you're going with this!"

"Why not save us all time and tell the court yourself?"

Another pause. A deep breath.

"Pilda."

"Pilda?"

"She was... She..."

After a few moments of floundering followed by silence, Felix *hmm*ed. "I actually have an account of what happened to her here," he said, stabbing a finger down on his desk. "I obtained this from Pilda herself, who was too poorly to travel to court. Shall I read it, witness? Spare you the…" He waved a hand at Gort, who did not respond.

Felix began without waiting for a reply.

"I was working on the plane bench one day. The wood-plane was old and rickety. I'd told Gort about it three times that week, but he wouldn't replace it. Just kept saying we had to keep going, or we wouldn't get the boat done in time. I think I was five hours into my sixth day of double shifts when I hit a knot in the plank, and the plane shattered, causing my hand to…"

He stopped, looking at Gort. "It gets fairly graphic from this point on. Need I continue?"

"What point are you trying to make, mister?" he mumbled.

"What happened to Pilda after her accident? Pilda, who was four months pregnant at the time?"

"I…"

"Please speak up."

He raised his face to Felix, eyes shining.

"I asked her to keep working."

"Or?"

"Don't make me…" Gort's voice trailed off.

Felix read the piece of paper. "You said to her: 'keep working, or I'll…' do what?"

Gort whispered something.

"Please speak up. What did you threaten to do?"

"…not pay her."

A few intakes of breath rose from the onlookers behind them.

"You didn't offer to take her to the local healer?"

"No."

"Or tend to her wounds yourself?"

"No."

"Or at least give her the afternoon off to tend them herself?"

"No."

"And all because you did not replace an old, faulty tool. For what reason? Money, I presume?"

Gort shrugged. "She is - was - my best wood-planer."

"Indeed. So, you ignore their pleas to replace old and broken equipment, while threatening them to work double shifts, even if and when they injure themselves on the aforementioned faulty equipment. All the while paying yourself a handsome wage. And despite this behaviour, you still attest that you have your employees' best interests at heart?"

"Yes…"

"…I see."

There was a long silence. Felix the Prosecutor stared at Gort, who did not meet his eye. Eventually, he continued.

"Tell me how you found the witch."

It turns out it had been simple enough. Gort had been complaining of his predicament to a few regulars in the pub, and his lamentations had carried to the corner of the room, in which perched a stranger passing through the village. Once the pub was all but vacated, this stranger approached the slightly-tipsy Gort and offered to put him in contact with a mutual friend who could help… for a small fee, of course. Gort had graciously accepted.

"You were not perhaps apprehensive of spending even more money, with no guarantee of any tangible return?"

"Well, he did lead me to the witch though, didn't he, so it was tangible, wasn't it?" Clearly irritated, Gort's manner had begun to shift back to belligerent. Felix didn't care.

"That is beside the point. A gambler who strikes lucky once should not rely on that luck. I suggest that you got lucky. Was this the first time you'd solicited the services of a stranger?"

"I beg your pardon?"

"Is this the first time that, upon meeting a stranger while in a state of mild intoxication, who offered a seemingly instant solution to an impossible problem, you have willingly parted with your dwindling supply of money in exchange for this stranger's services?"

"Yes! I mean, no. Whatever. I've never done this sort of thing before. Er, except for once, but I spotted that was a scam before I handed over any cash. Er, any more cash." His bluster deflated slightly with each self-correction.

Felix raised an eyebrow.

"So, to clarify: you did hand over money to a scamster?"

Gort fiddled with his cuff. "Uh, yes."

Felix sighed and began pacing.

"So you found this so-called 'mutual friend', who offered to assist. What did they say, exactly?"

After a cough, the witness wiped his mouth. "They said they had a spell that could make any of my employees twice as efficient at working. That it could double their productivity."

"And this, in your eyes, was a solution to your problem?"

Gort snorted. "Yes! Of course! I would try it on my best employee, my hardest worker, that is, and if it goes well, then I'd return to the witch and purchase her services for any other employees who were willing to undergo the spell." Felix stopped walking.

"Interesting choice of words. 'Willing to undergo' the spell. Was it a dangerous spell?"

"No! They assured me that there was no chance of injury or... worse. Not even any discomfort, other than providing the initial blood sample, which would barely sting at all. No worse than a bramble scratch." Felix interlaced his fingers.

"What did you think 'doubling efficiency' meant?"

"Well, that we could get twice as much work done."

"More specifically and literally, I mean. What did you think the spell would actually do?"

Gort shuffled a little. "Well, I didn't know, but I assumed it would make them move twice as quickly or make them twice as strong, or something. I didn't ask. It all seemed too good to be true, so I didn't want to know too many details in case it wasn't..."

Felix stopped him with a raised finger.

"Run that past me again. You didn't know what the spell was going to do, and you deliberately didn't ask, because you didn't want to hear the truth if the truth was inconvenient to you?"

"Well... It sounds bad when you put it that way, but that's not what it... I..."

Felix waited for a more complete answer. When none was forthcoming, he shook his head. "This spell could have been anything.

Anything! A spell that sprouted extra limbs, or an extra head. Perhaps it made them run twice as fast, at the cost of half of their lifespan. Or, as this was just a random meeting with an unchecked magic-user, it could have been a sick individual who just wanted to curse a few gullible citizens for their own twisted amusement while making a quick profit. Did it not cross your mind *at all* that what you were doing was potentially dangerous?"

"It did." Gort's brow was creased in irritation.

"And did it influence your decision in any way? For we both know that you still received these services, despite deliberately and intentionally avoiding any details that might burst this bubble of an idea."

"It did influence me! I negotiated a money-back guarantee if anything went wrong," said Gort. "They were reluctant, at first, but..."

He stopped upon seeing Felix's face, as if hearing himself speak for the first time. His default expression of irritation shifted glacially to one of horror. "Oh," he said.

"Oh, indeed," said Felix. He let the moment fester for a few merciless seconds.

"Did you tell Erran what you were going to do with this spell?"

Gort swallowed, his eyes flicking to Perran. They flicked back. "I... That is..."

"It's a simple yes or no question, witness. Did you, having concocted this plan, inform Erran of your intentions, along with the possible side-effects of what could happen?"

Gort did not reply.

"You could not inform Erran of the side-effects, Mr Redspun, because you did not know what the side-effects were going to be. You could not warn him of the procedure and the results of the spell because you did not know them. You did not *want* to know them. Am I correct?"

Gort looked down at his shoes. He nodded.

"Please speak up, witness. Am I correct?"

"Yes."

Felix waited a moment before continuing.

"I'd like to ask you about what happened after you obtained the sample from Erran and handed it to the witch. Bearing in mind, of course, that you didn't know what the spell did, and Erran certainly didn't. It was, I think, a great testament to the trust Erran placed in you that he went along with your scheme without pressing you for details. Trust that, perhaps, is running a little thin these days." The supervisor did not reply. "So you handed the vial of blood to the witch. Then what happened?"

Gort's face had fallen, as had his voice. No more the belligerent bombast of the righteously indignant. Now, Gort sounded like a man who has just been told a beloved friend has had an unfortunate accident.

"When I went back to the witch a few hours later, I saw Erran. I was very surprised, as I assumed Erran must have followed me there, snuck around me, then introduced himself to the witch. But something seemed a little off about him, like he'd just woken up from a week-long sleep."

"And then what?"

"Then the witch introduced me to my newest worker. She said that he was just like the original in practically every respect; a hard worker, intelligent, and with all the memories and knowledge of the original. The only difference being, this was a being created by magic, instead of by more traditional methods."

"So you learned the witch had made a doublekin - that is, a copy of a person created by magic. And what was your initial reaction? Gort?"

Gort had lowered his head.

"What was your initial reaction upon learning that you had just created a living, breathing copy of one of your oldest friends, without his consent? A being that believed it had a wife and child to go home to? A life. A life that was going to be in serious jeopardy when these two duplicates of each other met, which they inevitably were going to. What was your initial reaction?"

Gort sighed. "...I felt delighted that the spell had worked, and couldn't wait to tell Erran."

Those watching in the crowd murmured. A few words rose above the others. *Deluded. Idiot. Careless.* Felix ignored them and carried on.

"Did the idea of potential complications ever cross your mind?"

"No."

"I see. So this doublekin was created as an exact duplicate of Erran, down to the last hair, and with no plan, no safety net, no thought at all as to how this new creature would act in the world?"

"No, for goodness sake, no. Is that what you want to hear?" Felix was not going to slow down now. He raised a clenched fist in front of him, swinging it slightly for emphasis.

"But you *did* make sure to secure yourself a money back guarantee."

"Well…"

Felix didn't give him a chance to finish.

"And then witnessing the exchange between this duplicate and the original Erran, you saw the conflict. The altercation. You knew one of them, the clone, had struck down his double, and was rushing back to his 'family.' You knew this. Then when Erran tried to go back to his family and explain the terrible series of events that had just happened, only to find this doublekin had got there first and was proclaiming the original Erran was instead the clone… what did you do?"

"I… I thought that…" His eyes blinked and he coughed. "I mean, I didn't know which one was the clone…"

"I don't think that's true, Mr Redspun. But, even if there was some confusion and you were indeed unaware of which one was which, surely the right thing to do would be to explain the situation to everyone the moment the pitchforks were taken out and shaken. The moment one man's life and family were on the line. There would have been a way to resolve this, surely, if you had but spoken up. So, did you?"

A hesitation.

"I will ask again. When you returned to the village to see one Erran standing protectively with his family and one on the floor, knowing that there was every chance that the one on the floor was the original, what - did - you - do?" He pointed a finger at the witness with each word.

"I…"

"I have it in my client's witness statement. Would you like me to read it?" Without waiting, Felix unrolled a piece of parchment that he retrieved from his desk and began.

"My friend and employer Gort then added his voice to the mob, shouting for my exile. Even when I stumbled over to him directly, he ignored my pleas and treated me like a monster."

Felix rolled the paper up. "I suggest that it is no surprise that the doublekin sought out what it considered its family and home. Mr Gort Redspun. If you woke up one day and found out you were a magical clone, and the original version of yourself was not intending to share your family with you... what would you do?"

Losoja, who had been watching the questioning with barely controlled professional detachment, tapped her desk and rose. "Objection. Your Honour, this is not relevant."

"Prosecutor?"

"Yes, Your Honour. I withdraw the question. The situation was abundantly clear to you, witness, that you were one of four people in the world who knew what had happened. The witch, who was long gone. The two Errans, both dead set against each other. And you. The only one who could have resolved this conflict, or, better yet, prevented it from happening in the first place in all manner of ways. Yet you didn't."

A pause. He then gestured at the two Errans. "We know one of these is a clone. We are trying to prove which is the real one. I have a feeling that there is a chance that you know, but I can't prove that. I can only appeal to your morality. I only have your word, which, based on the evidence, I do not count on. My final question to you. In your heart, what do you think we should do?"

Losoja rose again. "Objection. My client is not a judge, and it is not his judgement that we are seeking."

The judge grunted in an affirmative way.

After hesitating just long enough so he couldn't be called improper or contemptuous, Felix straightened. He neatened his cuffs and smoothed his hair. "Understood, Your Honour. I withdraw that question."

Felix moved back to this desk and leaned against it. He had gotten so wrapped up in his own indignation that he found he was quite angry. He'd gotten carried away. *Two sustained objections in his last two questions? Not a good look.* The anger he felt had surprised him more than he was expecting. He took a few deep breaths and watched the defence making some notes, no doubt reacting to his sloppiness in preparation for their own cross-examination.

After a long sigh, Felix stood again. "I have one last question. Perhaps the simplest one, and one I have already asked," he said. Walking to the centre of the floor, Felix placed himself equidistant between the defendant and the plaintiff. The Erran and the Erran.

"Which of these is the original Erran?"

Gort's eyes flicked between the two of them. One, well-dressed and smartly presented, sitting upright next to Defence Counsel Losoja with his hands folded in his lap, the picture of uncertain dignity and quiet introspection. The other, ragged, dishevelled, nervous, desperate, hunched over, staring back at him with tear-filled eyes that twitched spasmodically. Gort swallowed. He started raising a finger to point at the one to Felix's left; the smartly dressed Erran.

Felix fixed him with his hardest glare. The witness whimpered.

He lowered his hand. "I don't know," he said in a small voice.

I'm not going to get anything better than that.

"No more questions," Felix said, returning to his seat.

But I got what I wanted.

12 - The Supervisor II

The defence lawyer, Losoja, was pacing. A lot of lawyers paced. That's why there was a killing to be made for cobblers that specialised in lawyer's shoes. The combination of requiring smart formalwear that had the durability of mountain-climbing boots meant most lawyers paid more for their shoes than the rest of their regalia.

Felix had been in this profession long enough to know Losoja was new at this. Yet, for all that, it wasn't nervousness that gave her away. What was it then? Her optimism? She stopped suddenly and held a finger up.

"It is the prosecution's argument that you, without any concern for your employees, created a duplicato of the plaintiff, Erran. It is now your opportunity, Gort, to explain your side of the story."

"Well, Mr Redspun?" said Losoja. Gort rubbed his eyes and looked up.

"Why should I? I said it already."

She blinked. "Mr Redspun, you have been cross-examined by the prosecution, yes, but now-"

"Why bother?" he coughed, then waved a hand at her dismissively. "Fine, just get on with it," he said, a harsh edge to his voice. Felix realised the man was barely keeping it together.

Perhaps I was too hard on him...

He looked at Perran, sitting a few chairs down from him. The man didn't look victorious or smug. He simply looked broken. How could he not be? Watching him hardened Felix's resolve once more.

"I'd like to ask about the pressure placed upon you to complete these orders," said Losoja. "You mentioned before that the Prince was demanding you to complete his warships. Did the Prince ever make you feel pressured or fearful if you did not meet his deadlines?"

"I know what you're tryin' to do," said Gort, sniffing. "Tryin' to find some justification for what I done. There ain't none."

"Mr Redspun. No charges have been raised against you, and you are not on trial here. I would advise you to answer my questions fully and openly. The sooner you do, the sooner you can be out of here."

Gort was clearly upset. He kept glancing at Perran. Felix's Erran. *He knows. I know he knows. He knows I know. Yet unless he actually says it...*

"Tell me about the Prince..."

Losoja began painting a valiant attempt at a narrative that placed Gort as the victim; a web of pressures from all directions forcing a poor, desperate man to take drastic measures. Unfortunately, Gort was not playing along. Masking her frustration well, Losoja gave up on that tactic when it was clear it was going nowhere.

"About the altercation my colleague mentioned," she said. "The scuffle between Erran and the duplicato. As you have attested in your own statement taken before this trial - a statement you have sworn is true - you say you are certain that you witnessed the original Erran strike the clone down and exit, leaving the clone on the floor. Can you explain the event as you recall it?"

"I... don't know any more."

Felix, despite being on the opposite side, felt stirrings of pity for Losoja. He knew what she was doing. She was trying to remind the judge of the facts as the witnesses of the defence had tried to establish them: the original struck first, and the clone was left behind. However... Gort was not the witness he once was. Losoja tried to coax something out of Gort but soon gave up.

"Thank you for your time, Mr Redspun," she said, before addressing the judge. "No further questions."

A grunt from the judge, and the lead bailiff acknowledged this by standing up. "Thank you, witness," he said. "You may go. The court thanks you for-"

Gort suddenly stood, the feet of his chair scraping loudly, and strode out of the room, not once looking at Erran nor anyone else.

"-your valued... oh well," said the bailiff. He glanced at the judge, who raised at first five fingers, then a clenched fist, and finally two fingers in a swift sequence of well rehearsed hand gestures. The bailiff turned back to the court. "The court shall take a ten minute break. Ten minutes." Judge Deccana tapped her gavel and retired to her chambers.

"That seemed to go well," Helda said to Yetty, nudging her on the arm. "I wouldn't want to be that guy right now," she said, jerking a thumb at the door.

"The thing is," said Yetty in response. "It perhaps doesn't matter that much. He didn't give us any definitive proof that our Erran is the real deal. Did you see what he did do, though?"

Helda looked around and frowned. "Muddied the waters?"

Yetty nodded and smiled. "He created space for doubt."

~

"How are you doing, Erran?" asked Felix when they were outside. The man was clutching a mug of tea and looking thoroughly downtrodden. He shrugged.

"Not Perran?" he grunted. "It wasn't easy seeing them just sat there. What if they reject me again?"

"Who?"

"My family."

Obviously! Idiot lawyer!

"Ah yes, of course. I can only imagine."

"Is it… going well? The case?"

Felix considered this. "On balance, I think so. It's hard to say, but we have at least created some doubt, which is good."

"Mm." He took a sip. "But we haven't actually proven that I'm the real one."

"No, not yet."

Erran hesitated, evidently trying to figure out how to phrase something. "I've noticed that you've never actually asked me for proof. You never doubted my word."

"Proof of what?"

"That I'm the real Erran."

Felix tilted his head to the side to consider this argument. "That's because it doesn't matter."

271

"What?"

"You assure me you are the original, and so I shall fight your corner with that being my perspective, because I am your lawyer. Even if you were the duplicato- I mean, doublekin, you are still entitled to some sort of quality of life, and I am still your lawyer, and will still represent you as best as I can."

He leaned in. "Incidentally, if you actually *are* the duplic- doublekin, now really is the time to mention it."

"But I thought you said it wouldn't matter?"

"It doesn't. I just prefer my clients to be honest with me."

Erran hesitated. "I'm not the doublekin."

Felix smiled. "Good. Right, we're back. You're doing great," he said, patting Erran on the shoulder. "Chin up." Erran gave him a tired smile in return, then they both re-entered the courtroom.

Journal Entry G - The Hunt

Reference case [GvB&S] (Glu v. NorBak&SheSwo), year 1332, Judge Ki presiding.

Ignoring squeals of rage and snarls of fury, the adventurer swings her mighty sword, and the vile beast is slain in one fell swipe. She takes a bloody trophy and returns home a hero, a legend, swathed in glory and cheered by all.

So far, so ordinary. But let me tell it to you in a different way.

An innocent creature is minding its own business in the swamps of Great Orterpul when a woman, armed to the teeth, strides in and attacks it. Despite pleas of mercy and cries of fear, the stranger kills the creature in cold blood, collects parts of its body for her own bizarre purposes, and leaves the body to rot.

A small figure in a broad black robe had knocked on the door to Lunchers one day, and asked to speak to someone. Upon being let in, they accepted a drink of cool water, then they lowered their hood and we saw that they weren't human, but rather, a Nosgoot: that is, a rarely-seen swamp-dwelling humanoid found around Orterpul in the North Country. After taking us all in with large, bulbous eyes, our visitor nervously wringed his three-fingered hands and shifted his weight from webbed foot to webbed foot. He explained to us, in heavily accented Common, that when his wife hadn't returned one evening, he went to seek her out, and found her slain, her decapitated body lying abandoned in the swamp. Nosgoot can talk to trees, he told us, after a fashion, and they had told him the story, at which point he had broken down in tears. He reasoned with himself that if he attempted to approach the perpetrators, he himself would also be slain. But what could he do?

Through some series of carefully asked questions and months of trekking, the Nosgoot, named Gluk, had found us. "Swamp-friends," he had said, pointing at me. "Swamp-friends?"

"Uh, yes, I'm a swamp-friend," I said, tapping my chest with a finger. An image of Great Croaker came to mind. I hadn't thought about that psychic frog in ages. I hoped he was well, wherever he was.

"Please help me," Gluk said, his wet eyes quivering, gripping onto my sleeve. "I fear for my children and family."

We took the case on, of course. We asked what the possible motivation could be. Gluk said he didn't know. He did tell us that some time ago a few younger humans had explored his swamp, tried to steal Gluk's store of mushrooms and what he called *precious metals*, so Gluk and his wife had chased them off. No one had been hurt, though.

After getting as much detail as we could from Gluk, we made enquiries of our own. The guild of bounty hunters in Northtown let us look through their records, and after a while we found it, Samskipti bless the record-keepers. A ragged piece of paper with some words scrawled on it.

Wanted: someone to slay the foul swamp-beasts of Orterpul. Reward: two silvers, a hot meal, and all the ale you can drink in one night.
-Baker

With a little more digging, we were also able to find this 'Baker', plus the person who had completed the contract; a veteran to the scene named Shezza Swordmaiden. I would like to have seen their faces when a representative of the court knocked on their door and politely asked that they appear to explain their actions.

Baker was first. A bitter looking man. We asked him on whose authority he had raised the bounty in the first place, and who gave him the right to order the death of another. He scoffed at us.

"What do you mean? It was a monster causin' a menace to us, that's what bloody right I had."

"Causing a menace? How?"

He'd shifted a little.

"Well, it was stealing our pigs and that."

We had called a telmatological biologist (a very serious looking word which apparently means 'someone who studies in swamps') as an expert witness earlier in the case. She'd been a wild looking woman with fierce eyes and zero inclination to hide her disgust for the defendants. She established for the record that Nosgoot are shy, quiet, and tend to avoid humans as much as possible. They had a fondness for shiny objects, typically metal, and they were strictly herbivorous, living solely off of mushrooms and moss.

(Well, that means they're not strictly herbivorous, Furbo informed me afterwards, neither are they completely fungivorous. I tried to tell him that lawyers don't care about the details, but he missed the joke and gave me a lecture. Either way, it was clear what she meant.)

Anyway, back to the point. It simply wasn't in the best interests of Nosgoot to interact with humans, well, at all.

After I reminded Baker of this, I stroked my chin in thought.

"So what use would a family of Nosgoot have for pigs?" I asked. I used words like 'family' deliberately to remind them that there was a family. A mother. A father. A life. Each time I did I had to stop myself from looking at Gluk, who would sink a little further into his chair, and wrap himself in his cloak a little more.

Baker's face drew into a scowl. "How the bloody hell would I know? All I knows is they're a menace and needs to be wiped out. Can't barely walk down the road without seeing one."

"And even if that were true - which I find hard to believe given their nature and relative scarcity - why is that a problem?" I said.

"Just look at them!"

I let that response hang in the air like the bad smell it was.

Shezza herself was next. She was remarkable in her cavalier attitude to such matters as morality. She had rolled her eyes when I suggested that mindlessly killing some peaceful, sentient creatures just because someone offered her a meagre reward to do so was, perhaps, problematic. After I asked her what her justification was, she sighed. Flinging her hands in the air in exasperation, she tried to explain it to me.

"It's like this, right," she said, in a heady brogue. "The world's a dangerous place, full of all sorts of bastards. Some scurry about on eight legs and drip poisonous slime from teeth as long as my leg. Others wear cheap suits and stand in courtrooms harassing bounty hunters about stuff no one cares about." She settled back, leaning against her chair, resting one grizzled leg over another. "It's my job to go out there and take on the fights that others aren't able to, facing the real monsters and villains. Real danger," she spat. "Not something I'd expect you to understand."

"Oh, you'd be surprised," I said. "But returning to the matter in hand. What due diligence did you undergo when taking on this bounty? How did you know that the target was a legitimate and legal target, and not the victim of misunderstanding or malice?"

She had scoffed. "Go and tell it to the trees, they'll listen better."

"I really think you would do well to answer my questions," I said, trying not to let my frustration boil over. She lowered her feet and leaned towards me.

"Or what?"

Well, I tried.

"You are not a witness in this case," I explained - in what seemed to me like a calm, rational tone but I have since been told was 'a little intense' - "But rather a suspect of both Conspiracy to Murder and Murder itself. I am giving you a chance to explain yourself. All you have done so far is gloat about how guilty you are. Are you sure this is how you want the case to go?"

That changed her tone. She stood up. "Murder?"

I nodded. "Murder. Nosgoot are protected. In fact, they share the same protection status as Goblins and Vowels; i.e., members of the Union, and therefore the same right to life as humanity itself. People often turn a blind eye to them and their rights, but I'm not people." I took a step towards the rapidly paling adventurer. "So I ask you again: What is your justification?"

I'm glad to say that since the conclusion of that case (in which both Shezza and Baker were given custodial sentences), the rules on 'bounty hunting' have been tightened. One can still post a bounty, of course, but only according to strict criteria, set out and enforced by the Guild of Bounty Hunters. If you take on an illegal bounty, you are just as culpable as the person who posted it.

If in doubt, put down the sword.

~journal entry ends

13 - The Witch

Felix stood and addressed the judge.

"Your Honour, I call the witch Hazel to the stand."

Tracking the witch down had been complicated and time-consuming. So much so that Felix himself hadn't been able to spare the time to do the tracking-down himself. The office of Lunchers & Co had had to hire the services of a 'sniffer'; a magically-attuned tracer of spells and spellcasters. (They usually preferred to be called Spelltrackers, but everyone called them sniffers.) Dago, one of the office clerks, had been sent with the sniffer to the pub that Perran believed Gort had been to with the instruction to hang around for a few nights and follow any likely leads.

On the second night, a suspicious looking figure matching the description of the go-between (given by Gort) walked in the door to the pub. After quietly conversing with the figure, and with Dago explaining in great detail (though not exactly *completely* truthfully) that now the sniffer had his 'scent', and they'd be able to track him to the end of the earth. The suggestion of alerting the authorities to the go-between's questionable activities was never fully expressed, but the implication was more than enough for him to relinquish the details of the witch and her location to the pair. Once in possession of this, Felix had sent her an official summons to be called as a witness, and trusted that she would turn up when requested.

Refusing to appear when called was an offence, punishable by time in His August Majesty's finest prison-houses. Despite this, earlier in the day, in the courtroom, a bailiff had warned Felix that this particular witness had been, in his words, unenthusiastic about appearing.

"She was not keen, not at all, sir," he'd said. "Well, at first. She was totally against it, getting all sorts of lairy at us. Then she went off in a huff, and I heard her talking to herself behind a closed door. After that, she came out all compliant as you like, and we didn't hear a peep from her after."

"And you're quite sure there was no one else in the cottage?"

"Quite sure, sir. We did a quick sweep afterwards. No one had left, and no one was hiding."

Who did she talk to… and how?

The witness was heading down the pathway between the seats towards the stand with a placid expression. Felix watched her. She appeared normal enough, as far as witches go. Though, saying that, every witch he'd met had been fairly abnormal in one way or another, so he wasn't sure exactly what a 'normal' witch was.

"Racelsus," he said quietly, then he thought rather than spoke: *What are you getting?*

Not much, came the reply in his mind.

She a fraud?

Oh no, she's a witch all right. Just not a very powerful one. Does that make me sound like a quidnunc?

A what?

You don't use that word anymore? How podsnappery.

Rass…

Sorry, what was the question?

Felix looked at the witness once again.

But she cast a duplication spell, didn't she? That sounds like quite a difficult spell to cast.

It is, replied Racelsus.

So…?

So the question is: who helped her?

"Hmm," he said out loud.

"Eh?" said Furbo, shaking himself to focus. "Did you say something, lad?"

"What's a quidnunc, Furbo?"

The old scholar gave Racelsus a pointed look. "She is."

Once the witness was settled, Felix took a long look at her. She was of middling years, with a deep splash of grey in her otherwise light brown hair. It hung around her in frizzy waves, almost obscuring a weather-beaten and sun-deepened face. She was dressed simply, in a plain brown and grey dress with a white shawl, and she stared at Felix with an expression of total neutrality.

Nothing to be worried about, he thought. *Just a witch of unknown means and powers, here under duress.*

"Witness," said Felix, walking over to her, forcing a smile onto his face.

"Hello," she said in a cheery reply, utterly at odds with her face.

"Please state your name and occupation."

"Hazel, and I'm a witch." Unlike her expression, her manner, in as much as one can tell from a handful of words, seemed open and helpful.

"Thank you. And how long have you been practising witchcraft?"

"Thirty years or so."

"And can you confirm that this man over here," Felix pointed at where Gort was nervously sitting near the back of the room, "approached you several weeks ago and asked you to perform a spell?"

"Yes."

"And you were performing this for payment?"

"I was indeed."

All going well so far... Felix allowed himself a brief moment of optimistic relief. *A good start.*

"And what was the spell he asked you to perform?"

"A spell of..." Hazel stopped speaking abruptly, her mouth still slightly open. Felix waited. The judge waited. Everyone in the room waited.

"...Of?" he prompted. The optimism fizzled away. Hazel's expression was still neutral. She turned her head to consider Felix and gave a small shrug.

"Nope, sorry, I can't remember."

Fighting off his initial reaction to scoff, Felix sighed. "Witness. Be serious. You have been a practising witch for three decades, and are doubtless therefore respectfully proficient at your art -" he ignored the *clack* from somewhere behind him "- and I must admit I find it quite hard to believe that you would not remember performing what is by all accounts a complicated and dangerous spell, less than one month ago. Do you agree?"

"Objection, Your Honour," said Losoja, standing up.

What did I say?

"On?" said the judge.

"Leading the witness. We have had no evidence to suggest that the duplication spell was complicated or dangerous."

The judge considered this. "Prosecutor?"

"My apologies," said Felix, inclining his head. He felt Racelsus give him the brain-speak equivalent of a nudge on the elbow for attention.

It is dangerous and complicated, though.

I know, he replied. *I just have to prove it, apparently.*

I could-?

I don't think that's wise.

You're no fun.

"I shall adjust my question," he said out loud, then turned to the witness. "Do you agree that it would be quite hard to believe that a witch who had been practising for thirty years would forget entirely the nature of a spell performed for a client mere weeks ago?" He took a breath, having nearly run out at the end of that surprisingly long sentence. No mean feat, considering he didn't need to breathe.

The witch blinked, evidently trying to work out the question. "I do, yes," she said, eventually.

"Good. Then, I repeat the question: What was the nature of the spell that the man we indicated earlier asked you to perform?"

She tutted. "Sorry. It has slipped my mind."

The judge *harrumph*ed. "Witness," she said, leaning over, her voice low and gravelly. "I do not for *one* moment believe that you have *no recollection whatsoever* of the events in question. If you do not answer to the best of your ability then I shall seriously consider holding you in contempt of court, and possibly trying you for deliberate Misleading of Justice. Do I make myself quite clear?"

Felix was shocked. To hear so many words from Judge Deccana was like hearing Prosecutor Ettyson burst into song.

"Yes, quite," said the witch, frowning. This change in expression, coupled with the judge's sudden loquacity, was threatening to send Felix into a spiral of shock from which he might never recover. The judge settled back, opening a hand to Felix. He shook off his stupefaction and turned to Hazel.

"In that case, for the final time: What was the spell that Supervisor Gort Redspun asked you to perform for him three weeks ago?"

The witch looked at the judge and her eyes narrowed. "I cannot recall."

"Enough," said the judge. "Bailiff. Perhaps a few hours with chains around her ankles will help to jog her memory."

One of the armoured bailiffs trotted over to Hazel and gestured for her to follow. She did, not even looking at Felix, and was led to a space usually reserved for the most dangerous of criminals, or any victims of the judge's ire. A shackle was attached to her ankles, which was then attached to the floor via a strong iron ring.

The judge tapped her gavel on the wooden plate. "Prosecutor. Please continue. I would suggest that we try to question the witness Hazel later on."

*She must be **really** irritated to be using so many words.*

"Thank you, Your Honour," said Felix. He glanced at the witch, who seemed unperturbed by the events happening around and to her.

She refuses to testify. Then she suddenly decides to come, before delivering an empty testimony that lands her in just as much hot water as not turning up. What is her angle? Who did she speak to?

14 - Shimma

This would be their last witness, the one that Felix had been building up to. Felix mulled over their position as everyone filed back into the courtroom. The problem with this case was the evidence.

There wasn't any.

There was no biological way to distinguish Perran and Derran, at least none that he or his team had uncovered. According to Racelsus, there was no spell that would identify which was the original and which was the doublekin, at least no spell known to her. They shared the same memories, and had the same feelings. So, in Felix's mind, It was all about fostering doubt. Muddying the waters. Then, when the only thing people were sure of is they didn't know which one was which or what was real, Felix would call their last witness.

He hoped to Habeus it was enough.

Habeus...

The God of Justice stared impassively down at Felix from a carving behind the judge. Above his stern, bearded face was a much smaller carving: that of a blindfolded figure clasping a set of scales. A shiver passed through Felix.

Haven't seen either of those since... that day.

The judge had settled herself down and was waiting for him.

Can't dwell on the past right now. I'll have time for that later.

He cleared his throat and wished he'd taken a sip of water.

"For our next witness, the prosecution calls Shimma Powley."

Shimma Powley watched Felix from the dock with grave suspicion.

She chewed on something evidently gristly, so gristly that it required chewing even when giving evidence. Felix was mesmerised by the disgusting combination of the rhythmic motion of the lump in her cheek and the wet, squelching sound it made as it was worked upon. It was like watching a cow chewing the cud, if the cow was ill with the lurg.

283

Focus!

"All you need to do, Ms Powley, is answer my questions truthfully and completely, to the best of your ability. Okay?"

The old woman squinted at him.

"I 'shpose," she mumbled, swapping sides with a slurp. Felix suppressed a shudder.

My star witness... I get all the luck.

"Firstly, what is your full name and occupation?"

"Eh?"

"What I mean is," said Felix, trying not to miss a beat, "what is your job?"

She looked at him like he was stupid. "Shlop," she said, spraying a fine mist of spittle with the 'sh'.

"Thank you," said Felix, glad he was out of range. He stepped closer to the witness. "And your name?"

"Shimma."

"Perfect," said Felix, regretting stepping forward. He deftly produced a hanky and wiped himself down. "Thank you, witness. Do you remember what you were doing on the... ninth of First Autumn?"

Felix was convinced that every time he needed to give a date that he would get it wrong, no matter how often he went over it beforehand. This meant an involuntary pause before each date suggested, just to make sure.

"Vinna'sh Day?" she said.

"Yes," said Felix.

Shimma coughed. "Yesh."

"Pardon?"

"Yesh."

"Yesh, I mean yes, to what?"

"What?"

Felix entertained the idea of throttling his star witness. Instead, he decided to start again.

"To clarify: do you remember what you were doing on Vinna's Day, First Autumn the eigh- ninth?"

"Yesh, I already told you, yesh!"

"...Can you please tell us?"

"Workin' in the shlop."

"And which shop is this?"

"My shlop, o' course. Are you denshe?"

Felix forced down another small pang of irritation. Was his witness being awkward on purpose? Or was it just her nature? He took a long look at her.

Her face was weatherworn and leathery, the same face you saw on old sailors or mercenaries, and she had the manners to go with it. Around her scrawny neck were a few loose stone necklaces, and her grey and white hair was cropped short. He noticed she was missing an earlobe. It looked as if something had bitten it off.

As he examined her she stopped chewing to spit out a lump of something definitely not worth scrutiny and eyed him up as if she wanted to start a fight.

This woman runs the village sweet shop?

Though, now Felix thought about it, perhaps she had a reason to be a little uneasy. If she'd heard the way Felix had spoken to Gort, perhaps she had been steeling herself for a verbal bruising.

That was different. You're a witness and have done nothing wrong. Mr Redspun, on the other hand... He deserved everything I gave him.

Felix rolled his neck to stretch it out. *I've stared down scarier people than you, Shimma, and I'm not finished.*

"And do you remember the customers you had on that particular day, Vinna's Day, First Autumn the, uh, ninth?"

"Aye. Can I go now?"

"Not yet, witness. These customers on that day. Was Erran Morrit one of them?"

She squinted at him, then to both Derran and Perran, and started chewing again. "He were. Him'n his wife'n their little girl. I wondered why they washn't workin, being it a day of honesht work, but 'shnot my business."

Derran had leaned over and started talking to Losoja in hushed, hurried whispers. Felix ignored them.

"And what happened when they visited?"

"They bought some shweets, what do you think happened?"

"What sort?"

"Hard toffeesh."

"That's it?"

"Aye."

"Your Honour," said Losoja, rising to her feet. "Sweet shops are full of many varied kinds of sweets. How is it that this witness is so easily able to recall the exact purchases made by a specific customer several weeks ago? Does she have some sort of ledger, detailing each purchase for each customer? There was no receipt given in evidence."

The judge looked at Felix, who looked at his witness. "Witness? How do you know it was hard toffees and only hard toffees that my client purchased?" Shimma reached into her mouth and pulled out a warped, mushed, brown lump. She held it up.

"Cos that's all I make." With that she popped it back into her mouth and continued chewing with a wet smacking sound.

Losoja had the good grace to at least look abashed. "I withdraw my objection." The moment she sat down, Derran resumed his frantic whispering. The Defence Counsel waved him down with a hand, nodding and then shaking her head.

"What time was this?"

"Mid mornin'. I know it was cosh that'sh when I usually take my daily exshpulsionsh, and I was feelin' the need when they came in." Felix, along with the rest of the courtroom, decided that more detail on that particular point was not required.

"After he bought these sweets," said Felix, deftly continuing with his original line of questioning to the relief of everyone in earshot, "what happened afterwards?"

"He 'et one too quick, damn fool."

A quick glance at Derran, who was frowning. "Why is that a foolish thing to do?" said Felix, tapping his chin in thought.

"You hash to shuck them first. Warm them up, don't ya?" This was accompanied by a repulsive slurp as if to emphasise the point.

"Why is that?" said Felix.

"If you don't, you'll do what that damn fool done."

"Which was *what*, witness?"

Shimma flung her hands up in the air in exacerbation. "He went and broke hish tooth on it, didn't he? Right there in the shlop. Yowled like a wounded dog, great big lummoxsh."

The defendant, the double, sat up suddenly, looking panicked.

"What happened then?" said Felix, masking back his eagerness to get to the point behind a gossamer-thin veneer of professionalism.

"He pulled the damn thing out and chucked it on the floor outshide. Birdsh probably nabbed it."

"The toffee?"

"The tooth."

"And so-"

A pained grunt came from the defendant's bench. The double had his hand in his mouth, and was tugging and prodding his teeth, one at a time, and evidently hurting himself in the process. Felix wasted no time. He pointed an accusing finger at Derran, just as the man cried out after a particularly hard tug.

"Your Honour, I move that you stop the defendant from doing what he is doing. He is attempting, I believe, to figure out which is the most likely tooth that was lost and-"

The judge raised a hand to stop him. "Bailiffs, restrain the defendant," she said, and flicked a hand at the bench. Three armed bailiffs swooped down onto the double, despite his lawyer's protestations, and held his arms back, one of them on each of his arms, while the third held the double's head up. "None of that, now," Felix heard one mumble.

Felix turned back to the judge. "I ask you, Your Honour: what is that man doing if not what I have just suggested? If he were innocent, why try to mutilate yourself to match the testimony? And, if I may be so facetious, his own lawyer has not yet performed cross examination, and so it may turn out my witness is wholly unreliable and their testimony useless."

"Oi," said Shimma. "Charming."

"And, assuming this is a distinct possibility, why would an innocent man leap at the first opportunity to do what he is trying to do: i.e. change his appearance to match this testimony? Because of this-"

"Your Honour," said Losoja, flustered, jumping to her feet, pointedly not looking at her witness, who was at this moment struggling to yank his own teeth while being restrained by three guards. "I must insist-"

"Later," said the judge. She waved at Felix. "Continue."

"Thank you," said Felix. "The facts of the case are as thus: We know the doublekin was created on the eig- ninth, the ninth of First Autumn. We know that there was at least several hours between the sample being taken from the original and the double being created from that sample. Therefore it follows that the double was a copy of Erran *at the moment the sample was taken.* What this means is that if something were to have happened to Erran in the meantime - that is, between the sample being taken and the whole confrontation in which Gort Redspun was a witness - and that something has left a physical mark on Erran, then we can use that to determine the original."

He spun and gestured to his witness. "Shimma Powley has testified under oath that she saw my client, Erran, break his tooth on the morning of the day after the sample was taken, but before the altercation with his double. I suggest that Derran has just realised that this means the original Erran will have a missing tooth - something which *he does not have*. He is trying, therefore, to break his own tooth and thus render this evidence - the only evidence that can provide direct, biological proof - inadmissible. But I would suggest that by his very actions he has in fact doomed himself. I suggest that it was the behaviour of someone willing to go to any lengths to hide their dark secret - that they know they are the double, and that they know the jig is up."

"I am inclined to agree, Mr Sacramentum," said the judge, with practical garrulity. She stood. "Each Erran shall be examined, and the Erran with the cracked tooth shall be declared the original." She snapped her fingers, the sound carrying further than Felix thought it would. "Bailiff, call for the doctor."

"Your Honour," said Losoja, not looking at her client. Her jaw was set and her eyes were like magma. "I have not been given the chance to cross examine the witness, a right to which I and my client are entitled!"

Judge Deccana gave her a withering stare. To her credit, Losoja only shrivelled a little bit.

"You are… entitled to, of course," said the judge, icily. "But at this juncture, do you believe it will help you - or your client - in any way?"

Losoja's mouth twitched, betraying her almost-calm expression. After a few heartbeats, she finally glanced at her Derran, then at Felix, then at the floor, crestfallen. "I withdraw my request, Your Honour," she said, her voice quiet.

Deccana snapped her fingers, and one of the few remaining armoured bailiffs who wasn't grappling with Derran or eyeing up Hazel hurried off to obey her orders. Within a few moments, Derran stopped struggling and went limp. A few words were exchanged between himself and Losoja, who gave him a hard look and a grave nod. She turned to the judge.

"The doctor will not be necessary, Your Honour," she said. It was at this point Felix realised Derran was sobbing. Despite everything, despite fighting for this exact conclusion, he couldn't help but feel pity for the double, who hadn't asked to be created, and who had done what most other people would have done.

"Because?" said the judge, seemingly immune to Felix's internal commiserations. Losoja bowed her head. "In the face of new evidence, my client wishes to confess that he is the double."

A murmur of muttered conversation bubbled over the room. Erran's wife, who had sidled back into the room with her child during the ruckus, and was situated a row behind Derran, sat in stony silence. Jylin had a grim expression on her face, eyes shining, and Pella, who barely understood what was going on, knew at least enough to know that something terrible was happening to her parents. Perran watched them both with undisguised yearning.

Judge Deccana looked straight at Derran, and gestured for the bailiffs to release him, which they did. He rolled his shoulders and stretched his neck. "This is true?" the judge asked. Derran nodded.

"Then this is at an end," said the judge, lifting her gavel.

"Your Honour," said Losoja, bowing her head again but raising her hands in supplication. "My client wishes to make a proposal." The judge frowned, then lowered her gavel.

"To whom?"

"To Perran."

All eyes turned to Perran, who blinked slowly at his counterpart. All except Deccana, who aimed her steely gaze at Felix. "Does your client agree to hear the terms?"

"I-"

"Yes," said Perran, standing with an arm resting on Felix's to stay him. "What is the proposal?"

"You know what I'm feeling," said Derran. His voice was low and harsh. "And exactly what I'm thinking." Perran nodded. "And what I'm about to ask." Perran nodded again. "Well? What say you?"

"...it's not up to me." They both as one looked to Jylin. "If she agrees then so do I." With the thought arriving like a burst of light, Felix understood at once what they were thinking.

They want to share their life. Doubles of their wife and child.

Jylin glared at Perran, then Derran, then back again. "What are you saying? Both of you?"

"It won't hurt," said Derran. "You barely feel a thing. Neither of you would." Jylin stood up and clutched Pella's hand, leading her back through the corridor between the chairs. "Jylin!" said both Errans at once, in the same tone of voice. She didn't look back as she left.

Derran tried to follow, but the two nearest bailiffs grabbed him again. They turned him to face the judge, who had a face like thunder.

Felix didn't know how this case would end. The best case scenario for the doublekin would be some sort of life-sharing agreement, but judging on how his family reacted, and the judge's face that looked unlikely. *In that case, it'll probably be some form of exile, and a prohibition on the doublekin ever making contact with the family of his progenitor.*

He thought about how he would feel if this happened to him. He concluded within a few seconds that he would feel pretty horrible. Despite winning the case, he felt no joy.

"Your Honour," said Losoja, rising to her feet. "Your Honour, please. On behalf of my client I beg for leniency."

Leniency?

She couldn't meet that terrible look from the judge. "This was a complicated and psychologically distressing case for my client in particular, who-"

"No deal," the judge said, and slammed her gavel on the plate. Felix looked up. Deccana had risen. "The doublekin shall be put to death."

15 - To Death

Felix felt ice in his guts. *Death?* Was it because of him? His prosecution? Has he led a man to his death for acting how any man might? Derran's face fell into despair, and he thrashed his body around.

"No!" he said, and the bailiffs grabbed him tighter. "Please!" A bailiff, the one who had spoken earlier, clamped a hand around his mouth and drew a dagger. "Enough," he said. "Let's be off with you."

Losoja had turned away from him. Her face was screwed up as she sat on the chair by the defence's desk. Judge Deccana had stood up, and was turning to leave. Losoja stood, as was the proper custom when the judge did. Felix copied her instinctively, but his mind was racing. Felix glanced over to Perran, who was looking almost as upset as Derran. Felix was here to represent his client's interests, it's true, but to put a man to the executioner's block as a result of his success? *This isn't right. Have judges always been this gung-ho?*

Felix thought back to the final moments of John Dagger's case. Judgement had been passed, an experienced and respected judge had done their duty as they saw fit for the good of the realm, and Felix had stuck his nose in it and told them to get stuffed.

Here we go again.

"Your Honour!"

Before Felix had a chance to change his mind, he was leaning forward on the desk, hands bunched into fists. He straightened. "This is not the only way. There is… precedent."

Judge Deccana had stopped, and turned very slowly to face Felix. "Prosecutor. Case concluded."

Other judges would have bellowed at me. Other judges had. But those three words… If I had a heart, it would have shuddered.

Felix steeled himself. He wasn't doing this for himself. He represented the downtrodden, the misused, the abused, the voiceless - even if they happened to be his client's opponent.

A.R. Turner

"Your Honour, I would be remiss in my duty if I felt a miscarriage of justice were about to occur and I stood by and did nothing." Deccana barked a single, humourless laugh.

"Injustice?" she growled. "A man has been duplicated. His double is a mistake. He will spread chaos wherever he goes, for he should not exist. He will succumb to temptation to visit his family again, and undoubtedly take drastic measures to return them to him. For his own family's sake, he must not be allowed to live."

Okay, then. Let's try this. Felix closed his eyes as he let the memory of the case flood through his mind, filtering out the details he needed. His eyes flicked open.

"*GurTen v. GurTen/GurTen*," said Felix, waiting. The Judge frowned.

"Purnisto," she said.

"Yes, Your Honour. A case in which a wizardess - Gurrinko - split themselves into three separate parts. In that case, it was ruled that the spell be undone, and the three separate parts reunited together to form the whole once again."

"No. Purnisto did no such thing," Deccana said, folding her arms. "You misremember."

Felix cursed himself. "Perhaps not, Your Honour, but he did rule that if the soul splinters agreed to reunite, to merge, then they should. I think the same could be done here. The double and the original reformed into one." He noticed all eyes were on him. Not just the eyes of an interested audience or an irritated defence counsel. Derran's desperate eyes. Losoja's calculating eyes. Deccana's furious eyes.

"Prosecutor, surely that is the same as killing the double, is it not? He will cease to be."

"Your Honour, that is the opposite of what will happen. He will continue to live." He turned to regard Hazel, the witch. She was still sitting as before, hands shackled, feet manacled, on the bench to the defence's side of the courtroom. "I believe some manner of spell could be conducted to reunite the two parts together, provided the witch Hazel is cooperative." Hazel did not react. He turned to Perran. "That, and my client agrees."

Perran stood. "I do. I wish to reunite." The guard covering Derran's mouth moved his hand. "I wish to reunite as well," he said through gasps. The guards holding him released their grip, and he stumbled forwards. He shuffled a few steps towards Perran.

The judge looked between them both. Then she looked at Felix. For a long minute she stared at him.

"Prosecutor, you are undermining your own argument," she said.

"Your Honour, I don't care."

That did bring a small smile from Deccana, which instantly vanished. She shrugged. "I see no reason why this could not be attempted. If it fails…"

"I understand," said Perran. "There are risks, but I - we - are willing." Derran nodded.

The judge inclined her head. "In light of new arguments, I shall adjust my ruling thus. If-"

"No!" screamed Derran.

Derran suddenly flew at Perran, teeth gritted, eyes wide, thrusting his outstretched hand straight into his face. Perran grunted as he was flung backwards. A boom and a crackle, and a spear of blue energy flew at the space Perran had been, piercing the head of his doublekin, causing it to spasm and spark. Derran's body crumpled to the floor, landing in a heap beside Perran, who began to wail. The witch Hazel who had failed to testify was standing, unshackled, thick chains in a broken heap on the ground by her feet. A light steam rising from her outstretched fingers, which were pointed at the witness stand. Chaos erupted as those in the audience began to scream and rush for the exits. Losoja threw herself to the floor. Felix felt a great wash of power come from the witch, and felt a similar one come from the direction of Racelsus. He snapped his head around and saw the skull actually hovering a few inches above the base of her cage, eyes glowing slightly. Hazel turned to face her, and the two witches glared at one another. After a few seconds, Racelsus gasped, and Hazel gritted her teeth, raising her hands higher. The power coming from Racelsus stopped, and she landed back on the ground with a rattle.

Felix took a step to stand between them. Hazel's mouth curled into a cruel smile, but it was ripped from her face by the sounds of charging feet.

The bailiffs, brave to a man, began to charge towards the witch, who scowled, threw her hands to the ground and vanished in a cloud of crackling vapour. *If Rass hadn't bought them those precious few seconds... if they hadn't charged when they did...*

Too many dreadful outcomes. Felix pushed them from his mind and ran over to Racelsus.

"Rass! Rass, are you okay?"

Ugh, she spoke directly into his mind.

"Are you okay, you ridiculous witch?!"

Yes, I'm okay. The voice in his head sounded strained. *Just winded... Oof.*

Meanwhile, leaping from his seat, Furbo hobbled over to Derran, Helda following at a protective distance, but even the most cursory of glances confirmed the worst. Despite this, the old scholar pressed a hand to what was left of Derran's neck and another to his slack open mouth.

"He's gone," he said, shaking his head. Perran sobbed and crawled over, cradling the body of his clone in his arms.

The judge had stood up, bellowing orders to the assembled squad of bailiffs and guardspeople. "No one exits or enters without my leave. You there! I want a sniffer in here, right away, before the trail vanishes! There should be one down in the lower staff chambers, or failing that Rutter's Row. I need a wizard of at *least* fourth class, or, failing that, a cursebreaker. You! Go to Kicksham's and find one. Tell them it's on *urgent* court business. You!" she said, pointing a finger at Felix.

"Uh, Your Honour?" he said.

"What the hell was that?"

"Uh, I'm sorry, Your Honour, I didn't-"

"Did you vet her before bringing her here, or what?"

"If I may," said Racelsus, loud enough to be heard over the chaos of armoured guards rushing about, despite her voice sounding strained. "I believe she was using Petunia's True Hiding."

The judge narrowed her eyes. "Explain."

"It's a spell that serves only one purpose: concealing your own powers from being detected by others who might otherwise sense you. Once she unveiled herself, her true power was revealed."

"How powerful is she?"

Racelsus clacked and coughed. "Very."

"Hm." The judge tapped her fingers on the desk, before shaking her head. She turned to the nearest bailiff, a man desperately trying to convince a row of indignant old men to stay in their seats, and shouted at him. "Where the hell is that sniffer?"

16 - Conclusive

In a small room set aside for lawyers, their teams and their clients, Felix, Yetty, Helda, Furbo, Racelsus and Erran waited. It had been gently suggested that they proceed there for their own safety, and they had not argued. Yetty had lit a pipe before producing a spare from an inner pocket, lightning that too, and handing it to Erran. Instead of smoking it, he was holding it, watching the smoke drift up in a thin stream.

"Well," said Helda, desperate to break the silence. "You won, at least. You'll get to go back to your home, now. So, that's good." Erran did not look up, and Helda frowned and fidgeted.

Felix ran over the events in his mind. Who was that witness? What was her aim? He had arrived upon several ideas that seemed to form a logical thread. As if sensing his thoughts, Furbo clasped his hands together and asked the question:

"Why?"

Yetty chewed her pipe. "It doesn't make sense." She looked up at Felix. "Does it?"

"Erran", Felix said, speaking low. He grimaced. "This next part will be hard to hear. I apologise in advance for that." Erran did not react. Felix clasped his own hands together and rested them on the desk in front of him. "Here's what I think." He paused. "This witch, Hazel, turned up today to kill you, Erran." Erran held his head in his hands and moaned.

"Why?" he said. "I haven't done anything."

Yetty was frowning at Felix. "Why then," she said, "didn't she strike right away? She clearly had the power to do so. She could have killed him at any time."

"I believe she came here with one goal. If she could not achieve that, then she had another, lesser goal. Her goal was to get the wrong Erran declared to be the double, then executed or exiled cleanly. She wanted to win the case legally."

"Why?"

"Because she wanted a doublekin to be out there in the world, undetected." Felix blinked, shaking off the tiredness he had not realised he felt.

"But *why?*" said Yetty.

"That's the part I am less sure of." Felix chewed his lip. "But think about it. She is the sort of a woman to offer her services to strangers, and for a low fee. Gort Redspun was in financial trouble, so the price can't have been expensive. Yet the spell is complex and expensive, magically speaking. Right, Rass?"

"Yes," the skull purred. "Nothing comes for free, magic least of all, and spellcasters are avaricious, more oft than not."

"So I can only conclude that for her the most important thing wasn't to make money, but to create willing doubles. Doubles that supplant their originals. As for her higher goal..." he looked at his hands, unclasping and clasping his fingers. "That... I have no idea."

Yetty sighed. "And her backup plan?"

"If she could not get the double to supplant the original without anyone knowing, then by erasing the original, the double would be able to take over regardless. Either way, Perran was not going to walk away."

"Which is why she turned up in the first place," said Yetty. "After some convincing... From who?"

"Exactly. That 'who' is a concern. But as to why she didn't testify, it's because she didn't need to. She just needed to be in the courtroom."

"If she had just spectated, there's a chance someone, perhaps Gort, might have recognised her and accidentally singled her out."

"So she had to testify, or at least, give that impression. She wanted to do nothing to help Perran though, so she said nothing and did nothing."

"Clever," said Furbo. His voice became muffled and distant. "Worryingly so. Someone is playing a long, dangerous game." Felix's vision started to blur and he blinked slowly. The room was spinning.

"I need..." he said, then shook his head as if fending off sleep. The others in the room looked at him. He heard one of them speak, but couldn't hear the words. "I need to go." A fuzzy blur reached out to take his arm, but before they could, he vanished.

~

Yetty withdrew her hand, her face falling.

"Uh, does he do that often?" said Erran, glancing up from his examination of the pipe. The ember in the bowl had died down with no one to smoke it, and so the smoke itself was practically non-existent.

"Yes," said Yetty. "We won't see him again for a while."

"On the plus side," said Racelsus, "it means your case is concluded... as if that wasn't obvious already."

"But he just... and what about that witch?" he asked. "My family? Are we safe? What if they don't accept me back..."

"They will, I'm sure," replied Racelsus in a soothing tone. "They will. As for Hazel... she is no longer your concern. I don't think she will come after you. There would be no point." She clacked her teeth. "No, she is a problem for the judiciary, and quite a problem I think she is going to be."

"Will they ever find her?" said Helda, trying and failing to hide her unease. "Wasn't there a sniffer or something?"

"A witch that powerful? If she does not want to be found, she will not be found," said Racelsus. After a pause, she added: "I'd be more worried if they *do*."

Journal Entry H - Wonky

Reference case [E.FDvXX] (EFleDal v. XanXel), year 1337, Judge Oppo presiding.

I've never used a magical staff in anger, or indeed in any other state of emotion. Although, a few of my previous cases would have been much more straight-forward if I could have simply lowered an arcane cane and blasted my opponent into the ether, if perhaps a little more unethically resolved. From my limited experience, however, I understand that they're fairly expensive, and, as you shall see, potentially temperamental.

I think you'll agree that if you had a shortlist of desirably reliable objects, a magical staff would be fairly high on that list.

Some staves, I am led to understand, will tap into the latent or practised magical energies that swirl and eddy in the soul of the wielder. Some are much less picky about who brandishes the stick and will unleash merry hell on anyone stupid enough to wave it about. The experienced and safety-conscious Relictus will contain the infused magic behind layers of balanced containment or nullification magic to stop any - and I want you to imagine all possible repercussions as I use this word - accidents. That way a skilled wizard or similar can 'open' the container and let the magic flow out, before 'sealing' it in again.

On the flip side, you will find bargain-basement Relic-makers who will pump out heaving bundles of the stuff, slipshod and downright dangerous that they are. When you skip the nuisance steps of 'safety' and 'care', it's amazing how quickly you can whip together a magical 'point-stick-at-thing-and-thing-goes-ouch'.

My client was the Elder of Fleety-Dale, a sparse but charming enough town in the West Country that was as poor as it was rural. The town had pooled their money to buy a magical staff to deter bandits. They'd bought it at great expense from a reputable staff-dealer, but had complained that the staff seemed 'cheap and prone to splinters', and none of the villagers could get it to do what it was meant to - fire beams of brilliant, burning light at would-be attackers. The staff-maker, Lady Xele's Finest Staves, had dismissed their claims out of hand as fabrications. Enter Lunchers.

"So you made this?" I asked, glancing up at her.

"We did," Lady Xele replied. I wandered over to it and examined the woodwork closely.

"It certainly looks good quality," I said, examining the latticework filigree on the shaft. "The artwork is very detailed."

"Of course," Lady Xele scoffed at me. "Xele's staves are the best, bluntly, in the West Country." Those in the audience gave a polite smatter of laughter at the slogan.

I lifted the staff and held it out to the defendant, who flinched almost imperceptibly. I asked if she would hold it, which she did with some hesitancy.

"And this is one of yours?" I asked. She glanced at it briefly, turning it so it glinted in the light. She closed her eyes and the staff glowed briefly for a few seconds, a thin vein of light blue power flickered along it, pulsing in the crystal at the top. She opened her eyes and the glowing stopped.

"Yes, without question. This signet at the bottom is my own personal logo - impossible to recreate, you know. The patterns are a sophisticated design that only I would recognise." She held up her hand, showing her elaborate signet ring to me. On it was a ghastly over-embroidered 'X', replete with leaves, sparks and lightning bolts.

"Additionally, the magic used to infuse it is known only to me. This is a Light-Beam Emitter, I'd say of perhaps middle-high to high power. Yes, high. Definitely high. Jycetium-inlaced eaglewood with deep ecto-orichalcum etching, estimated seven thousand year life-span. Multi-lifetime guarantee," she said with a wink to the crowd, who lapped it up.

"So, fairly robust?"

"Naturally," she said. I raised my hands, palm spread upwards.

"One of the premium models?" I ventured.

"Indeed," she said. "One of our most reliable staves."

"Designed for heavy combat situations? Fighting off bandits, and the like?" I asked. Lady Xele gave me a suspicious look. "Answer the question, please."

"Yes," she said, offering nothing else.

I nodded, taking the staff back from her, then took ten steps away until I was standing in the centre of the concourse. I held the staff in a loose hand, like a child might idly hold a broom. Every eye followed me.

"Jycetium-inlaced eaglewood with ecto-orichalcum etching, designed for heavy combat," I mused.

Forgive me a touch of theatre.

I twirled to face Lady Xele, swirled the staff around my head and brought it down on my knee. The staff snapped clean in two pieces. I held the bottom in my left hand and the top in my right, the crystal starting to spark slightly.

"Jycetium-infused-" I said, snapping the lower half into half again. "-eaglewood-" now the top half, "-with ecto-orichalcum etching," I finished, twisting the heavy crystal, popping it from the top of the staff with almost zero effort. "Designed for heavy combat." I let all the pieces drop from my hands to bounce and rattle on the floor. "Remind me how long that guarantee was, again?"

Lady Xele was purple with repressed indignity. "It must be a fake," she growled through gritted teeth.

Her lawyer leapt to her feet, his jowl quivering. "I object to this farce! It is clearly a forgery! Lady Xele is known for her quality and workmanship. This is a ruse of some kind, no doubt constructed for this so-called lawyer's sick amusement."

"My honourable colleague suggests this is a fake?" I asked, my eyebrows raised in surprise. The other lawyer could see where this was going before Lady Xele could.

"Obviously!" he all but shouted.

I had prepared for this. "I asked the defendant if this was a staff of her own making, and she said yes." The penny had not quite dropped.

"And?" he said.

"So either I'm so good at forgery that I can trick the great Lady Xele into believing a fake of my own creation is one of hers, or an alternative is true." I looked at him. "I see two options. One: Lady Xele cannot tell her own work from that of a fraudster who creates inferior stock, or two: Lady Xele creates stock of such inferior quality that I, a mere, feeble lawyer, can overpower it."

I let the words hang in the air. All I could hear was the grinding of Lady Xele's teeth.

"So, Lady Xele, I ask you. Which is it?" I asked.

I let her and her lawyer stew for a few moments before I shrugged.

"I can actually provide the answer myself, in this case. Half an hour before the case was due to start, I walked across the street and knocked on the door of the first 'Staffmaker Extraordinaire' I could find, that of one Kiko Lollop, who I will now call as a witness."

I gestured to the doorway and an usher nodded to someone out of sight.

Kiko Lollop appeared from behind a corner and shuffled forward, covering an ill sounding cough with the back of her hand. Once in the dock, she blew her nose on her sleeve, then sniffed with a lumpy sounding *splek* sound. She paused, leaned over and spat wetly on the floor, somewhere mercifully hidden behind the dock itself.

"Where'sit then?" she said, wiping her nose on her hands, or perhaps her hands on her nose.

"Just over there, madam," I said, gesturing to the small, expensive pile of kindling on the floor.

"You broke it, then? No refunds," she said, narrowing her eyes at me.

"I don't expect one, madam. Now, how much would it cost me for, say, three more of the exact same type, and how long would it take to make them?"

Kiko squinted her eyes and paused for a second. "Call it… twelve silvers a pop and I could have them ready by night after tomorrow. We got quite a big order going on, ya see."

"Do you get many requests of this sort?" I asked. "Fancy looking staves like this?"

"Oh, yes," Kiko Lollop said. "We gets asked to copy all sorts. Doctor Oola's, Jacobson's, y'know, high end stuff. Course, they don't work, not really, but you gets what you pay for. Oh it glows a pretty colour all right, but if a bear comes running at you it's no good to anyone, not unless you want to distract it with a fancy light."

"So your goods are not combat appropriate?"

"Oh no, not a bit. Only thing you could kill with one of mine is a gnat, and that's only if it was standing still. No, they're for show only."

I nodded.

"Do you ever get requests to copy the works of Lady Xele's?"

She hawked and spat again. "Funny you should mention that, actually," said Kiko, leaning forward. "Never a request before, then out of nowhere a month back I gets an order for - and I ain't joking - four hundred of the buggers. Exact copies of the one there on the floor. Some uptight gentleman with this massive moustache asked for it. Paid quarter up front, which is a bit unusual, but it was a big order weren't it? So I let it go, more fool me. Then, when we'd finished, the rest was meant to be paid on completion, but he didn't ever bloody pay, did he?"

I nodded as if this was something that happened to me daily and I understood the irritation of being swindled out of my hard-worked forgeries.

"Can you see the man now, by chance?" I asked. She went wide-eyed at the prospect of confronting the man who had stolen from her, and started glaring around the room, her jaw jutting forward. Within a moment, she had settled on Mr Jenkins, who was failing to conceal his face behind his collars. "You!" she shouted, pointing at him. "We's got unfinished business!"

Two of the bailiffs had to hold her back and the man flinched. He made an attempt to leave, but the judge ordered him to stay, which he did. What choice did he have? When the bailiffs had calmed her down, my questions continued.

"Do you know *why* this huge order for four hundred replica staves was placed?"

"They are not replicas, merely forgeries," said the other lawyer standing up. I gave him a thin smile. "Your Honour?"

"Was that an official objection, or merely a comment of your own?" said the judge. The other lawyer's face turned red.

"Objection," he said quietly. "I would like to state that the use of terminology is not correct."

I nodded. "Let me rephrase, witness. Why did someone order this many staves from you?"

Lady Xele glared at the nervous man in her employ with a mixture of hatred and vengeance.

"Obvious, I think," said the witness "*Someone* wants to make 'em on the cheap and flog them for way too much." She shrugged. "None of my business, really, I just make 'em look nice."

"Objection." Lady Xele's lawyer stood up, eyeing me, face twisted in a sneer. "The witness admits to crime via forgery, rendering her testimony inadmissible. My learned colleague's witness admits to forging the work of my client?"

I countered. "Your Honour, I would say that if it was *my learned colleague's* client who was ordering the goods, it wasn't forgery, it was commission."

"You have no proof my client ordered it," he said, all but jabbing a finger at me.

"The witness has selected your client's associate out of a room of strangers as the one who placed the order. Are you accusing her of lying under oath?"

He turned to look at the witness, who did not look like she was in the mood to be accused of lying. Her baleful eye fell on the lawyer, daring him to voice the challenge. "Uhm... Per... perhaps she was merely mistaken? There is, ah, after all, no concrete... proof." He seemed to wilt as he said it, avoiding the gaze of the woman in the dock.

Lollop herself gave a menacing grunt. "I gots this signet as well," said Lollop. "He gave it to me to stamp into the bottom of each staff to make it look good and proper." She fished about in her bodice in a manner not usually seen in courtrooms before producing a small stamp with a stout wooden handle. After wiping it on her sleeve, she held it out to me, but a throat-clearing from the dais suggested the judge wanted to see it instead. A bailiff took it from the witness and handed it up, where the judge took it, examined it, then pressed it into a sheaf of paper hidden on his desk. He held out his hand to Lady Xele.

"Your signet ring, please."

Lady Xele bristled a little, but twisted the ring from her finger. She glowered at me as she handed it to a bailiff, who passed it to the judge. He nodded, then pressed the ring into the paper again. After a nod to himself, the judge handed the paper to the bailiff who took it back to Lady Xele. The judge stood up to address them.

"Now, if the defendant would kindly indicate to me which of these was her personal, unforgeable signet and which of these is the obvious forgery, I believe we can conclude this case and find in her favour."

He paused.

"However, if she cannot… I regret to inform her that I believe that someone in her retinue is committing fraud. And, it might be in the best interests of the kingdom to instruct the courts to pursue this. It might not. What will remain to be seen is whether it is she herself who is behind it, or perhaps someone in her employ. I would certainly not risk my entire business on a guess…"

He paused again.

"Unless she has anything she wishes to declare, now, to the court?"

Lady Xele blinked twice and started whispering to her lawyer. Her associate attempted to speak but was pointed at by the lawyer and ignored. He started to pale. After a minute, the lawyer stood up.

"Your Honour, we must conclude that someone in Lady Xele's employ, one Wernand Fulcrum, must have been colluding with outside forces to defraud Lady Xele's good name and reputation for his own purposes."

The judge nodded as if this had been what he expected. "As for the matter in hand, concerning Fleety-Dale?"

Lady Xele inclined her head. "I shall *personally* oversee the creation of a replacement staff for them, offered at a severe discount-" The judge coughed. "-by which I mean, of course, free of charge… I would not want them to *suffer* for the actions of one stupid man." She glowered at me. I smiled back.

"I expect to hear of their receipt of their new staff by the end of next week, or there shall be consequences. As for Mr Fulcrum…" said the judge. He gestured and two bailiffs seized him. "We shall hold him in temporary accommodation until all this is *sorted out.*" He struck the plate with his gavel.

"Dismissed," he said.

~journal entry ends

Part Three: Deos

1 - A Visit From Death

I *wonder if I will ever find out what happened to Hazel. I hope Erran and his* *family return to normality. I wish I could be there to help.*

After his customary indeterminate-length existential crisis, Felix propped himself up onto an elbow, then up onto his feet.

No use moping.

Felix stretched his arms outwards and let out a sigh, trying not to focus on the questions he would not find answers to. "What's the plan today, then? Same old same old?" he said to the air. The grey grass and grey sky didn't comment.

Home, sweet home.

"Oh, okay, be that way." As was usual, Felix began walking in whichever direction he was facing. The endless plain had no beginning or end, as far as he could tell, and was identical in terms of features in every direction. He walked, deliberately thinking of nothing in particular.

Time was impossible to judge here, usually. That being said, it never felt like it was too long before he stumbled across someone in need of help. His feet weren't tired, nor was he bored, but it seemed he'd been walking for far longer than normal, and yet had still seen no sign of anyone. That was strange.

Was it just there was no one left to help? That didn't seem likely. Something didn't add up. And what was this odd… sensation? This itch behind the eyes, barely perceptible? He stopped walking, began looking around. Why, and for what, he didn't know. Involuntarily he thought of Jurrekker, the demon that had killed him. Had he found Felix? Would he want to finish the job?

Did I imagine all of that? It seems so long ago, and so distant…

He became aware of a sound, which unsettled him. Normally there were no sounds in this place, other than his own ramblings. He turned this way and that, looking for the source of it. It sounded like fabric rustling in the wind. A subtle sound, but in a silent world, a subtle sound can scream.

All of a sudden *something* caused him to shudder. He turned slowly and saw a shadow. It was roughly the size of a coffin lid, and stood gently moving in the breeze, like silk draped over an arch. *Jurrekker?* If Felix had had a heart, it would have frozen in fear. Something about this archway jabbed at a primal urge within him. The urge to flee.

Before his mind could relay this message to his feet, the veil parted, and a figure stepped through. The figure of a woman, dressed in old-fashioned clothes and carrying a basket, her hair set in a thick brown braid that hung in front of her.

"Who..?" he managed to splutter, before his words died in his mouth. She fixed Felix with depthless black eyes set in a haughty stare. Her face seemed at once ancient and ageless, beautiful and unbearable. All at once it hit him. The braid. That face. The basket. The terrible, terrible weight of those eyes.

"You're-" he said, choking on the words.

"I am," she said, in a voice like... like...

Felix swallowed and forced his voice to remain steady. "And what is the Goddess of Death doing visiting me?"

Skrida, Goddess of Death, The Final End, Soul-Harvester, Wife of Solhiti the God of Life and Fire, sighed, and pinched the bridge of her nose. "I need a lawyer."

~

It took a few moments for it all to sink in. Felix was reminded of a moment in his life where he had first met the celestial being, Cherinda, and she had quite literally descended from the skies and told him that he was humanity's last hope. He'd felt pretty out of his depth then, but at least he felt he could cross off *heavenly command to fulfil divine purpose* from his bucket list. But...

I'd better say something. Something befitting the moment.

"You need... a lawyer?" he said. Skrida sighed again.

"And to think you came highly recommended." She lowered herself onto a chair that had materialised. It looked to be made of swirling shadows. "Yes, I need a lawyer."

"What for, Your, er, Holiness?"

Was that the right honorific for talking to a God? Habeus was always behind the judge's chair, so 'Your Honour' seemed appropriate. The only other time he was talking to the God of Justice was when Felix had been at death's door, and at the time Habeus hadn't seemed to mind any skipping of ceremony.

"I'm not a priest, thank the sun," she said, then scowled at that. A dark scowl, the scowl of, well, the Goddess of Death. Felix felt uneasy watching it. Abruptly, her face returned to its plain expression. "Just call me Lady Skrida," she said, waving a hand, causing another chair to appear. "And take a seat."

"Of course, my apologies, Lady Skrida." Felix lowered himself onto it. It wasn't comfortable, but it would take a braver man than him to ask the Goddess of Death to conjure him a pillow. "Forgive me asking again, but what do you need a lawyer for?"

"I'm getting a divorce."

Now, Felix was not particularly devout. Even having a literal brush with Gods and other minor deities had not inspired him to study the pantheon and its thirteen members, or try to understand the many branches and cross-overs of the interwoven family of Gods that ruled over the entire cosmos. That being said, he had a fairly good idea of the basics, mostly thanks to a combination of Furbo's unsolicited but well-intentioned lectures, and Helda's borderline blasphemous but theologically educational outbursts of swearing. As a result, he knew that Skrida, Goddess of Death was wed to Solhiti, God of Life, and had been since time immemorial.

He had also never heard of any couple (or throuple, or quadruple - these *were* gods we were talking about) getting *divorced*.

"From... Solhiti?" he ventured.

The darkness flashed on her face again, but vanished within a second. "Yes. He and I are treading different paths these days, and as such have chosen to end our matrimonial commitment."

"If I may be so bold… why?"

"*Because*," she said, in a voice as cold as the grave. "He is a philandering, selfish, boorish, aggressive, irritating, lying, unreliable, untrustworthy sack of offal."

"And-"

"And Samveru is making us jump through all these bloody hoops!"

Felix wracked his brain. *Samveru, Samveru… The god - or goddess? - of… what?*

Something clicked. "Samveru, the Goddess of Marriage and Commitment?"

She gave him an awful smile that froze his heart. "The very same. Gods, I hate her sometimes." She waved a hand and a goblet appeared from a twist of black smoke. She took a sip. "It took me an absolute *age* to even discuss the idea in the first place, you know. 'Oh it can't be done, oh it's going to cause a schism, oh what will the humans think', blah blah blah. Can I tempt you?" she said, waving a hand, causing another goblet to appear in front of Felix.

"Oh, thank you," he said. *Whatever it is won't kill me*, he reasoned, reaching for it. *Uh, I hope.* He took a tiny sip. It tasted the way a spring sunrise looks after a storm. "That's smooth," he said, eyes wide, swirling the goblet around.

"Isn't it though?" she replied. *Was that a smile?*

For a few moments they sat in silence. Felix decided to let Skrida be the next one to speak, and so focussed on his drink instead of on the enormity of what was happening to him.

"So, after Samveru *finally* agreed to entertain the concept," she said with a sigh, "there were the practicalities."

"What sort of thing?"

"Oh, you know. Who gets to keep which relic. How the temples get divided up. And, not forgetting, Solhiti is the God of All The Cosmos, and so I am surely entitled to half of that, right?" She took another sip. More of the family tree of the Pantheon was coming back to Felix.

Did Solhiti and Skrida have any children? I'll try to find out in a subtle way.

Felix attempted to look casual. "Oh, and I suppose there is a question of custody of any children-"

At that word, Skrida's fist tightening and her goblet snapped at the stem.

Or maybe I'll just jump right into the dragon's mouth.

Skrida slowly released her grip, letting the goblet fall to the floor with a quiet thump. Felix watched it land with a heavy thump. *That was metal.* When Skrida spoke next, her voice had transcended all human levels of discomfort, and had leapt straight into 'primal fear of the unknown' levels. It sounded like the planet dying.

"That... *abomination*... that *aberration*... is getting... *nothing*." Shadows were gathering behind Skrida, looming over her, flowing from her.

"Uhm," said Felix in a small voice, and she glared at him. He suddenly felt the way a rabbit might feel if he stumbled accidentally onto a lion's dinnerplate. "I..."

She took a deep breath and in a heartbeat the shadows vanished, and normal Skrida was sitting in her chair again. A swirl of her hand and a fresh goblet appeared. "I know what you might be thinking. The histories are full of examples of my husband's... dalliances. All these years I turned a blind eye to them. I had to. For the good of the cosmos. But this last one... To actually bring the result of such... utter disrespect! Such mockery! To actually bring the offspring of one of these extra-marital *flings* into our home and announce him as his rightful and proper heir! That was the last straw, the *absolute* last."

She sipped once more then threw the goblet behind her. "That's when I knew I'd had enough. He had to go. But not without giving me what is mine by right. And, as you can imagine, an ego as big as his, he doesn't want to give me a pebble. I know what *those two* are like... I need to represent myself properly or they'll trick me into agreeing to something I don't want to." A wave of her hand and a much larger horn-shaped vessel appeared. Felix took his opportunity.

"There is... well, in the human world, there is precedent for divorce. Even the divorce of Kings or Queens. It's happened before. Surely

Habeus could oversee that the correct and proper course of action is followed?"

"That old fuddy-duddy?" she snorted, wiping her mouth. "No, he wouldn't do it. Said it wouldn't be *proper*. Pft." She tipped the horn back, sloshing the priceless drink of the gods all over the grass.

"Habeus said... Well, I'm sure he had his reasons," Felix said, not quite believing himself. "So Samveru is presiding, and it is you and Solhiti as the two parties. So if I were to represent you, and I'm not saying that I'm doing that yet, but just suppose I was... Who is representing Solhiti?"

She gave him a look as if he were utterly stupid. "Habeus, of course. Who else?"

~

"Habeus!?" said Felix, finding his breath suddenly a little harder to take, which was unusual, as he didn't need to breathe. "Habeus is his lawyer?"

"Well yes, of course. They're brothers, so..."

Felix took a long swig. Only upon the third gulp did he realise his own goblet had turned into a long drinking horn. He was grateful for it.

"Look, I don't know if I'm the right man for this," he said, swirling the contents of the horn. His fear of the displeasure of the Goddess of Death was starting to wilt in the face of the potential ire of the King of the Gods plus the God of Justice and Judgement joining forces against him. "What can I possibly do against those two?"

"You came highly recommended," said Skrida. "From none other than Habeus himself, in fact. And I've heard your name bandied about a little since then, too."

Felix didn't even register the compliment. He was still in terrified-panic mode.

"But... What... When... If..."

"Maybe this will settle your nerves." Skrida clapped her hands and the drinks vanished. She leaned in close to him. "I haven't told you what I will do for you yet."

"What you will..?"

"The boon I shall grant you," she said conspiratorially. "It has been known for gods to grant mortals boons." Skrida eyed Felix up and down. "Mortals, and... others. I wouldn't expect you to do this for nothing, of course." She leant back, surveying him like a farmer would look at a cow at a market that he suspected had the rot. "Your..." she waved a hand at him. "...situation. It's complicated. That much I can see. Are you dead? Are you alive? I imagine it's hard for you to get your head around."

It was.

"It is."

"If you accept my offer of employment, and conclude the case to my satisfaction, that is, successfully divorce me from my dreadful husband, and ensure I get what I want, I shall return you to the world of the living, complete and correct in every way, the same as you were before your unfortunate run in with that brute Jurrekker."

Felix's mouth opened of its own accord. He shut it again. "You could... return me?"

"I could," she said, and raised an eyebrow. "I could do it right now. I would do so with as much effort as it takes me to brush my hair." To illustrate the point she smoothed her black hair backwards with a languid hand. "A simple flick of a finger and you shall be back among the living. Breathing, cuddling, shaking hands, feeling the warmth of physical affection. No more yearning for this drab and dreary place. The flick of a finger." She tapped a finger on her glass. "What was it you said... Ah yes. That you'd kill for a cider?" She sat back, saying nothing, watching him with cold eyes.

Felix forced himself to calm down. "...Could you just do that for me now? If it is of such little effort for you?" He did not hold out much hope for this particular line of enquiry. *It was worth a try.*

She smiled at him, and it was the warm smile of a comfortable chair after a long, busy day. "Of course I could. But I won't. Not unless you do what I ask and get me what I want." She fixed him with those terrible eyes again. "That is my offer. Help me, and I shall restore you. Don't, or fail, and I shall not."

He thought about the offer. A return to life. What greater gift could he ask for? The ability to be able to just exist without this yearn to return.

Without having to focus his will just to pick up a pencil. To hold and be held.

"Or, if you refuse, I might just make your un-life a torment for eternity," she added sweetly. "In fact, I'll definitely do that."

Felix gave her a weak smile. "Lady Skrida, you have yourself a deal." He rubbed his eyes. "I'll need my team," he said. The Goddess of Death tossed her head, flicking her hair behind her.

"Allow me to kill two birds with one stone. As I understand it, you have only been manifesting in the physical realm to aid and assist mortals that are in peril, yes? Very noble. To remind you of what is at stake, I will allow you to walk amongst the living until the case is concluded." Felix's heartless chest skipped a beat. Skrida caught his expression and smirked. "Not *alive*, of course. Not yet. Just *present*. You may then also spend this time with your team." She leaned back, opening her arms wide. "Am I not magnanimous? I grant you a boon already, giving you early access to the rewards of your servitude before you have even earned it." When Felix did not reply, her smile melted into a neutral expression.

"A messenger shall fetch you when the time comes." A black portal swirled behind her, and she stood up, turning to leave. She stopped halfway, having noticed what Felix was doing. He had his hand held out, trembling imperceptibly, expression serious and earnest.

"I will represent you in your divorce case," he said quietly. "I will do my utmost to get you the result you want, and if I am successful, then my restoration to life will act as payment, only... if I am unsuccessful, then I shall accept the punishment you mete out." Skrida slid her gaze from his hand to his eyes, then raised an eyebrow at him.

"So very formal," she said.

"I look forward to working together," said Felix, inching his quivering hand closer towards her.

She smiled broadly, and turned fully to him. She took his hand and shook it once firmly. "How quaint," she said. Her grip felt like the cold grip of death, because, when you thought about it, it was.

2 - A Return

The sign above the door to Lunchers & Co still needed touching up. The paint was still flaking, the wood still warping. In the darkness of the evening, it looked almost like a prop for a gaudy horror play. Repainting it was certainly on someone's list, whether Dago's, or Mr Luncher's, or perhaps Felix's own list, lying forgotten, yellowing and curling at the bottom of a drawer somewhere. Every time someone properly noticed the sign, it moved up a place on the list. But, as other things kept cropping up, it was always pushed down again. Felix tilted his head.

You know what? I like it as it is.

It wasn't laziness, it was charm through imperfection.

Yes. Imperfect charm. Not laziness. Nope.

Felix raised a hand to turn the handle, then decided against it. It was never clear how long he had been away between cases. The biggest fear he had was that he'd return and find forty years had passed, or longer, and those he held closest to him would have either died of old age, or worse, forgotten him.

Racelsus would always be there, I suppose. If she hadn't gone mad.

Madder, I mean.

The weather-beaten sign and run-down cobbles outside the shop seemed ageless, so he had no clue how long it had been until he spoke to the staff. Was the sign mouldier than the last time he looked at it? Were those new cracks in the wall? He steeled himself to enter, then chickened out.

Stop delaying the inevitable. You'll have to do it eventually.

"Fine!" he said out loud, and knocked, willing his hand to connect physically with the door.

After a few moments, the door opened. The familiar waft of pipe-smoke and claustrophobia hit him like a wet flannel. The smallness of the office meant that anyone coming or going was in the eyeshot of basically everyone, so he was not surprised to see everyone looking.

319

"Felix!" said Yetty, stepping back and gesturing for him to enter. Felix sighed in relief. "Why are you knocking?" she continued. "And sighing?"

Furbo and Helda waved at him as they chatted over a cup of something steaming, while Dago and Merindhe were locked in some intense debate or other, almost hidden from view by one of the desks in the back. The desk the clerks used was the most paper-laden of all, though their newest staff member, John Dagger, was performing a vital yet perhaps the most demeaning legal job there was: acting as a paperweight.

Felix felt the tension ooze out of him. "Hi, Yetty, everyone. How long was I gone this time?"

Yetty and Helda exchanged a glance. Furbo checked an old clock that was taking up valuable wall space. "Well, the case with Erran concluded perhaps three hours ago."

"Three hours? That's much faster than usual."

Skrida doesn't muck around, thought Felix, walking to a stool. He perched on it. "How is Erran?"

Yetty's expression told him everything. "He's gone back to his village with his family. Well, they took a cart, and he walked. I'm sure they'll all be fine." She narrowed her eyes at Felix. "What is it? You're not normally this unsettled when you visit."

Visit... Is that all I am now? A visitor?

He sighed. "We have a new client."

Furbo reached for a biscuit. "Anyone we know?"

"Her name is Skrida."

"Huh funny sort of a name, that."

"Why?" said Yetty, reaching for a biscuit as well. Furbo dunked his into his drink.

"Well, my dear, Skrida is the name of the Goddess of Death. To give a child that name is to invite either bad luck or the wrath of the goddess, potentially." He lifted his hand to take a bite, but his biscuit wasn't there. He fished around in his cup with a long finger. "Odd sort of name, for sure. So, what does she need help with, my lad?"

"She's getting a divorce."

"Oh? Bit unusual for your, hm, typical clientele. On what grounds?"

"The husband is a bit of a sleazy, selfish, disrespectful, greedy, arrogant arsehole, basically."

Furbo tutted and shook his head. "Oh, I see. All too common, sadly. Poor lass." He lifted his cup to take a sip. "Who's the husband?"

"Solhiti."

Furbo spluttered, which degenerated into hacking coughs. Helda thumped him on the back until the old man raised a hand to stop her and looked up. Red-eyed, Furbo stared at Felix and spoke in a raspy voice. *"What did you say?"*

Felix sighed and reached for a biscuit of his own. "Tell me about it."

3 - Prep

Once Furbo had calmed down, the crew met up in the 'war room' - that is, the room that had the one table that was not covered in junk. Yetty, Furbo and Helda were sat around the table, with Racelsus and John perched on top in their respective housings. Dago and Merindhe were stood against the wall, and Mr and Mrs Luncher hovered in the doorway, drawn downstairs by the commotion.

"So," said Felix, hands in his pockets, standing in front of the blank blackboard that took up most of the far wall. "Then she told me a messenger would herald me when the time came."

"What will this herald look like?" said Yetty. The eyes of everyone moved to Furbo, who was nursing a heavy mug of tea. He glanced around them all with wide eyes and raised eyebrows.

"Beats me if I know!" he said, a little too loudly. "Perhaps it'll be a floating cupcake with little bat wings. Who knows anything anymore? Gods getting divorced, Gods popping over to Felix's for a visit. What next?" His eye twitched and he frowned down into his mug. Helda leaned over, nudging him with a shoulder.

"Puh-lease," she said. "The one time when we are all desperate for a little more historical context, and suddenly you're mister sarcastic?"

"What do you mean 'the one time'?"

"Furbo," said Felix. "Anything you can give us will help."

The old scholar looked him in the eye and saw just how earnest Felix was. He tutted and sighed. "Okay, my lad, I understand. It's just it's all quite a lot for me. I've studied these gods and goddesses for my whole adult life. To me, they were always distant things, you know. That whole thing with Habeus rocked me, that's true, though at least *that* was consistent with my readings. With the status quo. But to hear that not just any god, but the two most powerful, terrible gods are fundamentally changing the fabric of the pantheon… why, that just makes me feel all wrong."

He shook his head and placed his mug on the table. For a few moments he stared at it in silence. "I've been used to them looking the same, acting the same, being the same forever. As they were for my teachers, and theirs, all the way backwards. And now... it's all different." When he looked up, his eyes shone. "It just takes me a little getting used to, I think."

Mrs Luncher strode over to him and patted him on the arm. "I understand how you feel. The other day, a certain senior member of this faculty who shall remain nameless decided on a whim to change the upholstery in our bedroom. It wasn't that the new furniture was bad, it was just different."

How is that the same? thought Felix.

To his astonishment, Furbo gripped Mrs Luncher's firm, pale hand with both of his dark, gnarled ones. "Yes! That's exactly it!"

Felix shared a puzzled look with Yetty and Helda, who shrugged. That shrug said a lot. It said: *I know, but what's the harm?*

"It's okay, Furbo," said Felix. "I understand that this is all a bit weird. We can take our time with it though, take it piece by piece. Okay?" Furbo nodded, rubbing his eyes.

"I'll be okay in a minute," he said.

"We can take a break if you like?"

"No, no, I'm alright, I'm fine." He sniffed and smoothed down his lapel. With a smile he clapped his hands together. "Right, what was it you wanted to know? Ah, Skrida's herald. Now, the scriptures are vague in some aspects, but we definitely know she'll have ram's horns. Or, er, antlers."

~

"Divorce is the legal separation of two or more married individuals," said Felix, staring at a blackboard that simply said '*Divorce?*' on it. "It can happen for many reasons, but typically it's when one or both of the parties feel there are irreconcilable differences between the two parties."

"Or the couple find themselves on opposite sides of a civil war," said Yetty, with distressing casualness.

"What?" said Felix, blinking.

"There's precedent. Around eight hundred years ago a civil war broke out over Fowermolde-"

"The Lover's War," said Furbo.

"Right, and there were loads of couples that found themselves straddling the divide - those who sided with the first King, and those who sided with the second. As it was a civil war, the law of the land was still the same for both sides, and in those days you had to have both parties agreeing to the divorce. A lot of these people wanted to get divorced and remarry, but legally they couldn't, so they had to come up with some legal way to do it, because neither side wanted to tick off the judiciary, who were at that time headed by Judge Taclia the Bellicose. Remember the Arm of the Jurisprudent Father? The army that was under the control of the head judge? Strange times. After all the divorce laws got updated, this one sort of just got forgotten, and is technically still in statute."

Felix closed his mouth and shook his head, amazed. "How do you know all that?"

Yetty shrugged.

"Well, let's try and *not* start a civil war in heaven. That would be a bad move all round, I think. Has anyone here been divorced?" said Felix. He involuntarily found himself looking at Mrs Luncher, who met his gaze, prompting Felix to look somewhere, anywhere else.

"I have," said Racelsus.

"You have?" said Yetty. "When?"

"Last week," the witch clacked. "When do you think?"

"Okay," said Felix, resting a foot on the edge of a chair and resting his hands on his knee. "Tell me about it. What happened? What did the courts do?"

Racelsus gave a little chuckle. "Well, we didn't really settle it in court. My brother walked in on him treating me unkindly so he took him into another room, gave him a talking to, and I never saw him again."

Yetty leaned forward, resting her elbows on her lap, holding her head in her hands. "So you're still married?"

"Technically, I suppose, but he'll be long dead by now. Hm, I don't think that was as helpful as you might have wanted it, was it, Felix?"

After a pause, Felix shrugged. "Well, it was diverting, at least. Back to the case in hand, though." He tapped his chin. "Skrida told me that she wanted to leave Solhiti because of a number of reasons. She also told me that Samveru, Goddess of Union, was fundamentally opposed to the idea, but is willing to hear her case under certain conditions."

"Sounds stupid to me," said Helda, crossing her arms. "Lady wants to leave, let her leave."

Felix nodded. "If it were that simple... I didn't explain myself properly. She can *in theory* leave, but if she does that, she more-or-less forfeits her godhood. She won't be able to live amongst the gods, won't be able to enjoy being worshipped, except by underground cults that will no-doubt be the target of quite serious retribution by 'loyal' followers of Solhiti, and she won't get what she believes is her due - half of all the cosmos."

"I don't wish to be rude," said Merindhe, taking her weight off the wall and twisting her back to stretch it out. "Much as I like seeing ungrateful husbands getting their due... the Goddess of Death isn't quite what I'd call an underdog, right? Not the sort of clientele that Lunchers normally handles. So why are we helping her?"

Felix gave a dry laugh. "Have you ever tried to say no to a god? They can be quite pushy."

"But why us? There must be a thousand other lawyers she could go to. No offence meant to the room, but why not somewhere like Jurviles, with their gold-plated doorknobs and whatnot?"

"Somehow, Lady Skrida got my name," said Felix. "She sought me out specifically, on, er, someone's recommendation, apparently." Felix's words came out a slowing mumble as he tried to explain this modestly. "Habeus was busy, and so she wanted me to help." As he moved on to a topic he was far more comfortable with, praising his friends and colleagues, his usual manner of speech returned. "I wouldn't be a tenth of the lawyer I am without you guys helping me, so I thought I'd come here after I'd accepted. I couldn't really say no. You see... I mean, because... That is, if you'd rather not get involved, I'd understand..." Felix found it hard to vocalise what he wanted to say. He became aware of Racelsus's eyes upon him. Or, her sockets. Her voice spoke into his mind.

She offered you your life back, didn't she?
He dropped his eyes. *Yes.*
Do you want your life back?
Yes.
Then that's all the reason we need.
I can't ask-
Quiet.

Racelsus clacked loudly. "Lady Skrida, Goddess of Death, has offered Felix his life and body back should we be successful. Presumably, she will enact severe punishment if he is not. I think I speak for everyone here when I say that is reason enough for the crew of Lunchers & Co to offer whatever help they can, for in this, Felix, *you* are the one in need."

"Hear hear!" yelled everyone else in various volumes, all of which were loud and boisterous. Racelsus continued.

"It matters not whether we are helping two gods get a divorce, or simply correcting a spelling mistake on a written contract between two bakers. If through its resolution we are able to give you back that which you desire and that which was stolen, then we will do it."

"Hear hear!" John's tinny voice was the loudest, in the way a triangle can cut through an orchestra.

"Every one of us has been helped by you, some of us - myself included - directly. The rest, through the small things you do every time you return to us. The things you say, the things you do. The way you embody the philosophy of Lunchers & Co. You have saved us all in ways you didn't even realise. So, we are behind you. No matter what."

"Hear hear!"

Felix looked from face to face, each gazing back at him with furious intensity. Even Mrs Zwelee, caretaker and all-round helpful presence had poked her head around the doorway, behind the smiling eyes of Mr Luncher. She nodded to him. He cleared his throat to stop his voice from trembling. "Then we have a case to prepare." He turned to the blackboard, then back again. "Thank you all-"

"Oh shush, for the love of the gods!" said Racelsus, and everyone, including Felix, laughed loudly and for a long time.

327

4 - Arrival

A week or so had passed. The staff at Lunchers had been working long days and late nights to learn everything they could about the Pantheon, from the great cosmological events that formed reality to their bitter internecine arguments to their favourite tipples. When they weren't researching theology, they were poring over divorce precedent; reasons, arguments, history, loopholes.

On the morning of the eighth day, a gentle knock tapped at the door. Felix heard the quiet footsteps of Mrs Zwelee as she went to open it, then a few muffled voices, and the sound of footsteps drawing nearer. The door to the room he was working in opened, but Felix kept his eyes on the book he was reading, pressing a finger on a line.

"One second," he said, trying not to lose his trail of thought.

"Such strange circles you move in these days, Felix," came a musical voice that Felix recognised instantly. He looked up and beheld a figure standing resplendent in the doorway. The figure of a woman, dressed entirely in white, an aura of serenity wreathing her like a haze. A faint golden glow was washing from her, and she returned his gaze with a smile playing on her face.

"Cherinda!" he said, jumping to his feet, all thoughts of research forgotten. He took a step towards her and narrowed his eyes at her in false suspicion. "Since when did you use doors?"

She ignored his question and glided over to where he stood, then embraced him. He felt a calm sense of relief, of being unburdened, wash over him as she did so. He was aware of not having to manifest himself to feel the embrace, and surrendered to the feeling of it, realising he had been needing it for a long time. *Has it been so long since I felt relaxed?*

Cherinda the Celestial had appeared to Felix once before. She had been the herald commanded to find a human willing to defend humanity in front of Habeus, the God of Judgement, in the case brought by the demon, Jurrekker. After the tragic outcome of that day, Felix had not seen or heard from her since.

After a while, she pulled back from their embrace and held him by the shoulders, and the soothing feeling melted away. She looked deep into his eyes.

"Felix, you look dreadful."

"Thanks," he said, smiling. "I feel it, too." Cherinda was not smiling, and Felix felt his own grin wavering. Her brow wrinkled in concern as she regarded him.

"Goodness, I can't believe what's happened to you. Your soul is… well, it's hard to say what it is. But gods, it must be so painful."

It is.

"It was." Felix shrugged. "At least I'm still walking and talking, so I can't complain." She was still staring at him, and Felix suddenly felt exposed, like he was standing on a stage beneath a great spotlight. "Look, I'm fine, okay," he snapped, a little irritably, then immediately regretted it. "Sorry. It's this case. It's been playing on my mind. It's really good to see you again."

"And you," she said, the smile returning. A brief silence stretched between them.

"Can I offer you a cup of tea?" said Felix. "Or a biscuit? You liked the minty ones, yes?"

After a few moments, they were both settled down around the table, steaming mugs in hand. Helda and Racelsus had joined them. Helda was not making a massive effort to hide her distaste. Cherinda looked over to her and smiled. Helda grimaced in return, causing the celestial's eyes to nervously flick to Felix and back.

"Um, hello Helda, Racelsus," she said. "How are you both?"

"You know," Helda said, tapping a meaty finger on the desk. "Since you up-and-vanished, we ain't had a chance to have a chat to you about something. What with everything that happened before, it sort of all got caught up in the moment, but since that's all settled…"

She laced her fingers together and adopted an expression much like a judge might when asking a defendant exactly why he had decided to murder his dearest friend over an argument about breakfast. Cherinda looked a little unsure.

"What is it, Helda?" she said, her hands nervously smoothing an imaginary crease from her perfect robes. Helda narrowed her eyes.

"You changed sides at the end," she said, her voice low and cold. "You abstained."

"Helda-" said Felix, but Helda waved him down.

"Old Habeus called the vote about whether to end humanity. You'd been against it all this time, but all of a sudden you abstained, which threw the whole case up the swanny. You almost killed us all!" Her voice had been rising with each sentence, and she was almost shouting by the end. "You betrayed us! Why should we ever speak to you again?"

Cherinda's aura blazed red, and her face screwed up in fury. Her eyes flashed a deep crimson as she bared her teeth. Felix had never seen her like this and flinched back. Racelsus clacked, out of fear or anger, Felix couldn't say, but Helda stood firm, meeting that dread gaze. "You dare?" Cherinda said in a voice utterly at odds with the mellifluous tone her voice normally had. "Question my judgement? Me, a Celestial?"

"How could you?" said Helda, not budging an inch, her voice cracked and breaking with emotion. "How?" she shout-whispered.

The furious celestial hesitated, then at once her aura changed from red to blue. Her angry barks transformed into bitter sobs, and she held her head in her hands.

"I'm so sorry," she said, in a small voice. "I am. It was all those terrible things I heard and saw, and that prosecutor, Jeast... All of the arguments he made... the more I heard and the more I saw, the less certain I became." She looked up and her eyes were no longer red with cosmic fire, but with tears. "I made a terrible mistake, and every day I am wretched with the memory of it. I'm so sorry, Helda. Felix. Racelsus. Everyone."

Helda, who had been sitting there with a face of impassive disgust, felt her resolve to keep up the air of the wounded party crumble. After a moment her expression melted and she sighed, then shuffled her chair over to the weeping Celestial and placed an arm around her shoulder, resting her other hand on Cherinda's forearm.

"There, there. It all worked out in the end, didn't it? No need to cry," she said, gently stroking her arm. Cherinda looked up at her, unhidden shock on her face.

"You forgive me? Already?" she said, wiping her eyes.

Helda shrugged. "Yes."

"How? Why?"

Racelsus clicked. "Human nature. We don't like to wallow in negativity, generally speaking. We like to get it all off of our chests - provided we have chests, that is - and once all the bad stuff has been aired, forgive and forget, usually over a cup of something potent."

Cherinda looked from the skull to Helda, to Felix, back to Helda. "Really?"

Helda smiled, and hugged the Celestial close. "Really. All is forgiven. I just wanted to make you squirm a bit. Pub?"

"Pub?" said Cherinda, the word not quite finding recognition on those heavenly lips, so used to poetry and philosophy - the irony being, of course, that poets and philosophers were usually so used to pubs.

"Later," said Felix, eliciting an eye-roll from Helda. "Cherinda," he said gently. "You haven't actually told us why you're here."

Cherinda took a breath. "Yes, I realise that. Well, I've heard about your upcoming case with…" She hesitated. "With the goddess Skrida." She smoothed her dress again. "I've been asked to fetch you."

Felix sat up. "Oh, I wasn't expecting this so soon. Do I have time to pack?" He stood, looking around the room with sudden nervous energy. "Where are my notes? Oh, for a few more days of planning… How long do we have?" he said, looking at Cherinda earnestly.

The Celestial blushed a little. "Well…" she said, lowering her eyes. She looked at her hands and mumbled something inaudible.

"Speak up," said Felix, trying not to sound rude but failing. "Cherinda, I need to know."

"She said," said Racelsus, her voice taking on a note of jollity. "Oh, that's funny. I like that a lot."

"What's funny?" said Helda. Racelsus laughed, which sounded like a pole being dragged along a wooden fence.

"Do you want to tell them or shall I?" she said, to Cherinda. The Celestial cleared her throat, then sat up straight, but didn't make eye contact with anyone.

"I told them," she said, "that I would fetch you all and bring you to the divine realm for the case. They asked me how long it would take, and I said it would take, um, a week."

"A week?" said Felix, confused. "But you can do that whole teleporty thing you did for us the last time. We could be up there in minutes, right?"

Cherinda blushed again. "Well, perhaps, yes, that's the case, if I were to do that, then we could, but…" her voice trailed off into more inaudible mumbles.

"What she is trying to say," said Racelsus. "Is that our good and honest Celestial here told a little white lie in order to get you all a bit more time."

"Not just that!" snapped Cherinda at Racelsus, her voice loud and emotional but her aura a sheepish pink. "I also wanted to spend some time with you all again. Time is so ephemeral to the gods, and so I thought they wouldn't notice if I took a little longer than is strictly necessary… what? Why are you looking at me that way? What's so funny?" She directed this last comment at Felix, who was trying and failing to stifle a chuckle. He let it out, then reined it in.

"It's good to see you again Cherinda," he said, and meant it.

~

They caught up over the next few days, and Felix used this opportunity to learn as much as he could about the workings of the courtroom of the divine. Cherinda was happy to divulge what she knew, though when it came to discussions of specific gods, she was careful with her words.

"They are famously prideful," she said. "Prideful, boastful, self-absorbed, jealous, insecure, paranoid, cosmically powerful beings. A difficult combination, you know. Even Habeus can be like that, but he is by far the most reasonable of them all."

"They sound lovely…" said Felix, scribbling some notes.

"They're not lovely. Weren't you listening?" Cherinda waited for his reply with an earnest face.

"I was being sar… never mind," said Felix. "Sorry. Carry on, please."

The celestial sighed. "I mean, that's not fair. They can be lovely. They can be the kindest, sweetest, most generous beings in all creation... when they're in the mood. But they have to be in the mood. And even then, they can be spiteful just for the fun of it. They might bless you with the power of flight, but then take away your eyes. In fact, she did that once. That was Skrida," she added, with a significant look at Felix. "You have to be careful with her."

"Thank you, I will. Say, why didn't I see any of them during the whole case with Jurrekker? I saw Habeus, of course, but none of the other gods."

Cherinda gave a snort - another gesture he'd not seen from her before. Where was she learning all these bad manners? He eyed Racelsus, who he could have sworn eyed him back.

"Mortal goings-on are usually so far beneath them they don't even bother to check what's happening year-to-year. I wouldn't be surprised if half of them didn't even know the case was happening."

"Do we matter that little to them?" said Felix.

"In a word: yes. I'm sorry if it sounds harsh, but it's the truth, at least to them. Myself, I couldn't disagree more." She reached over, took Felix's hand and squeezed it.

~

"Well," said Cherinda, peering out the window at the midday sun several days later. "It's time to go. Do you have everything?"

Felix looked around. He had a stack of papers, and Furbo, Helda, and Racelsus were standing with him, with the rest of the staff standing a few steps away. They were all in the garden behind the firm.

"Yes I do," he said. Turning to Mr and Mrs Luncher, he nodded, and they nodded back.

"Good luck," Mrs Luncher said. "But I don't think you'll need it."

Felix smiled, then addressed John, who was sitting in his customary wooden block, which was being held by Dago. "You're sure you don't want to come, John?"

The dagger chuckled. "Oh, no, I'm fine, thank you. One mortal realm is quite enough for me. Besides, someone has to keep an eye on those two ruffians."

Dago tutted. "That's not a nice way to talk about them. They're right there, you know," he said, jerking a thumb at Mr and Mrs Luncher. Merindhe elbowed him in the ribs.

Felix turned back to Cherinda. "We're ready."

For the second time in his life - if this was still the same life - Felix felt the horrible sensation of being warped through reality. It was just as infinite and just as instant as before, with the same effect on his inner plumbing. His insides felt squeezed and twisted, hot and prickled, a bubbling, boiling, squirming, turgid, sloshing bag of queasy nausea.

"Oh gods," he said, retching. "I'm a bloody ghost, for goodness sake, why can I still be sick?" he moaned between heaves. It was then that he realised what he was being sick on, and immediately felt like a slug on the plate of the Dowager Countess at a royal dinner party.

"Oh, er, sorry," he said, looking around for something to clean up the mess. In doing so, he saw the Realm of the Gods for the first time, and was struck dumb by it, his nausea forgotten. Impossibly fine architecture of pure, white marble formed detailed statues and archways that soared above them. Every surface was tinted with gold or jewels, even the very ground they walked on, or were sick on. The sun was a brilliant bright white, yet not painful to look upon.

This is the most amazing thing I've ever seen, he thought, and then heard the distinctive sound of vomit being ejected onto the paving, and turned to see Helda on all fours, Furbo patting her on the back.

"There there," he said. "Let it all out, lass."

Not the most dignified entrance… Hopefully no-one saw that.

He looked around. They appeared to be alone, just Cherinda, Felix, Helda, Furbo and Racelsus. Felix sighed in relief.

Cherinda, who had been politely ignoring all the sick, smiled at them. "Shall we go? Follow me."

She led them through a grove filled with beautiful trees of every hue and colour, with great, juicy looking fruit that lowered itself on branches as they passed. "Don't eat it," she said as Helda, her nausea forgotten, reached up. She recoiled her hand as if bitten by a snake.

"Why?"

"Trust me," she replied, and elaborated no further.

After a short while, in which they saw no sign of anyone else, they came to an enormous white-stone building with a small door in the side of it. Cherinda stopped and turned to face them.

"I can't come with you, I'm afraid." She held a hand up to cease any protest. "Things work differently up here. I'm not... high up enough. But I have brought you here, to the door of the courtroom itself. Right through there, and keep going, basically." She smiled at Felix, and folded him into a hug. "You'll be fine, Felix," she said, bathing him in a comforting sense of relaxation.

"You think?" he said, allowing himself a little flutter of worry. She pulled herself back and nodded.

"Yes. I've seen you work. Have faith."

And with that she nodded at them all, walked past them, took three steps then vanished, fading into thin air. Felix swallowed his nerves, but they bobbed up again.

Okay, here we go.

He pushed the small door open and walked in.

Journal Entry I - The Orb

Reference case [RHvOA] (RenHar v. OalArt), year 1338, Judge Uewellin presiding.

There's something about people with power who abuse it that really narks me off.

"Oh wow," I hear you cry. "Felix with his profound views, whatever nugget will he share with us next."

Yes, alright, so far so obvious, but indulge me. It's something about the assumption that just because they have more money than you or a bigger house or a fancy orb that they are cleverer, or stronger, or more logical, or more trustworthy, or-

Sorry? Oh, orb? Yes, I'll get to that in a moment.

You put someone's name above the door and he employs a few people and suddenly he's a tyrant. Then their poor employees have to balance wanting to push this new overlord off a bridge with wanting to feed their families. So, they endure. They endure tyranny in all its forms. They endure overwork, or unfair blame. They endure inappropriate comments and enquiries of an unprofessional nature. Bullying, harassment, terrible jokes, boorishness, arrogance. They endure, because if they do not, *they* are the ones that lose out.

Like I said, narks me off.

I've gotten a little off track. Orbs. That's where we were, right? Orbs.

So, before the whole me-being-killed thing, there was this wizard named Oal who claimed he invented an orb that could answer any question posed to it. Pretty handy. A man, called Renn, heard about this, marched over to Oal and demanded to see it working. No problem, says Oal, and takes Renn to see the orb, whereupon I'm sure there was much muted lifting of silken cowls and twitching of candles in breezeless dungeons. The orb itself was simple enough. A large-ish perfect sphere of shining dark glass, resting on a cushion.

After a ponder, Renn starts with the questions. How can one measure the maximum wind load that a windmill can withstand?

Almost immediately, the orb responded, stating with confidence words such as density, drag, wind pressure and so forth, and how to use them to calculate precisely the answer to Renn's question.

What about the schematics for a device that could throw a two hundred pound stone block one thousand feet? In mere seconds, the orb's surface was covered in intricate white lines demonstrating how this could be achieved.

Renn's eyes lit up, and he took out his money bag.

Now, Renn was an engineer. Or rather, he employed engineers to work out complicated problems.

You can probably see where this is going.

Sir, Oal had protested. I must advise that the orb should only be used in an advisory capacity, and is no substitute for real worldly experience.

Renn took out his other money bag. Papers were signed, and the orb was sold.

Within a day, twelve engineers, along with their support staff, apprentices, supervisors and various others were sacked. Makko Renn's Engineering Services downsized from a team of thirty to a team of one and a bit. Renn could answer any question, solve any issue, in a fraction of the time it took for a team of highly skilled, reliable, careful engineers to work it out.

Eventually, after Renn presumably woke from sleeping on his giant hoard of gold, he received a visit from a group of very serious looking men, wanting to know why their bridge fell down. And while they're here, why is the new watchtower leaning so precariously? And why were the walls and floors in the city's new post office bulging?

Oal explained to me what was happening over coffee, after I'd agreed to represent him.

"Here's the shortfall of the orb," he said. "It has immense amounts of knowledge. I fed it by rolling it over books. You open the pages then roll it over, you see? Then it sort of sucks the information in, and stores it."

"Mmhm," I say.

"So it knows basically everything that's been written down, right? But it doesn't have real world experience. When you ask it a question, it will give you the exact answer, without any consideration of anything else. And sometimes, it assumes it knows the answer, but it doesn't quite have enough information, so it just sort of... guesses."

He took a sip. "Imagine you ask it to build you the perfect school. It would probably give you a series of cages suspended above a pond. Perfect. The kids can't escape, so they have to focus. You can dunk them to wash them or punish them. Easy to clean, cheap to maintain."

"But," I said, "the parents probably wouldn't be keen."

"Exactly," he said, then fidgeted with his cup. "Do you think we'll win?"

"Well, you never told him it would answer the questions correctly, and besides, you told him that it was for general advisory and inspirational purposes, yes? Not specifics? And got him to sign something to that effect?"

"Yes, I did."

"Then that bit of carefulness has saved you a lot of hassle. Did the orb advise you to do that?" I added, joking.

"Yes," said Oal, deadpan. I blinked.

"It can do legal advice, too?"

"Oh yes. But, the law isn't just memorising huge amounts of information and recalling them, right? So you have nothing to worry about," he chuckled.

I like to think I hid my slight choking on my biscuit as a normal, everyday laughing cough. If Oal did see it, he was polite enough not to mention.

"Besides," he said, calling over the waiter and pulling out his wallet. "I'm not sure the world is ready for the orb, yet. Most of the people who use it just think it's a joke and ask it to compose silly poems about pigeons and the like. I'll keep working on it. It'll change the world one day."

We won the case, of course, based on what I mentioned above. Renn was held responsible for the issues caused and forced to pay to repair them. Funnily enough, a new firm was employed to fix the messes, consisting of exactly everyone who Renn fired. I learned that there's 'mates rates', and apparently there's also 'foes fees'. Who knew?

Another thing I learned was to occasionally check the paper for available jobs like gravedigger or baker's apprentice. I thought it might come in handy to have a practical hands-dirty fall-back trade. Just in case.

~journal entry ends

5 - The Courtroom

They made their way down a simple, narrow corridor and through a plain wooden doorway adorned with nothing but the occasional meagre lantern. Felix had to admit he was a little disappointed. *I expected a little more... well, godliness.*

As they opened the doorway however, and made their way into the main courtroom, he changed his mind instantly. They emerged through a small entrance in the side of the courtroom, and each of them stopped dead when they entered.

For the second time in his life - or, unlife - Felix walked into a courtroom from another world. The first was Placenamia Courtroom, where the case was the demon Jurrekker versus the whole of humanity. He had entered that familiar courtroom to find it changed; everything seemed *more* than it was before. The most striking had been those in the audience. Whereas normally people from the local town or city would mill about in the aisles, watching justice get meted out upon their peers (either through a sense of civic pride or schadenfreude), in the case for humanity, those watching were drawn from all aspects of the higher plane, from mysterious black vortexes of abstract consciousness to divinely ascended turtles.

What he saw now was completely different.

A beautifully paved floor sparkled with gold-infused marble; each brick hewn and shaped as if by a master sculptor. Each chair (of which there seemed countless), arranged for those in attendance to observe the goings-on in the court, was shaped from living wood, which seemed to have grown into the perfect shape for prime comfort, twisting and turning with fluid sentience. Instead of cushions, thick, fluffy moss had sprouted anywhere where someone might sit or rest an arm. Every surface, from the desks of the lawyers to the barriers that separated the seating area from the concourse, were made of the same brilliant shining marble, with golden filigree describing intricate floral patterns down every vertical support column. And the judge's dais... Felix had met some ostentatious judges before, those who turned up to court insisting on wearing their largest, most flouncy robes, but this desk would have made even High Judge Oscaro 'Ostentation' Felleby blush and look away.

Firstly, it was enormous. A massive, vertical wall of pure gold, etched and embossed with, as far as Felix could tell, an entire history of the gods and how they came to be, every scene beautifully realised in breathtaking detail. The light shone from every raised surface, giving the impression of a sunrise over a small, golden sea. At the top, the wall swelled out, forming almost a castle-like crenellation of flamboyance, as the golden wall morphed into a series of golden birds of paradise. Felix could see a gavel hovering above the desk. Instead of the small, simple wooden hammer that Habeus had wielded, this was a monster. Gold, of course, with every surface studded with jewels and interlaced with mother-of-pearl. It was possibly the most garish thing Felix had ever seen, and he'd seen Helda's 'out-on-the-town' outfit.

"I suppose we're the first ones here," said Helda. She turned to look at Furbo, who was staring with unashamed fascination. "Oh, here we go," Helda muttered, then considered something. "Actually, how often do you get to see a carving as, well, *this* as this?" She nudged Furbo. "Why don't you go over and take a closer look? I'll keep watch."

Furbo flicked his eyes away to look at her, then back again. "You think I can?"

"Sure! What are they going to do exactly?"

"Oh, but I mustn't..."

Helda sighed and all but frog-marched Furbo over to the carving, to minimal resistance. Felix tried not to grin, but cracked when he heard the old scholar quietly moan: "Oh Helda, just look at the carving of that sheep..."

As he looked about him, Felix found his head threatening to spin. The sheer enormity of what he was about to do took his brain in both hands and shook it about. His walking slowed, his blinking sped up, and he clenched and unclenched his fists without awareness.

"Easy," said Racelsus, in a quiet voice that only he could hear. Not whispered into his mind, just spoken quietly. "You'll be fine."

"Will I?" he muttered back, a note of panic entering his voice. He glanced up and was met with an unfathomably high ceiling studded with stars, despite them being inside. Each of the constellations was highlighted in shining coruscations, sparkling and pulsing like starlight through a snowflake. "I think I'm out of my depth. Just look at that bloody ceiling. I can't cope."

"That's what you said last time," she said. "And that time it was the whole of humanity that was at stake. This time, the stakes are much lower."

"It's my eternal soul on the line!"

"Exactly! Only one, whereas last time it was millions."

"Oh gods…"

She sighed, and Felix felt something brush against his emotional panic, the same way a cat brushes against your outstretched hand and sends a little warm sensation through your arm and into your heart. It was not unlike what it felt like when Cherinda embraced him, but lesser, somehow. He heard Racelsus's voice floating to him.

"You'll be fine. It's just any other case on any other day, only the scenery is a little more garish. Well, a lot more. It's pretty much as garish as you can go. Do you think they'll make me a birdcage out of gold, if I ask?"

"Rass!"

"Oh, you're no fun. Feel any better, by the way?"

"I do. Have you been copying Cherinda?"

Racelsus *hmph*ed. "Not copying… just watching. Is it working? It's harder than it looks."

Felix felt the comforting feeling wobble a little, sending a wave of nausea through him. "Yes, it feels great, thanks."

"Good, so long as… Hmm, wait" she said. "Can you feel that?"

Felix fought the nausea down. "I feel, ugh, wonderful."

"No, not that."

The sickly comforting feeling disappeared from Felix instantly, to his relief. "What are you talking about Rass?"

She clacked her teeth. "They're on their way."

As if on cue, the main doors to the auditorium opened unaided, and a string of godlings, spirits and other divine persons began walking in. Some were solemn-faced, others were laughing and chatting. One had no face at all. All shapes and sizes, all colours and hairstyles, all outfits or lack thereof.

The gods had arrived.

No, not gods.

An old memory of Cherinda, a mere Celestial (and therefore considered beneath these strutting divinities), came to him. It was a few months ago, and they were chatting over what to expect in Felix's then-imminent case defending humanity.

When you enter the court, she had said, *you'll see all manner of Higher Beings, Felix. Don't be afraid; you'll be safe as long as you're with your chaperone - in other words, me.*

Higher Beings? What kind of Higher Beings? he had asked.

Oh, all sorts. Celestials, probably not. Demons, probably. Spirits, almost certainly. Some particularly talented sorcerers, astral projections, shamans, dream-walkers, manifest nightmares... Oh, and Habeus as well.

No other gods?

She had laughed. *Oh, most gods won't get out of bed for something as trifling as the extinction of humanity. No, count yourself lucky that the only god you'll ever meet is Habeus. The others are a... well, they're deserving of their reputations, particularly the nasty ones. Especially the pantheon. If you're ever unlucky enough to meet a godling, avert your eyes, say nothing, and hope they leave you alone.*

What if I meet a member of the pantheon?

The smile had faded. *Fall on your knees and beg for mercy.*

Felix wished the Celestial could be near him now. Wherever Cherinda went, a warm sense of peace followed. Now, instead of her calming aura, he was going to be sat next to Skrida, who was a smidge less cordial and a lot more sinister.

None of the parade entering seemed to stand out to him. Furbo - who had since retreated reluctantly back to Felix's side - had told him that he'd spot the members of the pantheon a mile off. He remembered the old man's crinkled face as he figured out how to phrase this delicate matter.

Habeus is, well, unique in his… modest appearance. The rest - and I do hope none of them are listening, as this is perhaps a little blasphemous - really do like to show off.

Felix steeled his nerves. Despite everything, he was a little star-struck. It's not every day you might meet the creator of, well, everything. There was no sign of the pantheon, yet. More and more minor deities and their hangers-on were filling the seats, some with drinks, others with food, one with what looked like a lyre.

You'll be safe as long as you are with your chaperone…

Felix felt his palms itch. He darted his eyes around the crowd milling into the room. Where was Skrida? What might they do if he was discovered without his client to vouch for him? Would they punish him? His mind filled with images of all manner of eternal torment.

Oh gods.

"What do you think of the decor, Felix?" came a low voice behind him. He swirled to find Skrida there, not an arm's reach away, smiling at him. She was dressed in a frilled and patterned dress of black silk, studded with amethysts and complete with gloves and veil. *Where had she come from? Had she been waiting? Can she read my mind?*

A series of wholly inappropriate thoughts immediately paraded themselves in his consciousness, the tamest of which was the one about Prosecutor Ettyson and the pig-wrangling. Felix did his best to force them behind a veil of nothing.

"Well?" Skrida prompted.

"It's, uh, very, well, well covered and appropriate." She raised an eyebrow. He coughed. "That is to say, that, uh, I love it. It's so, well, exquisitely carved." She rolled her eyes.

"Wonderful," she said. "I personally think it's hideous." She dropped onto a chair next to him, gesturing to him to sit. She waved a disinterested hand at the procession of divinity. "Don't *goggle* at them, you're embarrassing me."

Felix was vaguely aware of Furbo sitting behind Skrida. He was very red in the face, and Helda was gripping his hand and patting his arm. He hoped she didn't turn around. As if reading his thoughts, the Goddess of

Death turned slowly in her chair to face the old scholar. He squeaked as she met his gaze.

"Do you still want me to free you from your torment, mortal?"

"I'm s-sorry?" said Furbo in a tiny voice. She regarded him coldly, and her eyes started to gently pulse with pale blue light. "You begged for death not long ago. I can fulfil your desire." She raised a finger which began to glow purple. "Yes?"

"No!" said Helda.

"He was exaggerating, as mortals are wont to do," came the voice of Racelsus, more nervous and frantic than normal. "He didn't mean it. He was, well, you see, he was, uh, hungover."

"Hungover?" said Skrida.

"Uh, yes. That is to say, he was ill. He got better. He no longer wishes for death." She clacked. "Thank you for the offer, though."

Her eyes returned to normal, but Skrida moved her finger to point at the skull. "As for you, witch. Perhaps we should have a little chat later. Your own situation is... peculiar."

Racelsus made no reply.

Skrida arched an eyebrow at the trio, then shook her head and faced forward once more. She leaned in closer to Felix, who was suddenly filled with the smell of her. She smelled of cold winter evenings. "A strange following you have," she whispered.

He chewed his lip and placed his palms on his knees. "Sorry about that," he said, and she waved her hand irritably.

"I know this is all quite a lot to take in. Well, take it in, and fast. My darling husband and his idiotic band of simpleton friends will be here soon. Gah. I just want this over with."

As she silently fumed and stared forwards, looking anywhere but the parade of entering divinity, Felix took a look at her. There was some *aura* about her that wasn't present with the other minor gods. Was it because she was a member of the pantheon? Or was she a member of the pantheon because of this... quality? Something palpable emanated from her in waves. Something primal... something terrifying.

She tossed her head, causing Felix to flinch. She didn't notice. Instead she turned her head to the door and tutted. The background hum of the voices of those entering the courtroom increased in excitement and volume. "Oh, here we go," Skrida said. "Brace yourself…"

A ripple of cheers and applause, and a new figure passed through the doors. The crowd moved closer to him, extending hands and raising glasses. The figure returned each smile, each wave, and tapped his own glass against any offered to him with a laugh and a wink. He was tall and powerfully built, with curly brown hair and a smile as broad and welcoming as a harvest festival. There was a brightness about him. Whether it was the way he moved and acted, or perhaps a genuine emanation of light, Felix couldn't say.

"My husband's cousin," Skrida said, scowling. "He makes me retch." Her face remained locked in a frown, and showed no sign of actually retching. The god glanced over their way and gave a beaming smile, accompanied by a wave of such exaggerated greeting that it moved straight past ludicrous and straight into endearing. He strode over, the crowd moving back to let him approach. Within a few moments, he was standing behind their desk, staring at Skrida.

"Noble cousin," he said, in a voice full of camaraderie seasoned with good-natured mischief. "A pleasure to be in your exquisite company once again." As Felix watched, his kind, open eyes seemed to grow harder and more intense, his wide smile seeming more a rictus grin than a pleasant welcome.

Skrida sighed. "Well met, Gaman," she said with complete indifference. The god's eyes slid to Felix, who, far from feeling nervous being under that gaze, suddenly felt light and at ease. He almost laughed with relief.

"And who is this dapper gentleman?" said Gaman, extending a hand. "I don't believe I've had the pleasure."

"I'm Felix Sacramentum, Your Godliness," said Felix, taking the hand and shaking it. The grip was firm and warm, but not crushing. "I am Lady Skrida's lawyer today." As he said the words, the warmth within him wilted, and a note of worry sprouted in his core. Gaman's expression never changed, but something about his demeanour did.

"I see," said Gaman. "Well, good luck with that, Felix." The words *'you'll need it'* were not voiced, but Felix felt them nonetheless. Gaman nodded once more to Skrida, then turned back to his adoring followers.

"Helda, pinch me," said Furbo quietly.

A couple had entered, arm in arm, and those around them were bowing their heads as they passed. The female of the pair wore a green robe seemingly made of flowers, with a mantle of feathers around her shoulders. Her partner was bedecked in some of the heaviest plate armour Felix had ever seen, reminding him of one of Felix's first major cases: that of Bupp the Despoiler. This god made Bupp look like a lightly-armoured skirmisher.

Gaman approached them and bowed, taking the female god's hand in his and kissing it. The other god, and clearly her paramour, watched them both with a face like thunder. As Gaman rose, he shared a look with the other god, then the two men simply walked past one another.

"B-Berjast and Fridur," whispered Furbo. "The God of War and the Goddess of Peace." Skrida turned around and appraised him for the first time.

"A scholar?" she said, and Furbo's face went even redder.

"Yes, ma'am," he spluttered. She leaned over.

"So you'll be able to tell me how they are related to me, then?"

Furbo nodded, clasping his hands together. "Of course, My Lady. Berjast is the brother of Ferdaloga, who is your father by marriage, making Lord Berjast your uncle by marriage, and Lady Fridur your aunt. Their daughter, the lady Dyr, is your second cousin."

Skrida raised an eyebrow. "I don't know whether I'm impressed or bored. Certainly you know more than most of this rabble." Furbo tried to speak but no sound came out. She turned back to Felix and leaned over to speak quietly.

"Gaman and Berjast have always been at each other's throats. You see, Gaman has always loved Fridur, but Berjast got there first. That, and it doesn't help that Gaman is a pathological mocker, and Berjast has the sense of humour of a turnip, and a pathetic sense of pride matched only by my husband."

"Oh, I see," said Felix, trying to act as if gossip among the gods was a perfectly normal thing to talk about with, well, another god.

"One of these days they're going to actually draw steel and try to kill one another, and when they do… my money's on Gaman. Berjast might be the God of War, but Gaman has hidden talents, and can be tenacious if the mood suits him. Fridur would never forgive him, though… at least not in public." She gave him a knowing look, then settled back.

The river of those entering the court had started to trickle to a light stream. The nerves were starting to return. He closed his eyes and tried to focus. He heard a few quiet, shuffling footsteps.

"My Lady Skrida," came a familiar voice.

"Habeus," said Skrida.

Felix snapped his eyes open and stood. He turned to face the God of Justice. He looked exactly as he had remembered. Black robe, tied in a knotted belt. Great beard tied in a knot, swinging freely as he walked. It bounced off of his robe as he moved. Habeus was smiling at him.

"Felix," he said. "I'm glad to see you well." Felix swallowed.

"Your Honour," he said, and Habeus nodded.

"No need for that here. Today, you might refer to me as 'my learned colleague', or 'my opponent.'" That sent a shiver of nerves down Felix's spectral spine, and Habeus raised a hand in greeting to Racelsus, who clacked her teeth in reply. He turned his gaze back to Felix.

"It'll be strange not being the one in the large chair today, I must admit. But. I've been looking forward to this," he said, with a tiny twinkle in his ancient eye. "It should be a bit of fun, don't you think?"

"Uh, perhaps," said Felix, aware of his client sitting right behind him, trying to forget that Habeus knew practically everything about practically everything, legally speaking. Every argument, every precedent, every loophole… "I will certainly be doing my best, Your- uh, Sir."

"Oh, I have no doubt about it." He leaned in a touch. "So shall I." He let that hang in the air a moment. "Well," he said, standing up straight again. "I had best go and get ready." He nodded once to them all, then turned and shuffled off. Skrida waited until he was out of earshot.

"Old idiot," she said. "Far too caught up in the past."

Felix said nothing. As he watched Habeus take a seat, he saw him look up to the judge's dais and raise a hand. Felix followed his gaze, and found a goddess waving back to him. She was dressed in a simple robe of white, and had a crown of rings resting upon a mass of tight, grey curls. Beneath her hair was a stern expression that brooked no argument. Felix hadn't seen her arrive.

That must be Samveru, Goddess of Union. She looks... serious. It's not like I've not worked with serious judge's before though.

As he was thinking of all the judges he had ever stood before, a hush filled the room. Every voice had stopped, and every head turned to the doorway. A bright light was beaming from somewhere behind those doors, casting a web of shadows in all directions away from it.

A few gasps and murmurs of appreciation floated into the air as a figure stepped through the threshold. He had the physique of a body-builder, all rippling muscle and powerful movement. His hair was bright, almost white-blond, and his two matching enormous moustaches swept from his face like walrus tusks. Instantly Felix was filled with a sense of complete and total awe. *This is him! It has to be!*

Furbo squeaked and Solhiti, The Great Creator, King of the Gods turned their way. Instead of eyes, he had two blazing, burning points of light. Two miniature suns, flaming and boiling, glaring and blinding. It hurt Felix to look at them. He gave them all, his wife included, the most cursory of glances, then continued walking. Those godlings and other divine beings that had not taken their seats bowed low and backed away from him, and he ignored them. He strode to Habeus's side, and lowered himself onto a chair. Habeus looked small and old next to the imposing figure of the King of the Gods. He leaned over and started muttering to Habeus, who spoke back in a low voice. Solhiti shook his head and crossed his arms.

Gradually, a low-level background conversation started up again, and eventually people were talking amongst themselves, with more excited animation than before. It was like sitting in a theatre minutes before the curtains rise. Felix suppressed a shudder.

They're here for the drama. The drama that I'm going to be poking with a stick. What the hell have I gotten myself into?

"Look at him there, the great lummox," muttered Skrida, rolling her eyes and tutting. "What an arse."

Felix did not know how to respond.

~

A few minutes later, once Helda had roused Furbo from his stupor, Felix took stock. The great golden doors had closed, the room was packed, and all the major players were present. His own client, the manifestation of Death, was impatiently waiting for the proceedings to start - proceedings in which Felix would state the case for favourable treatment for her in her divorce from Solhiti, The Great Creator, King of the Cosmos, who was sat in a chair not twenty feet away.

Relax, said Racelsus straight into his mind. Her voice was low, soothing. *Breathe. You've done the prep. Trust in the process.*

Felix breathed and nodded.

"What the witch said," said Skrida, examining her nails. "You'll be fine and all that. Gods, mortals are so *needy.*"

"You... heard me?" said Racelsus. Skrida laughed. "Of course. Why, were you trying to be secretive?" The witch did not reply.

The background noise quietened down, and Felix looked up. Samveru, the judge in this case, had risen, and was holding a hand up for attention.

Such presence... Such respect... Such elegant poise. She's unlike any judge I've ever seen.

Judges came in all shapes and sizes, all manners and personalities, but until this moment Felix hadn't realised they were all lacking *something.* That special aspect to them that Samveru had in spades. She could have silenced a hurricane with that gesture.

Once utter silence had fallen, she lowered her hand. Felix found himself filled with excited nervousness to hear this paragon of order, this pillar of propriety, this avatar of deference speak. In a voice rich with maturity and poise, she began.

"We are gathered here today in front of esteemed friends and beloved family to witness the union of…" she stopped, and frowned. "No, hang on a minute. It'll come to me."

Oh, she's just like the other judges after all.

She snapped a finger. "That's right, the other thing." She scowled first at Solhiti then at Skrida. "You two. Before we begin, I suggest, one more time, that you put aside your petty squabbles, whatever they may be, and leave this room as a contented - married - couple, and cease this farce."

"I'm game if she is," came a voice like the rumble of clouds, and Solhiti turned to face his wife. "What do you say, oh-my-sweet-one?"

Skrida twisted her mouth and looked as if she might spit fire. Felix touched her arm with a hand, and she shifted her glare from her husband to Felix, who recoiled at that look. "Lady Skrida, I must insist you resist the urge to hurl insults at the opposition," he said. "It will feel satisfying now, but it will only hurt our case if they are able to paint you as emotional and easily riled."

A few tense seconds passed in which it felt as if her eyes bored into his very soul (which, given the circumstances, was entirely possible), but she eventually tutted and rolled her eyes. She faced Samveru and spoke in a reasonable voice. "That is not going to happen, Samveru."

"Farce it is, then," said Samveru, and reached up to pluck the jewelled gavel from the air above her. She struck the surface in front of her, causing a resounding metallic *twing* to ring out. Once the sound had finished ringing in Felix's ears, Samveru raised her hands.

"This hearing is in session." She paused. "The facts are as thus: The King of the Gods, Solhiti, and his wife, Skrida, have declared that their matrimonial bonds should be severed. Skrida, the instigator of this wanton dismissal of the sanctity of such commitments, not content with simply breaking countless aeons of tradition by going her own way, has insisted that the realms, tributes, lands, titles and other such attributions that belong to Solhiti - him being the bearer and holder of the vast majority of such things - should be split evenly between herself and her husband." Samveru glared at Skrida. "Do I have the shape of that about right?"

"You do," said Felix, responding before Skrida had a chance. She shot him an icy glare, which caused his insides to recoil instinctively, but he found the courage to lean in and whisper.

"Lady Skrida, I advise you to let me do the talking unless you are specifically called upon." She scowled at him, but said nothing.

Samveru turned to Solhiti. "And you agree?" Habeus stood up. "We do insofar as that which you have explained. We do not, of course, agree with Lady Skrida's desire."

"And what is Solhiti's opinion of this... scenario?"

Habeus shook his head slowly, his great, knotted beard swinging from side to side.

"My client regrets the state of affairs, but is of the mind that his wife's mind cannot and will not be changed. That being the case, he will not resist her in seeking a separation, although his heart breaks into pieces because of it. He is acquiescing to this formal hearing so that the matter may be put to bed, once and for all."

"Well," said Samveru. "Now I shall lay out *my* thoughts on the matter." She took a breath, stretching out the silence. "If the Lady Skrida wishes to stake a claim on that which belongs to Solhiti, then she should remain linked with him by marriage. *If*," she said, raising a hand to quell a scathing reply from the Goddess of Death, who had looked as if to speak. "*If* she does not wish to do so, then I shall allow her to break her holy union vow. However, in order for her to have any sort of claim to anything that belongs to her husband, then she must prove to me that she has the right to claim it, and that she was forced to seek a termination of this marriage, as opposed to simply wanting this... *'divorce'* for her own convenience, or as an attempt to seize that which she feels is hers, but that which has until this moment belonged firmly within her husband's influence." She paused for a breath. "Simply put, she must prove to me that what she is doing is not selfishly motivated. She must show to me that any reasonable person would seek to end this marriage based on what she has experienced. Then, and only then, shall I grant her request by the power that the cosmos has vested in me. Are we all understood?"

"Yes, Your Honour," said Felix, rising. Samveru appraised him, then nodded. She turned to the other side, who were conferring between themselves. A gentle murmur of conversation floated from the assembled godlings from the gallery while they did so, for they did for several minutes. Felix lowered himself again, caught Skrida's furious eye, and she leaned over to angry-whisper at him.

"To expect me to grovel and beg for what is rightfully mine... the absolute indignity of it." She scowled at the opposition, still in quiet talk. "What are they even talking about?" she said. Felix looked over at them and considered.

"They're probably not really saying anything, but just making it look like they're having a deep conversation. That way, when they finally agree to the judge's terms, it will seem as if they've made some gracious concession."

It's what I would have done in their situation.

Skrida raised an eyebrow at him. "You think they'd be so childishly manipulative?"

"Uh... It's possible."

Skrida shook her head. "I think you're right. He's just showing his unscrupulous side, as usual."

Habeus rose to his feet. "We have no issue, Your Honour. We believe that Lady Skrida, and her legal counsel representing her, will be unable to prove either point, and so we have no problem with the terms."

"Good. Took you long enough," said Samveru with a sigh. "Okay then, now that we understand, we may begin in earnest." She pointed at Felix. "You there. Mister...?"

"Sacramentum, Your Honour."

"Yes, indeed. Please lay out your opening argument."

Felix's mouth, despite being made of light, or ectoplasm, or whatever, was dry. He wished he'd taken a drink of water while he'd had the chance.

"Understood, Your Honour." He took several steps to the centre of the space between the bench and the gallery, and bowed. While he was bowed, he gave himself five seconds of sheer, utter, complete mind-numbing panic, letting it fizz and swirl around him like a thunderstorm. By the time he had risen, his face was calm, his hands weren't shaking, and he was ready to begin.

6 - Opening Statements

Felix took one last breath, and was shocked to realise that it felt different. The effort he was used to expending to manifest his physical presence was reduced somehow. He wasn't alive, that was certain, but something felt more present, fuller, like a glass filled with muddy river water instead of clear rainwater. Translucent, not transparent.

Focus, idiot! Navel-gaze later!

He could feel the weight of hundreds of pairs of eyes resting on his back. Each pair belonged to a being that considered him, on any other day, to be worthless. A mere mortal, prancing about on earth with whatever inane, fleeting life he might scratch out for himself before expiring a heartbeat later. Who was this meagre spark? This feckless nothing? Beneath even registry, let alone consideration.

But now? Now, he was the main event. They waited to hear him speak. They wanted to see the gormless face of the upstart *human* who fancied standing up to Solhiti. Did they just want to see what happened to him, what petty revenge the King of the Gods would mete out once he was through? Were they expecting him to break down in blubbering sobs and weep for mercy?

Were they here to witness the actual case, the potential realignment of their celestial power structure? Or just for the show? Felix felt he knew the answer.

I'll give them a bloody show all right.

The breath eased from him in a long release and he began.

"Your Honour, honoured guests, learned colleagues. Marriage, whether between the most prestigious of gods or the lowliest of mortals, is not something lightly entered into. It is a bond, a union, forged in passion and strengthened in love. Many, many beings from all over the realms enter into such unions filled with hope and joy, and thus remain that way until the end of their days. Each of those days is spent in showing their significant other the love and warmth that they feel for them, through deep affection, meaningful gestures, quiet earnestness and mutual

355

respect." Samveru's eyes had brightened as Felix spoke, and she was nodding along. Their eyes met, and a nervous flutter tickled Felix's innards.

She's not going to like this part.

"Alas," said Felix, "not all such unions are destined to last. There may come a time where one, or perhaps both, or however many members of this union there are, begin to act in ways that are less harmonious to the marriage. Perhaps they stop showing physical affection. Perhaps they stop showering their partner with compliments. Perhaps they stop listening to their beloved's problems. It can take many forms. These actions can build over time, and, as has been witnessed many times before, can lead to an irrevocable breakdown in the relationship. In such sad times, a divorce can be the only realistic option to maintain - or, more likely, restore - any semblance of happiness for anyone within the marriage."

Samveru's face had hardened with every word he said, shifting from surprise to disappointment, and was now a hair's breadth from outright disgust.

She's really not going to like this part.

"...Furthermore," said Felix. "Such gradual breakdowns, while common, are not the only route to marital dissolution. Sometimes, one partner or the other can break the ties of marital bliss with a single action, or a string of actions. Perhaps through some crime, like murder or theft. Perhaps through infidelity, or violence. In such cases, to remain in such a marriage is not only a source of unhappiness, but can be outrightly impossible."

The Goddess of Marriage and Union's expression had darkened even further. Felix felt an itch behind his collar.

Is she making me sweat? How can I sweat, I'm a bloody ghost!

"It is our intention today to display, through evidence given in testimony from a number of witnesses, that for her to remain in her marriage would be impossible. We intend to prove that, due to abominable treatment by her husband, seeking a divorce is the only course available to Lady Skrida, and that any reasonable person - divine or no - would feel the same way. And, this being the case, why should she see aeons of her hard work in helping her husband shape and rule the cosmos disregarded? She is entitled, as are we all, to the fruits of the sweat of her brow."

Do gods sweat? Oh god, stop thinking about sweat! Focus!

"Thus we shall not only demonstrate that to leave the marriage is the only option available to her, but that she deserves *at least* half of that which her husband claims is solely his by no other virtue than his simple say-so."

"My learned colleague over there will attempt to suggest that my client is being dramatic, and that she is not being forced out against her will. That she is petulantly storming off, leaving behind all that she is entitled to. It is my hope that by the time we are done, you will see the truth of it, and grant my client the divorce she deserves, according to the terms she deserves."

He turned and lowered himself into his chair, ignoring the murmurs from the gallery as each godling discussed this with their neighbours. He couldn't look Skrida in the eye for fear of seeing her disappointment. After a moment he sensed her looking at him. He took a breath, keeping his gaze straight forward, and braced himself.

"Very good," Skrida said in a low voice, in the same way someone might say to a dog that had just rolled over. "There's hope for your immortal soul yet, Mr Sacramentum."

For the first time in his memory, Felix felt both elated and greatly disturbed. Elated because his client, the Goddess of Death, had been impressed by his words. Disturbed, because of the casual way she reminded him of what was at stake, and how it was entirely within her hands to grant it.

Or torment him for eternity.

He turned to look at her and gave as good of a smile as he could muster.

"Thank you," he said, but she was already looking away. Habeus had taken to his feet and was shuffling to the space on the floor that Felix had stood.

~

357

Habeus had reached the centre of the concourse and come to a stop, his back bent slightly, in no hurry to begin. Everyone, Felix included, was watching the old man stand there, his knotted beard swaying gently, the light shining from his bald head. Felix had to remind himself that this stooping old man was a member of the Pantheon, because, well, he didn't look like it.

If you passed him in the street, you might think he was lost. Maybe this won't be so bad after all. There was that time when I was able to outsmart him... sort of.

In the case where humanity had been on trial, Felix had pointed out that Habeus had contradicted himself by saying humanity would be able to appeal, but only once they were eradicated. That had opened a crack in the sentence that Felix had wormed his way into, eventually spinning the case from a certain defeat to a borderline victory.

A flush of confidence coursed through Felix, and he felt his features settle into a smile. *I can do this.*

All of a sudden Habeus stood up straight, unfurling like some great bearded plant, his steepled fingers pressed together, and Felix's breath caught in his chest. He was used to seeing Habeus as an ancient old man, hunched over and almost frail looking, and while his heavy-lidded eyes held infinite wisdom and experience, the presence Habeus exuded was that of the learned teacher or grandfather. Looking at him now was like looking at a new man.

God, Felix reminded himself. *Not man.*

This Habeus was not hunched over and sleepy-eyed. His back was straight, his head held high, his expression severe, his eyes burning with bright intelligence. This was a great scholar at the height of his powers, not a tired teacher worn thin by time. He looked like a powerful sorcerer, or an enlightened philosopher, or a master tactician ripped straight from the storybooks. The realisation of what he was up against hit Felix like a brick.

In a booming voice full of confidence and music, Habeus spoke.

"My client, Solhiti, bears an immeasurable burden. He has, for time incalculable, without complaint or protestation, single-handedly shouldered the well-being of the entire cosmos, and everyone and everything in it."

Am I really about to object to an opening statement made by the God of Law and Lawyers?

Felix stood, raising a hand. His mouth felt dry and he coughed.

"I object, Your Honour."

Samveru stared at him. "What is this?" she snarled. "This interruption? Habeus quietly sat and listened to your entire speech without making so much as a squeak, and yet we are only moments into his and you are *interrupting* him? Such petulance!"

Felix felt the wind vanish from his sails. "Uh, I apologise, Your Honour, but such things are common in a court of law." Samveru peered at him, then looked over to Habeus. "It is?"

"Yes, noble cousin," he said. "Typically, if a statement or question breaks one or other of the pre-established rules, such as by being irrelevant, then it is within the rights of the opposition lawyer to bring that up and ask for the judge to intervene, often by insisting that the offending lawyer alter their words, or retract them entirely."

Samveru's expression did not change. It was as if she was convinced that she was the butt of some joke. "Well, then upon what grounds is this lawyer objecting?" she said, pointing at Felix.

"You will have to ask him that," said Habeus, turning to him. Standing as he was, presenting as his opponent mid-objection, Felix got his second sense of just how challenging being pitted against Habeus was going to be. There was a gentle fire in his eyes that displayed an intensity that Felix hadn't noticed when Habeus was sitting on the bench.

Samveru stared at him, eyebrows raised. "Well?" she said.

"Well," said Felix, withering a smidgeon. "I believe my honoured colleague is being misleading. He has suggested that Solhiti has assumed sole responsibility for every aspect of the cosmos, but, as can be understood by simply looking around, that is not the case. You, yourself, are in charge of marriage and unions, for example."

Samveru's expression shifted from suspicion to realisation. "Ah, that's true. You're an astute one, hm?" She waggled a finger at him, and Felix had no idea how to respond, so he just stood there. Samveru turned to his opponent. "Well, Habeus? What do you have to say to that, eh?"

Habeus bowed his head. "What my colleague is saying is true, up to a point. Solhiti bears responsibility for everything on the macroscale, and part of that government is trusting those around him to perform their own duties. One would not suggest that a general should perform the same duties as a sergeant, but one would still suggest that the general has responsibility for the army as a whole."

"A good point as well," said Samveru, nodding.

A long silence stretched.

"Cousin," said Habeus. "It is now up to you to determine whether to sustain the objection, that is, agree, forcing me to adjust my wording, or to overrule it, disagreeing with it, and allowing me to continue."

"Oh," said Samveru. She straightened her robe and adjusted her headpiece. "Okay then. Well, overruled. It's obvious that Solhiti doesn't manage every single thing that ever happens."

"Understood, Your Honour," said Felix, lowering himself to his seat." Habeus watched him sit down. Was that a smile on his face?

"As I was saying," said Habeus. "My client has shouldered this formidable burden since the dawn of creation, or as near as it makes no difference-" he said, raising a hand to Felix, who was about to object again, "-asking nothing in return. When it was suggested that the as-yet unmarried Lady Skrida become his wife, such boundless joy and euphoria filled his soul that he accepted instantly."

Solhiti did not look like the sort of a person to experience boundless joy or euphoria. He looked like the sort of person who punched boundless joy out of people.

"Bolstered by his wife's support, the burden eased slightly. Not through shared work, but through the knowledge that a friendly ear and kind embrace was waiting at the end of every day."

Skrida did not look like the sort of person to lend a friendly ear or offer a kind embrace. She looked like the sort of a person who collected friendly ears in a bucket.

A true match for one another.

"Through no fault of his own, this marriage, sadly, has run its course. The Lady Skrida became more distant and remote, overambitious and impossible to satisfy, and, despite my client's every effort to salvage the relationship, it is his final wish to see his wife happily into her new life. To suggest that she is in some way not only *entitled* but simply *able* to seize some of the burden of rule is both inaccurate and, frankly, dangerous. Simply put, it would kill her and damage the cosmic realm."

Felix looked at Skrida, who was gripping her hands together so tightly her knuckles went white. Despite this, her expression remained neutral, almost placid. Habeus continued.

"It is therefore prudent that this marriage be ceased simply and quickly, with the understanding that Lady Skrida instigated such proceedings of her own free will, and therefore she should return to her duties that my client has graciously allowed her to continue with."

"Allowed?" hissed Skrida, the facade cracking. "Allowed?!"

Felix leaned over. "Please, Lady Skrida, try to contain-"

She turned to him, her face blooming into a rictus snarl of hatred. Within a few seconds the horrible expression had melted back into indifference. "Hm," she said, staring straight forward, leaving Felix both wide-eyed and blinking.

Habeus in the meantime was standing, hands clasped behind his back. "In summary, Lady Skrida may leave. Of course she may. But she may not dictate the terms of her departure. She may not fill her pockets as she leaves." He paused. "The door is open to her. That is all."

Felix dared not look at Skrida. Habeus returned to his seat. Samveru watched him go, then once again plucked the gavel from the air, *ting*ing it against the plate in front of her. She pointed a finger at Felix.

"I think it's time for some of this evidence, Mr Sacramentum."

7 - Skrida, The Goddess of Death I

"I would like to start by allowing my client to explain her feelings on the matter in her own words," said Felix.

"That seems eminently sensible," said Samveru. "Though I would say that almost everyone in this room has doubtless heard Lady Skrida complain at length about her husband already."

Felix ignored the ripple of titters behind him. "That may well be the case, Your Honour, but I feel it would benefit her case if such discussions were expressed openly and officially, in front of the court, so we can address them officially."

"Very well, proceed." Samveru leaned back. Felix gestured to his client, and she rose, all black robes and detached menace. She moved like a black stormcloud, smoothly striding over to the witness stand without a sound. She took a seat.

"Witness," said Felix. "Please state your name and occupation for the record," he said.

"What record?" asked Samveru. Felix looked around and noticed there was no-one taking notes.

"A point of order," said Habeus, standing. He held up a hand and made eye contact with someone in the crowd, then beckoned. A figure began moving through the assembled seating, gingerly stepping around the many godlings and other divinities that were sprawled on their chairs, drinks held in loose hands. As they approached, Felix saw it was the figure of a young woman.

"Muna," said Habeus. The woman, Muna presumably, bowed her head. "Uncle," she said.

Is everyone here related?

"Would you mind, Muna?" said Habeus, and Muna nodded, then pulled a chair seemingly out of thin air. She lowered the chair off to the side of the concourse, then settled into it, and stared at Felix, hands folded in her lap. She did not blink.

"Uh, hello," Felix said. She did not react. "Are you going to be taking the court record?"

Muna didn't even blink.

"Lad," said Furbo, behind him. "She's the patron God of Memory." Felix looked at him with a 'what exactly do I do with that information' expression.

"She doesn't need to write anything down, is what I'm saying."

"She stores it all up here," said Habeus to Felix, tapping his bald head. "I'll write it all down later."

Write it all..? Felix remembered the great rack stuffed full of The Books of Precedent. He had seen them when waiting for Jurrekker's court case to start. Floor to ceiling, wall to wall, an archive to make any librarian shudder. Every legal case ever heard, and every judgement passed on them.

Did Habeus hand-write all of them?

"You may proceed," said Samveru.

But there were hundreds of them… thousands, even. He must have wrists of steel. Felix suddenly saw himself in his mind, trying to arm-wrestle the God of Judgement, and sweating while Habeus barely tensed his huge wrists.

"I said, you may proceed," said Samveru again, snapping Felix back to focus.

"Yes, of course. Wait, should I repeat my opening for the record?"

"No," said Habeus. "She was listening the whole time."

"Then why-"

"Ahem," said Samveru. "Do get on with it."

"At once," Felix said, with a nod of acknowledgement, rolling his own wrists in a few circles to loosen them up.

Focus.

Felix turned back to his witness, trying to seem unintimidated. It wasn't easy. Skrida considered him without expression. "Witness, please state your name and occupation." Those words were a ritual for him, a comfort, though once he had spoken it he regretted it. It was obvious who she was, and now everyone would think he was some sort of egotistical idiot. However, Felix remembered where he was, and so acting in a way he might normally consider egotistical was probably the norm amongst gods and godlings. His client didn't seem to mind, other than rolling her eyes.

"If I must." She paused for effect, sweeping her eyes over the assembled audience. In a deep voice, she boomed: "I am Skrida, Goddess of Death, Soul-Gatherer, The Inescapable, The Patient One, She-Who-Waits… I am The Final End."

A chill had passed down Felix's spine. "Thank you, Lady Skrida." He mentally shook himself, forcing himself to talk normally, not like someone about to question the physical and magical embodiment of death in all forms. "I shall now ask you a series of questions, and please answer with as much detail as you see fit."

"Ask away," said Skrida, picking her nails, her voice much more conversational.

"How long have you been married to Solhiti, King of the Gods?"

The witness splayed her fingers out in front of her as if she were at a salon, examining her work. "That's not easy to say. We gods do not measure time in the same sense as you mortals do. For us, there is no beginning, and no end… other than me, of course." She gave him a terrifying smile, then returned to her grooming.

"So, is it fair to say that you have been married a long time?"

"Yes. We have been married since before the first grub crawled along the ground."

"And how did you meet?"

She sighed. "When the First Primordial was overthrown by the Second, its soul was split into fourteen equal pieces, and we both coalesced into being at the same time, along with our cousins. After the Second had absorbed the fourteenth piece, and started trying to do the same to my recently birthed family, Solhiti seized it and held it down while I killed it - the First True Death - and you could say a certain spark flickered between us at that moment. I remember when he first saw me after that dreadful day. He fetched me a drink from a golden goblet, and at that point I knew." She smiled. "We were engaged that day and married shortly after."

"And was it a loving marriage?" said Felix.

"I object," said Habeus, standing. His voice cut through the air like a warhorn, and Felix had to stop himself from flinching. "There is no 'was'."

"Pardon?" said Samveru, seemingly as confused as Felix was by this sentence. Habeus shook his head, his beard shifting.

"It is important to note that it is still a marriage until such time as it is declared annulled." Samveru looked at Felix and raised an eyebrow. Felix looked at Habeus, standing as he was, fire in his eyes.

He's enjoying this. How long has it been since he's been able to stand on this side of the bench?

"Your Honour," said Felix, polite despite the situation. "I was referring to the fact that it *was loving* and is no longer, not that it was a *marriage* and is no longer."

"And is that what our judge has understood it to mean, I wonder?" said Habeus, stroking his chin.

Both of them looked at Samveru, who tilted a heavily decorated head to the side in thought. After a moment she nodded. "It is still a marriage. Rephrase your question, mortal."

I do wish they'd stop calling me that, especially as I'm currently... well, you know.

"Of course, Your Honour. Witness, in the time after you were first married, would you have described the marriage as a loving one?" Felix looked to Samveru for approval, and she nodded. Habeus lowered himself back into his chair.

"I would," said Skrida, quietly. "For a time, it was bliss. Caring, attentive, not to mention he was a fantastic lover." Skrida paused and Felix looked at his shoes, unwilling to interrupt, yet unsure of how to continue. Mercifully, Skrida saved him the trouble. With a smile, she said: "He made me feel like I was the only woman in the cosmos."

"And when did this behaviour change?" said Felix.

Skrida's warm smile froze then melted. "I started to notice small things. He didn't talk to me as much. Well, I thought, he's busy, creating the world, crafting humanity, striking the spark from his internal furnace. That has to take it out of someone. So, I overlooked it. But it became more difficult. He seemed... closed up. I thought: what had I done? Did he not love me anymore?"

She scowled. "Then, after a period of time in which he barely spoke to me at all, during which I blamed myself and internalised all of this hatred, suddenly one night he perked right up. He instantly lost his moody streak and returned to his bubbly, ebullient self. Old Solhiti once again." Felix risked a glance at the King of the Gods, who looked about as ebullient as an angry rhinoceros.

"What happened then, witness?"

"For a time, bliss. Harmony. Then, it hit me. Why the sudden return to happiness? I certainly hadn't changed anything. My routines were the same as ever. Something, somewhere must have given him joy. Something that-" She paused, holding a clenched fist to her mouth, then appeared to regain herself. "Something that wasn't me."

She closed her eyes. "At first, I assumed it was some breakthrough in his work. But as I asked around, there had been no significant changes. No new life forms. No new planets. Just... same old same old. So, I thought, perhaps he was feeling joy at the achievements of one of his family? And so, once again, I asked around. Had anyone achieved anything of late that they were particularly proud of? Of course, there were some responses, but none that would have bothered Sol much. Then I spoke to..."

She let a long breath out. "Her."

The atmosphere had chilled. The very air was literally colder. It was difficult for Felix to continue, but he steeled his nerves and asked the one word question that screamed to be asked. "Her?"

"I will speak *her* name only once," she growled. After a pause, in which the temperature seemed to drop again, she spoke one word with such venom that Felix's spine tingled anew, seemingly stabbing each syllable and dragging it across the flames.

"Opekktur."

A few heads in the audience swivelled, hoping to catch a glimpse of the named goddess, had she been brave or nosey enough to attend, but none were able to find her. She was almost certainly avoiding today's proceedings.

Sensible move, by the sounds of it.

"And who is-"

"Don't say her name!" snarled Skrida, jabbing two fingers at him. "Do not!"

"V-very well, my apologies." He forced himself to meet Skrida's gaze and tried to impress upon her their previous tactical discussions by raising his eyebrows. For a moment she focussed her fury on him, but soon relented, closing her eyes and breathing deeply. The temperature thawed a touch. "For the benefit of the court, who is this person?" said Felix.

Skrida did not speak. After a moment, Felix nervously smoothed his jacket. "Please, witness. It is important."

His client took a deep breath, then pointed a long finger at Furbo. "You there. Scholar. Explain." Furbo leapt to his feet, took a nervous swallow, then began speaking in a quick voice.

"Ope-uh, the lady in question is the Goddess of Mystery and the Unknown. Each of the texts describe her as aloof, distant, unbearably beau- ah, unbearably, uh, mysterious. Her patron animal is the owl." He gave a short bow then sat down again quickly.

"Thank you, uh, expert witness," said Felix, trying despite everything to follow standard court protocol, even if he seemed to be the only one doing so. He turned back to Skrida.

"And what happened when you spoke to this person?"

"She got very nervous when I approached. I assumed it was my reputation… but she hadn't been that way with me before. When I attempted to ask her about her projects, she didn't make eye contact, and answered with short words. For the Goddess of Mystery and Secrets, she's normally a blabbermouth."

Felix began to pace. "And this made you suspicious?"

"Yes. Not about… what eventually turned out to be the truth. I was generally suspicious. I knew she was hiding something. I went home and asked Solhiti about it."

Felix chanced a quick look at Habeus, who was sitting there watching them. *I wonder if he'll bring that up later. 'Generally suspicious' is a term ripe for digging. What's his plan?*

"What did you say to him?" he said, returning to his witness, who was clearly fighting to keep her feelings under control.

"I asked him why he thought... *she* was acting so strangely towards me."

"And what did he say?"

"He said to... He said..." she was gritting her teeth. "He told me to mind my own business, and to butt out. Me! His own wife!" With a force of will, she calmed her face, and allowed a placid, neutral expression to wash over it.

"And then what did you do?"

"Somehow, I did. I swallowed my suspicions. I pretended nothing was wrong. Inside, though..." she pressed a closed hand to her chest. "That niggling feeling never went away."

"And what happened next?"

"I noticed over time that more and more of the gods and goddesses I spoke to became distant with me. Almost... nervous. Each time I asked Solhiti about it, and each time he told me I was being ridiculous. Each time I tried to believe it. Each time another needle in my heart."

Felix nodded. "How did this all come to a head?"

She took a long, slow breath. "I have never wanted children. I have no interest in preserving a legacy. I don't want to handle the... Practicalities. This is something that Solhiti has known since we first became married."

She closed her eyes. "Once, I was walking, as I do, through the Dappled Meadows. While I was there, I met a young man I had never met before. At first, all I could see was his silhouette. I thought it was my husband at first. He had the same physique. The same bearing. As I approached, I noticed it was not him. The hair was the wrong colour. The eyes were... or rather, they weren't..."

She paused. "Whoever it was, I didn't know him. I asked him his name. Rokkri, he said. I asked him who his parents were. He looked me square in the eye, and proudly announced his father was Solhiti, the Sun himself."

She clenched a fist, then unclenched it, resting her hands on the surface in front of her. "My entire world came crashing down. I went and sought out my husband at once. I found him at... *her* dwelling. They were sipping nectar and laughing. I asked him who Rokkri was, and... and..."

"And what?"

"He told me that Rokkri was his son, and his heir, and if I had a problem with it, then I needed to deal with it myself."

Skrida's fingers dug into the marble bannister of the witness stand. It cracked under her grip. With a cool voice, she said: "As you can imagine, I became… upset."

"I can imagine," said Felix, with a tiny smile.

"What does that mean, mortal?" she said to him, her eyes furious, and he shuddered, his smile scurrying behind a veil of obeisance.

"Uh, nothing, Lady Skrida." She scowled, then continued.

"Those I tried to confide in gave me such looks. Such pitying looks. Then it struck me. They knew! They all knew! I was the last to know! Liaison after liaison, affair after affair… they bubbled up through the floor. Everywhere I turned, I learned of another. And everyone knew. Except me. Me!"

The bannister shattered in her grip. "From that moment, I knew I could not stay married to this… *ogre*. This excuse for a man! The man I loved had long gone. I sought help from Samveru to sever me from the binds to this abominable creature, but she told me I could not. So I went to our cousin, the noble Habeus, and he said that in the mortal world they have a process by which marriage can be cancelled. I confronted Samveru again, and she eventually agreed, on the grounds that I can prove it is the only course available to me."

She looked up at Solhiti with eyes as black as death. "And so here I am. I am here for what is mine. My freedom, and for my share. For have I not worked as hard as he has?"

Felix waited for a few breaths, then took a few steps over to Skrida. Her body heaved with each breath. Quietly, he leaned over to her.

"Are you okay, Lady Skrida?" he said quietly.

Her breathing stopped, and she slowly looked at him. "What?"

"Are you okay? Would you like me to call for a break in the proceedings?"

She regarded him for some time. Eventually she relaxed a little, and sat back. With a wave of her hand, the marble rubble reformed into a perfect, unbroken bannister. "No," she said.

"Are you ready to answer their questions?" he said gently.

She narrowed her eyes, took a breath, and nodded. "I'm fine," she said.

Felix hesitated, then nodded. He returned to the centre of the concourse. "I have no further questions for this witness, Your Honour."

Samveru was looking at her hands. After a moment she nodded. "Very well. I understand that the opposition will now ask some questions." She could not look at either Felix or Skrida. "Go on, then."

Felix sat down and watched as Habeus stood. He seemed unmoved by what Skrida had said, and instead marched over to the centre of the room. With no preamble or qualification, he turned to her.

"Witness. You are a liar."

8 - Skrida, The Goddess of Death II

"They will ask you questions," said Felix, several days before. He was sitting alone with Skrida in a dark room of grey wood. "Horrible questions designed to get a rise from you. They will trap you with convoluted phrases in order to trick you. Whereas my questions will be open-ended, theirs will be closed. They will try to get you to answer 'yes' or 'no' in ways that are designed to trip you up and agree to things that you do not agree with. They will try to unbalance you. To irritate and frustrate you. They *want* you to overreact, and will do anything they can to make you do it. Their whole case, I think, will rest on the sort of person they can paint you to be. So they will have one aim: to discredit and besmirch you."

Skrida gazed at him unblinking. She had not reacted to his words in any way. *Was she unsurprised? Did she not care? Is she just good at masking her emotions when it suits her?*

"Notice I said 'can'. You have the opportunity to deny them the satisfaction of getting their way. It won't be easy." Again, Skrida did not reply. She studied her fingernails. Felix lowered his eyes and interlaced his fingers. "Lady Skrida. If I may be so bold as to offer some advice."

She scoffed. "Well, that is why I am retaining your services, is it not?"

"Yes, I suppose so. Three key points." Felix relaxed his grip and held a finger up.

"One: Do not answer anything that is not a direct question. Feel free to ask them: 'is that a question?' or look at me if you are unsure."

"I am never unsure of anything," she said. Felix raised a second finger and continued.

"Two: Trust me. I am, as I am often reminded, a mere mortal. But I know the law, and I know how these things go. You have instructed me for a reason, so I ask that you trust me, even if it seems that I'm making a mistake. It's all part of the performance."

She raised an eyebrow. "And the third thing?"

The most important thing, and the hardest thing to say to any client, especially a god...

Felix lifted his gaze and met her eyes. He lifted a third finger.

"Don't lose your temper." She looked at him and laughed, a laugh full of mirth and warmth.

"Oh, don't worry on that account. Lose my temper, indeed," she said, wiping an eye with a finger.

~

"How DARE you, you snivelling *worm* of a man," screeched Skrida, who had flung her chair back and was enveloped in a swirling mass of obsidian shadows. "*You* accuse *me* of spreading falsehood? Me? I will have your snake-tongue for that, you treacherous viper! I'll split your soul into six and feed them to the darkness!"

Samveru rolled her eyes, Habeus looked a touch nervous. The shadows around Skrida darkened and coalesced into spikes while she continued spitting her curses. The room started to rattle.

Felix, said Racelsus. *You might want to do something.*

"What on earth do you propose?" he whispered at her. "I'm a little out of my depth!" There was a minor sense of uneasy conversation rippling through the audience.

"I will tear this whole farcical den of sneaks into-"

A burst of light accompanied by an enormous *crack*ing sound, and Felix threw his hands in front of his eyes. When the bright red smears over his vision cleared, he saw Solhiti standing up, light blaring from him in a golden aura.

"Cease this tantrum," he said. The light bled from him, fizzling against the darkness where they met. Skrida's face, twisted in a rictus snarl of fury, met the stern, passive face of her husband.

Suddenly, the darkness vanished entirely. Skrida was sitting, looking bored, examining her nails. She said nothing. Solhiti said nothing. The King of the Gods retook his seat, and Habeus took a few nervous steps towards Skrida.

"Witness," he said. "You must answer my questions."

She looked at him sweetly and gave a small smile. "You haven't asked me any yet."

I'm counting that as a victory.

Hearing an irritated hiss, Felix turned to Racelsus.

"I wish I was able to cover my eyes," said Racelsus. "Or close them. I miss eyelids."

"I'm willing to bet no one has ever said that sentence before," said Felix, trying to forget the terror he had just felt.

"I have, a few times. Great things, eyelids. Make the most of them."

Habeus was not rising to the bait. He had not spoken for a few moments, and neither had Skrida. Eventually he interlaced his fingers.

"You stated earlier that you have never wanted children. This has always been the case?"

"Yes it has."

"You also say that you made this plain to Solhiti. How did you do that?"

Skrida shuffled slightly. "I told him on the day we were betrothed."

"What did you say?"

"I said to him, plain as I say to you: I do not want children."

"And how did he take it?"

Skrida frowned. "He was..." she paused. "He considered my words, then said: 'I understand.' Then he said he would love and cherish me for eternity, with or without children."

Felix heard it the moment she said it.

"Those were his exact words?"

"Yes! I remember them as clear as yesterday."

"And this was a condition to your marriage?"

"Of course. I told him in no uncertain terms that if he were to impress upon me the prospect of children, I would end the marriage."

Habeus nodded, folding his arms. "So you acknowledge that Solhiti made no such claim to desire a childless future?"

Skrida stared at him. "What?"

"He agreed that you didn't want children, but he never said the same of himself. You are shaking your head, witness."

"No," she said. "No. You're wrong."

"Did it not occur to you that the king of the gods would want an heir?"

"He never said as much to me."

"But he never said the opposite?"

"I - that is… Well, he inferred it."

"How?"

Skrida was scowling. "Look, the point is we were married with the understanding that I did not want children. How complicated is that to get your thick head around?"

"And why is it that you don't want children, witness?"

Felix stood, speaking before Skrida had a chance to reply. "Objection, Your Honour. Irrelevance. The reasoning behind my client's decision is moot; the fact is, she did not want them, and made such intentions clear."

Samveru scratched the tip of her nose. "I admit I have always been curious… Personally, I have children, and believe it is my duty to do so, and encourage others to do so too." She paused, deep in thought. "But I find myself agreeing with Mr Sacramentum. Unless, Habeus, you can confirm to me that the answer to such a question is of paramount importance to your case?"

Habeus bowed his head. "It can be circumvented."

"Very well. Your objection is sustained. Please move on, Habeus."

It was still an odd experience for Felix, managing to successfully object to a point the God of Lawyers had made. He had assumed Habeus would be prim and proper, precise and authoritative, making no mistakes and presenting no weaknesses. It turns out he's just as ready to play dirty as any lawyer Felix had met.

Habeus himself had wandered to the middle of the area in front of the witness stand and had interlaced his fingers again.

"Witness, what is easier: living, or dying?"

Skrida raised an eyebrow. "What sort of a question is that?"

"One that I would like you to answer."

"Why?"

"Please answer my question, Lady Skrida."

She flicked her hair back. "Dying is simpler. Accepting death is much harder than living."

"But many are not given the choice, are they?"

"Just what are you getting at?" said Skrida.

"You said something earlier: that you've 'worked as hard as he has'. He being my client, of course: Solhiti, King of the Gods and God of Life."

"I have."

"I see. Tell me witness, what do you think of the realm of Gaman, the God of Revels and Celebration? Do you think he works as hard as you do?"

Skrida snorted. "No. I suspect he'd agree."

A gentle chuckle from the audience, which Felix saw was Gaman himself.

"And do you think that I, God of Justice and Law, work as hard as Berjast, The God of War?"

"Hardly," said Skrida. "Your point?"

"My point is that the Pantheon may have divided all of creation amongst ourselves, but our remits and responsibilities are not equal, as you yourself have just agreed. Solhiti's remit and responsibilities, even half of those responsibilities, are more than any other god, even a god as formidable as yourself, could handle."

"No, I disagree."

"You do?"

"I do."

"Death is simpler than life. Your own words. Therefore, does it not follow that to manage the realm of Death is simpler than managing the realm of Life?"

Skrida scowled at him, but said nothing.

"Why not give us a run-through of your responsibilities now, then? A day in the life, or death, as it were."

Skrida took a moment to think.

"I don't have to explain myself to you, Habeus. How I manage my affairs is my own business."

"Quite true, quite true... But I put it to you that the realm you manage, that of the silent souls of the departed, is not a complicated place. You welcome souls as they arrive, and keep them where they should not wander. My client Solhiti on the other hand..."

Habeus turned to consider the King of the Gods.

"The creation of life is infinitely more complicated than the ending of it. To plant a seed that sprouts a sapling takes many careful months, where the slightest mistake can lead to ruin. To nurture that sapling to a tree that bears fruit takes *years*. To simply kill the tree… anyone with a few minutes to spare can do it. The same of course is true for other forms of life."

"But," said Felix, standing up.

"*Excuse* me?" scathed Samveru, narrowing her eyes at him. Felix felt himself blushing as he inclined his head.

"Ahem, uhm, objection…"

Samveru sat back, shaking her head. "That's better. Come on, you all made these silly rules, the least you can do is follow them." She waved a hand in his vague direction. "You were saying?"

"I was saying," said Felix, ignoring the burning sensation in the tips of his ears, "that the taking of life is a moral difficulty. Any person, human or otherwise, with an understanding of morality knows that it is not a simple, easy thing to take a life. In fact, many who do so regret it for the rest of their days."

"And who do you think is responsible for that moral quandary?" said Habeus. "Life knows that life is precious, and so fights to protect itself. It is not Death's doing that one feels guilt."

More bloody philosophy.

"Furthermore, many animals that do not have this higher understanding do not baulk at the taking of life. Indeed, for many forms of life, it is necessary. Carnivorous species, for example. For them, the taking of life is not just simple, but necessary."

Habeus was in his stride, and Felix didn't know how to stop him. The old god was pacing, in time honoured lawyer tradition.

"What's more, there are species that even delight in killing. Human beings, to use my learned colleague's example, are not averse to the thrill of the hunt, are they? Or to the occasional ritual sacrifice? The joy of mortal combat, or a public hanging? How easy it is to seal off that nagging guilt in those circumstances."

Felix lowered himself back to his seat, with the feeling he'd walked right into the place that Habeus wanted him. He was struggling to find anything to say.

"Now consider the new parent, trying to raise their child from birth. How many brand new mothers have you found who are enjoying their newfound child-rearing duties? The constant nagging anxieties, the relentless, monotonous, tedious caregiving, the thankless, sleepless, crushing, *boringness* of it all. Ask them if it's easy to create and nurture a life."

"The creation of life is the most enjoyable part," said Felix, standing again. "As has been established in many forms of art since life began."

"The planting of the seed, yes," said Habeus. "But find me a poem about the raising of the sapling." Felix chewed his lip and sat down again, defeated.

"And if you are going to object, please say so first," said Habeus. "Ideally with the reason as to *why* you are doing so. Disagreeing with your opposing counsel is not valid grounds for objection, unless they are contravening protocol. Was I contravening protocol?"

Felix felt the colour rising to his cheeks, somehow. He said nothing. Habeus sighed, then returned to his desk and leaned back against it, arms folded over his beard.

"No, the taking of life is simpler, quicker, easier. It stands to reason then that the management of the celestial plane in which this duty is undertaken is much simpler, quicker and easier than that of its opposite. It's simply logical."

His eyes flashed. "So this is why I suggest that you were not truthful, witness, as you know this, and to suggest that your responsibilities are as great as that of Habeus, God of Life, is either ignorant or arrogant. Which are you?"

"You don't have to answer that," said Felix, pointing at Habeus but looking at Skrida.

"Why not?" said Samveru.

"It's, well," said Felix, rising slowly. Was he really about to complain about the conduct of the God of Law?

Yes.

A.R. Turner

"It's considered bad form to harass the witness in such a direct manner," he said, not looking at Habeus.

"It does seem a little pointed," said Samveru.

"I retract that last question," said Habeus. "But I do have another point to make. You said, witness, that once you were suspicious of my client's involvement with Opekktur-" he ignored the *crack* as the bannister beneath Skrida's fingers broke again "- that you 'swallowed your suspicions' and 'pretended nothing was wrong.' Now, I can call on a dozen witnesses or more who can attest to you badgering them endlessly about your suspicions." He swept his hand over the watching crowd as he did so. "Do you want me to, or would you like to simply admit that you were not perhaps as good at pretending as you suggested?"

Do I object? If I do, and Habeus calls upon these apparent witnesses, it looks bad. If I don't, I might look incompetent, and it looks bad either way. Should I-

Skrida snorted a derisive laugh. "I could have been much worse. I spoke to those I thought I trusted, it's true" She smiled and blinked at him, in a mocking exaggeration of coquettish ditzyness. "Can you blame someone in my complicated position?"

"Perhaps, perhaps not," said Habeus, not reacting at all to her showboating. "But I can accuse you of lying in your testimony for your own benefit."

That snapped Skrida back to her menacing scowl. Felix could hear her teeth grinding from where he sat. *Ouch.*

Habeus returned to his seat and conferred briefly with Solhiti. "We are satisfied that the witness did not provide full and truthful testimony, was incorrect in her assumptions of equal responsibility, *and* incorrect in her belief in her ability to oversee a truly equal share. Fundamentally, conclusively, and in summary, she is incorrect. We hope that Your Honour will remember that when considering any notion of equal divisions of the kingdoms." A brief pause. "I have no further questions, Your Honour."

Skrida had watched the last few minutes with a miserable scowl on her face. When Habeus had said this last part, she stood up and returned to the desk that Felix was at. Felix leaned over to whisper to her.

"I don't want to talk about it," said Skrida, grinding her teeth.

"Fair enough," said Felix.

They sat in silence for a few moments while Samveru made some notes.

"Who's next?" she said, and Felix rose.

Journal Entry J - Oath

Reference case [NA] (NA)

Do you feel so strongly about an ideal that you'd cast aside your entire life to pursue it? Quite a heavy question, I know. I'll give you a few minutes to think about it. While we're waiting, though, let me tell you about the Squires of Gyre's Ruin.

These cheerful chappies were founded somewhere on the border of the North and West Countries on a single, strange principle: grief-fuelled battle rage. It was a single moment some five hundred years ago during the siege that formed the climax of the The Ruin of Gyre, a series of terrible battles fought somewhere up north. Apparently, King Yuwa, standing in the breach against the tide of enemy soldiers, saw his five sons all cut down within thirty seconds of each other. This sent him into such a tornado of grief and despair, mixed with utter existential fury. Witnesses claimed he flew into the enemy ranks, a swirling dervish of righteous punishment, and single-handedly broke the innumerable warriors that had taken everything from him.

He was never seen or heard from again - presumably cut to ribbons somewhere is my guess - but, as is often the case with these sorts of things, a cult sprung up worshipping him. Those who had lost loved ones would congregate, on the one hand offering each other support, on the other, channelling their grief and turmoil into such reckless bravery and combat prowess that any army quartermaster would fall over themselves in order to attract them to their cause. Their goal? Why, a heroic death, of course. They sought to emulate their great unwitting paragon, their hero: King Yuwa.

For hundreds of years, the Squires of Gyre found themselves fighting in dozens of wars for dozens of causes. Their loyalty was often won by the ruler who promised the most to them - not in terms of money, as such, but in temples and guild halls - sanctified spaces for them to mourn their losses and gird themselves for battle. And a small allowance, of course, but that was *purely* for such necessities such as food, or weapons, or clothes, or wine, or fine sweets from the South Country… You get the picture.

Here's the problem though - their numbers were dwindling.

As the generations progressed, this old-fashioned and frankly macabre cult waned in popularity, like so many others. Without members, the regiments were smaller and less ferocious, and therefore less desirable… which meant less income for those at the top.

What's worse: Crime-levels over in New Gyre were at an all-time-low. Hardly anyone got murdered anymore, and the strong guilds of Wanderers or other wild vigilantes were methodically ridding the wilderness of beasts and monsters, making the chances of losing a loved one to a terrible attack by man or beast fairly slim. So, those morbid followers attracted to the cult for whatever reason would often have experienced little to no grief in their lifetime, certainly not to the level of previous generations, (often no more than a family pet,) and so were not so receptive to the grief-meditations that had so successfully transformed their members into grinning psychotic murder machines.

So, what to do? And where do I come in? Ah, well spotted…

After years of decline, suddenly their numbers were swelling. Dozens then hundreds of young, strong men and women, seeking the heroic and romantic end that the Cult of Gyre promised. It coincided with a dreadful spike in crime throughout the city - specifically, random, unrelated, brutal murders.

A rather tired and nervous looking officer of the city guard came to see me in Lunchers one afternoon, while I was working on another case. By his cloak and boots he'd travelled a long way indeed. Mrs Luncher came down to meet him, and it turned out they were old acquaintances that still kept in touch. Once he was settled with a steaming mug of something, and after a series of reassurances that he was *quite* safe, he finally removed his helmet, smoothed his grey hair back and asked a simple question:

"If you had to arrest a prolific and ever-more-popular psychotic murder-cult, how would you do it without plunging the city into chaos?"

I don't think they covered that one in my legal training, I said.

He revealed that they'd stumbled upon some evidence that suggested the cult, before its surge in popularity and membership, had begun orchestrating quite the masterful recruitment drive. It started with a number of pamphlets and plays, in which the heroic Squires of Gyre's Ruin were painted with tragic, romantic appeal. Then a fairly famous young actress had apparently joined the cult for 'personal reasons'. Lastly, and this is where the law does have something to say, they organised a systematic and methodical campaign of assassination against a predetermined swathe of what it deemed impressionable, emotionally vulnerable (but athletically gifted) individuals. These victims, struck with sudden, meaningless grief, flocked to the arms of the Temples of Gyre's Ruin, to be welcomed with open arms into the cult. More members, more prowess, more temples, more sweetmeats.

It all came to light when an enterprising young sergeant got a hunch and had the idea of trying to go undercover. She would sigh heavily at the local theatres, complaining of her boredom at her unequalled athletic achievements as loud as was socially acceptable, before moaning about how her parents always left the window open when they slept, downstairs at the back of the house, just by the big apple tree, can't miss it.

Sure enough, two nights later, a tiny creak, some gentle footsteps followed by a whistle and a crack, and our sergeant stood over the unconscious body of a priest of the Cult of Gyre.

No lawyer in the city was brave enough to prosecute, and this captain was worried that if he tried to represent it *pro se*, as in, the city guard represent themselves, some silver-tongued lawyer hired by the cult would exonerate them. Either way, he was concerned about safety. Not his own, to his credit, but that of any unlucky civilian dragged into this case… But something had to be done before more people were killed. He couldn't quite meet my eyes when he said the next part.

"So, I thought… What if I found a lawyer that wasn't so concerned about, uh, being, well, you know…" he asked. I exchanged a look with Mrs Luncher. *They really do keep in touch. They must have been close.*

"Killed?" I replied. He at least looked embarrassed. I sighed and agreed to represent the city of New Gyre in prosecuting their murder cult.

What did I have to fear exactly? I'd just have to figure out how to remain in the material world long enough to oversee it.

In the time between other cases, I was able to make good progress on it. I have my box of case notes, my opening speeches, my evidence, witnesses lined up... But any dates we have scheduled keep getting postponed or cancelled. After the fifth or sixth time, we started asking around. The evidence is overwhelming. Why can't we get this over the line?

It turns out no judge wants to be the one to deliver the obvious judgement in the open-and-shut case of The City vs The Psychotic Death Cult Murder Maniacs Club, and so they keep using every bureaucratic trick in the book to shunt it down the road or fob it off on each other. To rise to the top of the judiciary, you have to be able to cunningly bend bureaucracy to your will, and there are none greater skilled in the art of legal smoke and mirror tactics than judges. There's every chance this case will never be heard. It's almost a shame. I was quite interested to see what they would try to do to me.

~journal entry ends

9 - The Others - *before*

"He'll be here exactly when he said he will," said Cherinda, several days earlier. "So you can stop fidgeting."

"Sorry," said Felix, who still fidgeted. "I suppose I'm a little nervous to meet another god after all this time. First Habeus, then Skrida…"

"Samsvara is lovely," said Cherinda. "Well, not lovely as such, but he isn't horrid. He's just… well, he doesn't waste time." She looked a little awkward. "Don't take it personally."

Felix looked down at the list in his hand. Over a couple of days, the team, Cherinda and Furbo in particular, had concocted a list of potential witnesses in Skrida's case. Each one of them an all-powerful god or goddess, ageless, divine, beyond mortal understanding. From where Felix was standing, at this point they were just letters on a page, and names on a list.

Just a few letters. No big deal. But would they all agree to testify? Would any?

The problem with conducting a case in which one of the participants is the literal King of the Gods is that many people get a little squeamish at the idea of testifying against his character.

Felix checked the clock on the wall. It showed three minutes past noon.

"He's late," said Felix. Cherinda glanced at the clock.

"Your clock is wrong, I think," she said.

"That's more likely than him being delayed?"

"Felix, he's the God of News. He is the messenger of the Gods. He isn't late."

It struck Felix suddenly that he was about to welcome a God into the office of Lunchers & Co for the first time. Panic seized him.

I wish I'd swept the floors! Should I offer him tea?

A single, bold knock sounded on the front door, and then the door opened. In a blur of motion, a figure appeared in front of Felix and Cherinda. He was a thin looking man with the look of one who spends most of their time outdoors. He had his hand outstretched. Felix blinked, recovered, then took the proffered hand to shake.

The God recoiled, wiping his hand on his robe. "Your list," is all he said. Felix laughed nervously, then handed the list over. Samsvara looked him up and down, then vanished in a streak of colour.

"That wasn't so bad, was it?" he said, turning to Cherinda. The celestial shrugged.

"That was pretty friendly for him, actually," she said.

Anxiety bubbled up Felix's innards. "So," he said, desperate to distract himself. "What now? We just wait around? Will he get a reply back to us in time?"

Cherinda smiled, and some of Felix's anxiety melted away. "Oh, I think so." Felix took a seat and tried not to think about the interminable waiting that was bound to follow. Deciding to use the time more fruitfully, he went to the kitchen to boil a kettle.

The water came to boil, and he poured a cup of coffee for himself and a tea for Cherinda. As he was walking back to the meeting room, he was surprised to hear another bold knock on the front door. It opened, and there stood Samsvara, waiting, an impatient look on his face. He handed the list back to Felix, who, despite his surprise, expertly shifted both steaming cups to one hand in order to receive it.

"Uh," is all he had time to say.

"I've crossed out everyone who said 'no'," Samsvara said.

"You've spoken to everyone already?" said Felix, scanning the list, forgetting where he was or who he was talking to. He glanced up and Samsvara raised an eyebrow at him.

"Of course," said Felix, trying not to let his embarrassment shine through. The God of Messages examined his nails. "Was that all?" he said.

Felix looked at the list again, counting the names that weren't crossed out. *Not a lot... Is it enough?*

Realising the God of News was waiting for him, he blinked. "Oh, apologies, no that's all, thank you."

"Your clock is one hundred and sixteen seconds slow, by the way," said Samsvara. "I could... No, never mind."

Felix glanced at the clock. "Funny, I-"

Before he could finish the sentence, Samsvara was gone in a burst of wind, causing Felix's hair to ruffle and his list to flutter. He drew his eyes down to his list yet again, hoping it might have magically changed in the preceding seconds.

It hadn't.

Taking out a pencil, he started drawing a few lines to connect those gods who were willing to testify.

"Maybe if she... or could he be willing to..?" he muttered to himself. After a few minutes, he sighed. It was going to be a leaky boat, and no mistake. But with enough strategic plugging, they might just make it through.

Who to call first...

"Who's making all that whooshing?" came a voice from upstairs. Possibly Mrs Luncher. "Some of us are trying to get some work done up here."

"Sorry," said Felix, not paying attention in the slightest to what was said or who was saying it. He chewed his lip as he read the list again.

Pickings were slim. Each of those that remained on his list were likely either making some point of how they don't fear Solhiti, or perhaps were too insane to realise the danger of it.

"Felix? Did I hear the kettle?" said Cherinda.

His eyes settled on one particular name.

"Felix?"

"Oh, sorry," he said again, shoving the list under an arm and taking a cup in each hand once again. He handed one to Cherinda - a pure mint tea - and put the other on the table.

"Useful?" said the Celestial, blowing on her cup.

"Mm," was all he said.

"He fixed the clock, by the looks of it. That was nice of him. He must like you."

"Mm."

"Any name jumping out?"

"...Mm?"

Cherinda took a sip as he looked again at the list, his eyes drawn to that name again. That name...

"Rangt," he read. Cherinda spluttered in her tea, coughing as delicately as she could. She dabbed at her mouth with the edge of her robe.

"I feel I must say again… Are you… absolutely sure about that one?"

"Hmmm…" said Felix.

Rangt…

It was worth a shot. Cherinda's aura was a pale blue.

"You do know, don't you?" she said, after a pause.

"Hm?"

"That he's… well…"

"He's what?" said Felix, looking up.

10 - Rangt, The God Of Lies

"**I** call Master Rangt to the stand."

To a chorus of sharp intakes of breath, Rangt, God of Lies, sprang up, handed his goblet to someone nearby and started to make his way forward. He was wreathed in black rags, the fabric floating behind him as he walked. His expression was earnest and open, with bright eyes and a smiling mouth. The god was completely hairless, reminding Felix of the prosecutor that worked with Jurrekker.

Jeast... That's a name I haven't thought about in a long time. I wonder what he's up to these days. He's not here, is he?

He scanned the crowd while Rangt took to the stand. *No sign of him... just being paranoid.*

Before Felix could prepare his best questioning pose, he felt a tap on his arm. Turning, he found Furbo had shuffled over.

"My boy, are you sure this line of questioning is sensible? Rangt is the God of Lies. The legends tell that he cannot speak two successive truths, or two successive fictions."

A sinking feeling gurgled in Felix's stomach. "I thought his thing was that he could only lie?" he said, with a last dredge of optimism.

"No, lad. Common misconception."

"Ah. Not to worry."

Argh! Worry!

He watched the god make his way to the stand. "Cannot speak two consecutive truths or two consecutive lies, you say?" *If I could... If I'm careful...* "Okay," he said, grinning. "I can handle this."

"Good luck, lad," said Furbo, unable to hide his concern. He looked as if he wanted to say something else, but refrained. Both of them turned to Skrida, who was regarding them with some scepticism. "Trust me," Felix said, and his client rolled her eyes, before letting them rest on Rangt.

Approaching the concourse, Felix opened his arms.

"Your Honour," he said. "As you are aware, the witness Rangt has a particular style of answering questions-"

"Oh, I'm familiar with my nephew Rangt." Samveru's eyes sparkled. "This should be interesting. Proceed."

Felix stood, taking a deep breath. The God of Lies was watching him, a helpful look in his eyes, almost eager to help, too eager, like how Furbo gets when you ask him a question about history or when Helda sees you struggling with a sealed jar.

Let's see if he starts with the truth.

"Witness," said Felix.

"Hello," said Rangt. His voice was bright and cheerful.

"Please state your name and occupation."

"Felix Sacramentum, and I'm a lawyer practising at Lunchers & Co Legal Firm, except I'm dead. I was orphaned at a young age when my parents were wrongly accused of-"

"Thank you, witness," said Felix both too quickly and too loudly. *He's trying to unsettle me. Why?* Felix took another breath, or whatever he took in place of breath. *Open-ended questions are a bad idea.*

"You are the God of Lies, yes?"

"Yes."

"Thank you. And your name?"

"I just said, my name is Gerridge, and I'm an orphan. Shall I tell you where I'm hiding?"

Felix heard a small yelp from behind him. "No, witness, that will not be required."

"Oh, okay. It's Whitewood, by the by. Little cave by the River Way, if I remember correctly," he said with a wink to Helda and Furbo, who were clenching their jaws and letting their mouths hang open, respectively.

Was that a lie? Or the truth?

The yelp had morphed into distressed muttering. He swivelled to look at Helda and Furbo. The former was frantically gripping her hands together, the latter talking frantically under his breath to her. He heard Racelsus's low voice, but couldn't hear the words. *I can't talk to them right now.* He needed to drag this back to the case at hand, but... Furbo and Helda were some of his closest friends. The loss of Gerridge was one of the hardest things they'd ever had to face. Years spent tracking down their adopted son, not knowing if he was even alive... How could Felix ignore that?

Felix considered Rangt, who was quite happily watching him in return. He guessed the god was lying... but what if he wasn't? Was this truth-lie-truth method absolute? Could it change or deviate? What constituted a truth? When did he change to the lie? Could it stretch over several sentences, or was each sentence different?

One thing at a time. Focus.

He heard Helda choke back a sob.

One thing at a time.

"Witness," said Felix, his voice hardening. "Do you know my client Skrida, and her husband, Solhiti?"

"I've literally never heard of either of them," said Rangt, with a shrug.

"And you are the nephew of the judge, Samveru?"

"Yes. I'm also her uncle."

Either I've lost track of when he's lying or the gods have a messed up family tree.

Felix turned to the judge, who had the same look that a long-suffering parent gets when their child misbehaves. He could almost hear her saying *'Oh, isn't he naughty! Oh well.'*

Focus.

"I'd like to ask you about a specific event that occurred some time ago, between yourself and Solhiti."

"Is that a question?"

Deliberately not. "No."

"Okay, just checking." Rangt regarded Felix with complete neutrality. *What is his game... simple mischief?*

"Would you say you have a close bond, you and Solhiti?"

"We're inseparable, like brothers."

"And do you often talk about your lives, your concerns, worries etcetera?"

"No, we don't talk often."

"When was the last time you spoke together?"

"About fifteen seconds ago."

"And what did you speak about?"

"This case."

Felix took a moment to think. Was he the only one feeling his brain sizzling with tracking this bizarre conversation? He began pacing to buy some time. *So they talk often, and have recently talked about this case... Wait, is it that they don't talk often? Gods, my head hurts.*

He rubbed his temples. *No sense sneaking around the big questions. I think he's going to lie next, so better ask another small one, then onto the main event. Just anything to get past the lie.*

"Do you..." he caught Furbo in the corner of his eye. "...have any hair?"

"Objection," said Habeus. "This is not relevant."

"I agree," said Samveru. "Unless I am missing something?"

"Uh, no, Your Honour. I was... Well..."

Habeus shook his head. "I believe my colleague is attempting to confuse or trip up the witness by asking irrelevant questions. I would suggest that you insist that he ask only pertinent questions from now on, with no repetitions or deviation from the case at hand."

"Agreed. Mr Sacramentum, any breaking of these rules will result in my immense displeasure," said Samveru, giving him a steady, serious glare.

"Understood, Your Honour." *That's me told... Okay, I'll have to be smarter about this.*

Wait, did he actually answer the question? Is he about to lie or tell the truth? I need to ask something that doesn't actually matter but might seem like it could...

"Witness, how long have you known my client, Lady Skrida?"

"I've only just met her today."

Aha!

"Thank you. Did Solhiti ever approach you and tell you he wanted to end his marriage to Skrida?" Rangt opened his mouth to speak.

"Objection," said Habeus. "Is the witness prepared to answer the question?"

"Yes," said Rangt.

"My apologies," said Habeus, bowing his head. "I misheard something, and thus rescind my objection."

Samveru shook her head. "You're getting old, Habeus. Mr Sacramentum, please ask your question again."

Tricky old...

"Witness, I'll restate my question. But first, can you hear me okay?"

"No," said Rangt, raising an eyebrow.

"Excellent. My question: Did Solhiti ever approach you and tell you he wanted to end his marriage to Skrida?"

"Well," said Rangt. "There was a time when he came to me and we had a long, heartfelt conversation about his relationship with his wife."

"And what was said?" said Felix, too quickly, before cursing himself.

"He said that he loved her with his whole heart and would never consider ending the marriage under any circumstances."

"Can, hm, can you please repeat yourself witness?"

"He said: that he loved her with his whole heart and would never consider ending the marriage under any circumstances."

Gah, I thought that would work.

"Your Honour," said Habeus, rising. "I do not know what game Mr Sacramentum is attempting, but all I am hearing is the same answers repeating."

"My patience is running thin," said Samveru. "Is there much more of this, Mr Sacramentum?"

"Uh, not much more, Your Honour."

"Hmm. Two more questions, then move on."

She can do that? Samveru was glaring at him. *Okay, maybe I'd best not tick off the judge. Make them count. Wait, is this first one a lie? Or truth? No time for that.*

"Witness," said Felix, thinking furiously. "Do you believe that any sane god in the same situation as Skrida could reasonably be expected to stay married to Solhiti?"

Rangt considered this. "I believe," he said, slowly, "that Solhiti is a god that anyone would be delighted to be married to, and they would spend every waking moment blessing their good fortune with every breath they had. He is a kind, generous god, and, from what I have seen, a kind and compassionate husband, through and through. He is, in summary, virtuous, noble, upstanding, honest and worthy." He closed his eyes, a small smile on his lips.

Yes! That's what I've been waiting for. A golden arrow.

"Finally," said Felix, fighting back the urge to punch the air. "Is your name Rangt?"

Rangt's eyes flicked open and he stared at Felix. "Yes," he said, with a wink.

Felix took his seat, feeling slightly elated, and Habeus stood. The God of Law stared at Rangt, who returned the gaze with an open smile. The smile of someone who likes to help, can help, and will help.

"The truth," said the God of Justice without preamble. "It is rather important when dealing with matters concerning the law. Would you agree, witness?"

"Oh yes, absolutely," said Rangt, nodding.

"Good." Habeus put his hands behind his back.

"Witness, answer me: Is this statement false?"

Rangt blinked, his smile wobbling slightly. After a brief hesitation, he swallowed. "...Yes," he said, uncertain. "That is... No. Well... Uhm."

Habeus continued. "Are you going to lie in your next statement, witness?"

The God of Lies scratched his head. "I..." He chewed his lip, his eyes twitching a smidge. "N... ye... hmm..."

"What about in your last one?"

Rangt opened his mouth to speak, but stopped. "Well," he said, then he frowned. "It's..." He stopped making sound, his mouth opening and closing of its own accord.

"What's this idiot doing?" said Skrida, leaning over to Felix.

"The classic lawyer trick of making a witness look unreliable," he replied. "He's doing it by asking questions that are both true and false. Furbo once told me it's called 'dialetheism'."

"Sounds like 'being a deliberately difficult irritating pustule' to me."

"I hear it can be an interesting philosophical exercise."

"Ugh," said the Goddess of Death. Felix almost laughed. Rangt, on the other hand, looked to be in some distress.

"It appears to be working though, Lady Skrida," said Felix. "Poor Rangt doesn't know what to do."

The God of Lies was sweating and wringing his hands. His jaw was tensing, opening, closing, tensing.

"Are you a liar, witness?" said Habeus, his voice calm and level.

"Eeeennnfff," Rangt said. The sound came out as a long, strangulated whine. Habeus shook his head, turning to Samveru.

"This witness is clearly unreliable," he said. "Everything he has said is therefore suspect. Need I say more?"

Samveru sighed. "Okay, Rangt," she said. "You can go now."

Rangt, eyes bloodshot and twitching, stood up and strode off, muttering to himself. He walked into the crowd and beyond, disappearing through a door near the back.

"Will he be okay?" said Felix to himself. Skrida did not answer.

Samveru clapped once, the sound cutting through the gentle babble of the court. She reached up and took a hold of the gavel floating above her, then tapped it twice. "We shall have a short break. I will return once the hourglass is empty." With a gesture, a large hourglass materialised above her, hovering in midair. It turned, sending a thin stream of silver sand to the lower half. Samveru turned and descended down a staircase hidden from view.

Felix fiddled with his sleeve, trying to keep the concern from his face.

My golden arrow, so easily swatted away by Habeus. Serves me right for getting excited. I'd better try to say something encouraging.

"That, uh, well. Hmm," said Felix, drawing a blank while failing to hide the worry gnawing at his insides. Skrida did not look at him.

11 - Gaman, The God of Mirth I

Felix took a moment to take the room in, trying to sift the atmosphere through the sieve of his brain. How was it going? Was he coming across as a fool, or was he holding his own? Was he on the road to salvation, or damnation? He looked at Skrida, who was staring straight ahead, a downward curl to her mouth. Furbo and Helda looked haggard and worn. He caught Racelsus eye - well, socket - and she clacked her teeth, then spoke into his mind.

How are you holding up?

It could be worse… Couldn't it?

Sure. It could be a lot better, though.

You always know just how to perk me up.

It's why you brought me along, isn't it?

No, it was in case I needed a paperweight.

I didn't think you were the sort to be making a comment about a lady's weight.

Never! And if I see any, I certainly won't make any.

Felix let himself wear the grin he was feeling. Racelsus had a gift for making him smirk like an idiot at the wrong moments, but he had to admit that right now it cheered him up. Anything - everything - was easier to face after a friend has just made you laugh. Felix took a breath.

Anyway, time for the next one.

"I would like to call Lord Gaman to the stand," said Felix, standing. A small cheer went up from somewhere in the spectators area, and Gaman, the god who had introduced himself to Felix earlier, stood, a smile on his face. He slapped shoulders and gripped hands as he passed by the lesser godlings and heavenly figures, stopping occasionally to swap a few words of a joke, laughing heartily when one was offered in return.

The God of Mirth, Laughter and Merrymaking eventually made his way to the front area, where he waved openly at Habeus and Solhiti, both of which ignored him. Turning, the god first made eye contact with Skrida, who frowned, then second with Racelsus, who emitted a tiny girlish titter. Lastly, he met Felix's eye for a moment. Felix noticed that, despite laughter lines and a friendly face, Gaman's smile did not reach his eyes. *Am I imagining that? Is it my own bias? Am I just seeing the worst?* As Gaman continued to the witness stand, Felix shook off his uneasiness and looked at the witch.

"Are you okay, Rass?" he asked, in the way only a friend can in specific circumstances, often saved for pubs or other places where one might meet new people.

"Oh, yes, fine, thank you," she said, a little breathy. "Completely, completely fine. Gosh, he's got a nice smile, hasn't he?"

"You're damn right," said Helda, nudging the witch's cage.

I'm glad some people are having a good time.

Felix considered the God of Camaraderie. He had been surprised that Gaman hadn't turned him down. After going over the list, Felix had had a long talk with Furbo, going over each of the gods and their responses. When he had asked about why the God of Mirth might have been willing - or, rather, not *unwilling* - to talk, the old scholar turned pensive.

"I think it might be an old rivalry," he said. "Think about this, my boy. What is life? Is it the heat of the blood, or the light of the sun, or the joy in our hearts? Gaman has always considered himself to be the spark that encourages life to go out and explore, to grow, to find joy in companionship and solitude, in multiplying and dwindling. I think because of that, he has been envious of the position Solhiti has as the undisputed King of the Gods and Father of All Life."

"And he isn't scared of Solhiti?"

"No, he is not. For what would happen if Solhiti were to strike him down for impertinence? All joy would leave the cosmos, perhaps, and nothing would remain but grief and anger. Solhiti would have a rebellion on his hands, and his would be the first head on the chopping block as the one who stripped laughter and joy from the world."

"But surely that can't be the case," said Felix, fiddling with his cuffs. "If he *did*, uh, strike Gaman down, it's not like people - gods - couldn't suddenly feel happiness."

Furbo raised an eyebrow. "Oh? And how do you know that?"

Felix opened his mouth to speak, then paused. "Well, I don't… But that can't be right. Happiness is real, you can feel it. It couldn't just disappear. It's a part of us, separate from the influence of any god."

"Is it? Have you never felt yourself abruptly stripped of happiness and contentment, for one reason or another? Suddenly unable to find the joy in, well, anything?" He sighed. "It's said that's when Gaman turns his eyes from you. I tell you now, when he does, it hurts to go on." After a pause, he continued. "It's maybe why he thinks he should be the one true ruler. For without joy, what is life?"

Felix took his friend's hand and squeezed it. Furbo squeezed back.

"It might be even simpler than that," said Racelsus.

"Oh?" said Furbo.

"Maybe he just has the hots for Solhiti's woman?"

~

Back in the Courtroom, Felix shook himself from his reminiscing. Gaman was in the witness chair, waiting for him. Felix's mouth was dry. He moved his lips around in an attempt to relieve this, but gave up and started questioning.

"Witness," said Felix. "Please state your name and occupation."

"I am Gaman, and I am the God of Mirth," said Gaman, in a deep, rich voice. "And Joy and Happiness, Laughter and Lyrics, Jokes and Japes, Camaraderie and Community…" He smiled, a great, broad toothy grin that invited anyone near to join in. "And Smiles," he said, to a gentle titter from the audience.

Felix did not smile.

"I'd like to ask you some questions about Solhiti and Skrida," he said.

"Oh, so *that's* why we are here! I thought someone was getting married, or had died," he added with a wink. A few more laughs floated from the audience.

Oh, he's going to be one of those witnesses.

"Witness, how well do you know Solhiti?" said Felix, folding his hands over and resting them on his belt. Gaman leaned back on his chair.

"Very well. We are like brothers."

"How do you mean, like brothers?"

"We are cousins; they are like brothers."

More laughs, and Gaman winked at someone in the audience.

Spare me.

"Would you say you have known each other a long time?"

Gaman considered this. "I suppose so. Time is a complicated concept for immortal beings. But, if I had to give you a straight answer, I'd say: yes."

Felix nodded, then stroked his chin.

No sense dilly-dallying.

"Have you ever known Solhiti to forsake his marriage vows and to see anyone else?"

"He sees people all the time. He sees us right now."

"When I say 'see', I mean: romantically."

"Do you mean like smouldering gazes or lusty winks? That's how *I* would see someone romantically."

"I mean," said Felix, crossing his arms. "Did he ever copulate with someone other than his wife, Lady Skrida?"

Gaman narrowed his eyes at Felix. "Straight to it, eh? That wasn't much of a warm-up."

Felix didn't answer, and the God of Mirth gave a shrug.

"Okay, have it your way. Have I ever known Solhiti to forsake his marriage vows, you ask." He leaned back again, and produced a pipe from somewhere. After puffing on it once or twice, and blowing three perfect smoke rings of different sizes, he leaned forward. "My answer: Yes, I have. Many times."

Low murmurs from the audience. A few knowing glances were exchanged and many mouths were covered with many hands. It was a well-discussed topic of conversation, but never outwardly acknowledged. How could Gaman be so brazen about it? Gaman looked around at them, enjoying their reaction, but ignoring Solhiti's glaring. Felix only had eyes for Gaman. He was forming the right phrasing for the question he needed to ask, though he was thinking that perhaps the time for joking had passed, and hoped that Gaman would stop playing and give him a useful answer. He straightened up.

"You have seen Solhiti behave in this way with someone who was not his wife?"

"Isn't that the same question?"

Felix bit back the first reply he thought of, and instead smiled.

"I apologise. Lawyers have a habit of repeating themselves. It's just to make sure that we are completely and unarguably on the same page."

Gaman shrugged, his brown curls bouncing. "I thought it was because you charged by the hour."

A few more laughs rippled through the room, eager to fill the nervous atmosphere left by Gaman's last answer. Felix took a breath.

"I'm sorry if I'm starting to sound like a bore, witness, but could you please just answer the question?"

Gaman rolled his sparkling eyes. "Starting? You were starting, and now you've started. In fact, there might be an opening for the God of Bores, I could put a word in if you like?"

Felix maintained eye contact and said nothing else, and eventually Gaman sighed.

"Oh, fine. Yes, I have seen Solhiti behave in the aforementioned way with someone who was not his wife. Several someones, actually."

Felix nodded, and continued. "These 'someones'. Can you name who you have seen in this manner, witness?"

"I could, but it would take a very long time."

A ripple of nervous laughter passed through the courtroom. Solhiti did not laugh, and continued to stare at Gaman with undisguised irritation, like one might stare at a particularly loud and annoying fly in a sweetshop.

Felix leaned back on his desk. "I'd like to ask you about one specific time." He hesitated, glancing quickly at Furbo. *I hope you're right, or I'm going to look like quite the idiot.* "Do you remember the creation of the stars?"

Gaman nodded, his brown curls bouncing. "Ah, but I do." His voice took on a mellifluous tone, one of a master storyteller about to recount a tale worth the telling. "There was a great battle between the Pantheon and the fearful Undirbui, that is, those who dwelt beneath."

The tone of voice along with dramatic emphasis drew the courtroom in. Something about the way he spoke made Felix almost feel unwilling to interrupt. But he had a job to do, and it didn't involve listening to stories.

Well, it sort of does. But… Oh, never mind.

"And what happened after the battle?" he said, and Gaman raised an open palm above his head. With a swish of his hand, as if cutting off the head of some monstrous beast, he continued.

"Our battle was the stuff songs are made of. A swarm of foetid, bloated monstrosities bubbled and boiled from great fissures torn in the sky. I had my divine spear, Hlatursöngur, forged from the rarest of things, a smile from the moon goddess. It could slice a mountain in half as if it were a cloud, and yet, despite our strength at arms and the bonds of our kinship, the Pantheon found themselves overrun…"

When Gaman paused for dramatic effect, Felix seized his opportunity. "I see. What happened after the battle?"

A look of annoyance flashed on Gaman's face, but it vanished as soon as it arrived. He smiled instead. "I apologise, lawyer. I had forgotten that your kind are not stirred by tales of triumph against overwhelming odds and derring-do."

"I'm all for triumph against overwhelming odds, witness, but I just like the facts."

Felix felt a little bubble of satisfaction when he heard a few small titters from the crowd. He wasn't much for showboating, at least that's what he told himself, but sometimes you had to play the game. Gaman was looking at him as if he were a fifteen year old that had displayed how well he can tie his shoes. A look that said *Well done, I suppose, but I expected more.*

"Very well. I shall skip over the exciting parts and go straight to the pertinent facts. Yes?" His voice returned to normal. "After the slaying of these monstrous creatures, Solhiti seized them and threw them skywards, their bodies soaring up to become the stars. There they would ever look down upon those that had bested them. And might I say, my cousin has ever had a strong throwing arm," he said, winking to Solhiti, who did not respond in the slightest. Felix started to pace.

"When you and your fellow gods were victorious, what happened then?"

"Well, I organised a great celebration. A feast, with food, drinks, entertainment of all sorts. There were dancing moonbeams, and a wine of five-thousand flavours, a troupe of singing…" he stopped when he caught Felix's face. "…anyway. It was such a large and lavish affair that we ended up naming it: Stjörnuveisla."

"Thank you. And where was Solhiti during this festival?"

"He was either perched in the seat of honour, or moving around the crowds, sharing their warmth and relief. And helping himself to his fair share of drinks! We all made sure of that. He was the hero of the day, of course."

Felix nodded, mentally preparing himself for the next few questions. He glanced at his client, then fixed his eyes forward so he couldn't see his client at all.

"Did he spend any time with Opekktur that night?"

After a few moments of silence, Gaman leaned forward and spoke in a soft voice that nonetheless carried through the room.

"He did."

If Felix didn't know better, he'd have thought Gaman was enjoying himself. "What were they doing?" he asked.

"They were talking, but I couldn't hear what about. Then Solhiti fetched her a goblet of something to drink, which she accepted with a smile and a flutter of eyelashes."

"Fetched her a goblet in the same way that he had for his wife, Lady Skrida?" Felix could *feel* the tension emanating from his client as if it were an open window on a cold day. Gaman closed his eyes and nodded sadly.

"Yes, though, if I may, the goblet seemed a little bigger this time."

Felix dared not look at Skrida.

"What happened afterwards?"

"They walked off together. I don't know where exactly, but I didn't see them for some hours after that, and when I did, they looked mighty happy, and I would know."

"What do you think they were up to?"

"Objection," said Habeus. "Conjecture."

Samveru bobbed her head. "Good point."

Felix nodded. "I withdraw that question. Witness, did you say this had happened before?"

"Many times, many times." The pipe had returned, and Gaman put on the face of someone deep in thought as he smoked. "At the Feast of the First Rainbow, at the Third Moon Harvest festival, at the Solemn Passing Ceremony… My noble cousin has a weakness for a pretty face. I can't blame him. But, then again, I am not married." He met Solhiti's eyes for a long moment, unblinking. The tension built between them, and Felix got the impression this was not the first time they'd given each other such a stare. He broke the spell by speaking.

"Thank you, witness. I have no further questions. Your Honour, are these the actions of a man that respects his marriage? How would you feel if your husband was acting this way?" Without looking at Gaman or Solhiti, Felix made his way back to his seat. Settling down. He decided to let Skrida be the first to speak. She leaned over.

"If I could kill him I would," she said.

Felix didn't ask which one she meant.

"Habeus," said Samveru. "Would you like to question the witness?"

"I would, Your Honour," said the God of Justice, rising to his feet.

12 - Gaman, The God of Mirth II

Habeus stood and considered Gaman. The two men - *gods*, Felix reminded himself, *not men* - were physical opposites. Habeus was old and bearded, bald-headed with severe eyes and a mouth used to grimacing. Gaman smooth-skinned and curly haired, full of smiles, laughter and easy, languid confidence. Habeus steepled his fingers.

"The feast of Stjörnuveisla. A busy evening, by all accounts. Lots of comings and goings. Lots of conversations and celebration. Yes?"

"Yes," said Gaman. "A busy night indeed. You yourself became particularly merry, I remember." Gaman wiggled his eyebrows, mimed taking a sip from an invisible glass, then winked at someone watching from the crowd.

Habeus smiled. "Quite. You seem to have followed Solhiti's movements that night with some dedication."

"He was the hero of the hour. Why wouldn't I ensure he was well provisioned with victuals and potations?"

"Food and drink," Felix heard Furbo whisper behind him, presumably to Helda.

"Not the only hero, though," Habeus continued. "Plenty of gods distinguished themselves, yourself included, as you so elegantly explained earlier. Yet you watched Solhiti like a hawk. Why?"

"I don't think I watched him like a hawk. Perhaps more like a swan," said Gaman with a small smirk.

"Witness?" said Habeus. "What do you mean?"

"Nothing in particular. Look," he said with a sigh. "I am the God of Parties and Merrymaking. I was simply aware of everything that was happening during Stjörnuveisla, as would be expected, as it is my realm, yes?"

Habeus did not react. "What did you do after you saw Solhiti depart?"

"Nothing special. I moved among the partygoers, as per usual. Pouring drinks, sampling drinks, slapping backs, sampling more drinks, you know the drill."

"So you spoke to many of the guests that evening?"

"I did, as a matter of fact. Do you need your ears looked at, cousin?" He jammed a finger into his own ear and gave a great show of digging around, to which those in the audience chuckled.

"Did you speak to Skrida?"

Gaman leant forward, sitting in his chair properly for the first time, then he hesitated, narrowing his eyes. He glanced at the goddess in question. "I spoke to everyone at the party."

"But you only spoke to Skrida once Solhiti had left?"

"I cannot recall." Gaman's whole demeanour had changed. He was less gregarious all of a sudden. It was as if someone had taken the joke too far. Felix could feel the sudden shift in atmosphere as if it were a palpable, physical thing, like someone opening a barrel of rotten eggs in the middle of a flower garden.

"You just said that you know everything that happens at your parties," said Habeus. "Why don't you remember when you spoke to Skrida?"

Gaman shrugged. Habeus shook his head.

"Allow me to ask a slightly different question. Did you speak to Skrida after Solhiti left?"

"Yes."

"What did you speak about, witness?"

"This and that." Gaman waved a hand. "Talk of the battle."

"Did you say the words 'he'll never know'?"

Gaman froze. His hand that had waved lowered itself slowly to the tabletop. "What are you implying?" he said, slowly.

"I am implying nothing, witness. I am simply asking if you said some particular words," replied Habeus, matching Gaman's tone. Seeing this, Gaman leaned back again, his voice trying and failing to return to the easy, musical cadence it had before.

"Why those words specifically, eh? Who have you been talking to, you sneaky old so-and-so?" He delivered this line as if he were in a bad play, but no one was smiling with him. Habeus took a step closer to him.

"You haven't answered yet, witness. Who is 'he', and what will he never know?"

Gaman shrugged. "Probably Berjast making some boast or other. Are we done here?"

"Probably?" said Habeus.

"Probably," said Gaman.

"Witness." Habeus turned from Gaman and sought out a figure in the crowd. Evidently finding who he was looking for, he turned back to the God of Mirth. "Sannkalladur is sitting in one of the chairs over there. We have not called upon her as a courtesy, because we expect the truth to be spoken to us, openly, completely and without obfuscation."

Felix wracked his brain trying to remember that name.

What was it? Sannkalladur? Goddess of… Weather? No. Sann… God of Numbers?

He gave a pleading look over at Furbo, who leaned his way. "Truth," he said. "Rangt's sister."

"Of course, thanks, Furbo." He didn't know exactly what the Goddess of Truth would or could do to another god sitting in the witness chair, but he didn't imagine it was particularly pleasant… Though it would make everything a little easier.

Gaman's faux-pleasant expression had changed. His mouth was still holding a half-smile but his eyes were devoid of mirth. "You threaten me? Call me a liar?" It was as if an invisible dark cloud was gathering behind him. Felix tensed. Habeus did not.

"I have not accused you of anything," said the God of Law. "In fact, I am going out of my way to give you every opportunity to speak the truth. All I am saying is that we have at our disposal methods to corroborate that, and loathe as we are to use them, use them we shall if we deem it necessary. So, I ask you again." Habeus steepled his fingers once more. "Who is 'he' and what will he 'never know'?"

Gaman met the old man's eyes and scowled. All traces of jollity had completely vanished from the face of the God of Mirth, even the forced ones. "She's too good for him. The way he treats her is despicable," he spat.

"Who, witness?" said Habeus, his voice's volume rising to match Gaman's, but retaining its calm timbre.

"Solhiti, of course! The way he treats his beautiful wife makes me *sick*."

Voices rose in excited babble in the audience. There were rumours, of course, but to hear such proclamations out in the open… Gaman's gaze flicked around them, then to Skrida, then back to Habeus. The Goddess of Death narrowed her eyes. "Witness, what is your relationship with Lady Skrida?" said Habeus.

Gaman eyed up the Goddess of Death with undisguised longing. "There is no relationship between us," he said.

"But you wish there were?"

Gaman did not reply.

"Witness?"

The God of Smiles sighed. "We have spent many long hours in talk, the Lady Skrida and myself." He sounded wistful. "She makes me feel alive. Every hour in her company passes in but a moment." Felix stole a look at Skrida, who was studying her nails with disinterest. For him, every moment in her company made him want to scream and hide, but maybe she just wasn't his type.

Gaman looked at Habeus. "At the party, having just seen her so-called husband run off with some filly, I approached her and we shared a moment."

Felix chanced a glance at Skrida, who was stony faced. *A moment?*

"Perhaps I was a little merry from the atmosphere… But I told her how I felt and how I wanted her to leave Solhiti and be mine," said Gaman, his eyes sparkling. "I still do. Skrida-"

"Thank you witness," Habeus said, cutting him off. He turned to Samveru. "Does this sound like the behaviour of a woman planning to stay in her marriage?"

"I'm not finished," said Gaman. "She said no."

"Witness, I did not ask you a question," said Habeus. Gaman ignored him.

"She said no. She turned me down." Gaman sneered at Solhiti. "Despite everything, she remained loyal to you until the very end. Did you know that, O Great Sun God?"

Solhiti had taken to his feet. Gaman did the same. Both of their hands started to glow.

"Gentlemen," said Samveru, her booming voice filling the air. "I will *not* have fighting in my courtroom. Cease this bravado or I shall expel you."

The God of Mirth, looking in that moment more like the God of Anger, stared down the God of Life and Light. After a few moments, Gaman snorted, and waved a hand, dispelling the gathering light from it. "Jokes on me," he said. "But that's okay. So long as the general humour of the room is maintained, I can take a joke." He stepped around the stone rail that surrounded the witness chair, then walked off to find his seat. He looked at no one as he passed them.

13 - Samskipti, The Goddess of Communication

I

"Is it going well?"

Felix looked at Skrida, who was sitting next to him and fidgeting with her black, laced sleeve. She was picking at the impossibly fine thread-work lattices. Was she... nervous? Uncertain? It was the first time Felix had seen her show any sort of vulnerability. She seemed to notice his curious glance and quickly clasped her hands together and rested them on her lap.

"It is always hard to say," said Felix. "I knew a lawyer once who used to say: 'Guessing a judge's mind is like guessing what happens after you die; impossible to know for sure, but you'll worry about it forever regardless'."

"But I know what happens after you die," said Skrida, looking at him like he was thick. Felix blinked.

"Oh. Yes. I suppose you do."

"So that's a stupid saying, is it not?"

"Yes. Sorry. I'll have to think of a new one."

She crossed her arms, seemingly having abandoned nervous fretting for her typical haughty irritation. "So, is it going well?"

I don't think so.

"I think so," he said with a small smile, which was not returned. "It's time for our next witness."

Felix stood and caught Samveru's eye. She nodded at him.

"The next witness we would like to call is Lady Samskipti," he said.

~

A few heads turned as a figure started making her way to the witness area. She was old, with white hair arranged in an intricate braid. The Goddess of Tradition and Communication looked the very part of a stateswoman;

413

dignified, composed, respectable. As she settled into the seat, Felix was struck by the sight of her. She could have been a statue, carved by an artisan, perched outside a governmental palace, or intricately woven into a tapestry over a throne.

He realised after a moment that everyone was waiting for him to speak, and so pretended that he had been deep in thought, instead of deep in awe.

"Witness, please state your name and occupation," he said. Felix tried not to flinch as she regarded him with dark, grey eyes.

"Samskipti. I am the patron Goddess of Tradition and Communication of all forms." When she spoke, she sounded halfway between a warrior poet and a diplomat announcing a declaration of war. In the presence of this master communicator, Felix was immediately aware of the precise way he himself was speaking, and in being so, tried to speak normally, and in doing so, found himself speaking like he had forgotten how.

"Letters, talking, and the like, and that?" he said, inwardly cringing at himself. Samskipti regarded him without expression.

"Yes." She made no gesture, but it was clear from her subtle use of tonality and cadence that she wasn't finished. "It also includes singing, gesturing, the unspoken word, and the mutual understanding that passes between two of the same mind." She paused. "And cooking."

Felix almost stumbled, vocally speaking. "Cooking?"

"Yes. I like cooking."

A moment passed, in which Felix did not know what to say. Instead of addressing this, he continued with his original plan.

"Please tell us what you saw on the feast of Stjom, ahem, Stjörssm, excuse me, Stjörnuveisla."

She watched him struggle with the word and said nothing. "I saw Opekktur sitting alone by a shimmering pond. The pond of Svegladur, in fact."

"Had you seen what she was doing before?"

"Please don't end your sentence with a preposition," said Samskipti, instantly making Felix feel like a schoolchild again.

Between Samskipti biting my head off for my grammar and Skrida not wanting me to say the name Opekktur, I'll be lucky if I have an unblemished soul to work with…

Samskipti tutted at him. "With which to work, mortal."

Sorry, with which to work…

Felix blinked.

"Oh, uh, apologies." Was he blushing again? How could he do that with no blood? "Had you seen, ahem, Opekktur earlier that evening?"

Did I say that too loud? Don't look at Skrida, don't look at Skrida…

The Goddess of Words hadn't moved an inch since she took her seat, furthering the impression that she was carved out of marble. "I saw her briefly at the feast, before I left it," she said.

"Thank you. What was she doing there?"

"At the pond or at the feast?"

"The feast, please."

"She looked to me like she was waiting for someone. Or, something."

"After waiting for a while, what did you see Opekktur doing?"

"I wasn't waiting for a while."

"No, I mean, after Opekktur was waiting for a while, what did you then see her do?"

"Your sentence structuring needs some serious work," said Samskipti. "You say that this is your job?" She raised an eyebrow at Habeus. "I thought practising the law required precise and accurate use of language?"

It's like having a conversation with Furbo when he's drunk.

Habeus gave a *don't-look-at-me* shrug, to which Samskipti shook her head gently.

"If I could rephrase, witness," said Felix, trying not to let all of his credibility crumble into dust. "Could you please tell me what happened after you noticed Opekktur by the pond of… of…"

He blinked twice.

Svegladur, came a soft voice in his head.

"Svegladur," Felix said, to which Samskipti nodded in the way a teacher might when a stupid student finally remembered something told to him more than fifteen seconds ago. An unexpected fizzle of pride in Felix's chest bloomed and quickly died away.

Am I that desperate for praise? He thought.

Yes, came the voice of Racelsus again. Felix turned his head and frowned at the witch, who he swore was grinning gormlessly.

Bog off out of my brain, he thought. *For a skull you're awfully nosey.* He could almost see Racelsus pout. *Especially as you haven't even got a nose.*

Just trying to help...

He turned back to Samskipti, who was waiting for him to start listening with a disappointed look on her face. He should have known that the Goddess of Communication would know if he was distracted. Guiltily, he gave her a tiny, sheepish smile.

So much for praise... he thought. "When you are ready, witness," he said.

"When *I* am ready?" she shook her head and sighed, but continued. "As I turned to leave, I saw a great, golden swan descend from above. It landed on the water, and began gliding over to Opekktur."

"And then what?"

"It sang to her beautifully, and she sang back to it. She stroked the swan, and it smoothed its golden feathers against her. After a few moments of such petting, the two of them copulated."

"Copulated?"

"Yes. Gained carnal knowledge of each other. Embraced as lovers."

"Had sex?" said Felix.

She scoffed. "Yes, to put it in such base language. I take it you are not a poet, Mr Sacramentum?"

"Sadly not, witness," said Felix. "I am but a mere prosaic mortal, so such concepts are confusing to me. Do you mean they literally had sex with each other, despite being different species?"

Samskipti considered this for a moment, folding her arms and tilting her head back a little. She looked like an adult trying to think of the best way to explain a complicated concept in language a child could comprehend. "Yes, and no. Many divine beings can shapeshift, the greatest of which are able to adapt their forms in whichever way they see fit." She unfolded her arms and stared at Felix. "I shall let you imagine the details."

Felix shuddered. "Thank you. Now, as to why this is relevant to our proceedings today: I would like you to quickly clarify something for me."

"You mean: you would like me to clarify something quickly. Do not split your infinitives."

Felix forced a pained smile. "Thank you, witness. Yes, you are correct. You said the bird that you saw was a great, golden swan?"

"I did."

"I wonder, witness. Do you know the symbols of the god Solhiti?"

"Of course. A god of his calibre has many symbols. He has the sun itself. The hammer. The spark. The endless road. Solhiti has many symbols. Do you want me to name them all?"

"No, thank you. But if I may… Is a golden swan one of his symbols?"

Samskipti nodded solemnly. "Yes, it is."

Felix stole a glance at Habeus, who was watching intently.

"Is it therefore possible that the swan could have been Solhiti?"

"Objection," said Habeus. "This is conjecture."

Samveru peered at them, thinking. "I will allow the answer to this question, but make it clear that this is opinion, not fact."

Felix faced his witness again. "Witness. *In your opinion*, do you think that it is likely that the golden swan you saw was none other than the King of the Gods, Solhiti?"

Samskipti paused for a moment. "Yes, I believe it is possible."

"Why?"

"Because he can shapeshift. I have seen him take several forms over the aeons. One of his symbols is the golden swan. For any other god to ape that symbol would be inviting challenge, and I don't think any in the Pantheon is foolhardy enough to do that," she said, looking at Gaman, "or, at least, I didn't until today." She closed her eyes for a moment. "I have also heard many rumours about the relationship between Solhiti and various other divine beings, including Opekktur, and so therefore it is not a great logical leap to put the pieces together."

Felix nodded. "Thank you witness. I'd like to ask you another question." The Goddess of Poetry and History inclined her head. "You are the Goddess of Communication, as stated earlier. Have you been present whilst Solhiti and Skrida have been talking to one another?"

"…I have."

Excellent. This should be good…

"How would you describe their relationship?" said Felix.

"I would not. I am not a gossip," said Samskipti, staring at him.

Felix blinked. "I did not accuse you of being one."

"That is because I am not one. I will not conduct in a 'he-said-she-said,' and will not offer opinions on another god based on words shared with their partner."

"*Partner*," Skrida growled from somewhere behind Felix. Felix ignored her, and remained focussed on Samskipti.

"I see. May I ask why, witness?"

"I don't think it is very becoming."

Not very...

Felix fought back the urge to sigh, and instead inclined his head. "I understand. Those are the only questions I have. Thank you." He made his way back to his seat, where Habeus and Solhiti had been whispering. Solhiti gave an irritated wave of his hand, and the God of Justice took to his feet.

14 - Samskipti, The Goddess of Communication

II

"Witness," said Habeus.

"Good day," said Samskipti.

Seeing these two figures talking with one another made Felix feel like he was watching some ancient philosophers discussing the fabric of reality. Both seemed so confident in themselves and their experience. It was some combination of how they held themselves, the words they chose, their expressions, their unshakeable conviction.

Could I ever get that level of self-assurance? I suppose the fact I'm worrying about it answers my question.

"Samskipti," said Habeus. "You gave your opinion earlier that you believed a swan that you saw getting intimate with Opekktur may have been Solhiti, The Sun God."

"I did."

"And as Opekktur is not here to corroborate that, it cannot be verified. Would you agree?"

"I would, unless Solhiti publicly acknowledges my interpretation of events. Does he?"

Habeus looked back at Solhiti, who grunted and waved a dismissive hand at Habeus, a scowl on his face.

"He does not." Habeus rubbed a hand over his bald head, clearly in thought. "The swan that you saw. Can you describe it in any more detail?"

Samskipti considered for a moment, her eyes closed. "It was larger than an ordinary swan. The feathers were of radiant gold. It was perfectly proportioned, with an elegant neck and wings, a proud bill, and smooth legs. To summarise, the perfect swan, but golden."

"Thank you, witness." Habeus interlaced his fingers, and brought them up to rest against his chin. "The swan that you saw was not Solhiti."

A short murmur rippled through the crowd. Samskipti raised a sceptical eyebrow. She smoothed her robe down.

419

"As I stated earlier; I am not surprised that he claims that."

Habeus let his hands drop, then raised a finger. "It is not a mere claim. We shall prove it." He gestured to Solhiti, who stood, a face like thunder. Felix felt a wave of fear wash around his insides. Having been caught up in the cut-and-thrust of the case, it had been easy to forget just *who* he was up against. Solhiti, God of Life, was terrifying. Even the simple act of standing up emphasised his massive frame. The fact he wore a simple robe accentuated his powerful physical presence. Berjast, God of War, watching from the audience, matched the King of the Gods for size and was of course intimidating in his own very obvious way... but he was covered head to toe in huge, ornate plate armour. Solhiti's plain garb seemed to say: *I don't need it.*

He reminded Felix of the demonic figure of Elder Prastor, one of the witnesses in his case for humanity. The witness had been a shrivelled ancient man, until his true form had been revealed to be...

Felix's brow furrowed, his mind whirring. Now Felix thought about it, that figure had looked very similar to Solhiti. He hadn't had glowing eyes, as far as he remembered, but...

His focus snapped back to the present as Solhiti took five steps straight towards the witness stand, his heavy footsteps resounding through the silent courtroom. Samskipti's composure slipped by the smallest fraction as she shifted in her seat, the slightest quiver passing over her face, but before Solhiti reached her, he was suddenly consumed in a bright sphere of light. Felix had to shield his eyes.

"*Ffff-*" hissed Racelsus.

When the light dimmed, where Solhiti had stood was a bird. Not a beautiful golden swan, but a wretched, deformed monster of a bird. The feathers were grey, brown and white, and sticking out at unusual angles. The feet were enormous and ungainly, the wings short and stubby. The neck was ludicrously long and bare, and topped with a bald, gnarled looking head, with beady, boggled eyes. The bird was, in a word, hideous. It settled a baleful glare on Samskipti.

Habeus bowed his head. "The sad truth of the matter is that, for his many, many qualities, shapeshifting is not something that has come naturally to Solhiti. Despite his power in other areas, and despite the

Golden Swan being his sacred animal, the King of the Gods is unable to transform himself into one." To demonstrate this, Solhiti, in his bird form, took several steps around the concourse and flapped his small wings. Felix stood up.

"I object. How can we possibly know that this is true? Perhaps Solhiti is able to transform, but is unwilling to here in court."

Habeus whirled on him. "Do you accuse the King of the Gods to be a liar?" A few sharp intakes of breath sounded from the audience. Felix looked at Solhiti, who stared back at him. Even though the God of Fire was in this ridiculous form, the weight of that stare still felt like an anvil on his back. Felix felt his legs go wobbly and he lowered his eyes.

"I merely wish to verify this evidence," he said in a small voice. "It is my right to establish that." Habeus and Felix both looked at Samveru, who was resting steepling her fingertips together.

"It is possible," she said, "that Solhiti is being mistruthful. However, I have known him for a very long time. He is not the sort of a god that enjoys being humiliated. I therefore believe that he is not lying, for he would not willingly admit to being inadequate at something in such a public forum unless it were true." She looked over to the bird. "And you are making such a declaration of inadequacy, yes? You are stating to all here present that you are unable to shapeshift in the way that practically every other god can without issue?"

The bird's eyes flashed with fire as it glared at her. Samveru did not baulk. Slowly, the bird nodded, and Samveru did the same.

"We are, of course, willing to confirm with Sannkalladur," said Habeus.

"Understood. We need not engage the Goddess of Truth. With that in mind, I will accept this into evidence. The swan cannot have been Solhiti, because transforming himself into his own sacred animal is beyond his abilities."

Felix considered this. *So either he is lying and is willing to look like an incompetent in front of his subordinates in order to win this case, and is bluffing by offering to call on the Goddess of Truth…*

…or he is being truthful, and is not all-powerful.

Felix let out a long breath.

I'm glad I'm not religious. I feel like I'd be having some sort of crisis by now.

He shrugged and sat down. "I withdraw my objection," he said. He looked over at Skrida, who was rocking slightly next to him, barely suppressing a giggle.

"Oh goodness, that's funny," she said. "Oh, that will keep me going for a while." The bird had been consumed in another ball of light, and Solhiti, in his humanoid form, returned to his seat.

"So," said Samskipti, still sitting in the witness stand. "Who was the swan?"

Habeus sighed. "Unless Opekktur testifies, or the swan himself - or herself - does so, we shall never know. But it was not Solhiti." He tilted his head, then gave a small shrug. "I have no further questions." Samskipti got up and walked to retake her seat amongst the rest of the audience, but stopped when she reached Gaman. She leaned over and spoke a few quiet words, and Gaman's face went pale for a second. She then continued walking, while Gaman took a sip of the drink in his hand.

We'll never know indeed.

~

"Who is next?" said Samveru, fondling the golden gavel. Felix stood. He steadied his hands and forced them to unfurl.

"We would-"

He took a slow breath. The King of the Gods turned his head to face him, eyes blazing brightly. Felix felt like a stain on a lovely white shirt. No, less than that. He felt like a nameless, featureless pebble among millions. He cleared his throat.

"We would like to call Solhiti to testify."

His eyes met Felix's and he scowled. Habeus stood up and placed his palms on the table in front of him.

"No," he said.

15 - Threats

"I'm sorry?" said Felix, eyes darting from Solhiti to Habeus.

The God of Justice shook his head. "Solhiti will not testify."

"Why?" said Felix. Habeus raised his eyebrows.

"Surely you know this, Mr Sacramentum? The accused are not required to testify in their own case. That is their right. It is the case in your world, is it not?"

"Well, yes. But-"

"But nothing. Solhiti has declined to testify, and so he shall not."

A hum of excited conversation buzzed around the audience as the people watching gulped down this latest exciting development. The King of the Gods? Invoking his right to silence?

A moment ago he humiliated himself in front of everyone. What is he afraid of saying out loud? What could be so important and so necessary to remain a secret?

The image of Elder Prastor leapt into his mind again. After he had transformed, the possessed form of that old man had the same blond hair, the same physique as Solhiti. The same jawline. A relation? A son? Was… No, that would be ridiculous.

The King of the Gods wasn't a demon, was he?

That could be enough to split the pantheon. Would their loyalty to their ruler let them oversee such a revelation? Would there be an uprising? An overthrow? Are such distinctions even meaningful with such divinities?

A war in heaven…

He didn't need Furbo to tell him how bad that would be.

Samveru leaned forward in her chair. "You refuse to testify?"

"He does," said Habeus. "It is his right."

"Seems like a stupid right."

"On the contrary, it is vital."

The Goddess of Union tapped her fingers on the desk in front of her. "I cannot force him?"

423

"You could, but he could just as easily not reply to any questions."

"I see." She tapped faster, then ceased. "So what happens now?"

"Well," said Habeus. "If my learned colleague has any further witnesses, we invite him to call them up. If not, then we each summarise our positions, and you consider them, then deliver your judgement."

Samveru nodded. "Well, Mr Sacramentum? Did you have any other witnesses you wanted to call?"

"No, Your Honour. Solhiti was the final one."

"In that case," she said, sweeping her arm in front of her. "The floor is yours."

"Uh, Your Honour," said Felix.

"Yes?"

"I apologise, but it is usual at this stage of the proceedings to have a quick recess."

"A recess? Whatever for?"

"Well, to gather one's thoughts, consider the day's events, then accordingly close the argument based on that."

And, depending on the lawyer, take nervous toilet breaks or surreptitious swigs of fortifying liquids, or both. For me, I just need a five minute breather...

Samveru considered this, then swivelled her eyes to Habeus. "This is typical?"

"In cases in the mortal realm, yes, common enough." He shrugged. "However, I am good to continue on."

"Are you, Mr Sacramentum?" asked Samveru, her gaze returning to Felix. He bit his lip.

"I would be very much grateful to the court if a short recess could be called," he said, trying not to sound too pathetic. Samveru sighed then nodded.

"Oh, very well. You may have five minutes." She clapped her hands, and stood up. "Five minutes," she said, then disappeared behind her dais.

Felix glanced at Skrida, who was sitting impassively beside him. She had shown no reaction when Solhiti had refused to testify, which had surprised him. Perhaps she was as confused as he was. Perhaps she'd just run out of energy to care.

No, it can't be that. She runs on spite.

"Lady Skrida," he said. "I'm just going to confer with my team."

"Go on, then," she said, without looking at him.

He stood and walked down the bench towards them. They had mixed expressions. Furbo was still in a general state of awe at what was happening, and Helda was looking suspiciously at anyone and everyone. Racelsus looked as she ever did. They all looked up as he approached.

"Well," he said.

"Do you know what you're going to say, lad?" said Furbo, his voice a little wobbly.

"I think so."

"But you said you needed to confer with your team?" said Helda, and Racelsus chuckled. "What?" said Helda, looking at the skull.

"I think," said Racelsus, "that Felix needs another type of support."

Furbo and Helda exchanged a look, then each gripped one of Felix's hands. "You've done marvellously," said the old scholar.

"Really brilliant," said Helda.

"Passable," said Racelsus. "Four out of ten."

Felix raised his eyebrows. "That good?"

"It was the piteous whining that bumped it from a three," Racelsus continued.

"Maybe try some sort of interpretive dance?" said Helda. "To really seal the deal?"

"No, that won't do," said Furbo. "Stick to what works. Do it in song, my boy."

"I was thinking of just miming it all out?" said Felix.

"Why not all three?" said Racelsus. "Felix's closing statement: a performance of all varieties."

"Coming soon to a theatre near you?" asked Felix. Racelsus clacked.

"So long as you're not being tormented for eternity," she said.

"It sounds like an eternity of torment either way, where I'm sitting," said Helda, then she shrugged. "Might as well pick the one with an interval."

"No interval," said Felix. "Unbroken, four hour live performance."

They all stopped speaking and stood with each other for a moment.

"Thanks everyone," said Felix. "I needed this." They all smiled at him, and he smiled back. "Okay, I better get back to it."

"Good luck," said Furbo.

"You've got this," said Helda.

"Don't forget the encore," said Racelsus.

Felix turned from them and headed back to his place beside Skrida, who was looking at him curiously.

"What was all that about?" she said.

"Human stuff, Lady Skrida. It's hard to explain."

Skrida shook her head, baffled.

Felix stood up, and cleared his throat.

~

Felix took a look around the courtroom. How many eyes were on him right now? How many things had those eyes seen? Enormous cosmic events that Felix's fragile mortal mind could scarcely comprehend, and here he was, about to sum up the most important divorce case between the most important couple in existence.

"Your Honour," said Felix. "At the start of today's proceedings, I stated that I would show the court how the marriage between Skrida, Goddess of Death, and Solhiti, God of Life, had broken down irrevocably, and that it was the latter that was to blame. I said I would prove that Lady Skrida had no choice but to leave, and that anyone in her shoes would do the same. If I were able to prove these points, Your Honour indicated that our wishes would be granted: my client would be entitled to half the domain of Solhiti, and the union would be officially dissolved." Felix waited for acknowledgment of this, and Samveru nodded slowly.

"We have interviewed several witnesses who have attested the following: Solhiti had multiple affairs outside of his marriage, without his wife's knowledge and consent. Why without her consent? Because she would not give it. Why? Because she believed they were in a loving marriage. So, Solhiti did the easy thing that would mean he could have the best of both worlds: lie to his wife and hide the affairs."

Felix started to pace, for what he hoped was the last time. "Eventually, these affairs became less hidden. It got to the point where he was spotted, at least one time, perhaps multiple times, in crowded gatherings, going off for private liaisons with various people. Now, one could argue that to have an affair and hide it is bad enough. But at least the attempt to hide it suggests that the affair-haver knows it is wrong. To not even attempt to hide his own transgressions? It indicates a fundamental lack of respect for the sanctity of the union with, and feelings of, the one person who he should care about the most: his wife."

He stopped. "We know that these affairs are real because we have the proof: a child. Lady Skrida did not want children, and Solhiti knew this, and yet exploited her trust by having one with someone else."

Felix shook his head. "It is clear. Solhiti does not care for this union. He does not care for his wife. He merely wants what he believes is his, purely because he declares himself the King of the Gods. It is not right that he be rewarded for this behaviour. My client has no choice but to leave this sham of a marriage. Yet, in taking that brave step, is she to be punished by relinquishing all of that to which she is entitled? I do not think that is fair."

He returned to his seat. "I hope you feel the same way."

Samveru did not respond. "Thank you," was all she said. She pointed to Habeus. "And you?"

Habeus stood. "Thank you, Samveru." He walked slowly to the centre of the area in front of the judge's dais.

"Solhiti is a god of much responsibility. Heavy is his burden. It is far heavier, indeed, than any god - or mortal - could conceive. He has uncomplainingly led this government of gods and overseen the very universe since this role was thrust upon him. We must trust that he is wise and considered in his approach, and that he knows best.

"Solhiti was shocked and upset to learn of the conception of this case, and the intention of his beloved wife to seek separation from him. The suggestion that he had acted in ways that could be construed as harmful to her, especially in such a way that would cause her to want to leave, breaks his heart."

Felix glanced at Solhiti. He didn't look particularly heartbroken.

"I would also remind the court that this case is not one that Solhiti has brought forth. If it were up to him, he would quite happily undo all that has been done today and continue on in the same way as we all have been." Habeus gave Skrida a meaningful look. "It is still not too late."

She returned a gaze that could crack stone, and Habeus shook his head, then continued.

"However, if we disregard all that I have said above, and instead examine the evidence of this case, such as it is... There is no case to answer. What proof has been provided, other than the opinions of a select few members of the brotherhood of divinity? Some of which have an axe to grind and some of which are pathologically unreliable? Solhiti has acted true to his persona, as befits his unparalleled station and responsibility. A responsibility for *all, for* all." Habeus gestured with his arms, encompassing everything. His eyes met Solhiti's burning, unmoving ones, and Habeus's face slowly hardened.

"This has gone on long enough," He said, closing his fist. "Solhiti has gracefully given his wife the opportunity to simply leave. If being his spouse is so painful, she can simply leave. She gets nothing, however. She deserves nothing. She should be pleased that the King of the Cosmos extends to her this courtesy, for if she were any other person, *he would not.*"

A small ripple of unease fluttered through the courtroom as each and every member of the audience imagined being in Skrida's shoes. Solhiti did not have a long track record of mercy. Practically everyone and everything that had crossed him had lived to regret it. Not lived long, but regretted it all the same. So far, Solhiti had refrained from making outright threats in court.

That's probably why that one felt so...

Felix shuddered.

Real.

Habeus waited for a few more moments before he sat down. Samveru took a long breath, then she herself stood.

"And so now I move to consider my position?" she said, her voice infinitesimally smaller than before.

"Yes," said Habeus, settling his robes. "You may take as long as you wish. In fact, I remember once a case taking a full four months for the judge to-"

"I find for Lady Skrida."

An explosion of voices filled the room, from Habeus protesting, to the crowd chattering, to Helda cheering, to Skrida laughing. Even Felix himself found he was making some sort of noise, but he didn't know what it was.

My life! I can return!

His heart, despite not being there, was thumping with relief and excitement. An enormous smile split his face and he, quite without realising, found himself shaking hands vigorously with Lady Skrida. When he realised and tried to withdraw it, she laughed and pulled him into a victorious hug. When they pulled apart, she gave him the warmest smile he had ever seen. Felix didn't look over at Solhiti, but if he did, he'd have seen the King of the Gods forcing back a pained expression, not angry, more irritated, as if he had just gotten comfortable and realised he left his drink in the other room.

"I am not finished yet," came a piercing voice from the judge's chair. All voices died away and all eyes turned to her.

Samveru lifted a hand and the ostentatious gavel materialised in her grip. She moved as if to tap it on the plate in front of her. "The court finds for Lady Skrida, and hereby grants her all realms and titles as she desires, as authorised by the power vested in me upon formation of this union. I understand that to finalise this, I must now touch this hammer to the tabletop." She brought the gavel down at some speed, but froze with it an inch from touching the plate. Felix felt his smile drop a little.

What is she waiting for?

"I could quite easily do that," she said. "In fact, it would be the easiest thing I could do. Based on the arguments I've heard, I have no qualms about ruling that way." Her gavel was still hovering above the plate. It continued to hover, even when Samveru released it to steeple her fingers.

"Justice. An interesting word. My understanding - and do stop me if I'm off kilter here, Habeus - is that the only way true justice is achieved in this ritual of adversarial mud-slinging is if both sides present all of their facts. All of them. I don't believe that the court has had this happen. Yet." She sighed. "Still, if I am not presented with the arguments, then how can I achieve true justice? How indeed."

She placed a hand on the gavel's handle again, then glared at Solhiti. "I am giving anyone in the room one final chance," she said, "to add anything before I complete this sentence. This is the final opportunity." She gave them both a meaningful look, eyebrows raised. "I mean it."

Habeus frowned, and whispered to Solhiti. The two exchanged low, rumbling words, Solhiti's face growing more resigned with each exchange.

"Can she do that?" hissed Skrida to Felix, all trace of warmth vanished from her.

"Uh, in all honesty Lady Skrida, I have no idea. Normally the judge's word is law, so…"

He was interrupted by the sound of Habeus standing, hands placed on the table in front of him. He cleared his throat. "If Your Honour will permit us…" He paused. "Solhiti will testify."

"Oh, so he isn't too good for us anymore?" said Samveru, a mocking tone entering her voice. "Deigns to be subject to the authority of another, eh?"

Habeus and Solhiti said nothing.

"I thought as much," said Samveru. She withdrew the gavel and it winked out of existence. She leaned back. "Marriage is a sacred bond. Solhiti, as far as I am concerned, you have broken that bond, and so dishonoured yourself, your wife, and me. You are the King of the Gods, and so should be held to the *highest* of moral standards. You have taken this concept and torn it to shreds, for no other reason than your own immature compulsions.

"As I said earlier, despite initially being appalled with the idea of approving the severance of your union, having heard the case brought to be by Skrida and her team, I find it impossible to disagree with them." She jabbed a long finger in their direction. "Let that indicate to you the level of my displeasure."

She leaned forward. "But, due to your station, I will give you this one last chance - out of the respect I hold for your office, I hope you understand. I cannot believe that you, who so proudly rule over all of us, could be so unthinking." She pointed at Habeus. "Thus: I will allow you to testify. One chance to justify this abhorrent behaviour. One."

Felix's guts were filled suddenly with moths and butterflies. What had just happened? Just when he thought he had managed to, by some miracle, side-step the part of the case he feared the most…

He looked over at Habeus, who was whispering to Solhiti. Solhiti himself was staring at Felix, his eyes blazing, as he rose to his feet.

Journal Entry K - Charm

Reference case [PvVP] (Pit v. ValPer), year 1329, Judge Vimtio presiding.

Have you ever owned a lucky charm? Some trinket, totem or relic that you feel somehow improves the potential outcome of a day, date, spat or reunion? Maybe a runaway horse and cart sped past you once upon a time, narrowly avoiding your certain death by trampling by a hair's breadth, and you, quite suddenly and irrationally, decided that it must be because you were wearing that old pair of socks that you were considering throwing away the very previous evening? Since then, if you ever were in need of a gentle nudge of fate, you'd be sure to seek out those sad old socks, just in case. And, to make matters worse, perhaps one fateful day you misplaced them, only for some dreadful event to transpire. If only you'd had your lucky socks!

You can, naturally, purchase lucky items almost anywhere from trustworthy looking salespersons. No doubt they will spin you a tale of each of them, saying that this particular glass eye was worn by the terrible pirate Gurnard Cowe, and it saved his life when an arrow bounced off of it, see the mark? Or this here unassuming needle prodded a young man through his trouser leg one morning, waking him, only for him to find his barn was ablaze. Without the serendipitous stabbing, his livelihood would have been reduced to ash. That'll be seven silvers, please.

Whether 'luck' can be imbued into physical objects has been debated among certain circles for years. Most educated people nowadays will announce with some certainty that it is a fantasy, a ludicrous notion that only the gullible fall prey to. Yet, in secret, they will own a pair of lucky socks, I have no doubt.

A man with the unfortunate name of Pitty made a discovery one morning. Due to quite a regrettable sequence of events that I shan't repeat here, this poor gentleman found himself completely naked and facing certain death at the hands of a raging beast in the wilderness. An extraordinarily lucky series of events allowed him to escape, for which he thanked and blessed his lucky ring… which, upon examining his hand, he noticed had slipped off in the chaos. Thus, he concluded, rather astutely for a man in his circumstances, that luck was not some force that mankind could influence, but instead the mere belief that one was lucky was enough. The more one believed, the luckier one became. Whether he reached this logical deduction before or after he managed to get dressed, I never thought to ask.

Subsequently, Pitty started a business selling 'charms'. They were literally any old junk he could find for either free or next to free - rocks, leaves, bird skulls, teeth, plum stones - and he would sell them by the bucketload for a fraction of the price of a 'proper' charm. If questioned by the punters, Pitty gladly explained that his charms were just as magical as the next man's - that is to say, not at all - but he would go on to explain his theory on luck, and that by grasping this lucky pebble, and importantly, believing it was lucky, you too could experience good fortune.

He experienced success… much to the ire of his competitors, who tried to get him a) locked up, or at least b) forbidden from trading.

I defended him. I must admit I had a fun time pinning down some of these 'peddlers'. I remember one exchange in particular between us on the dock:

"So you claim, Miss Periwinkle, that each and every one of your lucky items are, well, lucky? Genuinely and completely?" said I, in my best lawyer voice.

"Yes! Unlike that blaggard's!" she replied, jabbing a ring-encrusted finger in the direction of Pitty.

"Forgive my ignorance, but answer me this: Are two luck charms more effective than one?"

"Why, yes, of course! The more you buy, I mean wear, the luckier you'll become!"

I nodded and gestured to my assistant by the door, who waved to someone out of sight. A gentle rumbling sound started in the distance.

"In that case," I said, "I have taken the liberty of purchasing every 'good luck charm' I could find in a three-league radius. Ah, here they are."

At the doorway, my associate pushed a heavy wooden cart. It was filled with all manner of tat - rocks, feathers, dolls, pins, hats, a horseshoe, socks, a hiltless dirk… Pitty stood up as the cart passed it, removed his latest 'good luck ring', threw me a wink, then tossed it on the pile before taking his seat again. On top of that pile was a rotating spice rack of small, black bottles.

"Nine of those bottles contain seasonal ales, courtesy of the village brewery." Her eyes widened. "One contains poison." I didn't look at the judge. "Shall we put your theory to the test?"

I'd like to say she meekly admitted that it was all a scam and I affected a cocky strut to the pub that evening, but it wasn't my lucky day. Standing to her feet, she spat on the floor.

"Certainly, but I'd insist you remove all but two bottles - the poison, and an ale."

I looked up at the judge, who had raised an eyebrow at me. A more, hm, emotionally balanced judge might have demanded I stop this charade, but Judge Nurmle seemed to be in an interested mood, and instead let me lie in the bed I had threatened to make. Either that, or he was drunk.

I looked at the bottles and chewed my lip.

Of course, they were all beer. Obviously, they were all beer. I'm not a bloody murderer. What could I do? We removed eight of the bottles, and this insane woman, with only a slight tremor in her hand, swiftly downed one of them in front of everyone. We all waited for the choking and spluttering that I knew was not going to come. Sighing, I turned to the judge and started to admit my deception, when a cough from the stand caused me to spin.

The plaintiff was on her knees, clutching at her neck. She wheezed, her face turning purple, then collapsed. In the furore that followed, I nearly got marched off to the block right there and then. She survived, thank Habeus, and after a few very awkward conversations between the judge, the local town guard and myself, I was cleared of attempted murder.

It had turned out that Miss Periwinkle was quite seriously allergic to a type of yellow mushroom called Dapperlings. Would you guess what the local brewhouse used to flavour their 'autumn ales'?

To this day, some of the staff at Lunchers do not believe that I didn't plan this whole thing. Some say it with disgust, one says it with admiration.

A.R. Turner

The case? Well, it was thrown out in the end. Quite tragic, really. The defendant, Pitty, was killed by a falling tree on the way home. It had nothing to do with the fact he wasn't wearing his lucky ring. It was just bad luck. Wasn't it?

~journal entry ends

16 - Solhiti, The God of The Sun

The King of the Gods straightened. With deliberate slowness, he stood, head high, back straight, and walked over to the stand. All eyes were on him as he lowered himself into the seat and folded his arms. He sat as still as stone, staring forward, ignoring Felix completely.

Where Samskipti had been a stately statue carved from marble, Solhiti was a stern and disapproving military hero glaring at his inept successors. He was a schoolmaster furious at a disappointing student. A grandfather scowling at a blundering son-in-law.

I could just not question him. We've already won based on the evidence once.

If he decided not to question him, then it would be down to whatever Habeus could pull out of his beard. By that point, it would be too late for Felix to go back and cross-examine him again. No, he would have to do it. He would have to interrogate the King of the Gods.

Was Felix really about to question this figurehead? This unapproachable bastion? Presumably Solhiti could destroy him with a flick of a finger, and who could stop him? Would any other god leap to his aid? Felix's stomach fluttered with anticipation, and he had to flex his fingers to hide the shaking. Helda handed him a glass of something, and he took a grateful sip.

Here goes nothing.

Felix placed the glass down and took a step forward.

"Witness, please state your name and-"

"You presume to speak directly to me?" growled Solhiti, snapping his gaze to Felix with eyes as bright as twin suns. It physically hurt to meet his gaze, and so Felix flinched away from him, squinting. "You, who are nothing, less than the blink of a weasel's eye, dare to presume to speak to me? Me, Solhiti, King of the Gods, the Great Creator?"

Nothing came out when Felix tried to speak. He cleared his throat and tried again.

"I, well-"

"Stop this *irritating* squeaking, mortal." Solhiti turned his head and brushed a hand away in a dismissive gesture. "Go and enjoy what little time you have to pursue the pointless flash of nothing you call your existence. Withdraw yourself from my presence immediately before I remove you myself."

Felix felt very small and completely out of his depth. Panic seized him. He squeezed his eyes shut and tried to focus, but could only think of escape.

What am I doing? I have to go. This was a mistake. I'm insane!

Felix.

He flicked his eyes open and looked at Racelsus, who was watching him from her cage on the desk.

Focus on me. Listen to my voice. Don't worry.

How can I not worry?! I'm about to cross-examine the bloody King of the Gods!

The same King of the Gods who split the earth into fragments in a rage, then joined them back together just because he could. The same god whose very core burns at the centre of the universe. The creator and the destroyer. The... the...

Focus on me, Felix. Look at him. He's just a bully. He's trying to intimidate you. Don't let him.

Trying? Trying!? He doesn't need to try! He's literally-

The King of the Gods, yes. But right now, he is also something else: your witness. I've seen you cross-examine murderers, demons, and dragons. Every one of them could have wiped you out with a moment's thought. What makes this guy any different?

Felix blinked and chanced a glance at Solhiti. He was sitting, cross-armed, scowling upwards. Two spots of bright light on the ceiling indicated where he was looking exactly.

This is different...

No, it isn't. A bully is a bully is a bully. If you don't stand up to him, who will? Anyway, what's he going to do, kill you?

Felix snorted, causing Solhiti's eyes to whip over to him. "Pathetic," the god rumbled, shaking his head and looking at Samveru. "This is a farce."

Now that Felix looked at the god, what could he see? A ridiculous moustache. An ultra-macho veneer of bravado that precisely nobody found appealing. A child-like arrogance that surpassed all arrogance. Someone convinced of their might-makes-right mentality.

A bully. He looked over to Racelsus.

Sometimes all you need is a brave face, she said.

Felix stood up tall and straightened his shoulders. With deliberate slowness, he forced a neutral expression onto his face. He cleared his throat, causing Solhiti to stare at him again. Without flinching, Felix met that burning gaze, ignoring the discomfort.

"I apologise if I have been unclear," he said. "But I asked if you could state your name."

Solhiti squinted his eyes at Felix. "You have some nerve, mortal."

"And you seem to have trouble grasping simple requests, witness."

Felix heard a few intakes of breath behind him. Whether from mortals or other gods, he didn't know. He didn't dare look in case his reserve melted into pudding. He still wasn't certain of the official term of address for gods, let alone the King of the Gods, but just calling them 'witness' certainly wasn't it. Solhiti pressed his fingers together until his knuckles cracked.

I'm dead.

Solhiti took a long breath, puffing up his chest.

Was that a tiny smirk, or did I imagine it?

"I am Solhiti, King of the Cosmos." He waved a hand at Felix, letting the breath out. "Ask your questions, lawyer."

Felix's mind instantly went blank. "I shall," he said, filling time, while the hamster on a wheel that was his brain ran as fast as its little legs could run. Lawyer and witness glared at each other, Solhiti assuming Felix was making some challenge, and Felix trying desperately to remember what he was going to ask.

Why don't you ask him about his relationship with his wife, came Racelsus's voice.

"How would you sum up your relationship with your wife?"

Solhiti grunted. "We are very much in love. Or, I thought we were. We were to rule the cosmos together for all eternity. Alas, she is done with me." His eyes met his wife's. Neither spoke.

"Alas, indeed," said Felix. "What do you think could have caused this breakdown in your relationship?"

"I do not know."

"I see. Well, let us work through the possibilities. Were you ever violent towards her?"

His eyes flashed red at him. "Never."

"Did she ever question your authority as ruler of the universe?"

"No." Another grunt, and a shift in his position. "Never in public."

"Thank you. Were you ever unfaithful to your wife?"

Solhiti hesitated.

"Witness," said Felix. "It is a simple question. We are considering reasons as to why the relationship between your wife and yourself has broken down. Unfaithfulness is a common reason why such things happen on earth, between mortals. I ask you again. Were you ever unfaithful to your wife?"

Solhiti sighed, and pinched the bridge of his nose with a thick thumb and forefinger. "Yes."

That shocked Felix, as well as eliciting a wave of excited babble through the assembled onlookers. He had been prepared to press this point in a dozen different ways. To parade the evidence of testimony, to hammer home the repeated affidavits about his dalliances. To do his damnedest to put the King of the Gods on the back foot, until he felt forced to admit his unfaithfulness. But for Solhiti to just admit it? That was the one thing Felix had not expected.

Skrida's jaw was clenched and she appeared to be trembling. "For years," she said, getting to her feet and jabbing a finger at him, "I have tried to get a straight answer out of you. Years. And yet, now? *Now* you offer it *plainly*?"

"Skrida," said Solhiti, his tone gentle. "Listen." His wife had stood up, her eyes smouldering with fury. Felix held a hand up to her, and she directed her ire at him.

"Lady Skrida," Felix said, walking over to her. "We must tread very carefully here. This may be a game plan to get you to act out of emotion, and therefore reduce your own credibility. I know you're upset, but please, try to hold onto it for a little while longer."

She stared at him and Felix felt that gaze penetrating his soul. "You expect me to-"

"Please," he said, and she blinked, unused to being interrupted. She stood silent, black fire smouldering in her gaze, then sighed in frustration and rolled her eyes.

"Make him pay for it," she scowled between grated teeth, then threw herself back onto her chair. Felix watched her, took a breath, then turned back to face Solhiti.

"Witness," said Felix. "Can you explain… why?"

Solhiti huffed out a breath. "I am immortal. I have existed since the first breath of the universe, or near enough. Do you have any idea of how long that is?"

Felix did not reply.

"Your concept of faithfulness is rooted in your biological limits, mortal. You have a limited time to scratch a meagre existence, and so you have created methods with your inane bureaucracy to enforce union with another. You deny your very nature. Surely you do not expect the gods to do the same?"

"Well, why not, witness?"

Solhiti snorted. "Listen to yourself. If you are given the entire scope of the universe and infinite time to entertain yourself, you would act as I have acted."

"Presumably between performing the duties required to rule over the cosmos?" said Felix. Solhiti glared at him.

"Indeed."

Felix started to pace. "Witness, what of love? Do you not wish to stay faithful for love?"

"Your concept of love is nothing but chemicals," said Solhiti.

Not this again…

"I'm sure the Lord Svegladur would disagree," said Felix, turning to the audience to see if the God of Love was watching. To his disappointment, he was not immediately obvious.

Drat.

Instead, he turned back to Solhiti. "Love is one of the cornerstones of life. It is the strongest emotion. It is what drives parents to care for their helpless young. It is what drives men to fight for one another. To endanger themselves to help a friend. If it is just a chemical, then so what? Perhaps life itself is a chemical, then. That doesn't make the sacrifices and commitments we make in its name any less real."

Solhiti said nothing.

"And besides," said Felix, coming to a stop. "It is because of you that we have love. You are the Great Creator, yes?"

"…yes," said Solhiti.

What was that pause? I can't get distracted yet.

"So you understand the importance of it among mortals? We are made in your image, so why do you feel you can be set apart from the laws you created for mortals?"

Solhiti scoffed. "I created you. I am therefore already above you. What I do for myself and what I have made for you are completely separate."

"'Do as I say and not as I do'?"

"In a manner of speaking," said Solhiti, crossing his arms.

This isn't getting me to where I want it to… Time to try something else.

"If you had no reason to be ashamed of your behaviour," said Felix. "Then why did you hide it from your wife?"

Solhiti turned to face Skrida, who was shooting pure daggers at him with her hard eyes. He sighed, and lowered his eyes.

"I wish there were another way," he said.

"What does that mean, witness?" said Felix. Solhiti did not reply.

"Witness," he said, more firmly. "You were married to one of the Pantheon. A beautiful, mesmerising goddess by all accounts, strong enough to match you in will and intellect. Why did you throw it all away?"

"I did not throw anything away," said Solhiti. "I had a good reason."

"To cheat on your wife?"

"Yes."

"And what is this 'good reason'?"

Solhiti let his eyes drift skywards and stare at the ceiling. He didn't respond for a moment. Eventually, he sighed.

"I did it to protect the cosmos."

Felix blinked.

That's a new one.

"Protect the cosmos?" said Felix, raising both of his eyebrows. "That is quite a claim. Unbelievable, some might suggest." He shook his head. "And just how does cheating on your wife help to protect the cosmos?"

Habeus stood. "Your Honour. The workings of the inner circle of the Pantheon are sacred and secret. As ruler of the known universe, Solhiti must consider things that no other creature may have to comprehend, and must deal with these things in unorthodox and creative ways. Are we really going to lay bare that which might best be left unsaid?"

Samveru leaned over. "Nice try, Habeus, but I think you know that we will have to hear this. It is vital to the case, is it not?" Habeus bowed his head. "I understand, Your Honour. But please ensure my objection is noted."

The King of the Gods watched this exchange, then rubbed his temples. "Here is the reason. The Pantheon needs an enemy." When he offered no more, Felix frowned.

"I'm afraid I don't follow," said Felix, uncertain. Solhiti sighed in exasperation, and fidgeted in his seat. He lifted his hands and held them apart, as if holding an invisible ball, then threw them up in the air. He grunted in frustration, then shook his head, his moustache flailing.

Why is he struggling so much?

"Witness-"

"Quiet, mortal," hissed Solhiti. He slammed a fist on the bannister in front of his seat, cracking it. "Blast it all." He rubbed a palm over his hair, eyeing Mona, God of Memory, who hadn't moved a muscle since being beckoned by Habeus. His eyes flitted to the crowd of minor godlings watching, in various states of gossip-fuelled exalted curiosity. He scowled, shook his head, took a huge breath, and began.

"When the First Primordial was destroyed, the Second was created, as were we, the Pantheon. We battled the Second Primordial and killed it. What followed was a period of time in which we scoured the cosmos for any trace of the Primordial or their spawn, and wiped them out. What do you people call it?" he said, pointing a heavy finger at Furbo, who squealed, then hopped to his feet, eyes boggling.

"The Hreinsun, Your Holiness," he said. Solhiti grunted.

"That's it. So we did. We found them all, and killed them all. For a time, there was peace, and it was good." He sighed. "Then, the gods started to get restless. They started arguing. Snipping at one another. I realised it was because our rule was absolute, and they were bored. No more challenges."

He paused. "So I created demonkind. I worked on it in secret with Rangt. Who was he going to tell? Who would believe him? We created a series of demons that, while never posing a threat to overthrow the gods, would nevertheless provide a challenge to our skills. We united once more, defeated them, and life was good for a while longer.

"Then of course the gods started to multiply. More gods equals more problems… Every aeon or so since, when tempers get a little frayed, I have brought about some calamity or other to keep them occupied. Oh, you know them. Scholar, list some for me." He gestured at Furbo again, who sprung to his feet once more.

"Uh, Svarthol?"

"Yes, the great big void that was going to consume everything. That was one of mine. Next."

"Let's see… Tvimenningur?"

Solhiti actually laughed. "That one was a mistake. An 'evil' duplicate of a god? Stupid, childish notion. But anyway, you get the idea. Diversions to keep everyone busy." He gave Felix a searching look. "Humanity was one, you know. A diversion. You were supposed to keep the gods busy for ages, but you all became so *boring*. You were much more fun when you were romping around the fields in tribes, building temples out of sticks and mud."

Charming.

Solhiti let out a loud breath that blustered his moustaches. "So, what next? I'd tried divine enemies, creating forms of life, exploding star cascades, alternate realities… I've been running out of ideas. Hence, my thinking was this: Instead of keeping everyone focussed on some outside threat of annihilation, why not keep them all busy with internal gossip? I'd rather have them all prattling on about nothing instead of plotting to overthrow me and spiral the universe into turmoil.

"Thus, I started flirting around. At first, I kept it subtle. But after a while, no one picked up on it, so I made it more obvious. Even invented a so-called bastard son! He's just an illusion. And, let's be honest... it's worked a treat. It's all anyone's been talking about for absolutely ages."

Felix shook his head, ready to tear this pathetic defence a new blowhole. "Of all the ridiculous reasoning... You are saying that the reason for your infidelities - which you do not deny - are to keep the gods from getting so bored that they *destroy the universe*? I have never heard such complete... such total..."

He had turned to look at his client, expecting to see a panorama of vehemence wrought on her face. Lady Skrida, far from being the seething avatar of repressed hatred that she was before, had turned doe-eyed and love-struck. Felix cleared his throat. "Lady Skrida... Are you okay?"

She ignored him. She only had eyes for her husband. "You would do all of that for the good of the cosmos?" she said in a small voice.

Solhiti nodded sagely. "I would, my love. For you. For without you, the cosmos is nothing regardless. So I state in front of all who are present. The Pantheon, the Godlings, the record, even the mortals." She sighed. Felix stared at her, then stared at Solhiti, then stared back at Skrida.

This can't be happening.

Skrida and Solhiti gazed at each other across the courtroom. Sparks sizzled from each of them; from Solhiti, bright and shining, from Skrida, dark and sinister. Yet, neither god paid any attention to them. They had only eyes for each other.

At an unspoken signal, they started moving towards each other. Skrida hurried over to Solhiti, running into his outstretched arms. "Oh, Sol," she said, pressing her face into his massive chest. "That's so thoughtful of you."

"Oh, my little Skrida," said the King of the Gods, squeezing her tightly. As they embraced, a collective sympathetic moan of romantic joy rose up from the gods watching. Samveru had a smile on her face as she watched the King and the Queen of the Gods hold one another.

Felix had to manually force his eyebrow to unfurrow and his mouth to shut. He faced Racelsus. "Am I going insane?" he asked.

She clacked. "If you are, then I am too. But I'm probably not a good yardstick." He turned to the rest of his team, where Furbo met his eye and shrugged.

"Gods are weird," he said, and for once, Felix completely agreed.

Samveru stood up and grasped the gavel from thin air. "I would like to suggest that this entire case is withdrawn. Any who object, speak now or forever hold your peace."

Should I say something? thought Felix nervously. *What would I even say?*

When no one spoke, Samveru smiled and slammed the heavily encrusted hammer onto the desk in front of her. "Dismissed!"

A great cheer went up from the assembled gods and godlings in the room. Felix turned to look at them all, stupefied.

I will never understand gods. Still…

Felix turned back, and stood watching the two gods that had mere hours ago been ready to rip each other's heads off whisper lovingly to one another. Solhiti was stroking his wife's hair, and she was running a finger up and down his arm. "All's well that ends well, I suppose," he said. A nagging feeling jabbed at his sense of well-being. He realised it was Racelsus gently but urgently prodding his mind.

I wouldn't get too cosy. We technically lost, you know. What does that mean for your deal?

Felix frowned. Well, sure, they lost, but the end result was that everyone literally kissed and made up. Surely that meant that… I mean, the gods wouldn't…

"Furbo," he said, and the old man leaned in to listen.

"Yes, lad?"

"Gods… they don't have a history of reneging on deals, do they?" Furbo's face fell a little. "Or going back on promises, not once they've agreed. That's not something the gods do is it?" With each word, Furbo's face fell further. "It isn't, is it?" said Felix, a note of nervous worry entering his voice.

"Uh, well, that's a good question… Uhm, you see…" His voice trailed off as Skrida extricated herself from her embrace and turned to face Felix. Her face was imperious, but noble. Superior, but genteel. Or was he just hoping it was?

"Mr Sacramentum."

"Uh, yes?" he said, trying to sound calm and failing. Her steady gaze and neutral face looked like she was posing for a statue of an empress.

"You represented me valiantly in all of these proceedings today, and for that I am grateful." Her face broke into a warm smile, her eyes shining.

"Thank you," said Felix, feeling relief spread through him.

"You will no doubt be wishing to return to your old life as soon as possible."

"Well, yes, Lady Skrida." Her smile widened.

"Of course," she said.

Thank goodness. No need to worry.

"But," she said, her blank expression returning.

But?

That one word sent an icy spear of fear straight through him like a pike on a frozen winter morning. "But?" he squeaked. Her face morphed into that of a disappointed teacher, or a childhood bully, or a vindictive psychopath.

"You said some very hurtful things about my husband that I simply cannot endure."

"But I was helping you, Lady Skrida!" Felix said, a draining feeling of panic washing through him. "It was for your case." She tilted her head.

"But I lost the case. The divorce didn't happen, and that was part of the deal that you and I made."

"Surely-" said Felix. He looked at Solhiti, who was watching him dispassionately, his arm around his wife. He looked at Samveru, who was examining her gavel. He looked at the crowd, who looked like they were enjoying how things were turning out by clashing cups and drinking excessively, with Gaman, God of Parties, producing shimmering cups of something from somewhere and passing them out to anyone and everyone. A few more sober or gossipy heads were craned to get a good look at him. Habeus was watching, his eyes narrowed.

"No more buts, I think." Skrida raised her hand. "You have blasphemed, and what is more, you have failed me." Her face had taken on a maniacal quality, eyes wide, a sadistic grin peeling back her face. "And so, you must pay the price. An eternity of mindless torment sounds good."

She lowered her hand at Felix, and a swirling black cloud of vapour started to coalesce around it. "You understand, of course. You let me down, Mr Sacramentum."

"But our deal!" said Felix, taking a step backwards. "We shook hands on it." At this, Habeus glanced up, his eyebrows drawing together in thought.

"You failed, mortal," crooned Skrida. "Don't worry, I'll poke my head around once every forty or fifty thousand years."

"I didn't fail," said Felix. "Don't you remember the wording?" He started to speak quickly and frantically, his eyes on the Death Goddess's black-magic-clad hands. Taking a cautious step backwards, he searched his memory for the words he spoke on the day he met Skrida, and started to recite them:

"'I will do my utmost to get you the result you want, and if I am successful, then my restoration to life will act as payment.'"

"Oh, be silent, already," said Skrida, walking towards him. The rest of the gods were watching him with a sense of amusement, except for Habeus, who was furrowing his brow.

"'Only if I am unsuccessful, then I shall accept the punishment you mete out.'"

"And?"

"I was not unsuccessful. You got the result you want."

He was aware that his voice was starting to sound desperate, no doubt playing into the stereotypical view the gods had of humans, of cowering, shivering, wretched, useless gadflies, but at that moment, he didn't care.

Skrida shook her head as he retreated. "It's too late to play with words, Mr Sacramentum. Far too late!" She whipped her hand backwards and flung it forward, swirling streaks of black snaking towards him. In that moment Felix thought of Ettyson, without knowing why. He closed his eyes and braced for the pain.

In a flash of light, visible even through his closed eyes, something dashed in front of Felix and lifted its arm, deflecting the blackness away to fizzle against the vaulted ceiling. Felix snapped his eyes open and found himself staring at the back of the bald head of the God of Justice, who had positioned himself between him and Skrida.

"What-" he sputtered.

"What is the meaning of this?" growled Skrida, readying another wave of black mist. "Move, old idiot."

"Those words you agreed to," said Habeus. "Only if he was unsuccessful... 'Only'. A very important qualifier."

Skrida was making no effort to hide her disgust. "So?"

"I cannot allow you to go against your word. When you agreed to Mr Sacramentum's terms, you two struck up a contract. I will not allow you to break it."

"How am I breaking it?" spat Skrida.

"I told you already. 'Only.' Only if he is unsuccessful can you punish him, and therefore can do so under no other circumstance."

"But he was unsuccessful in getting me a divorce!"

"But he was *not* unsuccessful in getting you the result you wanted."

"I *signed* nothing," said Skrida, after a brief hesitation. "No contract exists."

"You shook hands after Mr Sacramentum laid out the terms. That is a contract. If I do not defend the sanctity of such things, then I would be remiss in my position as the God of Law."

For a moment no one spoke. Felix, despite feeling massively out of his depth, felt the compulsion to speak. He took a step to the side, moving from the cover of Habeus. He was surprised at the calmness in his own voice.

"Please be reasonable. We can all walk away happy. You are joined once again with your husband, and the case is concluded. Why not draw a line under it and we can all move on?"

Skrida's eye twitched as she stared at him. Felix remembered all of the lectures he had been given over the past few weeks about the pride of the gods, especially the pantheon, and regretted his contribution immediately.

"You are nothing," snarled Skrida. "Your opinion is irrelevant." She turned once again to Habeus. "Now, for the last time, move."

Habeus took a step to once again place himself between Skrida and Felix. His eyes and hands started to glow. "No. There has to be meaning to these things. The mortal's soul is under my protection."

The Goddess of Death took a deep breath, but seemed unsure of what to say next. Despite their occasional fallings-out or arguments, no god in the history of the Pantheon had ever openly attacked another.

She has to back down. She has to.

Felix looked at Habeus. The God of Law and Justice exuded such a confident aura of power, even Felix, who was not particularly attuned to the magical arts, could feel it washing over him as if he were standing next to an open furnace. Even if Skrida did launch herself at him, how could Habeus lose?

Is this what the fervent feel like?

From where Felix was standing, Habeus was as steadfast as the mountain, as righteous as the ground, as commanding as the sun.

The sun...

Felix felt a knot in his stomach as he turned his gaze towards Solhiti, who was taking several small, languid steps to stand beside his wife. From Solhiti's open hand stretched a beam of light. That light slid downwards with a hiss until it touched the stone floor, hardening into the solid form of a handle. At the end of that handle, where it touched the ground, the light spread like melted gold, then gathered, blooming into a solid sphere of white-gold light, bright enough to burn the eyes, almost as bright as the Gaze of Solhiti himself. The God of Life and The Sun swung it upwards and held it, pointing the weapon forwards.

"This is Augnbrennari," he said in a low voice. "The Harnessed Star." The shadows shimmered and quivered as he shifted his grip. "I have not wielded it for many ages." He slowly aimed the weapon at Habeus. "Do not give me reason to do so again, brother. Stand aside."

Habeus flinched as that great hammer swung his way, but did not move. "No."

"You are no match for me, Habeus. You know this. Do not be a fool. For the love I bear you, I give you one chance to rescind."

Felix saw it, too. Where Habeus burned like a furnace, Solhiti glowed like, well, the sun. Felix bit his lip and prepared himself for the inevitable. He would tell Habeus to give him up, and throw himself on Skrida's mercy.

It wouldn't be the first time...

He opened his mouth to speak, but was distracted by what sounded like two anvils being bashed and scraped together. Another figure walked up to stand beside Habeus, causing the floor to shake as his heavy feet fell. Felix was stunned to see it was the massively armoured bulk of Berjast, the God of War, standing beside and completely dwarfing himself and Habeus.

"Now, now, O Wise And Noble King Of Mine," said Berjast, in a deep voice that rumbled out of his now-closed greathelm. "Let's not do anything we might regret."

"This isn't the time for your petty squabbles, Berjast," said Habeus quietly.

"Is that not what this is?" said Berjast, with a sardonic chuckle.

"Oh, give me a reason, Berjast," came the sing-song voice of Gaman, now standing beside Solhiti. Solhiti glanced at him, to which Gaman nodded once, and Solhiti grunted in assent. Gaman turned back to the God of War. "I've been wanting to put you in your place for aeons, you overgrown beetle, but you've always been too much of a coward to throw the first punch."

"Coward!?" roared Berjast. He slammed his mailed fists together and in a burst of red lightning two huge greatswords materialised in his grip. "You've been asking for this, O Stupid Smiling One."

On Gaman's other side, Berjast's partner, Fridur, the Goddess of Peace, had approached. She turned to face her husband with a cool, level stare. "You as well?" bellowed Berjast. "Traitorous witch!"

"One little mortal life," she replied. "To avert a conflict within the Pantheon. That seems like a simple trade."

A shiver ran down Felix's spine, and not just from the complete terror he was fighting off. The room had turned cold. A figure that Felix didn't recognise approached from behind him somewhere, and took her place next to Habeus. She was blue-skinned, and was surrounded in a light haze of frosted mist.

"Oh, great," spat Skrida. "Who woke up the ice queen?"

"Charming," said the newcomer. "How's the marriage, Skrida? Still going strong, I see?"

"This doesn't concern you, upstart."

"It doesn't? So there isn't a helpless person being bullied by a group of arrogant gods who really should just keep their conceited noses out of it?"

The goddess turned to Felix and gave him a smile.

"I'm Halka, by the way."

"Nice to meet you," said Felix, on reflex. "Uh, thanks."

"It's not my first time standing up to these pompous arses," she said, then turned back to them.

One by one more and more gods picked sides, with the rest of the Pantheon arriving as if summoned to stand on which side they felt like supporting. Each major God was followed by their subservient godlings and other divinities, each one weighing up which side had their greatest chance for survival, or which side would give them the most political rewards for standing with them. While many stood with Solhiti, many did not, including Samveru, Rangt, and Vinna, the God of Honest Work, who took a second to commend Felix on his fine job with that Erran character. Felix didn't register the compliment.

The tension in the air was threatening to rip his head in two.

Was this really happening? Was his fate about to cause a schism in the Pantheon? Were the realms of the gods about to be consumed in bloody battle, or even war? What would that mean for the mere mortals back on earth?

He looked to Furbo for advice, but the old man had passed out. Helda was fanning his face, whispering to Racelsus, frantically looking around the room, looking exactly how Felix felt.

"I will make this statement one final time," said Solhiti, lifting his hammer. "All of you in front of me: stand aside. Relinquish unto me the mortal you are shielding, and we shall say no more of this."

No one moved. Solhiti flexed his arms and grunted.

"Very well." He took a step forward. "We shall take him by force."

Felix closed his eyes and, despite himself, prayed. He didn't know who he prayed to, seeing as every god he knew was here already, and half of them wanted to kill him, but he prayed nonetheless.

Please...

He had a sensation of being yanked backwards, as if some great hand had grabbed him and flung him. A great rushing filled his ears, and when it stopped, he opened his eyes.

And saw nothing.

~

Felix could see nothing, hear nothing, smell nothing.

"Where am I?" said Felix. All he could see was an infinite blackness. Shifting his weight, he noticed the floor beneath his feet felt solid enough, smooth, like metal or stone.

"An interesting question."

A voice floated through him, leaving streaks in his awareness like ink in a pool.

"Who's there?" he said, his own voice sounding empty and harsh in comparison.

"A strange question$_{\text{question}}$," came the voice. It sounded like two voices speaking in unison. A high voice and a low voice, an octave apart. **"I am."**

"Please," Felix said. "I have to get back. My friends…"

"Oh, that can wait$_{\text{wait}}{}^{\text{wait}}$." A third voice joined the other two, sitting somewhere between them. The addition of this layer gave their words a semblance of harmony, like a chord on a harp being played. **"Everything can wait. Nothing is so urgent as to interrupt our conversation."** More voices joined the choir as it spoke, each adding a new level of richness and harmony to the others. It was quite the most beautiful sound Felix had ever heard.

"Who are you?" he said again, almost unwilling to foul the pure music of the air with his own monotonal voice.

"You called for me$_{\text{me}}{}^{\text{me}}$."

"I did?"

"You can call me Frumræd Eallwealda ap Sóþfæder tíw Andlícnis," the voices sang, then laughed, the laugh of the river as it splashes. **"If you can remember all that$_{\text{that}}{}^{\text{that}}$."**

Felix gave a nervous chuckle. "Uh, well… What about Frum?"

There was a pause.

"That is good enough. Frum. Hah. *Frum.*"

There was a short silence in which Felix heard no sound, not even the sound of his own breathing. His breathing was normally fairly silent anyway, what with having no breath.

"Who are you, Frum?" he said.

"They do not remember it."

"Who?"

"Your gods."

Felix blinked, not that it made any difference in the utter darkness. "You know them?"

"I created them. I created everything."

"Who created you?"

"A funny question."

Felix couldn't see what was so funny about it. "Uh, okay. What am I here for?"

"It all seems to be getting a little out of hand, don't you think?"

"What do you mean?"

"They intend to punish you for their own failings to mask their own inadequacies_{cies}^{cies}."

"Oh." Felix said.

"So I intend to voice to them my displeasure_e^e."

Felix chewed his lip. "Uh, okay. What does that mean?"

"I just thought I'd give you some warning."

"Well, thank you, Frum. You're, uh, very kind to want to help me."

"I am everything. Prepare yourself."

"Wait!"

Am I really talking to what I think I'm talking to? I could ask anything! The great mysteries of the universe! The hidden answers to the biggest questions?"

"Yes?_{Yes?}^{Yes?}"

"Can I ask you a question?"

"I know the question you will ask. It is: 'Why do ghosts have lower back pain?_{pain?}^{pain?}'"

"Eh?" said Felix.

"It is part of a tapestry to make them remember what it is to be alive_{alive}^{alive}."

No! That can't be the only question I get to ask!

"But-"

He wanted to continue speaking, but suddenly in a flash of exploding light, he was back in the courtroom. The eyes of the pantheon were on him, with Lady Skrida reaching a hand out to him.

He had somehow taken a few steps forward, and was now standing between Skrida and her allies and Habeus and his behind him. Habeus looked at him with a concerned face, but didn't move to help him.

A swirling string of black mist billowed from Skrida's hand, soaring towards Felix as he stood, transfixed. The look of arrogant triumph on her face melted when she watched the mist dissipate inches from touching Felix. With a scowl, she lifted her other hand, redoubling the effort, threatening to utterly consume Felix in waves of pulsating dark energy. Just as before the magic vanished. Solhiti was watching with an amused look on his face. His bright, sunlike eyes bore into Felix's, and for the first time, Felix felt no pain or fear in meeting that terrible gaze.

Incensed, Skrida whirled on her husband. "Do something, you great oaf! Strike this impudent mortal down!" Solhiti looked down at her and sighed. "Very well, wife. I will finish what you cannot." He shifted his grip, swirling the massive glowing hammer he held as if it weighed nothing, then took six powerful steps towards Felix, lifting the weapon above him. Felix lifted a hand in a futile attempt to protect himself, and Solhiti brought the great weapon down on him with enough force to split a planet.

As Augnbrennari slammed into Felix's outstretched arm, the weapon shattered, then with a flash of light, disappeared. Solhiti stared at his empty hand, utterly agog, then blinked at Felix. "What are you?" he whispered, his voice flitting between awe and murderous rage.

Damned if I know.

A feeling bubbled up within him, filling him with confidence. He heard a chorus of voices talking to him, each voice overlapping, unable to decipher them individually or make out any words. Opening his mouth, this chorus of voices came out. The loudest of these was his own voice, but the words were not from his mind.

"I am a reminder$_{\text{reminder}}{}^{\text{reminder}}$," he said, with a hundred voices. "You overstep yourselves$_{\text{selves}}{}^{\text{selves}}$."

At his words, some members of the pantheon sank to their knees. Some hid their fear, others did not. Solhiti clenched his fists, but Felix saw them shaking.

"Never again!" screamed Skrida, and a cloud darker than the void exploded from her, aimed in a wailing spear towards Felix. He lifted his hand and the blackness froze. Without his input, the spear turned, so the point was facing Skrida.

"It seems an example must be made," spoke ninety-nine voices from his own mouth. Skrida's face hardened into pure fury, daring him to strike her down.

"No, please!" came a voice, and Solhiti strode in front of his wife, arms outstretched. "Do not hurt her!"

Felix felt hesitation from within himself. The voices spoke to his mind in unison.

An interesting situation$_{\text{ation}}{}^{\text{ation}}$.

Felix replied in the way he would usually do so with Racelsus when she spoke into his mind. *Uh, yes. I'm a little out of my depth.*

In that case, stand back$_{\text{back}}{}^{\text{back}}$.

The black spear flew at Solhiti.

At the last second, it swerved, striking a hole in the wall of the courtroom and sailed off into the sky.

Why did you do that$_{\text{that}}{}^{\text{that}}$?

I did that?

You diverted it$_{\text{it}}{}^{\text{it.}}$.

Felix took a breath. *I didn't want to kill anyone.*

Not even those that would easily swat you without thinking$_{\text{ing}}{}^{\text{ing}}$?

Even those.

Hm$_m{}^m$.

Felix felt the immense power within him vanish, and he fell to his knees. Gasping, he felt a strong arm help him up. For a panicked moment, he thought it was Solhiti coming over to finish the job, but looking up, it was Helda. She helped him stand. Felix saw she had tears in her eyes. It was the first time he had seen her cry.

"Any of you try anything like that again and you'll be sorry!" she said, whirling on the gods and standing in front of Felix. "We lost him once already, we aren't losing him again!"

He heard footsteps behind him, and saw Furbo holding Racelsus's cage. The witch had fire in her eyes, Literal fire.

None of the gods made any move or spoke any words.

"And you!" said Helda, pointing at Skrida. "You struck a deal with Felix! Now fulfil your end, or else! Give him back his life!"

Skrida scrutinised them. She had a look that Felix hadn't seen before. Was that... Humility? She took a step towards them, then she turned to look at the gaping hole in the courtroom wall. In a small voice she spoke.

"That was you, wasn't it?"

Felix swallowed. "Er, it's complicated."

"I mean... if it wasn't for you, I'd be..." Skrida pointed at the hole, then clicked her fingers. "Gone."

"Uh, well, yes. I think so," said Felix.

The Goddess of Death looked at him for a long while, then nodded.

"A deal was struck. I will fulfil my end of it." She lifted a hand, causing Felix to flinch, but Helda held him strong. With closed eyes, she whispered a few syllables, and Felix felt immense heat burgeoning within him. It spread from his chest to his fingertips, causing him to gasp and shiver.

"What are you doing?" shouted Helda. "You're hurting him!"

Felix felt like he was going to explode, or burn to a crisp, or melt. The heat built up within him, and just when he thought he could take no more, it abruptly vanished. Helda's hands had blistered from the heat of him, but she hadn't let him drop. She gritted her teeth as she kept him from falling.

Felix took a shuddering step, testing his legs. They... ached.

"I'm... alive," he said. Helda folded him into a bone-crushing hug. "Ack! Don't kill me again-" he managed to force out through crushed lungs, and Helda let him go.

He wriggled out of her grasp, and looked up at Skrida, who was watching him with an expression he hadn't expected to see on her face.

Surely he was mistaken. It wasn't...

Gratitude?

"Thank you," she said, inclining her head. Solhiti took a step towards his wife and embraced her. He turned to Felix.

"Thank you, Felix," he said, gripping Skrida tightly.

"You're welcome," said Felix, unsure of what else to say. Solhiti looked at him expectantly, the silence lengthening. Eventually Felix said: "Anytime."

Solhiti smiled.

"I will send you all home," he said, then, releasing his wife, raised a hand.

"Already?" Felix wanted to say, but was interrupted.

In a burst of light, Felix and his companions vanished, appearing moments later in the front room of Lunchers & Co.

A shuffling sound from behind them and Dago and Merindhe leapt to their feet, smoothing their hair and straightening their clothes. "Blimey!" Merindhe said, a little too loudly. "What's with the, uh, sudden entrance?"

"Felix," said Racelsus, ignoring the two blushing aides.

"Rass?" said Felix.

"You know Solhiti was waiting for you to ask him for a boon."

"A boon?"

"You know, a gift from the gods? Where essentially anything could be yours? Power, wealth, immortality, that sort of thing?"

"Oh." Felix paused, then shrugged. "Never mind."

"Never mind!?" Racelsus yelled, then started swearing.

"What's all this language?" came a voice from upstairs, and Mrs Luncher descended the stairs. "Nice to see you're back with us," she said, looking at Felix.

"Uh, yes," he said, awkwardly patting himself. "Solid and accounted for, I think."

"Good good," she said, with a knowing smile. She gazed at her crack legal team, having faced gods-know-what and survived to tell the tale. "Who fancies a drink?" she said, and everyone announced that they did.

~

Solhiti stood amongst the Pantheon. Habeus was looking at him, but Solhiti could not meet his gaze. Each member was standing in their accustomed place. A silence cloaked them like a heavy blanket.

"That was very close," the God of Justice said eventually. "Without that young man's help, it would have gone very badly."

"Hm," said Solhiti. He studied each of the Pantheon in turn, settling finally on Habeus. "There are going to be some changes," he said.

17 - Taberna

Helda, her hands wrapped in bandages from where they had blistered, nudged the door to the Duck in Flagon open with her elbows. Behind her the crew of Lunchers & Co filed in and found spaces around a large wooden table.

"Burt!" Helda shouted, getting the attention of the barman/landlord/bouncer, then raised her bandaged hands. "Have you got any straws?"

~

It was dark in the Central Placenamia Office of Government. Dusk was approaching, and most of the staff had left, or were in the process of leaving. Most.

A figure in a smart suit, carrying a bundle of papers, walked through the front door. After a brief conversation with the security guard, he passed through a corridor and up a staircase. Upon entering this level, he located the manager of this floor and approached him. The suited figure said a few words to the manager, who paled. Both men headed to a door at the back of the floor, which was locked. The manager fished out a key from his inner pocket with a trembling hand, and unlocked the door. The two of them then headed up a second staircase, the suited man in front. At the top of the staircase waited a heavy, imposing door.

They hesitated. The suited man holding the folder nodded his head to the door, and the second man swallowed, then knocked. After a moment, a female voice called to them.

"Enter."

~

"Come on," said Dago, patting the space next to him. "Watch," he said, nudging Merindhe's arm. "I'm telling you, there's something fishy about all this."

Yetty walked smartly up to Burt, an open smile on her face.

"Hi, Burt," she said. Burt grunted in reply. "So, ah, I was wondering if I could order a glass of white wine?"

"Don't do wine," said Burt, spitting into a bucket that was out of eyeshot (though not out of earshot.)

"You sure?" said Yetty, glancing back to Dago. "No wine at all?"

"Don't. Do. Wine," said Burt, with, for him, enormous patience. "What d'ya want?"

"Um, just a beer please," said Yetty. She sighed in relief when Burt turned his back to grab her a pot. When she had been served, she scuttled back to the table.

"I don't understand it," she said. "She must have something on him. There she goes now."

Mrs Luncher, who had been outside taking the air, strolled back into the pub. She caught Burt's eye, and, without any apparent conjuring on his part, he produced a thin-stemmed glass filled with a pale wine-y liquid. He placed it on the bar, and Mrs Luncher collected it, then went back outside.

"I just don't get it," said Yetty, staring at her drink. "What's she got that I don't?" She sniffed. "Actually, don't answer that." She took a small sip, then grimaced at it, before turning to the two clerks.

"So, what's going on with you two, then?" She crossed two of her fingers together. "Hmmm?"

The two clerks blushed enormously, before muttering something non-committal.

"Mmhm," said Yetty, taking another sip and regretting it slightly less. She let them stew in silence while she watched Mr Luncher step outside for a smoke.

~

The manager pushed the door open and held it for the suited man, who walked in. The manager stayed outside. Around a table stood three more figures: two women and a man. The file-holder nodded to them each in turn, then placed his bundle on the table. He slid it from its folder and turned it so it faced the figure opposite him. The top of the paper had the words "Extremis" and "Immediate" in large, serious letters, followed by a long detailed description of charges written in a small, precise hand. At the bottom was space for three signatures.

~

"Gah!" shouted Yetty, before pointing an accusing finger behind her. "It's not fair when you nudge the darts mid-flight!"

"I'm not!" said the witch. "You're just terrible at this game."

Yetty scoffed then turned back to the board. She took her time aiming, sticking her tongue out of her mouth in concentration. Furbo glanced at Racelsus, and could have sworn the skull winked. The dart flew from Yetty's hand, and landed on exactly the spot that left her one point short of victory.

"Gah!" she yelled, clenching her fists.

"Oh no," said Racelsus, giggling. "Butterfingers."

"You're going on my list," said Yetty, before bursting into giggles as well.

~

The man took a pencil and signed his name. He then handed the paper to the woman next to him, who did the same. Lastly, the third woman, the woman who had spoken, picked the paper up and examined it more closely. She eyed the man in the suit, who returned her gaze without expression. Finally, she signed her name on the bottom of the page. Her signature was long, mostly because of all the titles before it.

~

"I tell you, I'm so famished I could finish off one of King Mutter the Fat's famous forty course banquets. What's on the menu today, then?" said Mr Luncher, reaching for a small set of spectacles that he kept in his front pocket. They weren't there, so he patted several other pockets, before finding them secreted in his waistcoat. He withdrew them, breathed on them, gave them a polish then set them on his nose. After blinking three times and adjusting them, he searched around the room, before spotting where the menu was written in chalk on a board above the bar. He rubbed his eyes, blinked again, then studied the menu. After a few seconds, he removed his glasses.

"Pie," he said, sliding them back into his pocket. He got to his feet. "Pie, anyone?"

Everyone agreed that pie would be wonderful, all except Felix, who had one small caveat.

"Just so long as it's not Froggoboggo pie," he said, laughing nervously. "Uh, not that there's anything wrong with that," he said, catching Helda and Racelsus's gaze. The two of them were in equal parts fond and protective of that particular delicacy, as Felix had found out once when trying to criticise it. "I'm just, well, not in the mood for, ah, that, um, today."

That particular pie was mostly swamp, wrapped in pastry, and was seen as a delicacy in some parts of the world. Notably, parts of the world Felix tried to avoid. There was just something about mushrooms, frogs and swampweed that didn't agree with him on a gastronomical level.

In the meantime, Mr Luncher had popped up to see Burt, exchanged some words, then returned.

"Good news," he said to Felix with a smile and a nod.

The suited figure inclined his head, then deftly slid the paper back into its folder. He turned to leave without speaking. The manager, who had been waiting outside, accompanied him down both sets of stairs, locking the door behind him. At the front door, he shook the suited man's hand, then watched him stride smartly away.

The manager had questions, of course, but he didn't voice them.

~

"Ya knows I don't fully understand your ways," said Burt, the landlord of the Duck In Flagon. "I ain't one of your learned types or whatnot. Never got a higher education, ya might say." He leaned closer, his foul breath washing over Felix. "But care t'explain to me why it is yer doing what yer doing?"

"It isn't what it looks like," said Felix, sweat beading on his forehead.

"It ain't? Because it looks like yer dunking a dagger in a pint o'beer, and looking mighty odd while doing it," said Burt.

"He... wanted to try it out," said Felix, nodding at the knife.

"Eh?"

"It might be easier if I just..." Felix slowly lifted his hand, a dripping John Dagger emerging from the cup. The dagger whistled.

"That was... well, that was shomething else!" the knife hiccupped. "Hoooweee!"

Burt squinted at John, then at Felix. With a movement far quicker than Felix expected, the massive barman deftly snatched the dagger from his hand and held it up in front of his huge, haggard face.

"Oh gods," John moaned. "Euurgh..."

"You old enough?" said Burt, to the dagger, his scowl mere inches from the blade.

"What's it to you, fatty?" said John. Burt's hand squeezed more tightly. "And you ever actshually wash your hands, or do you just rub 'em on whatever damp surface is in reach? I'm royalty, didn't you know, you have to reshpect me."

Felix, along with the rest of Lunchers - that is, those that were not currently face-first on the table, snoring - considered leaping to their feet and challenging Burt, but something about the terrifying publican wielding an enchanted weapon made them hesitate. For Felix, it was primarily not wanting to get himself murdered within hours of being brought back to life. That, and it was looking like a time-honoured tradition was about to be repeated in front of their eyes - the tradition of getting chucked out of a pub at least once in your life. Felix wanted to see

465

how John would handle it. So far, it was going brilliantly, so long as getting thrown out of the pub was your end game.

"You know," said Burt, his voice low, but still loud. "I served twenty-four years in the army. You learns a lot bein' on the front line that long. Facing down warlock-screamers, pirates of the southern isles, monsters you ain't never heard of, and men that put the rest o' them to shame." His voice lowered again. "You learns, for example, how t' dismantle a dagger in under five seconds so that no bugger will ever be able to hold it again. You learns how to snap a blade with nothin' but your fists, boots and teeth." He brought the dagger closer still, his voice almost a whisper. "And lastly, ya learn who t' give respect to, and when to shut yer mouth. Ya understand?"

"Yes," squeaked John, his voice tiny, tinny and trembling.

After a long second, Burt slowly placed John back into Felix's pint glass, blade down, then clomped away to his usual spot, glowering at people from behind the bar.

The crew of Lunchers shared glances, then all started laughing at once. Helda woke with a start, sitting bolt upright. "Who, what?" she spluttered. "Whassat?"

"John has been initiated," Dago, the clerk, said patting the dagger on the handle. As one, the crew lifted their various drinks and toasted him.

"Welcome, officially, to Lunchers & Co," said Mr Luncher with a smile.

~

A figure peered into the window of Lunchers & Co. Seeing nobody there, he opened the door and entered. He did what he was instructed to do, and quickly - pausing only to frown at the clock. He flicked a finger at it, then, satisfied, left quietly. He locked the door behind him, leaving no trace of his visit. None except the trace he wanted them to find, of course.

No one would have seen him. No one would have believed it if they had.

~

Furbo sat there, his mouth open. "You *what*."

"Uh, well, I reckon it might have been the, uh, next rank up. So to speak," said Felix, sipping his beer.

"Wait," said Helda, reed-straw hanging from her mouth, eyes blinking independently. "So like, the god that made the gods or something?"

"I think so." Felix stared down at his pint, which quivered viscously. "But then, who created him?"

"What," said Furbo, his voice intense, "did he say to you?"

"Hmm, well he introduced himself to me first of all. Oh, what was his name."

The old scholar let out an involuntary squeak. Felix, oblivious to the vein starting to throb on Furbo's head, was tapping the table with his finger, trying to jog his memory. A moment later, he clicked his fingers.

"Aha," he said, pointing at Furbo. "His name is Frum."

"Frum?" said Furbo. "Frum!?" he repeated. "You expect me to believe that this creator, this god amongst gods, this highest power, is called *Frum*!?"

"Well, his name was much longer than that, and more complicated, but I've forgotten it," said Felix with a shrug. "Ah well."

"I…" said Furbo. "When… You…"

"Something the matter?" Felix said, eyeing Furbo. "If I didn't know better, I'd say you're upset."

"Did… he say anything else to you?" the old man said between clenched teeth.

"Uh… Nothing important, I think. Something about back pain… but I can't really remember the rest. or I'd… have… remembered…"

Felix finally saw the look on Furbo's face, and felt a small flush of embarrassment. "Oh," he said. "I just realised that this sort of thing is probably the sort of thing you'd have wanted to know, isn't it?"

"You could say that!" said Furbo. "I've only been studying the gods and their many designs my whole bloody life! Then you accidentally meet a *new one*!? A *higher one*!? And then you *forget what you talked about*!?"

Felix chewed his lip. "Sorry," he said, with as much drunken genuineness as he could muster. Furbo, with one last twitch, took a deep breath, followed by a deep pull on his beer. He took another breath, then sighed.

"It's okay, my lad," he said, his normal soft tone returning. "It can't be helped. You were quite busy, after all." He hesitated, then put a hand on Felix's. "Maybe next time you meet the god of all gods, the highest of the high - the very *tip top* of the tower, so to speak - try to remember what they say to you, eh?"

~

When the manager returned to his desk, he lowered himself into a chair and breathed a long, slow breath. Curiosity could be a killer, and he had trained himself to ignore most of what he saw on the upper levels. Still, the ability to ignore information also depended on the ability to absorb it quickly and accurately, and the manager had a quick eye. A very quick eye. As he had shown the suited man into the room upstairs, in the general movements of door opening, walking, nodding of heads, polite gestures and hand shaking, the folder had flapped open for the briefest second. That was all the manager needed. He had noticed the name in small writing at the top of the bundle, a name that was never read out, yet had had its fate sealed all the same.

~

The night was nearing its end, and Felix was sitting on a wooden bench outside. The evening air was comfortable, with a gentle breeze and cloudless starlight.

"I never really thought about the admin," he said. "Of dying, you know?"

"Mhmm," said Mrs Luncher, nursing her glass.

"I should have taken out life insurance," he muttered. "No doubt it would have been voided anyway. Those things are designed by people in suits to make them all but useless. Oh well. Say, it's getting late. I might head back soon."

Mrs Luncher yawned. "Good idea, Felix." She stood and stretched. "Let's gather everyone up. Have you seen John?"

~

If anyone asked, he hadn't seen a name, of course. Unless he could somehow turn it to his advantage at a later date, he would never speak the name to anyone, or admit to having heard of it in any way, shape or form. He filed it in his mind amongst a long list of other names, the latest unfortunate to have their name written on such a form in such a building. From this moment on, the manager, for all intents and purposes, did not know the name written on the death warrant.

Still, despite this, that tiny spark of curiosity flashed briefly.

Who is... he thought, then shook his head, remembering the thickness of the folder and the words on the top.

*Who **was** Felix Sacramentum...*

18 - Partes

It was the morning after Felix's return to humanity, and once again he was lying in a heap on the floor.

"Nyerugh," he gurgled.

"Foofff…" grunted Helda biliously.

"Grnnh," whined Furbo.

"Shhhh," hissed Racelsus.

"Eeeeeech," whined John Dagger.

These pathetic outbursts were joined in chorus by Yetty, Dago and Merindhe. Even Mrs Luncher, when she performed her traditional bursting in to tear open the curtains, did it with a little less glee than usual. She still managed to glare down at her employees with just as much maternal derision.

"Breakfast?" was all she said.

"Yes!"

"Brilliant idea!"

"Nyerugh!"

After another meal at Gutcher's that was as much grease as it was plate, Felix and the others spent the late morning strolling the parks around Lunchers and cursing the sun for being bright, the birds for being loud, and just about anything and everyone for daring to exist in a way that wasn't completely dark and totally silent. Yet interspersed in this shared good-natured hatred of everything were endless shared joys. Reminiscing of a night that was hard to remember, excitement at a reunited future, and buckets of relief that everything turned out well in the end.

When they returned to the office of Lunchers & Co, a huge pot of coffee was brewed, and the staff gently moved piles of papers and books so they could perch, sit or generally lounge their pounding heads away.

A *ting* noise came from the clock in the meeting room, which was met with much complaint and cursing. At the same time, a separate *clonk*

471

sound came from a clock at the other side of the office, which was heckled in a similar way.

After a few moments, something clicked in Felix's head.

"You finally found the twisting turny thing to fix the clock then?" he said to Mr Luncher, who was in the kitchen.

"Hm?" he said, pouring the coffee.

"The clock," said Felix. "You fixed it."

"What? Oh no, lad, still can't find the blooming thingy for it." He entered the meeting room and handed Felix a cup of tea. Felix looked at it.

An idea came to him. It sent a momentary flicker of panic through his churning guts, which he tried to suppress, but failed.

"Did we get any post this morning?" he said.

"Just a letter about an investment I made a while back," said Mr Luncher, handing out the coffees in a series of mismatching mugs. "No good news on that front, sadly."

Felix got up and walked over to the front door. There were no letters jammed in the letterbox. Nothing on the floor.

"What are you looking for, lad?" asked Furbo.

"Just a thought," he said, eyeing the clock again. "I must be mistaken." He shook his head, and immediately regretted it. "Never mind," he said, and returned to his tea, which he had wished was coffee, but was still too polite to mention. He lifted the mug and blew on it, heading out of the meeting room and towards his desk.

As he went to take a sip of his drink, he noticed the package. It was resting atop a small pile of papers, in which it had blended in quite expertly with the various piles of paperwork and other junk that seemed to fill Lunchers, from the boards to the rafters. It was small-ish, unremarkable, except for the letter resting on top of it. Something about that letter seemed significant.

After a brief hesitation, which was largely spent looking for a mug-sized bit of free tabletop space, he put down his drink and lifted the letter. It felt heavy in his hand, and, despite not being an expert in these things, the paper seemed of incomparable quality. On the front of the envelope was written, in exquisite handwriting: "Felix Sacramentum, Lunchers & Co."

Mr Luncher, who was peering over his shoulder exclaimed happily. "Someone who got the apostrophe right, at least! Nice paper, that."

Felix ignored him. He turned the envelope over and saw the seal. "Furbo," he said. "Do you recognise this?"

Furbo rose with a groan and shuffled over. "Hmm," he said. "Sign of the guild of postmasters, I think. No, sorry, that's Samsvara's temple." He sidled back to his chair and slumped onto it. "Curious," was all he said, before closing his eyes and taking a huge sniff of his coffee, then sighing contentedly.

"Mind if I..?" came the voice of John Dagger. "That looks like it might slice really nice."

With a hand that only trembled slightly, Felix lifted John Dagger and opened the letter with him.

"Ooh, very nice indeed," said John. "Top quality stuff, that."

Felix put John back in his stand, then took a breath. He unfolded the letter and read it. As he did so, his eyes widened.

"Huh," was all he said.

"'Huh', what?" said Yetty. "Spare us the dramatics, please!"

Felix handed the letter to her, and Yetty flourished it in the style of a town crier before reading aloud.

"Dear Felix,

I apologise that I can't be there in propria persona.

Solhiti has made some changes within the Pantheon, one of which dictates that direct interaction between the gods and mortals is no longer permitted. I understand his reasoning, even if it means I must do via letter what I would prefer to do in person.

However, I was able to modify his edict slightly. While the gods may no longer directly influence the mortal world, Solhiti agreed that neither should the other divine races. This means that humanity is, for all intents and purposes, safe. At least, safe from the likes of Jurrekker. Not from itself.

I didn't get a chance to apologise for all that rotten business with Jurrekker. Rest assured I am still searching for him, and shall one day visit justice upon him.

It was a delight to stand opposite you in the courtroom. Your arguments were sound, and your examination was impressive. Well done.

One final thing. I want you to have something. I intend it both an award and an apology. I hope it serves to both encourage you and remind you.

Your friend,

Habeus"

Felix had, in the meantime, opened the small box and was staring at the contents. He lifted it slowly and held it up for all to see.

It was a plain wooden gavel resting in a bracket which was affixed to a board. On the board, in golden lettering, was written:

Representing the downtrodden, the misused, the abused, the voiceless. Lunchers & Co: Lawyers for the Underdog.

In smaller writing, beneath the hammer, it said:

By Divine Appointment.

THE END

A note from the author

Hello! If you've just finished the book and gone "What, who the heck was Halka?", then I just thought I'd tell you something you might find interesting. Many of the gods that appeared in this book (Solhiti, Skrida (albeit with a different name), and of course Halka herself,) appear in my short story, titled 'Halka', which can be found in the Winter of Wonder 2021 'Superhuman' edition, along with another collection of wonderful short stories by a selection of talented authors. You can find it at the link below or by checking out either the website of the Cloaked Press at https://www.cloakedpress.com/ or my own site: https://www.arturnerauthor.com/

The story itself concerns a young woman who is suddenly whisked away from her ordinary, mortal life and forced, against her will, to assume the mantle of Goddess of Winter; a job that no self-respecting god would ever choose to do. Some of the gods are warm and welcoming to the latest addition to the pantheon, and some of them, most decidedly, are not...

https://www.amazon.co.uk/gp/product/B09M82XVV3/

Another note from the author

You made it! Congratulations. No mean feat. Corpus was a meaty 140k words compared to the piffling 99k of Avocado, as my mum tells me she thinks of whenever she thinks about the book. Jokes on her, the book was actually named after the flea treatment I torment my cat with every month. If you haven't read Advocatus, then that's even more impressive, and I'd genuinely like to know what you thought as you read it, presumably with many furrowed brows and exclamations of 'who the heck was that?' and 'this story makes no sense!'

Books take many things. They take time, first of all, but more than that they take teamwork. Sure, I slapped a lot of words onto the page, but they would never have made it through the sieve of quality without the gentle jostling of the combined efforts of a few individuals. So, enormous thanks again to Anna, Dad and Tom for reading every word at least once, sometimes many more times, and pointing out when what I'd written was good, and when what I'd written was lumpy, misshapen clumps of floury bumf. Without their constant encouragement and necessary criticism, this book might have A) never been finished, and B) if it was finished, would have been half the book it could have been, despite being twice the length. Especial thanks to Dad who spent many hours with me on video calls making me justify every paragraph, every sentence and every word (even the name of *that* wizard in Act One). Thank you.

Thank you to the discerning minds at the Cloaked Press for taking that first gamble on me, all those years ago. One of these days, I'm sure we'll meet in person, and then I can get you to sign a book for me.

Thank you as well to everyone in my friendship group and beyond who took a chance and read the books I've written. Your kind words of support and effusive praise have humbled me, embarrassed me and encouraged me to keep going. You're all wonderful people. Yes, even you (you know who you are).

I'd also like to extend thanks to everyone who has read and reviewed the book on Amazon, Goodreads and beyond. The little sloops of independent publishers and authors, along with our self-publishing brothers-and-sisters in arms, can never hope to compete with the galleons and aircraft carriers of the big names in the ocean of publishing. That's why, if you enjoyed this book, I would encourage you to leave a review wherever you think best, and to do so for any others from small presses or self-published authors that you might come across. And, if this book made you apoplectic with rage, or struck you with a wave of ennui, do the same. You could recommend this book to others, or even lend them this copy to a friend (or enemy, if this book filled you with hate), though I'd say if you're reading the ebook version, make sure you know and trust the person before lending them your iPad.

-ART

A final note from the author, then he'll leave you alone

Indie publishing houses, small presses and self-published authors cannot compete with the large publishers with their armies of marketing gurus and mountains of money to throw around. On the other hand, small presses (and independent publishing) allow authors a huge amount of creative freedom. The downside is that it can be hard for small voices to be heard (or, in this case, read).

If you enjoyed this book, please consider leaving a rating or a short review of it on Amazon, Goodreads, Google, or even just scrawled with a compass onto the nearest tree/fence and/or picnic table. Sharing this book with a friend, either by lending them this copy or blackmailing them into buying their own, also helps tremendously. If you happen to live in South Wales, there are also some copies floating around the library services. If you don't, you should be able to convince your local library to stock a copy. Though, if you're reading this, you've probably already finished the book. Hm, must rethink this. Anyway.

The same is true of any small or independently published books you read.

Lastly, and this probably goes without saying, but if you happen to be a Netflix content scout or Hollywood producer, *do feel free to reach out, I won't mind.*

Okay, I'll go now. Thank you all, you are all beautiful people, and see you for the next instalment of the Culpa Magum series, coming sometime in the 21st Century (probably).

-ART

www.ingramcontent.com/pod-product-compliance
Lightning Source LLC
Chambersburg PA
CBHW061536190726
48289CB00004B/1068